Praise for *Trang Sen*

I0681730

from reviewers

This is the story of Trang Sen, or "white lotus," a brave and brilliant Vietnamese girl who had to grow up during the Vietnam War. Masterfully written by a diplomat who has extensive experience and knowledge of the cultures, the settings, and human psychology, the book follows Trang Sen's journey from her first encounter with an American in 1957, her teen years in the alleys of Saigon as the war raged, her coming-of-age and love-life as the war worsened, to her life in the late '70s after the U.S. army pullout from Vietnam.

Trang Sen is [one] of those very rare books that grab your attention from the first paragraphs, take you on a journey . . . entertain you, educate you, make you care about the people and the topics visited, and then leave you reeling, stunned . . . because the author has changed your understanding forever. Smith delves deep . . . she opens our eyes to what it was really like out there.

That war is over but others are still raging. *Trang Sen* is an excellent read for students, young people, and all adults who have the power to make a difference, because this book clearly shows why a war is never the right path towards problem solving, achieving peace, or preserving human dignity.

Ia Uaro, BookPleasures.com

Too few authors have addressed the fact that the American public is poorly informed about the conditions . . . of Vietnam . . . before the U.S. Military shoved down the door and pushed our way into a senseless and brutal mistake of a war. Perhaps if more authors did the obvious research needed to recreate pre-war Vietnam and explain Vietnamese customs that were so disregarded, perhaps there would be fewer wars staged under the banner of "democracy" that serves as a feeding trough for corporate greed.

Smith draws her characters well. . . Her graceful, simple style shows sensitivity to the essence of the Vietnamese people. She offers a lot to absorb while she spins her tale of family, sibling love, coming of age, and bravery in the face of many varied forms of danger.

Grady Harp, LiteraryAficionado.com & on Amazon.com (5 stars)

Trang Sen is a phenomenal novel that tells of a young girl discovering herself amidst war and life. The historical detail of the book is rich and flavorful, and more powerful is the simple way in which the story is told, without artifice. . . I highly recommend this poignant story to anyone wishing to relive a historic period through the eyes of a young innocent who was forced to grow up too early, and find her own way through life.

MyBookAddictionreviews.com (4 stars)

Trang Sen is a well-written, enticing story of a Vietnamese woman adjusting to a quickly changing world. Through the eyes of Trang Sen, the reader experiences life in Vietnam

Praise for *Trang Sen*

through the American occupation. . . [T]he journey is truly addictive.

Women who love romances would find this novel perfect for them, others for its historical accuracies and perspectives. *Trang Sen* is a novel for everyone.

Teri Davis, Midwest Book Review.

In *Trang Sen*, Sarah-Ann Smith puts a human face on a war that seems distant now, capturing the painful suffering of the Vietnamese and the problems and confusion faced by the ones who were brought to the United States. . . [S]he captures the trauma of Trang Sen's family, forced to give up their land, losing sons in the war and becoming refugees in a city teeming with the poor, desperate and hungry.

Relationships between American men and Vietnamese women were so commonplace they were almost the norm. . . Although *Trang Sen* is fiction, it rings true to that troubling time.

Carole Currie, *Asheville* (NC) *Citizen-Times*

from historians and academics

Americans tend to remember the Vietnam war as something painful that happened to us. We think much less about the experience or the much greater pain endured by the Vietnamese. In showing us that tragic time through the eyes of a Vietnamese woman growing up during the war, Sarah-Ann Smith also shows how Vietnamese lives were formed and deformed by that long travail, and about the kinds of choices so many were forced to make amid terrible circumstances.

Arnold R. Isaacs
author, *Without Honor* and *Vietnam Shadows*

Sarah-Ann Smith has introduced us to a small group of Vietnamese and American personalities caught in that ill-fated war. Though there are hints of later developments, at the last page they have just reached middle age, with one, Trang Sen's son, not yet old enough for high school. Half their lives await them but escape us. Can we somehow follow them, now that we care? Perhaps the author will have pity on our curiosity, and will follow up with a sequel. We can only hope.

Francis X. Winters, Professor Emeritus, School of Foreign Service, Georgetown Univ.
author, *The Year of the Hare*

Trang Sen, the heroine of Sarah-Ann Smith's novel, embarks on a journey that requires heartbreaking choices. The choices she makes and the people she meets along the way are brought sharply to life by Smith's spare prose and we find ourselves, like Trang Sen, hovering in that strange space and time where the passions of Americans and Vietnamese

Praise for *Trang Sen*

came together but could not find stable purchase.

Drawing on her own experiences as a former U. S. diplomat and an expert on Asian social and political life, Smith depicts her characters and their surroundings with unusual cross-cultural empathy and a keen eye for detail. Part coming-of-age tale, part historical drama, part love story, *Trang Sen* vividly portrays the human cost of war while celebrating the resilience and imagination of the human spirit.

Mary Beth Mills, Professor of Anthropology, Colby College
author, *Thai Women in the Global Labor Force: Consuming Desires, Contested Selves*

from readers

We can never know the throat-constricting terror these people suffered after we pulled out. The book got me to thinking about the "boat people" [and] brought me to tears as I read about Trang Sen's last day in Vietnam and the crush of people waiting to get on that plane. I could see it all.

Tom Abeln, President, Chapter 61
Veterans for Peace, St. Louis, MO

Trang Sen helped me relive our time in Vietnam. . . [It] captures the truth of what we saw and experienced more than anything I have read . . . [and] made me feel that I was there.
Nancy Hope, former Vietnam refugee camp volunteer

I've recently finished *Trang Sen*. I enjoyed it so much.

I have just finished reading your book and it is wonderful. I got nothing done yesterday and not a lot of sleep either.

I finished your book and felt, like Francis X. Winters, that my only regret was that it was the last page. . . I learned a great deal about the life and culture of the Vietnamese.

I read your book over the weekend and could hardly put it down. It was captivating and oh, so enlightening.

You have to know that you kept me up until 1:45 this morning. I had to finish the book.

A very intriguing story. I really felt like I knew more about the Vietnamese people when I finished. . . Thanks so much for the hours of being in another time and place.

Trang Sen

A novel of Vietnam

by
Sarah-Ann Smith

Pisgah Press, LLC
PO Box 1427
Candler, NC
www.pisgahpress.com

Pisgah Press was established in 2011 to publish and promote works of quality offering original ideas and insight into the human condition, the realm of knowledge, and the world around us.

Printed in the United States of America

Published by Pisgah Press, LLC
PO Box 1427, Candler, NC 28715
www.pisgahpress.com

Book & cover design: A. D. Reed, MyOwnEditor.com
Cover photos: courtesy USAF archives, US Navy Information Service

Library of Congress Cataloging-in-Publication Data
Smith, Sarah-Ann
Trang Sen/Sarah-Ann Smith

Library of Congress Control Number: 2014957486

Includes bibliographical references and index
ISBN-10: 1942016050
ISBN-13: 9781942016052
Fiction/General

Second Edition
March 2015

Acknowledgements

Trang Sen has been a years-long undertaking. Along the way countless friends have made comments and noted details I had overlooked, attention to which hopefully make the story more true to life. Thanks are due to all, for both their encouragement and their critique, and above all for hanging in there with me.

Thanks specifically to the Harcourt Road Writers for input at an early stage, and especially for forcing me finally to articulate, to myself as well as to them, what I wanted this book to be.

I could not have brought the novel into final form without the support, sharp editing eye, layout skills, and—most important—enthusiasm of A. D. Reed. He not only loved the story, but insisted that I be ruthless in cutting, changing, rearranging. However painful that process was at times, it has produced a better book. *Sine qua non.*

Though set in historical times and places, *Trang Sen* is not intended as a historical account of the Vietnam War. Except for mention of military and political leaders, the characters are fictitious. I simply wanted to tell a story of the soldiers and diplomats, and particularly of the hapless Vietnamese, caught in the maelstrom of the war and its aftermath.

Nevertheless, I have tried to be as accurate as possible about the milieu in which the novel is set. Frances Fitzgerald's *Fire in the Lake*; Gerald Hickey's *Village in Vietnam*; Arnold Isaacs' *Without Honor*; Stanley Karnow's *Vietnam: A History*; and Frank Snepp's *Decent Interval* were especially helpful in this regard. None should be considered responsible for unintended errors in fact or interpretation.

I have also tried to be accurate about life and events in Washington and Northern Virginia circa the mid-1970s. The one intentional anachronism is placing the release of *Star Wars* in 1976 rather than 1977 for the purposes of the story.

As this second edition of Trang Sen goes to press, I am grateful to my readers, many of whom shared their reactions with me, and to the many book clubs that invited me to take part in their discussions. The positive response has been both humbling and exhilarating.

I want once again to thank Pisgah Press's A.D. Reed, my editor and publisher, for his continuing support and unflagging zeal in promoting Trang Sen and giving it a place on his growing list of quality books.

Feedback from readers has demonstrated that whatever I intended, my novel illuminates for them the time and place that was wartime Saigon. Women my age have frequently thanked me for giving them an account of events that took place at a period in their own lives when, as they put it, they were so busy having babies that they paid no attention. Readers too young to remember those events also seem to have found the book enlightening.

This second edition coincides with the fortieth anniversary of the final U.S. departure from Saigon on April 30, 1975. By focusing on the events leading up to that moment, and their aftermath, from the perspective of the Vietnamese victims, perhaps my book may in some small way be an antidote to the hoopla and self-congratulation that could surround this anniversary.

Sarah-Ann Smith
December 2014

Author's Notes on Sources

Pp. 3-4 - The account of the Trung sisters is based on the website www. womeninworldhistory.com (accessed January 16, 2012). The Trieu Au account and words attributed to her are from info-facts.com/TrieuThiTrinh, written January 2007 (accessed January 16, 2012).

P. 85 - Theodora Lau, *The Handbook of Chinese Horoscopes*, New York: Harper Colophon Books, 1979, p. 161.

P. 104 - Nguyen Du, *The Tale of Kieu*, trans. Huynh Sanh Thong, New Haven: Yale University Press, 1983, pp. 161, 163. Used by permission.

P. 199 - *For the Good Times*
Words and Music by Kris Kristofferson
Copyright © 1968 by Universal Music - Careers
Copyright Renewed
International Copyright Secured All Rights Reserved
Reprinted by Permission of Hal Leonard Corporation.

P. 213 - John Berger and Jean Mohr, *Another Way of Telling*, cited in Edward W. Said, *Culture and Imperialism*, New York: Vintage Books, 1994, p. 334.

P. 279 - Hugo of St. Victor, *Didascalicon* (trans. Jerome Taylor), cited in Said, *Culture and Imperialism*, p. 335.

Pp. 279-280 - Jean-Paul Sartre, *Les Mouches* (*The Flies*), F. C. St. Aubyn and Robert G. Marshall, eds., New York: Harper & Row, 1963, p.105 (Act III, Scene II).

P. 293 - Sartre, *Les mouches*, p. 105 (trans. by the author).

TABLE OF CONTENTS

TRANG SEN

Prologue

Brave Women

YOU ASKED FOR a story to remember always.

Once long ago, a Chinese general conquered our people. He called himself our emperor and named our land Nam Viet. That is where our name came from, but we never called that man emperor. Many years after the general died, the Chinese forced our beloved Nam Viet to become a province of China. They set cruel rulers over us. We hated them, and fought them many times.

Now, when the Chinese had ruled us for more than a hundred years, a Chinese commander murdered the husband of a brave and aristocratic lady. That lady, whose own surname was Trung, begged her sister to help her avenge her murdered husband. The Trung sisters ran the Chinese out of our land, and our people made them queens.

But then the Chinese came back, with an even bigger army than before. Though our queens fought with great valor and determination, they were defeated. They committed suicide by throwing themselves into a river, to avoid rape and disgrace.

Such brave heroines surely could not die. Our people at that time believed they entered the realm of the immortals, built temples to them, and named a festival in their honor, the famous Trung sister-queens. You have seen those temples, and you know that festival.

After that, we hated the Chinese more than ever. Another woman warrior, Trieu Au, inspired by the valor of our glorious queens, led a revolt against the Chinese. She cried, "I only want to ride the wind and walk the waves, slay the big whale of the Eastern sea, clean up our frontiers, and save the people from drowning. Why should I bow my head, stoop over, and be a slave?" Ah, but she was splendid going into battle, in her golden armor and riding on her elephant. Alas, she was defeated. Vowing never to surrender, she too committed suicide.

Our people built temples to her as well. We still remember her gallant struggle.

CHAPTER 1

FISHING

THE CHILD SKIRTED the edge of the rice fields to retrieve the frayed bamboo pole, an old piece of net she had carefully mended, and a basket clumsily woven from pieces of palm frond she had scavenged from her family's newly thatched roof. She had planned her fishing adventure for days, and hidden everything outside the village, a few yards into the forest beyond the paddies — her special spot, known only to her and Kim Hoa. Maybe they would let her do it if she asked, but they said "no" so much, she had decided not to take the chance. And she knew they wouldn't let her use good fishing gear.

She had thought her father and brothers would never finish slurping their soup. At last, though, she and her mother could clear things away. She put the big screen cover over the leftovers to save for supper and tomorrow's breakfast. That done, she pretended to settle down with the others, to rest through the hottest part of the afternoon. When she had made sure her mother was dozing, she crept from the house on bare feet.

Clutching the ramshackle fishing things and keeping behind the rows of vegetable gardens in back of the houses, she made for a place along the broad river bank where no one could see her. A large overhanging tree and long tendrils of vines enhanced its seclusion and helped protect it from the sun's relentless heat. Near the bank, the water deepened into dark pools — a good place to fish.

She leaned against the tree and tied the corners of her net to one end of the pole, turning it into a simple trap. When pulled through the water, it was very easy for a fish to enter but almost impossible for it to escape. So long as the old piece of netting didn't disintegrate. She gently lowered the makeshift trap and dragged it slowly through the water as she walked along the bank.

For a few minutes nothing happened. Then the pole bent suddenly and she pulled the net up. A small silvery fish thrashed back and forth, scales gleaming. She slid one hand down the pole toward the net as she grabbed her basket, scooped the fish into it, then tied the basket to the tree and lowered it partway into the water.

When she had caught several small fish, she sat down with her back against the big tree. Lulled by the insistent humming of cicadas and the heat of the slowly lengthening afternoon, she drifted into a half-sleep.

Abruptly, she was wide awake. Not ten feet away, a khaki-colored shirt, a light tan arm reaching for the basket cord. She jumped to her feet, stared speechless at the man's close-cut blond hair. Startled, he turned, and she looked in wonder at his pale blue eyes.

He said something she couldn't understand, then, in halting Vietnamese, spoke to her. "These your fish? I buy. How much?"

She shook her head, then quickly lowered it, embarrassed.

"I not hurt. No be afraid. I like fish."

She shook her head again but slowly raised her eyes and stared at him once more.

"What your name? I Tom, from America."

"Phan," she mispronounced the name.

A branch snapped on the path. The American looked around as Trang Sen's brother came into the little clearing.

"Little Sister, what are you doing here?" Minh stopped in his tracks. "Who is he?"

"I don't know." She hadn't thought how she would explain what she had been doing.

"Want fish," said the American in his odd Vietnamese. "Be friends."

Trang Sen had an idea. "I was taking a walk. I thought it would be cool by the river. Then I saw him. He was pulling that fish basket out of the water."

Her brother eyed the stranger, a little bolder now. "Where did you get the basket?" He pointed to it, chuckling to himself at its dilapidated state. The man must have picked it up from someone's trash heap.

"Not understand. Want fish."

Minh thought a moment, avoiding the American's eyes. None of the village people would have left a basket of fish unattended, even this basket. Perhaps this odd-looking man had caught them.

He touched the basket. "Did you catch these?"

The American nodded vigorously.

"Ah. That's fine. They're your fish. They're good fish, very good to eat."

The man fumbled in his pocket, withdrew a wad of American bills and, peeling one off, held it out to Minh, saying, "I buy."

"Oh, no." The boy put his hands behind his back. "We don't want your money."

Then the man offered Trang Sen the bill. She was equally embarrassed, though for different reasons. "I don't want it. You'll like the fish." She was more courageous now that Minh was there.

"Can't take fish."

Minh was mystified. The only way out of this was retreat. "Let's go, Little Sister."

He caught her hand and pulled her along with him.

She looked over her shoulder for one last glimpse of the American, standing in confusion, the money still in his hand. She couldn't help grinning at him, odd as he seemed to her.

Trang Sen following her brother, the two walked single file along the path. "You shouldn't have gone off like that, little Lotus," he scolded her. "Ma-ma is looking for you."

"Ma-ma is always looking for me. I never get to do anything."

"What do you want to do, little one?"

"I want to go with Fourth Brother, to ride the buffalo."

He turned and looked at her. "You want too many things. You cause Ma-ma and Pa-pa more worry than all us boys together." But he smiled at her.

"Even than Eldest Brother?"

"Best not to mention that." He, the second son, could remember his older brother clearly. Eldest Brother had always been different from the rest, going off by himself, reading, thinking. He had been almost useless at the chores. Eldest Brother, Minh suddenly remembered, only liked to ride the water buffalo. Like Little Sister.

"Little Lotus, you must learn the things Ma-ma is trying to teach you. It's your fate. You mustn't fight against it."

"I will! I will fight! Why can't I do what you do?"

Why was she so stubborn? Where did she get these ideas? In a burst of adult sensibility, Minh understood his parents' fear for her. Where could such ideas lead?

MINH TOLD THE family about the American. "He talked like this — 'want fish, take money, be friend.'"

They laughed.

"But where did he come from?"

Their father explained. "The headman said the Americans have built a camp not far from here. They think the Communists will be here soon, and they want to train our boys to fight them."

"What is a Communist, Pa-pa?" asked Trang Sen.

He shrugged. "It's all politics, no need to have anything to do with us."

"But will we have to fight them?"

"I don't know." He looked away, out to the night sky.

Trang Sen lay in the hammock, her eyes wide open in the black darkness. She had pestered her parents until they finally allowed her to take her turn with her brothers sleeping in the single hammock. It was cooler than the plank beds built against the wall, and she liked being suspended in air, swinging back and forth.

Her thoughts spun around the American, as a moth, spellbound, draws ever closer to a flame. What would it be like to have hair the color of ripe rice? And those odd pale eyes, like the eyes of the fish in her science book, the ones that remained forever in the deepest parts of the ocean, their eyes bulging, useless sockets. He was so big, much taller even than Second Brother, who topped her father by half a head.

What was America like? Were all Americans like him, so big and pale? How did they keep from frying in the sun? The schoolteacher said America was big, even bigger than France, and much, much bigger than this country. He said it had lots of cowboys and policemen, who fought bad men. She hadn't been sure exactly what a cowboy was. She supposed Fourth Brother who rode the buffalo was a cowboy. That's what the teacher had called them, using the words for buffalo and boy. It was all very confusing.

All in all, the day had been most satisfying. Not only had she caught fish and seen an American, she had gotten herself out of what could have been yet another severe scolding — so smoothly that not even Second Brother suspected anything. The American had been most helpful, confusing Second Brother just by being there. And now she knew what Americans looked like.

CHAPTER 2

ELDEST BROTHER

April 25, 2005

Dear Kenneth,

I'm staring at your email asking me, for perhaps the thousandth time, to tell you how I got to know your mom and dad in Vietnam, and my take on what happened there. It's kind of odd to have opened the thing right now. Before I went to the computer I got a yen to put on some of my old LPs from the '60s and '70s; so I'm sitting here listening to Simon and Garfunkel — I know, ancient music to you. And, yes, I still have my old turntable, and I still listen to records sometimes. In this mood, I decided to write you the old-fashioned way, in pen and ink, via snail-mail. Regardless, your emails are always welcome.

Between my fit of musical nostalgia and the fact that it will be thirty years on Saturday that the last Americans left and the North Vietnamese army marched into Saigon, I suppose this is as good a time as any to take a look back.

It's hard for me to talk about those years. My chest still feels like it's being squeezed by a tight fist when I let myself think about the whole Vietnam mess. And I can't help wondering how many mistakes I

11

made because I was so very young — much younger than you are now —
and so unprepared to handle a lot of what was thrown at me.

Well, that's my feeble excuse for ignoring your question for so long.
I'll try to shed a bit of light for you, out of my own firsthand experience,
and also from what I heard from your mother. She was a lot more willing
to talk about herself back then. Except for one part of her life that I
finally managed to dig out of her.

I remember speculating with you one time about how things might
have been different if the U.S. hadn't picked up where the French left
off. But we did step in, and as early as 1957 we had several hundred
military advisors in South Vietnam. Your mother once told me it was
about that time — 1957 or 1958 — that she first encountered an
American.

In the years after that we got more and more involved. When I
went into the Foreign Service in June 1965 and began to learn more of
what we were doing, I was, to put it mildly, uneasy. I had just come
from Berkeley, after all, where the Free Speech Movement had turned the
whole place upside down. My sympathies were with the students who
were in the thick of things, but since I was heading for a government
career, I didn't get involved. But I don't need to go into the 1960s
student and civil rights stuff, since we've been over that many times.

Anyway, it looked to me as if things were going from bad to worse,
both for us and for South Vietnam. After the coup that overthrew
President Diem and his brother in November 1963, a few weeks before
President Kennedy was assassinated, the Saigon government very nearly
collapsed. Over the next year and a half there were four coups, and what
was left of the government became totally dependent on the U.S. The
coups ended about the time I arrived in the State Department, when
Nguyen Cao Ky, an air force Vice-Marshal, seized power.

By the time I started my first job, keeping up with Vietnamese
military affairs, General William Westmoreland had been commander of
the U.S. military advisory mission for a year. He was there until March
1968 — and by then a lot had unraveled, both in Vietnam and the U.S.
Out toward Tay Ninh — you know, where your mother's village was
— by the mid-1960s the so-called "safe area" was no farther than 20 or
30 miles from Saigon. All the villages out that way, including hers, were
infiltrated by the Viet Cong.

•

As you can imagine, the military chaos created a whole raft of social problems. With all the American soldiers in the country, prostitution became the number one way to make money. "Tea girls," as they were called, could be had for the asking. And by the time I got to Saigon, whole streets of shops were catering to the Americans, with everything for sale from cheap tourist doodads to tailor-made Western-style clothes like your Aunt Hoa made. And you wouldn't have believed the amount of black market stuff pilfered from the American commissaries, for sale in just about every other store.

In between following the military goings-on and briefing my superiors — who included practically everybody in the Department, since at that point I wasn't even on the ladder, much less climbing it — I found a kind of macabre humor in reading a little manual called "Short Course on Customs for Vietnam-Bound Personnel." It was a perfect example of how our arrogance kept messing up our understanding of the place even when we got all the facts right. Dense as I was then, I could see how offensive it was.

But it did give some useful information. The explanations about names and honorifics helped me when I read reports coming in from the Embassy. Such stuff as the simple fact, second nature to you, that Vietnamese have three names, that the surname comes first, and that they use their personal name, rather than their surname, with the appropriate honorific, even when that honorific is "President" or "General." It took me forever to keep the everyday honorifics straight — that "Co" was Miss, "Ong" was Mr., and that the wife used her husband's personal name with "Ba." Growing up with all this, you can't imagine what a big hurdle it was to me and most other Americans. I mean, imagine Americans calling their leaders President Michael or Governor Catherine!

I got interested in how personal names were chosen. I always thought it really odd that, when it came to naming you, as intellectual as she was even then, your mom reverted to the custom of calling children First Son, Second Son, and so forth. It was more amazing that she gave in to the superstition of skipping the number one. She explained to me one time not long after you were born, in all seriousness, that evil spirits always focus on the eldest boy. Calling you number two was the way to throw them off the track and keep them from hurting you, she said.

I'm going to have to stop for now. But I do want to add one more *thing. I know you've never understood why your mother won't talk with you about that time. There are good reasons why she wants to keep her memories buried deep. Maybe those will be clearer when you've heard some of what I'm going to tell you. Right now, let me just say this — your mother is a very brave woman, braver than you've ever realized. I hope you'll come to understand that too. And it seems important at the start of this little enterprise to say right out, I love both you and your family, and your mother, very deeply. If you didn't know that before, know it now!*

So, love and all that,

Uncle Blake

AS ALWAYS WHEN she stopped, she remembered, the memory suffocating.

The day her brothers left. Long before dawn, the village awake; small squares of light shining in the houses along the narrow path; the stream beyond the path touching with liquid black-brown the duller, brooding darkness of the forest beyond it. She slipped out of the house and ran to the far edge of the village to watch the road. An army truck rumbled toward her, olive-drab blot against the misty pre-dawn greyness. It slowly negotiated the turn into the path and edged along between the stream and the houses, to stop beside the council house. Its idling motor drowned out the forest sounds and spread a low fog of exhaust fumes. The headman sounded the large gong to call the villagers.

Trang Sen edged as close as she could. Minh came to stand beside her. "You'll have to help Pa-pa now. I told him you can help him."

"I don't want you to go."

Too soon they were ready to leave. She had a last glimpse of her brothers as they climbed into the back of the truck. Minh smiled at her, a small, uncertain smile. The truck, with some difficulty, backed out to the road, grinding its gears.

Now only Fourth Brother, Tho, was left. Now Trang Sen helped her father. And even with another daughter, Trang Mai, added, the house seemed empty. Her sister's arrival animated old dreams. The two of them could be like the Trung sisters, remembered forever. If Trang Mai ever grew up. Even the prospect of a companion heroine wasn't enough to make Trang Sen enjoy taking care of the child.

Trang Sen leaned on the plow, pushed her straw hat up and wiped her forehead with the back of her hand. She surveyed the dry, cracked fields, dotted with her relatives and neighbors, their black-clad figures and conical sun-hats splotches of dark and dull yellow against the red earth. By now, the fields should have been soft with the monsoon rains. Instead, they were sun-baked, rock-hard and impenetrable. From the forest the persistent drone of cicadas accented the shroud of heat.

Another memory, more remorseless.

Her father, his face blank. "Second Son has passed out of the world, taken by the guns." Her mother, wailing. "My good son, my good son."

Her father gazed at his wife's grief, his own tears locked somewhere inside.

After that, the nightmare, over and over. A black shadow, trying to swallow her. It had no shape, but was alive. Edged with red. Sometimes she cried out.

Once, her mother came to comfort her. "It's all right. Don't be afraid."

Trang Sen grew thin. But always she could push the plow. She wanted to push harder, faster, not letting herself stop to rest, to remember. She set her hat firmly forward, roused the two buffalo with a chucking sound, and lifted the long wooden plow handle, so much taller than she was. When she first started using it, her arms and shoulders ached from holding it steady as the buffalo pulled it across the field. Now, she easily settled the metal blade in the furrow and guided it forward. The straightest furrow in the village.

The war had given her what she wanted, to do what the boys did. It wasn't the way she had imagined. But she was proud of her plowing.

She kept on, plowing and remembering, back and forth, back and forth, her eyes on the line of trees at the edge of the field, shimmering in the white sunlight and alive with murmuring insects.

A LETTER CAME, from Long, the oldest son. "He's coming home," her father said.

Her mother was ecstatic. Her father was quiet, but he too was pleased.

Trang Sen could barely remember Long, but he was her hero, more than Minh. In her dreamy imaginings, sometimes the two of them rode side by side on ponderous elephants, majestic and beautiful, swaying high above the earth. Sometimes Eldest Brother led the way against undefined enemies. They killed tigers, rescued villagers from unnamed dangers. Eldest Brother was a stronger, wiser Trang Sen.

She watched her mother, the endless chores to be done over and over, seemingly forever, relieved only by an infrequent trip to the market in Tay Ninh, to buy staples like the baguettes they had all learned to like because of the French, or to sell a few dried peppers or the occasional fattened pig.

Her father's fate was little different. Eldest Brother had escaped, by going away to study, first to Saigon, then to France. She wanted to do that too. She could, she was sure. She was good at reading, good at everything at school. But she didn't go anymore. Too much school wasn't good for girls, her mother said. And there was no time, now.

She looked at her face in the shiny metal mirror, her mother's only treasure. What would Eldest Brother think of her, so thin and ugly, plowing all day?

She slipped out of the house after everyone else was asleep. Leaning against the thatched wall, she read by the light of a tiny oil wick. When, quite late, she went in, she couldn't sleep for the stifling heat. She moved restlessly on the bamboo mat, trying to find a cool spot, and finally went back outside. The moon was hidden by clouds. Maybe it would rain before it was too late after all.

IT DID RAIN, a day and night of steady soaking. After that, daily heavy showers. The earth grew spongy.

It was time to transfer the seedlings to the field. Her father had been tending them for weeks. He never allowed anyone else to do it. Trang Sen thought he willed the seeds to sprout, almost caressing the tiny plants with his long fingers until they grew up straight and tall, each one a perfect spike of new bright green.

Everyone helped plant, the fields thick with villagers, stooping knee- and elbow-deep in muddy water. Trang Sen's mother came, Trang Mai strapped to her back. They worked for three long days, backs aching from setting the tiny seedlings one by one in the flooded earth.

Trang Sen stood beside the house, sluicing dipperfuls of water over herself, spell-caught by the cool wetness on her sweat-soaked body and mud-caked limbs. A strange young man in western clothes came up the path. She thought at first he was an American. He had an odd way of walking — in long strides, moving his whole body. Lifting one foot, then the other, quite distinctly. Completely different from the short sliding steps, the gliding shuffle of the villagers, their upper bodies almost motionless. Maybe it was the shoes, she thought, that made him walk like that.

Chickens clucked frantically and scurried out of his way, as if they too knew this was a stranger. He looked straight ahead, toward their house at the end of the village. She wondered, a sharp pain of a thought, if he was coming for Fourth Brother.

She set the dipper down beside the big water jug, quickly put on her clothes and edged around to the front of the house. Her mother came out, Trang Mai on her hip.

Ba Cao also stared at the young man, then cried out. "First Son, First Son!"

She thrust Trang Mai into Trang Sen's arms and ran to the gate, Trang Sen's father and Tho behind her. Trang Sen followed, hanging back.

Greeting them all, Long turned to her. "You are Younger Sister."

She lowered her head, self-conscious. "Not now. This is Younger Sister." She held Trang Mai out to him.

"Ah, I've been away too long."

That evening Trang Sen listened to Long and her father talk, sitting at the low table, the only light the reddish glow from the candles on either side of the altar. It seemed they would talk all night.

"Not an easy time you've had, Pa-pa."

"Too much trouble, to be sure. With both your brothers gone, we work too hard. And with Second Son . . ." he hesitated.

"I came back to help. It was time to remember my duty — to you and our country."

Ong Cao shook his head. "About the country, I wouldn't know. We need a strong young man here. I'm getting old, I'd sleep easier knowing you're here to look out for the family."

"I'll work with you, for a time anyway. We must think about the country, too, though. While I was in France . . ."

Ong Cao interrupted him. "That's all too much for me, my son. It's more than I can do to keep up with this little village, with my own family."

Trang Sen thought something changed in Long's expression then, a momentary hesitation, the flick of a shutter.

She was fascinated by his educated, Saigon accent, his odd western-style clothes. Odder on her own brother than they would have been on a foreigner. In spite of his strangeness, or because of it, she was drawn to him. She would get him by himself, as soon as she could, she resolved, and ask him her own questions — why he wore those clothes, talked like that, walked like that.

He fell a few notches in her eyes when he started helping in the paddy field. His skill was negligible and never improved, no matter how hard he tried. But Ong Cao wanted him to do much of the work that had been hers. If Fourth Brother had usurped her place, she would have been angry. Not with him, though.

She explained things, over and over. "You have to keep getting the weeds out. But very gently. Don't pull up the rice."

He watched and nodded, tried it.

"No, no!" She almost shouted. "That's rice!"

She took the seedling from him, showed him the difference.

"How did you learn all this?"

"I don't know." Gathering courage, she added, "But I'd rather do what you do."

"And what do you mean by that?" His tone seemed unnecessarily sharp.

She opened her mouth, then closed it and looked down at the green shoots flickering in the shallow water. "Read," she whispered. "I want to read."

"Well, that should be easy enough. What do you want to read?"

She thought he was laughing at her. "I don't know. Will you help me?"

"We'll see."

To prove she was serious, she decided to ask Schoolmaster Co for help. Before she lost her courage, she set out to see him. She walked past the small school building in the middle of the village and opened the gate to the house next to it. "Master Co!"

The old man appeared in the doorway, his face hidden in the shadow of the roof overhang. "Little Sen?"

Trang Sen bowed respectfully.

"What would you be wanting, child?"

"I want to study, I need books, I want Eldest Brother to help me." She got it out in one breathless sentence.

Co frowned, annoyed. "You're going too fast for me, little Sen. Trinh Van Long . . . smartest boy I ever taught. But what of you? You left school long ago. Why start studying again?"

More slowly, Trang Sen tried to explain. "I want to go away to school, like Eldest Brother. I . . . I thought I'd ask him to help me. But I want to show him how good I am."

Co smiled a little. "No harm lending you books, I suppose. If you promise to bring them back. Tell your brother to come visit me."

"I will, I will."

"Come along to the school, then, child, and we'll see what we can find."

She struggled down the footpath, arms loaded with the books. Her cousin ran out to intercept her. "What are those for?"

Trang Sen explained.

"Are you still thinking of such crazy things?" Kim Hoa drew herself up in all her fourteen-year-old haughtiness. She was a dumpy, clumsy adolescent, a bit overweight, and useless behind a plow. But she was apprenticed to the village seamstress and was fast becoming an expert. Trang Sen claimed she could have embroidered the clothes of a queen if they had one.

"Never mind. Tell me about Cousin Long."

"He knows so much. But" — Trang Sen giggled — "nothing about planting rice. I'm better than he is!"

"Oh, Trang Sen. Always boasting. Anyone else would just be happy to have her brother back."

LONG AND TRANG Sen read together, huddled in a corner of the bed platform around the dim light of an oil lamp.

Ba Cao watched apprehensively. "I don't like it. They're too much alike." They both had the same dark, almost liquid, eyes, and the lock of hair that always seemed to stray out of place. She muttered and shook her head.

She required Trang Sen to look after Trang Mai more often.

Trang Sen obeyed, but complained. "Second Sister doesn't like me to carry her. She always cries."

"You must learn how to stop her crying. What kind of mother will you make? All this reading, no use. Look at me. Where would reading have gotten me?"

Trang Sen and Long walked together from the field, leading the buffalo. He looked back at them. "I used to like minding the buffalo, the only chore I was really willing to do. I liked swaying on his back. It seemed to me I was safe from the world then. I used to sit there thinking of all the wonderful things I would do. Then I thought I would really like to ride an elephant. Funny the ideas kids get."

"I thought that too." She had almost forgotten. The buffalo were just work animals now. "I thought I'd go to Saigon someday, get away from here. But I never thought what I'd do when I got there. I was just a kid."

He laughed. "You're still a kid."

She stood a little straighter. "I can plow better than most of the men."

"I know. You're teaching me. I would never learn to work the paddy fields before. I was afraid it would take me away from studying."

"I feel that way."

"But you must learn what Ma-ma is trying to teach you. Maybe she's right. Maybe this reading is a bad idea."

"No! It's the only thing I like!"

He didn't answer.

She was suddenly angry. "All of you grow up and leave, and I keep staying here. I used to want to work like the boys, but that's no fun either. One day Fourth Brother will go to the army. And who knows how long you'll stay?"

He said nothing.

She glanced at him. "You aren't leaving, are you? Please don't leave."

He shrugged. "I soon must. I mean to talk with Pa-pa."

"Then let me go, too, away from here!"

IN ALMOST INAUDIBLE, hissing whispers, Long and his father argued.

"I don't know anything about all these political ideas, but joining the Front is a bad idea, I tell you. I forbid it."

"Half the village council is helping them, one way or another."

"They do that to stay alive. The Front does nothing but frighten people. If you want to do anything, join the army. That's something to be proud of."

Long opened his mouth, then closed it. After a moment he said, "It isn't right to argue or disobey you, Pa-pa. But the Front wants to improve everybody's lives. We'd be better off with them in charge. Don't you want a better life?"

Ong Cao shrugged. "My life is fine as it is. Or was until they took my two sons away. That's what comes from all the meddling. Best to leave things alone."

He reached for his pipe, got up and went outside, his thin shoulders bent in an old man's stoop.

The next morning Long was gone. Her mother said Pa-pa had run him off. Her father said nothing. Guiltily, secretly, Trang Sen applauded. She had never seen anyone oppose her father. But the day was empty without Long.

To the relief of them all, he returned two days later. "I've done at least part of what you wanted, Pa-pa. I've joined the army."

Ong Cao nodded. His wife turned away to hide her fear.

Long had to report to the training camp the next day. "It's not far. I'll come back from time to time."

That night he joined Trang Sen on the narrow veranda that surrounded the house.

"Why do you care about the war? It just messes everything up."

"I want us in charge of our country again. That's all. I want the foreigners out."

"What about the Americans? I thought they were helping the army."

He ignored her question. "When I was in France I thought I'd join the Front. Most of the people I knew there have come back to do that. It's only because of Pa-pa I'm in the army. This way I'll be able to help you more. Since I was away so long, I owe that to all of you. There'll be some money to make things easier. These days it's no good depending on what we can sell in Tay Ninh."

He glanced at her. "Pa-pa still needs you now. But when the war is over, I know a convent school in Saigon, if you still want to go to school by then."

Tenuously connected thoughts spun through her head. He was going to help her. What if her parents refused? What if he changed his mind? What if the war kept on?

"I'm not sure you should do this," he was continuing, "but I can tell you're determined, and you can do the work. Master Co will help you. I've also talked with Pa-pa. They won't stand in your way." He chuckled. "Pa-pa saw it as a kind of bargain to keep me out of the Front."

"What if the war doesn't end?"

"It will."

But it got worse.

MASTER CO KEPT his promise, reluctantly acknowledging Trang Sen's ability. Sometimes he shook his head at the waste. If she had been born into a rich family, in Saigon, a place saturated with Western ideas. . . . All she really needed was to be a valuable wife for some village boy — if there were any left.

Her adolescent loveliness could not be hidden by the black peasant clothes or her scant attention to her appearance. Her cousin Kim Hoa reported, "They're all talking about you, all the mothers. They say you look like Auntie, so beautiful when she was your age." Kim Hoa felt no envy. She giggled. "They say you'll make some boy a good wife."

Trang Sen blushed.

She looked at Ba Cao with new eyes, and saw that her mother was still beautiful, though her hair had streaks of gray and she was worn down by all their troubles. Trang Sen examined herself in the polished mirror. Her oval face stared back at her, dominated by the brown eyes under eyebrows that slanted gently upward. She was pleased.

She had little interest in the few village boys still at home. Marriage was a threat to all her plans. But she had concocted a fantasy around the light-haired American. She lay awake, savoring it. He would come rescue her, lifting her in his strong arms and carrying her away to safety. She wore a filmy ao dai, which streamed behind them as he ran, her hair long and shining, catching the faint silver beams of the moonlight. The end of the fantasy always found them making love. Other times, she imagined herself having a baby. Not in the same dream.

LONG WAS FIRST stationed at the camp near their village, in charge of training young recruits. Educated, he had entered the officer corps. Because of this, his lot was easier than that of his brothers. He was deeply troubled.

"The training is no good," he told Trang Sen. "Useless against the Front. And they're so young, just boys. Cannon fodder, that's all I'm teaching them to be!"

She thought of Second Brother.

Then Long was transferred to Saigon, to the office of one of the generals working with the Americans. Trang Sen thought he was even more dissatisfied.

She felt the time had come to think about the school again. Tho was becoming a skillful farmer, and he was still too young for the army. She thought they could manage without her.

A DAWN-PALE SUN slowly emerged on the flat horizon. Mists of fog lay over the rice fields, rendered indistinct the more distant houses. The forest, lighted from behind, stood out darkly beyond the paddy, the line of tall palms swaying lazily in a slight breeze. Trang Sen stood at the edge of the veranda, savoring the momentary coolness.

Fourth Brother appeared, holding the reins of the buffalo, their father beside him. As she turned to follow them, she saw Long coming along the path. Observing him, Trang Sen felt the familiar surge of admiration. His slim body showed no spare flesh. Lately, too, she thought he seemed less foreign.

He called a greeting, and Ba Cao appeared in the doorway.

"I can stay for a few days. I'll change and come with you."

"You must have some breakfast first," Ba Cao insisted. "There's some nice dried fish from the market."

The others went on. Ba Cao set a steaming bowl of rice porridge and some small plates of condiments on the low table, then squatted down beside her son.

"How is First Sister? She's more beautiful every time I see her. Like you."

Ba Cao ignored the compliment. "That child is born to trouble. Pa-pa and I think it's time she married. But I don't know. She's never been one to agree to anything not to her liking. She will cause us all much grief."

"What about her studies?"

"If you ask me, she already knows too much. Men don't want wives smarter than they are. They don't even want their wives to be able to read."

"I was thinking of her really going to school, in Saigon." He held up his hand as she began to protest. "There's a convent school I know about. I think it's the only way to keep her out of trouble, as you say. She would never survive marrying someone in the village — if there were anyone for her to marry."

"Well, I never heard of such a thing. You'll have to speak with your father."

He rose, pulled the dark, pajama-type pants and top off a peg on the wall, and prepared to join the others in the paddy field.

He smiled as he turned around to his mother. "Don't worry."

Long told them about a new program to stop the Front from raiding villages. "The Americans call it strategic hamlets. Sometimes they leave a village where it is, but ours will have to be moved. Our soldiers will give us barbed wire to string around the edge of the village, and they'll give us whatever we need to build new houses and make the place safe. We'll have to do all the work ourselves."

"How is barbed wire going to protect us? Do they think in Saigon that the Communists don't know how to cut wire?" Ong Cao laughed grimly. "Where will this new place be? And what about our paddy fields? Will we lose the rice crop?"

"If they decide this area is too dangerous, you'll have to start new fields."

"First they take all my sons, now this."

Trang Sen thought of something else. "If everyone leaves the village, won't the Front come and use what's left, and take our rice when it's ripe?"

"Most likely. But there's nothing we can do."

Her anger flared. "Nothing we can do, always nothing we can do! They keep doing these stupid things, killing us, and we never do anything!" Almost in tears, she ran out the door.

Her father shook his head. "It's time that one was married, calmed down." He went on, talking to himself. "She will surely seem a desirable wife. Ma-ma has taught her well. Besides, she is beautiful — too beautiful perhaps. It's not easy, finding a husband these days. Maybe a widower, or someone rich enough to have a second wife."

Long hesitated. "What if she didn't agree?"

"She would have no choice." Ong Cao frowned. "But it could be a problem. First Daughter has a mind of her own."

Long mentioned the school. "I think the nuns would be delighted to find a girl as bright as she is."

Ong Cao pulled on his pipe. "Best she be married. Then our problems would be over."

"I wonder. I can't see her submitting to a husband she hadn't willingly married. There'd be all kinds of trouble between the two families. And she'd be miserable. Not, perhaps, the best way to reward her loyalty. She's worked as hard as any son."

"It's true. She's a good daughter."

"Saigon is dangerous, too many things could happen. Who would watch over her?" asked Ba Cao.

"The convent school is very strict. If anything, the nuns are stricter than most parents."

"I don't know, my son. We'll have to think about this."

Ba Cao only shook her head.

LONG KNEW WHERE to find her. At the edge of the forest, sitting back on her haunches, her head leaning on her arms.

"Do you feel better?"

She shrugged.

"You're right to be angry. If you could see the stupidity of the generals — and the blockheadedness of the Americans — to think an idea like this can work! It will just uproot everybody for nothing." His voice was tight.

She looked at him, surprised out of her own turmoil. He didn't often show even this much emotion.

They were silent for a while, listening to the tree frogs croaking and the hollow hoo, hoo of an owl deep in the forest. From time to time the velvet swish of bat wings passed above them.

"I would like you to be in Saigon. I must teach you about politics."

"I hate politics. That's where all the trouble starts."

"And that's why you must learn about it. It's all there is."

It had been a long time since he mentioned anything about her going to school. She was afraid to ask him more.

That night she lay on the plank bed, listening to her parents' low voices behind the thin partition of their sleeping alcove. She thought of Kim Hoa, soon to be married. Trang Sen didn't talk much with her anymore. The intended husband was the only son of an old family friend. Slightly lame from a childhood illness, he had escaped both the army and the Front.

He and his parents ran a small shop in the next village. They could use Kim Hoa, would add a tailoring shop to get the most out of her sewing talents. They had given handsome gifts. Kim Hoa's father could hardly refuse them.

Trang Sen shivered. Would her own father be any different? The same thing would not, must not, happen to her. She drifted off to sleep lapped in the fuzzy edges of the daydream of her American rescuer, strong and light and blue-eyed.

Before Long returned to Saigon, their father gave him permission to contact the convent school. "I haven't made up my mind," he warned. "I suppose it doesn't hurt to ask."

Ong Cao sat for long hours in the evenings staring at his unlit pipe, often squatting outside under the overhanging thatch, thinking.

Every day another village was moved, each one closer to their own. Then their turn came. They were to move to an abandoned sugar cane field a quarter mile or so on the other side of the stream. A stretch of forest separated it from their village. Part of an old French plantation, it had been depleted years ago. The French owners left before Trang Sen was born, but some of the villagers had worked there.

Long returned the day they moved. The villagers worked together, hurrying to get the roofs of the houses raised, the household goods under cover, before the afternoon rains began.

Trang Sen felt her own fate was part of the upheaval. She took his noon rice to Long, who was working on the barricade around the new village. She squatted beside him as he ate.

"I've talked with the Sisters at the convent school. Pa-pa said I could do that."

"Oh."

"It's not an easy thing for him to decide. He only said he'd think about it. But I think in the end he'll see it's a good thing. I told the nuns how you've studied on your own, and how well you've done. They're very impressed. They want you to come."

She blushed with excitement and pleasure. "They really said that?"

"Yes. But with Pa-pa . . ."

Elated, she interrupted, "You'll tell him how safe I'll be in a convent." She grinned at him.

After supper Long talked with their parents. Trang Sen pretended to read.

"It seems a good thing for First Sister now. Perhaps better than arranging a marriage, with all the good husband prospects away in the war."

Ong Cao nodded. "Yes, that also must be considered. What if we married her, only for her to become a widow?"

Ba Cao broke in. "This will lead to no good. She needs a husband to settle her down, the same as I did. I know about headstrong young girls. How can you two know?"

Her husband glanced at Trang Sen, drawing on his pipe. At last he turned back to Long. "It is a strange thing you're suggesting. But all is changing. It seems that this must change too. It may be that things will never be as they were, that this is the best way to prepare First Daughter for a new life."

Ba Cao raised her eyebrows in angry disapproval. Her husband shook his head, as if to deny her objections. "I can't stand against the changes. You may tell the Sisters she will come."

Trang Sen could bear it no longer. Slowly, very carefully, she closed her book, stood up, and walked out of the house. In this new place there was nowhere to go, no familiar forest path. She thought of Kim Hoa, but what could she say to Kim Hoa? She stood irresolute on the edge of the new-cut path, excitement and a strange new desolation churning inside her. To go away, to study, to see Saigon, all at once. She recalled the old dream, of riding on the elephant, side by side with Eldest Brother.

1963–1964

15,000 U.S. military advisors
in Vietnam by the end of 1963

CHAPTER 3

EXILES

MUTED LIGHT PENETRATED green shutters, closed against the afternoon heat. Trang Sen's voice droned through endless French verbs, the monotonous recitation hanging in the humid stillness and lulling Sister Louise into a sleepy stupor.

The girl's thoughts wandered from the verbal drill. Saigon, so disorderly. All the different people, so many foreigners — officials, diplomats, soldiers, journalists, all rushing around to some purpose unclear to her. And all the people from the dead villages, here with no home. Eldest Brother's patriotic passion, his anger, making sense here.

Sister Louise sat up straighter, trying, without success as usual, to look appropriately dignified despite her dumpiness, evident even beneath the heavy folds of her habit. "And now, *ma chère*, a little conversation."

Trang Sen liked this part best. If only she could learn faster.

"*Très bien, très bien.*" The Sister signaled that the lesson was over. Trang Sen bowed formally, as the students were taught to do. The Sister smiled, her blue eyes sparkling a little.

Sister Louise watched Trang Sen walk the length of the courtyard. She remembered the day the girl arrived, escorted by her brother, stiff with the unfamiliarity of her new ao dai. *Such an intelligent child. Mais oui, the most intelligent I've ever taught. And how quickly she learns the French. Her accent almost perfect already. . . . All these years, never sure why I came to this place, so godless, so beautiful, beautiful unto perdition. Such angry people — why do they hate us, who have given them so much? I, who have given them so much? I am weary, very weary, I long for home. But this child, beautiful like the land itself, yet without the lost innocence. It is perhaps for this I have been an exile here.*

Trang Sen climbed the stairs and walked along the open passageway. She turned and looked down at the courtyard, vivid with purple bougainvillea and clumps of red and cream poinsettias. Now, at the beginning of the dry season, everything was still luminous with myriad shades of green, punctuated by the bright flowers. The air, clearer and drier, held a hint of coolness. But she felt suffocated by the faded yellow stucco of the massive walls, at night longed for the air and openness of her home, its thatched roof and bare earthen floor.

Something gnawed at her when she thought of home. Her mother, so opposed to her going away, neglected all her other duties to get Trang Sen ready, as if she was preparing her for marriage . . . She remembered the last thing Ba Cao said, as she gave the new ao dai one final, straightening tug — "You are like me, little one. I only ask one thing, that you remember all I have tried to teach you. You have to learn what I did — to obey and submit. It is for your own good." Then, "There! You are beautiful. May your spirit be as beautiful." To Trang Sen's surprise, her mother's eyes had filled with tears.

When she mentioned the incident to Long, he only said, "Ma-ma is right. Someday you must learn those lessons." That annoyed her.

She heard shouting and scuffling from beyond the wall, not for the first time that day. This time, though, the noise came from just outside the gate. Some of the students were gathered around the porter. She ran down the stairs to join them.

The old porter resolutely guarded the entrance, his hunched back seeming a little straighter as he stood facing the girls. "No, no, you young ones stay inside. Very dangerous out there."

Sister Nguyen approached him. "What is it, Old Tranh?"

"Bad times." He looked around, as if he expected some blow to fall on him. His voice sank almost to a whisper. "With President Diem killed, he and his brother, too, a bad day for the likes of us. The Buddhists are out there celebrating."

Whatever else he might have said was cut off by the arrival of Sister Marie-Jean, the headmistress. "What is all this?" Her voice was sharp, her square face stern within the white wimple. All day she had insisted everyone stay in the compound, keeping their curiosity in check by the sheer force of her own will.

The Vietnamese Sister lowered her eyes in quickly assumed humility. She hesitated a moment, then suggested that Catholics would surely be in for a bad time.

"Nonsense. This has nothing to do with us." Sister Marie-Jean turned to the porter. "No one is to leave the compound without my permission. No one. Is that clear?" Then, turning to the little cluster of students, "All of you go back to your work," she commanded.

Trang Sen's head churned with curiosity. *Had Eldest Brother known about the generals' coup? What would happen now? Was it really dangerous out there?* The impulse to find out was too strong to resist.

The supper gong sounded. She joined the other girls chattering in the dining hall. Sister Marie-Jean rapped them to silence, asked the blessing and gave them the signal to be seated. Trang Sen spent the dinner hour perfecting a scheme to sneak out. She would wait until her roommates were asleep. How could she get past the porter? The wall was too high to climb over. Then she remembered the small gate behind the kitchen. It never seemed to be guarded.

She lay stiffly in bed until she was sure it was well past midnight, then stealthily dressed, abandoning the ao dai for the short tunic blouse she had worn in the village. The courtyard was cloaked in eerie shadows, the pale poinsettia blooms ghostly in the light of a sliver of moon. She slid swiftly around the arcade, through the deserted dining hall and kitchen, down the plank walk to the gate. It opened inward with a Western-style lock which could be set to stay open. But she needed something to tie the outside handle to the metal gatepost so it would look locked. She found a tail-piece from the strips of rattan used to tie the big rice bags closed, set the lock, carefully pulled the gate open and let herself out.

At the opening to the alley, she peered down the street in the direction of the presidential palace. All day there had been sporadic outbursts of shouting and sometimes gunshots, but the city seemed calm now. She headed toward Eldest Brother's quarters.

The intersections were guarded by heavily armed police. Avoiding those crossings, she took advantage of the relatively unpatrolled areas in between, crept along in the shadows of buildings and walls. As she slipped around the last corner, she heard voices behind her. She pressed against the compound wall and tried to think what to do next.

Someone suddenly seized her arms from behind and put a hand over her mouth. "Who are you? What are you doing out after curfew?"

She made muffled attempts to answer.

"Be still or you're dead!" He twisted her arms behind her back and reached for his pistol with the other hand.

"I was looking for my brother. He lives there." She inclined her head toward the gate. "He's General Le's aide."

"Your brother's name?"

"Trinh Van Long. Please . . ."

"Where did you say he lives?"

"In there." She nodded toward the gate again. "You have to ask the guards."

"Not so fast." He jerked her arms tighter. "Where's your identity card?"

Her identity card. She had forgotten it. She was now genuinely frightened. Terrible stories of people disappearing, of what happened to girls taken in by the police, froze her blood. "Please, have them call my brother."

He eyed her sharply. What if she was telling the truth? If anything happened to the sister of General Le's aide, then what?

"Come on." He pulled her toward the guard station.

"Halt there!" The guards angled rifles toward them, the dark grey barrels glinting dully in the sallow arc light.

"Ever seen this girl before? She says a Trinh Van Long's her brother."

"We have a Captain Long, sure enough. About her, hard to tell. You sure she's his sister?" Both guards snickered.

"Stop looking at me like that! Of course I'm his sister!"

The policeman tightened his grip on her again. "Quiet!" He turned back to the guards. "You'd better call Captain Long. If this girl's a fraud, she'll be punished, I promise you that."

Trang Sen began to wonder, nervously, what Eldest Brother would say.

The guard returned, followed by Long. His uniform was wrinkled, his hair rumpled, as if he had just gotten out of bed.

He looked at Trang Sen. "What is this?"

"Is she your sister, sir?"

"Yes, yes. Release her."

"Yes sir." The policeman jerked himself up straight, letting go of Trang Sen's wrists.

She stood rubbing them, avoiding Long's eyes.

"What are you doing here?" he repeated.

"I . . . I wanted to find you."

The police officer looked curiously at the two of them. Long turned to him, said curtly, "You may go."

The man bowed and scurried away.

"All right, come with me." He motioned her through the gate, then stopped and spoke with the guards.

His room was barely large enough for the narrow cot, a table and a small chair. He motioned her to the chair, then sat down on the cot facing her. "Explain."

"I heard about the coup. They said there were riots, that some generals had killed the President. I was afraid for you." She said it all very quickly, but finished a little more boldly. Maybe anxiety for him would get her out of this.

"Was that the only reason?" His voice was unsympathetic.

She looked away from him, her eyes hot with tears.

Bluntly, he went on, spitting the words out. "You know what could have happened to you out there. People picked up after curfew are never heard of again. Especially beautiful young girls. Especially without their identity cards."

She had no answer.

"How did you get out?"

She explained. "Oh, I have to go back. They'll discover about the gate if I don't get there before the cook."

He shook his head, but couldn't suppress a smile. "You aren't going to sneak back in. I'm taking you in the morning and you will explain this to Sister Marie-Jean."

"Oh, no, please. I promise not to do it again."

"No. When you went to the school, you understood the rules."

"But they like me so much! I don't want to disappoint them!"

"You already have," he commented drily.

He rose and pulled the blanket off the cot. "You can sleep here." He motioned her to the cot and spread the blanket out in the narrow floor space for himself, turned off the dim overhead bulb and lay down. Soon he was asleep. But she lay for a long time staring into the darkness.

THE PORTER COULDN'T conceal his surprise when he opened the gate. He stared at them. "What . . . how . . .?"

Long ignored his stuttering curiosity. "Please let Sister Marie-Jean know we're here. We'll wait until it's convenient for her to see us."

The old man grunted and slipped off toward the nuns' quarters.

A few minutes later he returned. "Sister will see you now."

Trang Sen trailed behind Long to the headmistress's office.

"What is this?" Sister Marie-Jean addressed the question to Long. "Her roommates discovered Trang Sen gone this morning, and Sister Li found the back gate unlocked."

He bowed. "We deeply apologize. Trang Sen will explain."

She looked at him and swallowed.

"Go ahead. Tell Sister Marie-Jean what happened."

Her eyes on the dark teak floor, Trang Sen told once more how she had left the compound, to find her brother, she said. She hesitated, not wanting to mention the policeman.

"Tell the whole thing."

Sister Marie-Jean's face grew more and more stern.

"I promise never to do it again, Sister."

"We'll see that you don't."

There was no comfort in the assurance.

The headmistress toyed with a pencil, then looked again at Trang Sen. "I want to talk with the Captain. You may wait outside."

She left the room, not daring to look at Eldest Brother.

"You do realize how serious this is, Captain Long?"

"Yes, Sister." He switched to French. "You understand, of course, that she meant no harm."

Sister Marie-Jean nodded. "But such behavior is grounds for dismissal, suspension at the very least. In her case I am reluctant to do either. I don't mind telling you, sir, in many years I have not seen so intelligent a child."

Long inclined his head.

"Until now she has given us no trouble. But I can't allow the other girls to think we take this lightly. If she were suspended for, perhaps, two months . . ." The headmistress left the sentence unfinished.

"I will be honest with you, Sister. It took a great deal of persuading to convince our parents to allow Trang Sen to come here. If she were to return home now, they would not allow her to come back. They would marry her as soon as possible, no doubt to some completely unsuitable villager. I am sorry, Sister."

"No, no, I'm grateful for your frankness. It would be deeply wrong to deny the child a chance to develop that fine mind." She glanced out the window at the blossom-laden branches of a tamarind tree arching over the wall. The lines of her face, etched by years of holding herself and all the school in order, seemed to soften a little. "I must give this some careful thought. . . . Please ask Trang Sen to come back in."

She was sitting hunched over on a bench against the wall, her hands clasped loosely in her lap, oblivious to the early-morning bustle in the courtyard. She looked up at him, her expression desolate. He smiled slightly as he motioned her inside.

"Trang Sen, an offense such as yours warrants dismissal."

The Sister paused to let that sink in.

"However, I have not yet decided what to do in your case. Until further notice you are confined to your room. You will leave only for meals, which you will eat at a table apart from the others. You will not attend classes. I suggest you reflect very seriously on how much the opportunity for an education means to you, and whether it is worth throwing away. I will let you know when I have decided on additional punishment. You may go now."

Trang Sen bowed and left the room, holding onto an appearance of dignity by a desperate effort. After a brief final exchange, Long followed her.

"There is nothing I can add to what Sister has said." His tone was gentle. She was both surprised and grateful.

She watched him until he disappeared through the gate, then went down the length of the compound to the dormitory. She sat on the edge of the bed, her chest constricted with the tears she would not release. To be dismissed. She couldn't go back to the village. She would run away. And never see Eldest Brother again? Her chest grew tighter at the thought. And Sister Louise. What would Sister Louise think of her now?

When she was summoned at last, four long days later, she stood before the headmistress with what she hoped was a proper combination of submission and pride.

"Well, Trang Sen, you've had some time to think about this. Have you come to any conclusions?"

"I was very stupid, Sister."

"And what about your studying?"

"I've tried to study myself, like I did at home. I do want to stay." Her voice caught in spite of herself.

"I'm going to give you a chance to do that. I am compelled to suspend you for two months" — Trang Sen's head dropped lower — "but you may stay here, confined to your room except for meals. I encourage you to study on your own."

The tears of relief were the hardest to suppress.

"I have told your brother of my decision. He can decide whether to inform your parents, since he has responsibility for you here."

Trang Sen bowed.

"And, Trang Sen, I'm sorry this happened." The headmistress looked sharply at her. "I rather suspect your actions several nights ago were not unlike earlier escapades. Just remember, you aren't in the village now and you're not a child anymore."

"Yes, Sister." Trang Sen blushed with shame.

But as soon as she left the Sister's office, unqualified relief swept over her. She could stay.

Her room was dark and airless, the shutters closed to keep out the beating sun. She studied until noon, then joined the others in the dining room. At her solitary table she finished her meal and waited to be dismissed. It was Sister Louise who rapped for their attention.

Trang Sen bowed as she filed past, several steps behind the others.

"Trang Sen."

She turned around. "Yes, Sister."

"Are you studying your French?"

"Yes, Sister. I studied most of the morning." She added, "I'm sorry this happened, Sister."

"I was surprised. You have been such a perfect student. But," Sister Louise couldn't keep her voice stern, "we shall go on from here. I look forward to the day when we resume our classes, *ma chère*."

Her roommates were in the room when she returned.

"What happened?" asked Thanh Thuy. "Did Sister say you could stay?"

"Yes." Trang Sen explained the punishment.

"Oh, how miserable."

"But it's such a relief. I was afraid they'd send me away. I could have never come back."

"I think I'd rather never come back." The three of them giggled.

Trang Sen turned to the stack of books on her desk.

THREE WEEKS, SHE counted as she walked across the courtyard. Its greenness was tinged now with dry-season dust around the edges. She had thought it would be easy. It is, she repeated to herself, far better than being sent away.

She was tired of listening to her roommates' endless chatter. Usually about some lieutenant or other. Bedtimes she retreated into her dream of the blond American. She could almost feel his arms around her as she drifted into sleep, lulled by the droning voices of the others.

"Sister." Trang Sen bowed as she passed one of the Vietnamese nuns.

Sister Nguyen returned the greeting frostily, her narrow face beneath the stiff wimple showing no warmth.

The maid Ba Tu was in Trang Sen's room. "Young miss." She accompanied the greeting with a low bow.

"No need for such formality, Ba Tu."

The maid pushed the mop back and forth.

"How long have you been in Saigon, Ba Tu?"

"I came last year, with my husband, miss, when the Front attacked our village."

"I miss our house in the village sometimes."

"Are you from a village, miss?"

"Yes." She thought of something else. "How old are you, Ba Tu?"

"I was born in the year of the dog."

"Seventeen, western-style," Trang Sen worked out, half to herself. "Not much older than me. I was born in the year of the rat. When were you married?"

"Two, maybe three years. I had a baby, but it died."

I could have been like Ba Tu. Except for Eldest Brother. "Did your parents find your husband for you?"

"No, miss, my parents are dead. I was living with my uncle. He was so mean I ran away. One day I found some work planting rice. The old man handing out the seedlings took a liking to me. He gave me a job that whole planting season. When he found out I was alone, he asked me to marry him. It wasn't the right way, miss, but what could I do? He said he would give me a home if I would take care of him in his old age. Then he got sick and after that our village burned. So we came to Saigon."

"Is he still sick?"

"He's a little better now, miss. On good days he drives a cyclo. And here I can work, so even if he's sick we eat."

The room seemed even drearier after Ba Tu left. *I could be friends with her, we're almost alike. But she's afraid of me.* Trang Sen suddenly longed for Kim Hoa. *She'll be married now, perhaps having a baby already.* Trang Sen almost envied her. She turned face down on the bed and wept.

One of her roommates, Thanh Thuy, came in to retrieve a book and found her there. She hesitantly patted Trang Sen's arm.

Trang Sen turned her head away.

"I'm sorry, I thought maybe I could help."

"No way to help," mumbled Trang Sen, then, "thank you," she added.

"We can talk more sometimes if you like."

Trang Sen nodded.

SHE LOOKED IN the mirror again and pushed back the wisp of unruly hair that always seemed to escape, forcing it to conform to the smooth line from forehead to ear. To look perfect.

Eldest Brother was coming for her. He would be proud of her — she had endured her punishment without complaint. And kept up with her studies, even without the help of the Sisters. They had all been pleased.

All, that is, except Sister Nguyen, in mathematics. That subject had been easiest of all. But Sister Nguyen was determined to be hard on her. In class she tried to fluster Trang Sen, refusing to acknowledge her correct answers. When Trang Sen eventually stammered a wrong reply, the Sister smiled broadly, her thin lips stretched to the breaking point. "We'll see if you can overcome your handicaps. With your weak background, well, I don't know."

Trang Sen had lowered her head, her face scarlet.

Sister Li came to the doorway. "Your brother is here."

Trang Sen followed the nun's flapping sandals along the passage and down the stairs.

Long smiled at her as she came across the courtyard. She couldn't help doing a little skip, despite her resolve to be sedate. His smile widened.

"I decided you should have a reward. I'm taking you to a French restaurant, one of my favorites."

Outside the gate all was honking horns and acrid exhaust fumes, people jostling past, young women sailing by on bicycles, their pastel-colored ao dais fluttering behind them.

"I could never be a nun."

"No." He chuckled at the idea. "You would have great difficulty being obedient."

"Not just that. It's so boring. No one ever dares anything in the convent. They're all like this." She made a face, pulling down the corners of her mouth and half closing her eyes. "They might as well be asleep, even the girls."

She shook her head at a beggar pestering them and dodged a reckless cyclo. The driver rang his bell hard and yelled at her.

"Just don't get run over your first day out. But the convent has its uses. You do still want to study, don't you?"

"Yes, yes, of course. It just feels good to be outside. I was going to be so dignified, too."

"No matter. Tonight is for enjoyment."

He guided her into a narrow side street off Le Thanh Ton. Halfway down the block, they came to a tiny restaurant, its open door flush with the sidewalk. Ceiling fans sluggishly stirred the warm air inside. The head waiter led them to a table against the back wall, somewhat isolated.

"My favorite table. He always gives me this one."

She looked at him curiously. "Do you often come here?"

"I miss France sometimes. So I come here. The owner is French, and we talk about Paris, and about Arles, where he lived."

"You've never told me much about France."

He stared past her. "I sometimes think I'm more at home there than here. The people tell you what they mean, none of this hinting and coming at things the long way around. I like that. And I like the seasons changing. . . . Ah, you don't know, Paris in the autumn, the leaves all gold and red and the air sharp with frost." He stopped. "Well, I'm Vietnamese. That's what I finally decided. So I came back. It's strange, though, I often feel I belong in neither place."

Momentarily, with a shiver, she thought he was talking about her.

He picked up the menu and studied it as the waiter came toward them.

"And a bottle of the Batard Montrachet," Long finished the order.

He turned to Trang Sen. "What about your two months?"

She told him how it had been. "Sister Louise . . . well, I disappointed her. I feel the worst about that. She's very kind, not angry. She says my French is better even without her lessons. I don't know, though. I couldn't catch much of what you were saying."

"Those were words you wouldn't likely have learned."

She went on. "But I don't understand. The Vietnamese Sisters seem to hate me, especially Sister Nguyen." She recounted the morning's grilling.

His silence was edged with anger.

At last he looked up, explained wearily. "I understand it, only too well. It's just like it was all those years the French ran the country. The French Sisters look down on our people. So our Sisters need someone to treat the same way. Then you come along. Not only are you from a village, but the French nuns give you special treatment. Even Sister Marie-Jean. She let you stay there because she knew you could never come back if she sent you away."

"Did you . . .?"

"We discussed it. But let me finish. You're actually treated better than the Vietnamese Sisters. And you're one of the few people they dare treat poorly. They'd never single out a wealthy Saigon girl." His voice had a bitter edge. "So we use up our energy sniping at each other instead of sticking together."

"You think the French Sisters are wrong? I think Sister Louise is wonderful! And why should the others be angry with me? I haven't done anything to them!"

"That's what I'm telling you. It doesn't matter what you do, how you feel about Sister Nguyen, or any of them."

She told him about Ba Tu. "I'm more like her than I am the others, but she's afraid of me."

"Another way we let ourselves be divided. You *are* like her, but she can't see that because you're part of the group she thinks is different."

"That can't be! I *will* make friends with her! She's just afraid because she's been alone and she's in this big city and her husband's sick and . . ."

"All right, all right. You *should* keep trying. I just want you to understand what's happening, that's all."

"I can see what you mean about the nuns, and I suppose about Ba Tu, but it still doesn't make any sense."

"No."

The waiter brought the first course and the wine. "A celebration tonight, Captain Long?" He glanced appreciatively at Trang Sen.

"My sister. Something of a celebration. Her first time to a French restaurant."

The waiter bowed. "Yes, I can see the resemblance. A beautiful young lady," he added, in Vietnamese, "and a kind brother." He turned away from the table.

"How do *you* feel?" she asked. "I mean, about the French. You seem to like them so much."

"I? I'm very drawn to them, to their culture, their ways. As you're finding out, what we get here is still a French education. And did you ever wonder where we got into the habit of eating bread and drinking coffee? That's because of the French, too. And I like all of it, but I get angry at the way they, and the Americans too, treat us — but here."

She had picked up a snail by the shell and was preparing to suck out the meat.

"Let me show you the French way to eat those. I know, I know." He forestalled her protest. "They're just snails. But in France they're considered a special delicacy. You hold the shell with this and pull the meat out, just so."

He watched her struggling and laughed.

"I don't see why you have to go through all this."

"You want to understand France, don't you? Perhaps someday you'll go there, and then you won't be embarrassed because you don't know how to eat. Come on, surely you can conquer a small snail, considering all the other things you've done." He grinned at her.

She picked up the tongs and fork again with determination. The shell skittered across the plate, but her second attempt was more successful. "It seems a lot of trouble for a snail."

"Ah, but they're not snails to the French, they're *escargots*. Doesn't that sound far more refined?"

Ignoring him, she concentrated on the snails. She had succeeded in getting two into her mouth when it dawned on her what he had said. She dropped the shell she had so carefully grasped with the tongs. "Me? Go to France? Is that what you said?"

"Would you like that? I was only teasing you. But sometimes I think going away is the only thing for you to do. It isn't unheard of in Saigon for a girl to go away to study. The only problem would be money."

She was even more surprised. "You've really thought about it."

"I suppose I have, at least a little."

"Where would I go? What would I do?"

He shook his head. "It was just a thought, probably not a very good one. Forget it."

But the idea was there now. She said nothing more, only devoted herself to the snails, which suddenly took on a new element of romance and promise. *Escargots*, he said they were called.

When she had eaten them all, she looked up. "What's been happening? No one ever talks of politics in the convent."

He was immediately somber. "I more or less agreed with the idea of the coup, Diem was so mixed up with the Americans. But the generals are in with the Americans thicker than Diem ever was. Now there's talk, which I'm afraid may be true, that the Americans actually put the generals up to what they did. And there's something about it that stinks, the way we're turning against each other. It's just like the convent, but with much more serious results. And no one does anything for the peasants — or they do the wrong thing. We're all a bunch of Saigon snobs and Paris intellectuals."

"But you . . ."

"I? I understand some of those things. It just doesn't matter because I'll never have the power for it to make any difference." He lowered his voice almost to a whisper. "I really think the country would be better off with a Communist government. At least Ho Chi Minh has a vision."

She didn't know enough to argue with him, or even if she should argue. "Do you think you should have joined the Front?"

"I don't know. The only thing I'm sure of is, we should be free of the Americans. Why did we throw out the French to let the Americans in?"

"Why do you hate the Americans? I rather like them."

"That's a foolish thing to say. What do you know about them? Have you ever even talked with an American?"

"No. Well, once, but I suppose that doesn't count."

"What are you talking about?"

She told him of her childhood encounter with the American by the river, elaborating on the way she had tricked him.

His eyes danced. "Did Second Brother know what was happening?"

"No, oh, no."

He chuckled. "We perhaps should let you handle the Americans." Then he was no longer joking. "You've always been like this, haven't you? Sneaking out that night was like all your other escapades — you do something first, then deal with the consequences later."

"I won't do that again."

"Oh, I'm sure you won't. But what will it be next?"

"I thought tonight was for enjoyment." She pouted. "And you haven't answered my question. Why do you hate the Americans?"

"All right. Tonight is for enjoyment. I did promise that. But I worry about you. Someday I'm afraid you'll land in real trouble."

She looked down at her plate. After a few moments he reached over and patted her hand. "I won't scold you again."

He took a long swallow of wine, rolling his tongue appreciatively around the flavor. "Why do I hate the Americans? I don't actually hate them, but I don't want them here."

He thought a bit. "I don't really like them either. They're so arrogant. The French are arrogant, too, but not in such a big, blustery way." He laughed. "Around Americans, I always feel that one of them is going to step on me with his big foot and crush me like a fly. He won't mean to, mind you, he just can't keep his big foot out of the way."

```
first U.S. combat units arrive, March 1965
       200,000 U.S. troops in Vietnam
                  by the end of 1965
```

CHAPTER 4

TO HONOR A FATHER

VERY EARLY, SISTER Li shook her awake, told her to go to the headmistress's office. Dressing swiftly, she tried to think what she could have done, to be summoned at such an extraordinary hour. It was Long, grim-faced, waiting there for her.

"Pa-pa is dead. I've gotten permission for you to go back to the village."

"Are you sure?" But of course he was.

Outside the massive wooden gate, sidewalk and street were filled with people pushing their way into the city — old men pulling carts loaded with household goods, women with knees bent under bundles suspended on long poles across their shoulders, babies strapped to their backs; phalanxes of slow-moving bicycles. Honking horns clashed with ringing cyclo bells and children's wails. Exhaust fumes hung like a quivering pall in the tepid air. Trang Sen covered her nose and mouth with her hand.

At the corner of Le Loi and Nguyen Hue, she got separated from Long. Frantic, she craned to see him over the mass of heads. At last he appeared, grabbed her hand. "Hold on, don't let go."

The bus terminal, jammed with people — small children clinging to their mothers, old people clutching small packs, bags and baskets, detritus of another life. They alone seemed to be leaving the city.

Suddenly frightened, "Is there fighting on our road?" she asked. She stumbled over someone's basket, would have fallen but for Long's tight grip.

"I don't know. If there is, they won't let the bus go."

But eventually their bus was honking and bludgeoning its way through the thicket of cyclos, lambrettas, and cars to the city's western outskirts.

"I hate to think of Ma-ma there alone. Soon Fourth Brother will be drafted — if he's not taken off by the Front first."

Long paused, then continued, almost to himself, and somewhat bitterly, she thought. "At least we know. These days parents die, sons are killed and no one finds out. It's only because of my precious position that the message got through." He looked past her out the window.

She wondered at his pain. She could feel nothing. Her family, the village, were like a dream.

The bus was stopped at a checkpoint. Long strained forward to hear what the cluster of uniformed men were saying. "They aren't letting buses through."

"Can't you tell them who you are?" He was wearing peasant clothes.

He shook his head. "I thought it would be safer this way. We'll have to walk."

The road would take them a long way around, and they would still have to cut back to the new village. They decided to take a chance crossing the abandoned rice fields — unflooded, dusty, overgrown with weeds — and go through the forest.

"We can pick up the path that connects with the one by our old place. It's probably not used much now."

Halfway across the open space he turned to look at her. "You shouldn't have worn the ao dai."

"I didn't think about it. Here, wait a minute." She halted and wound the ends around her waist, tying them together in a large loose knot so that her legs were unencumbered.

The harsh white sunlight washed out colors. The earth around them was a dull brick red, the distant trees a line of dusky gray-green. Red dust clung to their damp skin and invaded their eyes and noses.

At last they reached the forest. Long signaled her not to talk.

The elongating shadows darkened. The metallic calls of the drongo, the occasional screech of a monkey, were replaced by the night sounds of tree frogs, the *kyew-kyew* of the little brown owl, the high-pitched scraping of cicada wings.

A far away crane call echoed. Long halted. "That could have been a signal."

He looked at her ao dai again. "That will never do. They'll know we're not country people if they get too close, but we can at least fool them from a distance." He unfastened his shirt and pulled it over his head. "Put this on."

She obeyed without a word, her hands shaking. He buried the dress in a pile of leafy debris.

It was hard dark by the time they reached the edge of the forest. She was surprised to find their old rice field was still being used.

"We'd better not stay on the path from here on," whispered Long.

Crouching low, they skirted along the backs of the abandoned houses to a point where the stream beside their old village could be forded. They plunged in knee deep. Trang Sen bent down swiftly and splashed her sweating face and arms.

On the far side, they pushed through the overgrowth, avoiding the path. Another crane call sounded — and was answered from nearer by. Long motioned her to stop. A twig snapped on the path, then a line of shadowy figures filtered past. Occasional dull glints hinted that at least some were carrying weapons. Trang Sen pressed against the darkness of a tree, scarcely daring to breathe. The rough bark prickled her skin.

Finally the procession passed. They waited a few more minutes, then moved on.

At the village checkpoint a rough voice stopped them.

"Is it Ong Hai?"

The watchman came closer and peered at them through the darkness. "Ah, young Long, here to see about your poor mother." The old man shook his head. "Terrible times, these. Come on, both of you. I'm sorry about your honored father."

A candle shone dimly through the open door. Ba Cao sat beside a coffin in front of the altar, her head bowed.

"Ma-ma."

She looked up startled, then her face relaxed. "My son." Her lips trembled. "I prayed you would come."

She noticed they were streaked with sweat and dirt. "But how . . . what happened?"

"We're all right. We had to walk through the forest, that's all."

She turned to Trang Sen. "First Daughter. I have longed for you."

"Yes, Ma-ma, I too," Trang Sen lied. She stood in a pool of isolation, overwhelmed by the sense of strangeness that had surprised her earlier.

"Wash yourselves and put on some clean clothes. Then eat a little and rest. For once there's a bit of extra rice in the house."

Seated at the low table in the middle of the room, Trang Sen listened to the other two.

"Will Third Son come?"

Long shook his head. "I sent a message, but there's no such thing as leave these days." He didn't add that Quang's unit was involved in some of the heaviest fighting, north of Bien Hoa.

Trang Sen hadn't thought to ask about her brother. What was wrong with her?

Long spoke again. "Ma-ma, how did it happen?"

"Your father and Fourth Son were in our old rice field. It's been safe during the day, though the Front soldiers steal the rice at night, when it's too dangerous to go over there. Now they've started coming in the daytime too. Two men were killed last week. Your father was the third."

She shook her head. "I told him he shouldn't keep using that field, but here nothing grows well. Your father is a stubborn man. They were over there two days ago and some men with rifles came out of the forest, tried to steal the buffalo. Your father told them they couldn't have them. So they shot him, right there in the field."

Ba Cao spoke in a monotone, as if reciting a passage from memory. As if all her grief had been used up.

Long paused. "Then they didn't know who he was. I was afraid it might have been because of me."

His mother shook her head. "No, he angered them. He should have obeyed them."

But Trang Sen thought, *Maybe the buffalo aren't worth your life; but he did right.* For the first time she viewed her father with pride. His stoic grief when Second Brother died, his struggle as his world became more and more chaotic now seemed like courage to her. She thought of his agreeing to let her go to the school, recalled his words, *"It may be that this is the best way to prepare her for a new world, where all things are changing."* That seemed like courage too. She felt a sudden tenderness for him.

She got up and went out onto the verandah, squatting with her back against the wall of the house. The comfortable familiarity of that position overwhelmed her. She was home, but from across a gulf that made her forever a stranger. *Did Eldest Brother feel this way when he returned to the village?* She remembered their conversation at the French restaurant. Perhaps he felt the same, even about Vietnam itself. Would that be the case for her someday? Tears filled her eyes. She lifted her head and looked at the blurred outline of the dark forest against the darker sky, occasionally lighted by a far-off flare.

She stayed there for a long time listening to the quiet voices behind her, not hearing the words. Finally she went back in.

"It's time to wake Fourth Son to watch," her mother was saying.

"Don't wake him," said Long. "I'll watch."

"You're too tired."

"I couldn't sleep now. I'll sit here and think a little. If I want to sleep, I'll wake Fourth Brother."

She reluctantly agreed and went into the partitioned-off sleeping space she had shared with her husband. Trang Sen remained with Long beside their father's coffin. Eventually she crossed her arms on her knees, rested her head on them and slept.

Trang Mai's cry awakened her. She raised her head. The candles no longer glowed sharply, but were swallowed in a grey pre-dawn dimness. The few pieces of furniture emerged fuzzily, as through a mist.

She crossed over to the sleeping platform and hoisted the child onto her hip.

Tho peered sleepily over the edge of the hammock. "Eldest Brother, First Sister, I didn't know you were here." His voice no longer had its high-pitched little boy sound, was somewhat gravelly.

Long smiled. "It's good for you to sleep. It hasn't been easy, the last two days."

"No." He shook his head violently, as if to erase the memory.

Trang Sen looked at him. He was too young for this. But he was growing up. A sudden thought stabbed her. Troops would come one day, or the Front would come in the night. He would surely be taken away, perhaps to die like Second Brother. Momentarily, she felt something of Eldest Brother's bitterness.

THE WAKE WAS held that morning, the funeral in the afternoon. Mechanically, Trang Sen put on the white robe and took part in the public display of grief. But her own mourning had taken place the night before, when it seemed she found and lost her father all at once.

After the third-day ceremony, Long prepared to return to Saigon.

"Ma-ma, it's too dangerous for you to stay here any longer, especially for Fourth Brother. In Saigon, I can take care of you."

Trang Sen was to remain a few days, to guide them to the city.

Long lowered his voice. "Can we trust the headman?"

His mother's answer was almost inaudible. "I don't know. Some say the only way is to be for Saigon in the daytime and the Front at night. Some say that's what he does."

"I thought so." He paused. "That makes it important for no one to think you're leaving for good. I'll ask Uncle to look after things here. Then you can slip away when the time comes."

Ba Cao quizzed her daughter constantly on where they might be living, whether they could plant some rice, what it would be like in Saigon. It was another strangeness to be the experienced one. "It's not like that, Ma-ma," she kept saying.

Trang Sen insisted that they travel light. Finally, her mother agreed to take only the ancestors' altar and some food.

The night before they left, Trang Sen slipped out to the verandah after the others were asleep. She squatted on her haunches, looking dreamily at the night sky. Everything was ending. With Pa-pa dead, all of them going to Saigon, they would never come back again, any of them. She thought of Saigon, the chaos of that walk to the bus, in that world that seemed so far away, that time so long ago, but in reality not very far, only a few short miles from here.

Would she always be two different people, was there no link between this and the world she had chosen? She hungered for a connection — someone, something — to bridge that gap. She missed Kim Hoa, so real in this place that belonged to them both.

Her uncle had told her Kim Hoa was pregnant. She tried to imagine what it would be like, having her own baby. Why couldn't her life be simple like Kim Hoa's? And yet . . . such a life still made her shudder. She remembered the rest of what Uncle had said — Kim Hoa's in-laws had indeed opened a tailor shop, but they thought it should be doing better.

They were thinking of going to Saigon. She didn't ask whether Kim Hoa was content. *She probably doesn't mind*, thought Trang Sen, *she never complains about anything*.

She gave her uncle the name of her school, to tell Kim Hoa, if she came to Saigon.

THEY SET OUT early, Trang Mai on Trang Sen's hip. At the last minute Ba Cao ran back and retrieved the polished mirror. Remembering Trang Sen's continual harangues about baggage, she looked at her daughter almost defiantly. "I couldn't leave that."

Trang Sen nodded.

Tho turned out to be more helpful than perhaps even Long would have been. He seemed to understand automatically what to do, and his energy was apparently inexhaustible. He walked a few feet in front, parting the bushes for them. He would have outpaced them completely, but Trang Sen wouldn't allow him out of her sight. As she watched his narrow back bob up and down, she tried without much success to connect this emerging young man with the child she had left behind not very long before.

The forest trek was uneventful, though Trang Mai's occasional fit of fretful crying unnerved them. When they finally reached it, the highway appeared deserted.

They stumbled slowly forward as it grew dark. "We have to rest," said Ba Cao. "The baby can't go much farther."

In the stillness Trang Sen thought she heard something moving on the road behind them.

"Quick, off the road!" She pushed her mother toward the ditch. They scrambled down and crouched in ankle-deep muck. They didn't dare slap at the mosquitoes humming around them. Trang Sen closed her eyes against their insistent attack and hoped there were no snakes.

More distinct now, the sound was the wheels of a cart bumping along the road. They heard low voices. Trang Sen peeped over the edge of the ditch. She saw several families trailing behind a cart pulled by a decrepit water buffalo. "It's all right."

They climbed up the embankment and hailed the refugees as they came alongside.

The strangers' village had been burned the night before. "Our headman was stubborn," reflected the old man who appeared to be the leader. "He wouldn't do what the Front told him. Now we've lost everything, and he lost his life. We're headed for Saigon too. We don't have much food, but the child could ride in the cart. As long as the buffalo lasts." He chuckled. "It's so old and useless the Front didn't bother to steal it."

AT THE EDGE of the city Trang Sen hired a lambretta to take the four of them to Long's compound. Ba Cao stared dubiously at the tiny three-wheeled vehicle, its metal hardly thicker than a tin can, and glanced longingly back at the wooden cart.

"This will be faster," Trang Sen promised.

But for Ba Cao, unaccustomed to city traffic, it was a slow, nerve-racking ride.

Long greeted them with relief. "I've found a small house. It wasn't easy. But money helps."

That bitterness again, thought Trang Sen.

"It's rather far from this part of town. That may be safer, as we've had several bombs go off near here, just since I've been back." He looked anxiously at his mother. "It will be very different from the village. I hope it's all right."

Ba Cao looked dazed.

"We're very tired," said Trang Sen. "Could you take us there?"

He hailed two cyclos. Their way was west and slightly north of the part of the city Trang Sen knew. Just behind a large market, the cyclos halted at the entrance to a narrow alley that ran between two rows of low, French-style buildings. Eldest Brother led them single file to a gate a hundred feet or so from the street. It hung lopsided against a ramshackle bamboo fence. Inside was a bit of yard and a tiny old house built of wooden slats, unaccountably sandwiched between the fading mustard-colored stucco structures. A scraggly banana tree grew next to it. On either side of the rickety plank walk the yard was overgrown with weeds.

Inside, one window shutter swung on its hinges. Spider webs filled the corners of the main room and geckos scurried across the floor.

Long looked at them apologetically. "It's not too good, but I thought you'd like it better than an apartment. You can grow a few vegetables, Ma-ma."

Still speechless, Ba Cao peered through the gloom. The bare plank beds looked uninviting. A low table, covered with dust, was the only other furnishing. But Long had prepared a place for the altar, a narrow shelf attached high on the wall.

Ba Cao crossed the room, drew aside a curtain and examined the small kitchen. Then she set her bundle down on one of the beds. Allowing herself one small sigh, she began to issue orders.

"We'll need sleeping mats, and a rice pot, now. The rest can wait until tomorrow." She looked around again. "Where is the water? Surely there's a way to get water in Saigon."

Long nodded, relieved. "I'll take Fourth Brother and show him. Yesterday I saw some buckets, out in back, I think." He handed Trang Sen a wad of bills. "Go with Ma-ma to the market, get whatever you need."

Blue and white striped plastic awnings covered the market stalls. The walkways between the rows of vendors were narrow and muddy, soaked with the water used to wash vegetables and fill the tubs of live fish. There were stacks of every kind of fruit — rose-colored water apples, dark purple mangosteens, red-orange mangoes and the dun-colored, hairy rambutan. Bedraggled chickens sat morosely in cages, awaiting a certain fate. Great mounds of shrimps and fish filled the air with their salty, just-this-side-of-decay smell. Live eels swam in tubs beneath the tables. Chock-a-block with the food stalls were those selling kitchen utensils, sleeping mats, hammocks, clothing, plastic toys, furniture.

The crowds of noisy people jostling their way from stall to stall were too much for Ba Cao. Trang Sen made all the decisions, haggling with vendors over the price of kitchen equipment, food and bedding.

"It's all so expensive," her mother kept saying.

"What are these?" Ba Cao pointed at two elongated metal containers of bottled gas Trang Sen had just bought.

"They're gas for cooking. You won't need charcoal here. You connect this up, turn a handle, and there is the fire." Trang Sen had noticed two shiny new gas rings in their kitchen. "I'll show you."

Ba Cao shook her head. "Too much to learn . . ." she trailed off, her interest diverted by a meat seller chasing after a small boy, shouting "thief" and brandishing a cleaver over his head.

"What kind of place is this? Surely such a little child can't be a thief."

"You don't pay any attention to that, Ma-ma. Let's go. We have some vegetables for supper, and they're delivering the rice and the gas now. We can come back for the other things tomorrow."

The main road was harsh with the sound of horns and the roar of motorcycles, the latter spewing hot bursts of exhaust fumes. Ba Cao wrinkled her nose and covered her ears.

TRANG SEN BEGAN to think of returning to school.

She consulted Long. "Ma-ma seems to feel much better since she planted some vegetables, even though she can't use them yet. She doesn't like the taste of those she buys." Trang Sen's voice was impatient.

"Don't be too hard on her. She's had too many changes." He was thoughtful. "I hope it was right to bring them here."

"You haven't answered me about going back to school."

"I want you to go only for classes, and live here."

She felt the old trap begin to close once more. "I don't want to do that," she objected petulantly. "For a whole month almost I've helped them. I want to go back to school."

"I'm worried about them. Fourth Brother is too young . . ."

"He's no younger than I was when I plowed the fields all day," she interrupted hotly.

"That's true." He hesitated. "You're one of those people who have to take on more burdens because you can handle them. Think about it," he added harshly, "did Cousin Hoa, or any other girl, do as much as you? Because of you, Pa-pa and Ma-ma got along much better than the others. Fourth Brother will never be as dependable."

Hot tears were feverish behind her eyes. "You went away," she persisted. "You did what you wanted." She refused to look at him, and struggled not to let him see the tears.

"It was different then. The war wasn't the way it is now, and they didn't have so many troubles."

She looked at him sullenly.

"You're always complaining about the rules, and about your roommates. You would still be doing what you want. I'll make sure Ma-ma allows you to study."

"It will be like it was in the village," she retorted. "Ma-ma wants me to be like her. She doesn't understand."

"She understands more than you think," he responded sternly. "Most of the time she's right. Someday you'll have to learn that."

She only looked at him, her resentment a shield between them.

"They'll need you for a long time," he went on. "Fourth Brother too. The city is dangerous for boys his age. You've seen them running around, stealing, getting into trouble. Ma-ma will never be able to keep that from happening. I think you can."

For the first time, she was deeply angry with him.

SHE FORCED HER way off the bus, pushing against people trying to get off and on at the same time, almost falling as the door slammed shut. Her books scattered in the dust. She hurried to pick them up before they were trampled. A tanned arm, sparsely covered with light blond hair, reached out to help her.

He smiled at her startled look. "It seemed you could use some help," he said in fairly smooth Vietnamese.

She stood up, self-consciously straightening her ao dai. She was almost as tongue-tied as she had been on that long-ago day when she had met the American on the riverbank.

He collected the rest of the books and handed them to her, then walked beside her through the market. He was so friendly, she began to feel less shy.

They picked their way between the rows of stalls, stepping over or around the baskets of fruit, the chicken cages, and the pans of live fish that were overflowing into the narrow dirt walkway.

"I've come to this part of the city several times. There don't seem to be many students here, at least not wearing a convent-school ao dai. I was surprised to see you."

"I never see any Americans either. Why do you come here?"

"Oh, I go out on my own, try to go places where there aren't any Americans, to see how people really live."

She examined him covertly. Despite his uniform, he didn't fit her idea of an American soldier. Really quite short, he was not much taller than Eldest Brother. His hair was a light blondish brown, drab. It was combed in a straight line to the side, plastered close to his head. His eyes were a pale color, between blue and green. He wore glasses, which he kept taking off and wiping on the edge of his khaki shirt.

"I like Vietnam better than any place I've ever been," he was saying, rather extravagantly. "I wish this war wasn't going on. Then I would be able to see how beautiful it really is. Last week I went out into the country, took a bus west as far as it went. I love the rice fields and the palm trees, and the peasants with their oxen and wearing those wonderful pointed straw hats."

She giggled. "Those aren't oxen, they're water buffalo. Can't you tell the difference?"

"Well, no, I guess I can't." He tried to defend his mistake. "We don't have them in America."

At the edge of the market, Trang Sen spotted Tho leaning against a wall with some other boys. He looked at her in surprise.

She scowled at him and called out, "Does Ma-ma know you're here?"

It was his turn to scowl. "I was just going. She might not like what you're doing either."

"Go home," she hissed at him.

The American was smiling at this exchange. "Will you tell me your name? I'd like to talk with you again."

She shook her head, suddenly overwhelmed at her own boldness, walking through the market with this stranger. *What would Ma-ma say, or the nuns? Or Eldest Brother?*

She turned and almost ran from him. But later, remembering, she felt a secret thrill at having stumbled into the forbidden encounter.

Ba Cao COULDN'T manage anything beyond tending the little vegetable garden and dealing with the new cooking equipment. Trang Sen did all the marketing, and solved — or tried to solve — whatever problems came up.

There were enough of those. Tho had joined other rootless boys, aimlessly roaming and congregating on the edge of the busy market. Whenever she saw a small thief being chased through the marketplace, Trang Sen feared it would turn out to be her brother. It was time Trang Mai started school, but Ba Cao, remembering what she still considered the mistaken handling of Trang Sen, refused to send her.

Trang Sen tried to persuade Long to intervene, but when it came to criticizing his mother, he balked. Trang Sen's muted conflict with her annoyed him.

Trang Sen missed their conversations. She asked him why he no longer tried to teach her about politics. He shook his head and said what was happening was too depressing.

She thought it was exciting to have so many Americans everywhere, so tall and light — or, even stranger, black. They made Long angry. "We don't need all these foreign troops."

"But what about the Communists?"

"What about them? We're all Vietnamese. We all want peace and unity." It sounded like a rehearsed speech.

She kept thinking about the American she had met in the market. In her memory he seemed much handsomer. Over her books at night, her mind drifted into a daydream that he thought of her too. She imagined herself in love with him, could arouse an achy longing by the mere thought of his arm reaching out to help her. She focused on that light tan arm, was entranced by the memory of its golden hairs.

No one knew about that encounter except Tho. Trang Sen guessed his fear that she might get him into trouble prevented him from saying anything. He usually hung out with other boys only while she was at school. His mother would believe him if he told her he needed to check on the rice delivery at the market. But Trang Sen wasn't so easy to fool. He tried to be home before she returned.

SHE WAS READY to graduate from the middle school. To prepare for college, she needed two more years in the upper level. She had assumed Long would agree to that, but with his responsibilities for all of them, she wasn't sure now.

Sister Louise stopped her as she was leaving class. "Ma chère, what are your plans for next year?"

"I want to continue, Sister, but it may be that I must work to help my family."

The Sister shook her head. "That cannot be. You mustn't waste such intelligence. Though I have noticed that your mind doesn't seem to be on your studies lately."

Trang Sen blushed. "Sometimes it's hard to study at home, Sister."

"You must definitely keep on with your studies. Would you like to study in France someday?"

"Oh, yes, I want to go, to speak French, to see the beautiful places."

"But you must also have a goal, ma chère. It is one thing to study here for the sake of studying. To go to France would be more serious."

"Do you think someone like me, Vietnamese I mean, could study literature?"

"Of course, of course, it could all be arranged. Why not?" Sister Louise leaped ahead several years. "I could no doubt urge the college I myself attended to look with favor on your application. We must work hard together to prepare you." She spoke as if it were already settled.

Trang Sen was cautious again. "I have to talk with my brother."

Thanh Thuy, her former roommate, caught up to Trang Sen as she crossed the courtyard. Thanh Thuy occasionally sought her out and chatted with her, and Trang Sen warmed to her in spite of herself. She wasn't sure why the girl tried to keep up the relationship. Trang Sen told her little of her family, sure Thanh Thuy wouldn't understand a mother who couldn't cope with the city.

She smiled at her classmate now. The other girl squeezed her arm. "Tonight my parents are having a dinner for some American officers," she whispered. "My mother has specially asked permission for me to leave the school so I can be there. Sister doesn't know it's a big social event, with foreign men."

Trang Sen looked at her enviously. "If only I could meet some Americans." She thought of the "market man."

"That should be easy. Your brother could introduce you."

"I don't think so. He . . . he . . ." she began to explain, then thought better of telling Thanh Thuy how Eldest Brother felt about the Americans. "He doesn't know any very well."

"Nonsense. The Americans are dying to meet pretty girls. They don't need to be formally introduced." Thanh Thuy giggled self-consciously. "My mother wouldn't dare tell Father, but she thinks it wouldn't be a bad idea for me or one of my sisters to marry an American. Then, whatever happens here . . ."

"Thanh Thuy!" Trang Sen was amazed. "Your mother would actually agree for you to marry an American?"

"It's not so unusual." Thanh Thuy was somewhat defensive. "My aunt is married to an American colonel, and my mother's cousin is engaged to someone at the American Embassy. Surely you've met someone with an American husband, or at least seen some mixed couples in the street."

Trang Sen shook her head. "Only the tea-girls." She thought to herself that perhaps she hadn't noticed; she would have to look more carefully from now on. "Well, enjoy the dinner party. I hope you meet someone handsome."

Thanh Thuy grinned in answer. She gave Trang Sen's arm a final squeeze and dashed off.

Trang Sen walked slowly out the gate. She imagined Thanh Thuy gaily chatting with handsome officers, all with her parents' approval, and was jealous. It could never happen to her. Eldest Brother would be angry at her even imagining herself at such an event.

LONG SWUNG THE gate jauntily as he came through. He was carrying a net shopping bag bulging with packages. Laying it on the narrow tile counter in the kitchen, he began to unload it, held up a freshly killed chicken by its limp head. "For a little feast tonight," he explained.

Trang Mai came running in from outside and threw herself into his arms. She reached over to rub her finger along the scaly yellow skin of the chicken foot.

"But, my son, so expensive. A whole chicken." They hadn't seen such since they left the village.

"My expense, for celebration. I was promoted today."

"But of course it would happen. Such a fine son."

He laughed. "Well, they don't notice if one is a fine son. Besides, it may be that I'm not so fine. But here, I haven't shown you what else I brought." He pulled out an oblong package and carefully unwrapped a bottle of Chinese rice wine.

Even Ba Cao drank enough to become slightly tipsy. Long lingered after the meal, apparently reluctant to cut the evening short. But at last he stood up to go.

Trang Sen also stood up. "I'll walk with you through the market."

They walked in silence for a few minutes. She was afraid to ask him her question.

Finally, she said, "Sister Louise asked me what I want to do about the upper level."

"Well?"

"I told her I want to stay for it."

He said nothing for a few moments, then, "I can't see any use in that. You don't have a goal, and it's far too expensive."

"I think the convent would help me, especially if you asked them. And I *do* have a goal. I told Sister Louise I want to study literature. I've thought about it for a long time."

"Literature! What possible good could that do you?"

"Does it always have to be useful? Sister Louise didn't think it was such a bad idea. Besides, are you using what you studied?"

"It helps me understand what's going on."

"You could understand that by keeping your eyes open."

"The family needs you now, and I'm thinking what a future husband would want. If you learned to be a secretary, or perhaps even a bookkeeper, you would be able to bring in some money. It won't help your chances to find a husband if you're so over-educated," he added, unconsciously echoing their mother's argument.

"I don't think I ever want to get married." She spit the words at him. "Why should I want a husband telling me what to do?"

"Of course you want to get married. You should be grateful you've been allowed to do what you wanted for so long."

Her anger turned to tears. "I don't know why you don't like me anymore. I've done everything you said, and you never talk to me, except about the family. I wish they'd never come here!"

"You don't mean that, you shouldn't say such a thing. It's our duty to take care of them."

"I hate the way everything changed. You used to come see me and be nice to me. Now all you do is tell me something I need to do for them. Always for them!"

"It's only that I know I can depend on you. I thought we both understood that."

"I haven't complained, have I? Except . . . except . . ." She thought of their frequent arguments over her mother and Trang Mai. "But I've done everything you said. Even if I keep on going to school I'll still take care of them." She rubbed her face fiercely with the back of her hand.

"Perhaps I've expected too much. I do think about you, and worry about you. The safest thing for you is to get a job and learn to do something useful now. Two years from now we would be having the same conversation, and what you want would be even more impossible, because it would be to go to France. How can we send you to France?"

"But Sister Louise said —"

"Sister Louise is a romantic. She doesn't think about the practical side of things at all. She's had too much influence on you."

•

"Oh, no, I love Sister Louise."

He paused. "I do have something else to tell you." He was apologetic. "It's about the family again. About Fourth Brother."

"Are you going to send him to school?"

He laughed a little. "School is your solution to everything. No, for him it's too late. It may have always been too late. He doesn't have the intelligence or interest you and I have. You can't see it, but I think it's the same with Second Sister. No, the only solution is the army. I've talked with the officer in charge of the draft board for this section of the city. He has put Fourth Brother's name at the top of the list."

"Must it be so soon?" She remembered the result of her other brothers going away and shivered. "He's so young."

"Nothing will change. If he gets in trouble, as he'll surely do if he goes on like this, it will be too late. This is the only hope."

She felt very cold. "Don't you even care what happens to him? He might die, like Second Brother."

They had reached the bus stop on the other side of the market. He stopped, and was silent for a long time. She stood beside him, fighting tears and not sure why she wanted to cry, for herself, for Fourth Brother, for whom or what.

Finally he answered her. "Of course I care. There are no choices and I have to choose. And it's not the first time. Perhaps if they'd stayed in the village . . . Even you — bringing you here could be a kind of death for you, too." He turned his head away and stood clenching his fists. She had seen tears glistening in his eyes.

She shook her head to dispel the sudden vision his words had evoked — her own future, cold and lonely. But his desolation was unbearable. He was supposed to be always strong, always standing between her and the chaos that surged around them.

"Oh, no. I . . . I didn't understand." Desperately, she tried to comfort him. "If they had stayed there the Front would have surely taken him. He might even be dead now. It's not your fault. I'm sorry for what I said."

She reached out and gently touched his arm, remembering a time long ago when he had done the same to comfort her.

He struggled to control himself, his back stiff.

"I'm sorry," she said again, then, "I've spoiled your celebration."

He shook his head. "It was a foolish thing, my empty pride. It means nothing. But it made us happy for a while. Perhaps for the last time."

"Not the last time. The war will end someday."

"Sometimes I think it never will." He rubbed his face and looked at her, with his finger wiped a tear from her face. "Most times, you're the one who keeps me going. I remember your beautiful dream of charging off on an elephant to save our people."

"Do you remember that?" She was surprised. "It was a silly child's dream, so long ago."

"Not silly, very important. We should have such dreams. I did once, but now . . ."

A bus pulled up. He touched her cheek again. "My brave little sister. I leave much to you."

She watched him climb on the bus and waited there until it disappeared, then slowly turned toward home. She couldn't endure his pain. At the same time, guiltily, she cherished the thought of his tears, and his touch on her cheek.

SHE WAITED NERVOUSLY for the draft notice to arrive. Tho had angered her frequently since they came to Saigon, but now all she could remember were his charming baby ways when he was the youngest, his admiration of her as he followed along the edge of the field watching her plow. She remembered too his unexpected strength and good sense on the long trek through the forest the day they left the village, how he kept them going with his endless energy.

She began to understand why Long had done what he did. Perhaps there was a chance Tho would come out safe and whole on the other side.

When the notice came, Ba Cao was calm. She only said, "Another son gone. We become a family of women. Who is to care for us?"

"Eldest Brother is here, Ma-ma."

"He may also someday leave us."

"No, Ma-ma. I asked him. He said they need him here. Don't worry."

No matter how despondent, Ba Cao seemed automatically to set about preparing food for all the great changes of life. Tho's chagrin rose as he saw the ever-increasing jars and packages.

Trang Sen remembered it had been the same when her other brothers left. She reassured him. "Everyone's mother is doing the same."

He seemed almost relieved to be drafted, as if he too saw it as a way out.

Trang Sen decided to see him off. She had a fuzzy idea that she would give him some last-minute advice.

Before dawn, they threaded through the dark streets, picking their way around those still sleeping on the sidewalks. The city was already alive with the bustle and noise of market vendors, setting up shop wherever they could find an empty spot.

She could think of nothing to say, now that the final opportunity had come. Just as he was about to climb into the truck, she caught his sleeve. "I remember how you had grown up when I came back to the village, how you helped when we were walking through the forest. Go well and safely, my brother."

LONG WAS WAITING at the school gate. She immediately assumed something had happened to Tho.

He shook his head.

He guided her to a small noodle stand. They sat down at one of the empty tables, far back in its dark interior.

"They came for Fourth Brother."

"I know. How is Ma-ma?"

She shrugged. "She doesn't get so upset anymore."

When the waiter came, he ordered tea for her and a beer for himself. Drawing small circles with his finger in the water splashed from the teapot, he said, "I've been to talk with Sister Marie-Jean."

"Oh."

"She says there is a scholarship for you for the next two years. I've told her you may continue."

She thought she would be elated.

He looked up to see tears in her eyes. "It's a time to be happy, not sad. I have blood on my hands, even maybe Pa-pa's blood. I can't have your pain to pay for too. You perhaps are a flower I'm allowed to watch unfold, a white lotus in a river of blood."

For a long time she could say nothing, struggling not to cry. She searched for something to say to comfort him. "You have no blood to pay for. And I understand about Fourth Brother now. This was his only chance. I . . . I think he thought so too."

He stared at the water pattern on the table. "There *is* something else. I think we should not tell Ma-ma. Third Brother is dead."

She tried to absorb this. "But we must, he must be presented to the ancestors —"

"He was blown to bits." He slammed the words at her, not trying to soften them. "Nothing left. I overheard the commander of that battalion, telling about a whole unit being wiped out. He didn't know my brother was in it. They don't like to report such things. Bad for morale."

With an effort, she shut her mind to the image. "Couldn't we tell Ma-ma he is dead without telling her how? The ancestors . . ." She seldom thought of the old rituals these days, but the enormity of leaving her brother's soul to wander unclaimed was too much.

"What could we present to the ancestors? There's nothing there, I'm telling you."

"Why are you telling me?" She felt something very much like anger.

"If something should happen to me, someone should know."

"Don't say that!" She almost shouted it. "You're safe, here, nothing can happen to you."

He looked away from her. "Perhaps I wanted to tell someone who remembered him. He was a child when I left, still minding the buffalo."

She tried to think of something to say to dispel his anguish. "I'm glad you told me. I will honor him secretly, even if we can't present him to the ancestors."

U.S. troop strength almost
400,000 by year's end

CHAPTER 5

KIM HOA

TRANG SEN IGNORED the peddlers waving samples of their goods at her, paid no attention to the child-beggars grabbing at her tunic. This part of the city was a rabbit warren of shacks — self-made refugee shelters hastily thrown up wherever there was space. But in this one small neighborhood streets had been laid out and a few alleys cut through.

Someone had given the school porter a note for her, with Kim Hoa's name and the address of the tailor shop. It was beside an overpass and below the main road, squeezed between a tiny cookshop and what seemed to be an added-on extension of a small church. She had spotted it from above before working her way down the concrete bank. Some of the shacks were under the overpass, using it as a roof. Others leaned against the concrete pillars, which formed one wall of the meager shelters. The little tailor shop itself was hardly more than a narrow two-story shed with a flimsy roof patched together from scrap metal, and using the wall of the church as one of its side walls. It had a tiny upper balcony, covered by a piece of corrugated tin.

Trang Sen peered uncertainly into the darkness, eyes dazzled by the bright sun. A slight man limped toward her. Quite old, she thought.

"Can I help the young miss?"

"I'm looking for Trinh Kim Hoa. Are you her father-in-law?"

"Her . . . her husband." He blushed.

"I'm Trinh Trang Sen, her cousin."

He smiled then, widely. "She has hoped you would come. Sit down, she's at the market, will be back soon."

Trang Sen stood there a moment, uncertain. "Is the market far? I can go meet her."

"Not far." He limped to the door and pointed in the opposite direction from the overarching highway. "To the end of the street, then through the alley, and across the street behind this one."

She headed off the way he told her. She hadn't wanted to sit in the little room waiting with him.

She thought Kim Hoa would somehow make things better. If she wasn't worrying about her mother and Trang Mai, it was Fourth Brother. And always, looming in the background, an immovable mountain, the secret knowledge of Third Brother's death. But with Kim Hoa here . . .

She looked at the faces streaming past her. Would she recognize Kim Hoa after all this time? She would have the child with her, now a year or so old.

At the edge of the busy avenue, she waited for a chance to dash across to the market. A woman was standing on the other side, looking quite desperate, a child on her hip, her other arm weighed down with her purchases. She was noticeably pregnant. Can it really be Kim Hoa, so thin, and looking so old?

Trang Sen tried to catch her attention, then finally bolted through the traffic, dodging cyclos and motorcycles.

"Kim Hoa!"

"Trang Sen." Kim Hoa set her parcels down and made the traditional greeting as well as she could, hampered by the child.

"I wasn't sure it was you at first. Here, let me help." Trang Sen took the bags Kim Hoa had begun to pick up again. She chucked the chin of the toddler. He wavered toward tears, then relaxed into a gum-exposing grin. The two women laughed.

"What is he called?" Trang Sen asked.

"Van Hai," Kim Hoa answered, then said, "I was trying to cross the street. I'll never learn to do it."

"You'll get accustomed to it. Even Ma-ma can do that. Let's go." She took Kim Hoa's arm.

Kim Hoa allowed Trang Sen to pull her across, repressing the impulse to stop and stare at the vehicles barreling toward them. On the other side she caught her breath. "I can stand there and look all day. Yesterday my husband finally came to find me. But that's worse — he's too slow."

"How long have you been here? I've missed you terribly. How is Uncle? Your family?"

"Second Sister is home still. No one for her to marry. My brothers . . . two are dead. We don't know about the others. But Sixth Brother, he went off with the Front." Kim Hoa added in a whisper, "Pa-pa thinks the headman stole him. He thinks he buys peace by giving them our boys."

"Ma-ma said that might be happening. But when did you come? Are your husband's parents here?"

"A sad story. You mustn't mention it to my husband, it upsets him too much. There was some kind of sickness, people were dying. As if the war wasn't enough. The health people came from Tay Ninh, gave us medicine. But they used a needle and his mother and father wouldn't take it. Then they got sick and died. After that, my husband decided to come here. There was no reason to stay anymore. He sold the things in the store and now we have only the tailor shop. We've been here a few months."

"You should have let me know. We could have helped. Eldest Brother could have found you a place to live, the way he did for us."

Kim Hoa shook her head. "We have no money. You don't know how expensive houses are. Cousin Long must pay for yours." Kim Hoa continued, embarrassed, "I came to your school three times, before I got up courage to speak to the porter."

"So it was you. He just said a woman, and I thought . . ." She stopped. "Why didn't you ask him to call me?"

"I looked in, and there were all the girls in their ao dais, and . . . and I was afraid. I thought you might be ashamed of me, a country girl, no education. I watched the gate, hoping I'd see you leave, but I never did."

"Oh, Kim Hoa, I would never have been ashamed. I've missed you so much. Those girls at the school, I don't like them. I'm the one who's different, like you."

There were tears in Kim Hoa's eyes. "I kept remembering the last part of the time you were in the village. I thought you were angry with me, for getting married."

"I was never angry with you." Trang Sen forgot the times she had been. She tried to explain, to herself as much as to Kim Hoa. "I was only thinking about myself then. I couldn't bear Pa-pa finding a husband for me."

Kim Hoa smiled a little. "You're always the same. Dreaming of so many big things, then you really do them. So different from me."

Near the shop she lowered her voice. "We mustn't talk of the sad things in front of my husband." Then louder, "Come in, I'll make some tea."

They stooped to pass through the low doorway. The man stood up, a little unsteadily.

"My husband, Duong Van Chau."

Trang Sen bowed. "Ong Chau."

Kim Hoa put the baby down on the bed platform. She took the groceries from Trang Sen and retreated behind the curtain at the back of the room. Trang Sen picked the baby up and jostled him on her hip. "A fine son."

"We are very lucky. And you see there will soon be another." He added, "Please sit down. My wife is preparing a little refreshment. You will understand it isn't much. We are so poor, and Saigon is so expensive."

She sat on the edge of the platform, modestly folding her legs under her. He politely refrained from looking at her.

Kim Hoa reappeared, placed a tray with tea things beside Trang Sen. She had changed to a clean jacket and smoothed her hair, pulled back into a tight bun at the nape of her neck. *Perhaps it's her hair that makes her look so old*, Trang Sen thought.

In the presence of the husband, neither could think of anything to say. Warned not to mention sad things, Trang Sen was doubly speechless.

She wrote down her address and made Kim Hoa promise to come for a visit.

"I'll come. I hope I don't get lost. There are so many ways to go wrong."

Trang Sen hurried through the streets, dim with late afternoon shadows, her mind roiling with thoughts of Kim Hoa. *They'll surely starve.* She added Kim Hoa's money problems to her catalog of worries.

TRANG SEN ASKED, "Do many Americans come to the shop?"

Kim Hoa shook her head. "None. We're too far away. But it's too expensive to live closer in."

"This will never do. The Americans are the best customers. And I've seen what some of the tailors do — they cheat people, they don't know how to make the clothes. Someone as good as you could make lots of money."

Kim Hoa shrugged. "No solution."

"Well, there must be some way."

Trang Sen talked with Long. "Cousin Hoa, Ong Chau, they'll starve, hidden away in that alley where no one can even find their shop."

"I don't really know that part of the city. But you're right — I doubt if there are many customers there."

"They need to be near the Americans. Kim Hoa is really good. She could get rich."

"That might not be so easy, even if she's good. With so many tailors, how can the Americans find just one?"

"That's why she needs to be near them, so they don't have to hunt for her. Wouldn't you rather see your own cousin make a little money from the Americans than a stranger getting rich?"

"Let me think about it."

She wasn't sure what that meant, but the next week he came looking for Kim Hoa. She went with him to the tailor shop. Kim Hoa was taking an order for an ao dai. Ong Chau bustled about nervously, limping back and forth, offering cigarettes and impatiently waiting for Kim Hoa to prepare tea. He apparently saw Long as a business opportunity.

Kim Hoa's customer left and they chatted politely. Long eventually brought up what was on his mind. "Have you sewed western-style clothes?" he asked Kim Hoa.

"A little. A few Americans came from the army camp near the village. I made them suits, and silk shirts. Our officers sometimes wanted those too."

"How would you feel about working in someone else's shop?"

Ong Chau looked doubtful.

"I have a friend who runs a small shop on Nguyen Hue Road," he explained, "a perfect location, near the Rex Hotel. He has much business, and wants some help. He may even want a partner, but hasn't yet decided. I suggested you could work for him, learn a bit more about the western clothes."

Ong Chau defended them. "We are doing quite well here."

But Kim Hoa said, "No, we should consider this. We could always do better."

Ong Chau was obstinate. "We are satisfied here. You see that we have business. Now my wife will be busy making the ao dai for the lady, other people come, our reputation grows."

Kim Hoa squelched him. "You know that's not true. The lady is the first customer in weeks. Who knows when there will be another? How are we going to eat, I ask you?"

Ong Chau seemed almost afraid of her. *Could it be Kim Hoa who runs the household? Maybe she's not so soft after all*, thought Trang Sen.

Long chuckled as they walked down the street. "You never told me Cousin Hoa was a little tigress. I don't think we have to worry. She'll see that Ong Chau accepts my offer."

"She's not really a tigress. But," Trang Sen admitted, "I was surprised to hear her talk to him like that. I always thought she never said a word for herself."

"She seems to be doing that quite well now."

Trang Sen brought up the more important matter. "Does your friend really want a partner?"

"Definitely. I presented it the way I did to give both sides a chance to see if it works out."

When Trang Sen went back to the shop several days later, Ong Chau was alone.

"She has gone to work in the new place, started there two days ago. She's very late coming home, works so hard."

Kim Hoa quickly learned the unfamiliar clothing designs. Ong Ngoc's shop wasn't far from the convent, and Trang Sen began stopping by each afternoon. Soon she was as familiar with the various fabrics as Kim Hoa. She didn't have Kim Hoa's knack for design or color, but she was meticulous in keeping track of orders. With her ear for languages, she had picked up a smattering of English. She was the one who could best remember the strange sounds of the customers' names.

Long came in one afternoon while she was there. Emerging from the small office cubbyhole after talking with the tailor, he motioned Trang Sen to follow him out of the shop.

"Ong Ngoc is anxious to formalize the partnership. He says he hasn't found anyone with Kim Hoa's skills in all his years in the business."

"Didn't I tell you?"

"He'd like them to live above the shop, to keep an eye on things at night."

Trang Sen nodded.

"I'm prepared to lend them the money to buy into the business. I want you to offer Cousin Hoa the loan. It won't be so embarrassing for them to accept it that way."

When she presented Long's offer, Kim Hoa protested. "We could never accept this."

"Why not?"

"My husband would never agree."

"And you can't see that he does?"

Kim Hoa blushed. "I suppose I could if I decided it was worth it."

"Well, isn't this worth it — a chance to do so much better?"

"Cousin Long is very kind. You must tell him how grateful we are."

TRANG SEN EMERGED from the back of the shop. Kim Hoa and a customer were bent over a ring of swatches.

The man looked up and stared at her. "You," he finally said, "the one in the market."

She had never thought she would see him again. Face to face with him, her fantasies about him embarrassed her almost to the point of suffocating.

"I hardly recognized you, in your peasant clothes. But no one could forget that beautiful face."

She was even more embarrassed. She blushed and lowered her head. Kim Hoa looked from one to the other.

Trang Sen turned to her. "I'm going now."

"But, you were going to stay . . ."

She rushed out, leaving them both staring after her.

Why did he have to say that about my face? What will Kim Hoa think? I'm lucky Ong Chau and Ong Ngoc weren't there. Or Eldest Brother. Especially Eldest Brother.

She crossed the street at the end of the block and stopped around the corner of the end building. Cautiously she peered out. She had a good view of the front of the shop, could see him leave. If he came in her direction there would be plenty of time to get lost in the crowd.

When he finally emerged, he stood indecisively, eventually crossed the street and hailed a cyclo. Once he was out of sight, she went back to the shop.

"You said you were going home."

She ignored Kim Hoa's comment. Assuming casualness, she asked, "Did you make a sale?"

"Of course I made a sale. He would have bought the whole shop if that had been the only way he could come back and see you again."

"What did he say? Did he say anything?"

"Only that he met you once, but didn't know your name. He asked me your name. Did you meet him with Cousin Long?"

"Did you tell him my name?"

"No. When did you meet him? I was sure he knew Cousin Long."

"No. What's his name?"

Kim Hoa grinned at her. "I'll tell you only if you tell me what's happening. No, you don't." She slapped her hand over the order book as Trang Sen tried to snatch it.

"I just met him one day when he was walking through the market near our house, that's all. It was months ago, and I had really forgotten about it. I was surprised to see him, and there's no more to tell. Now will you tell me his name?"

"If that's all, why should you care?"

"Kim Hoa!" Trang Sen lunged for the book.

Kim Hoa held it out of her reach, then relented and looked at the order form. "Pil-inths, I think."

"Let me see." Trang Sen took the book and studied it for a moment. "Billins. A. Billins. That must be his surname," she added, half to herself.

"I think you like him."

"Of course I don't like him. I just happened to see him once before, that's all."

She noted when he would be coming back.

SISTER LOUISE HAD wanted to chat. For the first time ever, Trang Sen wanted to hurry away from her. She managed to be polite, but her impatience was evident. Sister Louise asked if she had an appointment. Although she said no, the Sister had dismissed her soon after, to Trang Sen's guilty relief.

She hadn't been sure she would go to the shop. But she convinced herself that she wasn't going to see the American, merely to help Kim Hoa. She must act as if she didn't remember him. And make very clear that she didn't appreciate remarks like the one about her face.

She hesitated in front of the shop window, stared at the bolts of brightly colored cloth, almost turned back before anyone saw her. But gathering courage, she peeked around the edge of the display window into the open door. Kim Hoa was alone.

Trying to appear as if it was an ordinary day, Trang Sen walked in. "What is there to do this afternoon?"

"Lots of work. You'll surely have to stay until I finish the fitting."

Trang Sen managed a blank expression. "Of course I'll stay." She picked up Van Hai and set the little boy on the side of the counter, apparently immersed in playing with him. She didn't turn her head when she heard the hard-soled footsteps.

He stopped a moment and caught his breath, started to come toward her, then seemed to think better of it and turned to Kim Hoa. Soon the two of them were intent on the fitting. He was obviously as skilled at ignoring Trang Sen as she was him.

Afterward he said to Kim Hoa, "Would you ask the young lady if I may say hello to her?"

Kim Hoa took Van Hai from Trang Sen. "You might as well be polite," she whispered.

Trang Sen went over to him.

"I've thought of you all the time since that day in the market."

"You mustn't say such things."

"I'm really sorry. I don't understand what is appropriate to say to young ladies here. In my country that would be a compliment."

She was silent.

"Will you tell me your name, where you live? I don't want to lose you again."

"I come here all the time."

"What are you studying now?"

She answered briefly.

He asked about her family. Soon they were talking as if they were old friends, the way they had that other day.

Ong Ngoc's arrival disconcerted her. "Mr. Billins has ordered a suit," she explained.

Billings noted that she knew his name, but he said nothing.

Ong Ngoc smiled slyly. "A fine young lady always helps business."

Trang Sen blushed and the American laughed. He turned to Kim Hoa. "I'll be back next week."

He left without glancing in Trang Sen's direction.

He ordered some other work after the suit was completed. She couldn't help thinking he did so to have an excuse to see her again. She decided to avoid the shop, but each time she knew he had an appointment, she couldn't stay away.

At night she dreamed of him. As in her adolescent fantasy, he carried her away from great danger. But in this dream he seemed to carry her into darkness, not to the beautiful new world she longed for. She would wake up, shivering until her passionate waking fantasies dispelled the cold emptiness of the dream.

As she turned into Nguyen Hue he caught up to her and fell into step beside her, panting. "You really must tell me your name. I could have called after you instead of running to catch you."

She laughed. "Then it would be too easy."

"I must say, Ba Chau is a very loyal friend. I've tried everything I know to get her to tell me."

"Perhaps someday I'll tell you. She never will."

"I don't understand that. Your culture is very confusing to me. You seem to fear I might steal you away."

"You really mustn't say things like that to me."

"There, I've done it again. Please don't stop talking with me. I'm glad I saw you here," he continued. "Today is the last day I'll be coming to the shop. I can't go on forever buying things, just to see you. I must find another way. Won't you tell me where you live?"

She shook her head. Her heart jumped when he said he wouldn't be coming back. She should refuse to listen to what he was saying, but all she could think was that she had been right about why he kept ordering more clothes.

"My mother would never let you see me." That wasn't the right answer either.

"Why? It's just a friendship between two people attracted to each other."

She blushed deep red. He had used a word that had a purely sexual connotation. "What do you think I am? If you want a tea-girl, go find one, down Tudo Street over there. There are enough for all the Americans!"

"I didn't call you a tea-girl. I don't think that."

"Then why did you use that word?"

"What word? I just said we —"

"Don't say it again, I don't want to hear it again."

"I'm sorry. Whatever I said, I didn't mean what you thought. Please, let's be friends. If you won't tell me where you live, at least tell me the name of your school."

He did seem sorry. "I'll tell you, but you must never come for me there, or let them see you. They are very strict at that school, and I could get into trouble."

"I promise."

"The Convent School of the Blessed Virgin."

"How will I know where it is?"

"I didn't promise to tell you that."

"You must at least tell me something I can call you, if you won't tell me your name."

"You can call me Co Sen."

"Sen. . . . It means lotus, doesn't it?"

She nodded and started to leave.

"Wait. Aren't you going to the shop?"

"Not now." She disappeared into the crowd, leaving him there.

June 15, 2005

Dear Kenneth,

Always good to hear from you. And I'm especially pleased to hear how well the kids are doing.

Sorry to be so long getting back to you. I got bogged down reading term papers and exams, then there were all the early garden chores waiting. And the late spring months are such a beautiful time here, it's really hard to stay inside. Even today, my attention keeps wandering. There's a family of western jays I can see from the window, and I'm fascinated by how hard that mother and father bird have to work to keep the little ones fed.

Let's see. To begin where I left off last time, by mid-1966 South
Vietnam was on the verge of civil war. And I don't mean between
communists and anti-communists either. A big part of the problem was
Nguyen Cao Ky's ham-handed way of making sure everybody knew who
had the power — namely, him. But he overstepped himself with the
Buddhists, and completely miscalculated their ability to make trouble.
Buddhist demonstrations turned violent in Saigon that spring. By late
May the conflict was ratcheted up a notch when self-immolations were
added to the protests.

As for me, I started Vietnamese language training in 1967, to go
out to Vietnam in 1968. I had mixed feelings about getting even more
involved in the mess we were making, but it was almost impossible for
those of us who had just come into the Service to avoid Vietnam.

So that brings us to 1968, a truly terrible year, both for Vietnam
and the U.S. Just to remind you of some of what was happening on this
side of the Pacific, anti-war protests kept spreading, and getting bigger
and more frequent. And the civil rights movement was veering much more
toward violence. At times it seemed the whole nation was at a boiling
point. Every once in a while it boiled over. That was the year Martin
Luther King, and then, just a couple of months later, Bobby Kennedy,
were both assassinated. Even now I can remember how hopeless I felt.

In Vietnam, as I think you know, at the beginning of the lunar new
year, the last day of January 1968, the Viet Cong and North Vietnamese
regulars attacked all over the south. In Saigon, they even invaded
the U.S. embassy. Actually, the embassy in those years was a pretty
dangerous place to work. Tet wasn't the only time it was attacked.

Anyway, the U.S. and Vietnamese military reaction was at least as
brutal as anything the Communists did. What I suppose we have to call
our side bombed sections of Saigon without any concern for civilian lives.
It was also during this same Tet attack that a photographer took that
famous picture of a South Vietnamese general shooting a VC prisoner in
the head on the streets of Saigon. That was Vietnam's shot heard — or
seen — around the world.

In the end, the Tet campaign was a loss for the Viet Cong and
Hanoi. They had seriously miscalculated popular support in the south.
To me, this proved that the only thing most ordinary Vietnamese
wanted was to be left alone. Ironically, though, the U.S. public was so

overwhelmed by television images of the violence, including that street execution, that they mistakenly concluded that the other side had won. The anti-war movement became even stronger, and really this was the beginning of the end. It was only a matter of time before American public opinion forced a pull-out.

Ah, yes, 1968 — quite a year for sure. The My Lai massacre followed Tet by less than two months. I was in language training at the time, and we only heard rumors of what had happened. The Pentagon of course wanted to keep the whole thing under wraps, and they succeeded for a while. The massacre didn't become public until a year and a half later.

I left for Saigon in late June, a couple of months before the Democratic convention that nominated Vice-President Humphrey. It was kind of a relief to be out of the mess of American politics right then. I was heartsick to think Bobby Kennedy wasn't the one standing there accepting the party's nomination. Well, you know Humphrey lost. Johnson's mistakes were too much for him. I now think they were also JFK's mistakes, but that wasn't so clear at the time.

Everybody assumed Nixon's election was a victory for the peace movement. Peace talks had already begun in Paris that May of 1968, and American voters thought Nixon's promise to pull out was more credible than anything Humphrey could offer. As it turned out, though, Nixon expanded the war — into Laos, then Cambodia.

In spite of the U.S. troop drawdown, there were still 15,000 American casualties between 1969 and 1971. And, not even counting South Vietnamese civilian casualties, more South Vietnamese troops were lost in those two years than the total number of Americans in the entire war. That's an important point to remember, Kenneth. We Americans find it incredibly difficult to worry about any casualties other than our own.

Ho Chi Minh died in September 1969, but the war went on. There were huge anti-war demonstrations in Washington, in October and again in November that year. (I hope all this doesn't sound too much like State Department jargon. It's hard not to slip back into that mode. But hey, I was a diplomat — what can I say?)

Of course, most of what I've been telling you was happening while I was right in the middle of it. I was, to put it gently, frustrated, and

I could hardly bear to see the suffering we were causing. Looking back, I'm not sure why I stayed in the Service. I guess I eased my guilt at being part of the problem by trying to learn as much as I could about Vietnam's history and culture, and most of all by getting to know the people. My friendship with your mother and, later, what was left of her family, became a big part of that.

Well, I'm sitting here looking out at the garden and can almost see the weeds growing, so I'll get this out to the mailbox and get to work on those little devils.

Take care of yourself. Like your mother, I'm afraid you work too hard, but I know you don't want to hear that, especially from me, who should be on your side!

All the best to Rachel and the kids,

Uncle Blake

SHE WENT FROM school to shop to home in a hazy dream. Sometimes Billings waited at the bus stand near the school, sometimes he walked along the street where he knew she would pass. Sometimes days went by and she didn't see him. *What if he never comes back?* she thought anxiously when that happened. *What if he's gone back to America?*

She tried to maintain a wall of formality with him. He told her his full name, Arthur Billings, and wanted her to call him Arthur. She refused, clinging to the more distant Ong Billings.

The street in front of the school was clogged with demonstrators, mostly university students. Peasants too, and a few Buddhist monks, their bright saffron robes punctuating the dark- and light-clothed crowd. Suddenly the demonstration became a full-scale riot. Club-wielding youths smashed cars and set fire to them, shouting, "Down with the Americans, down with Ky!"

She couldn't decide whether to try to push her way through to her bus stop or go back to the convent. She saw Billings struggling to reach her. He finally broke free and ran up beside her.

She had to shout for him to hear her. "You shouldn't be here. They're angry at the Americans."

"You shouldn't be here either. They aren't bothering to notice who gets in their way."

"I was going back to the school. Then I saw you."

"Go back. It's the safest place for you."

"What about you?"

"I'll manage all right." He pushed her toward the gate. Looking back one last time, she saw his light-brown head bobbing up and down, moving away from her. She turned and pulled the bell. The porter peeked out.

"It's me, Trang Sen. Let me in!"

He opened the door a narrow slit for her to squeeze through, then quickly slammed it shut and barred it again.

Students were standing in little clots in the courtyard. Thanh Thuy came up and clutched her arm. "I saw you leave. Why did you go out there? It's so dangerous."

"I thought I could get to the bus."

Thanh Thuy shook her head. "A bunch of hoodlums, that's what my father says."

"There were Buddhist monks with them. Do you suppose it could be another coup?"

Thanh Thuy squeezed Trang Sen's arm more tightly.

As quickly as it had materialized, the mob surged on. When Trang Sen left the compound once again, the only sign of disturbance was the smoking remains of gutted cars. *What happened to Billings*, she wondered. *Is he all right?* And this feeling against the Americans. She realized Eldest Brother wasn't the only one who didn't like them. As for her, she admitted to herself that she had taken the Americans for granted, and thought Premier Ky was the handsomest leader they could have. As empty-headed as her classmates.

Kim Hoa was standing at the shop door, looking up and down the street.

"Didn't the rioters come by here?"

Kim Hoa shook her head. "I heard they tried to set fire to those tea-girl places on Tudo Street."

"They came right down the street in front of the convent. Bil—" She stopped.

Kim Hoa looked at her curiously. "Have you seen Billins?"

"No, oh no. That wasn't what I said. You think about him too much."

"*I* think about him? You were the one who said —"

"I said nothing! I don't ever want to hear his name again, do you understand?"

Rather late, Long came to their house. "I was worried about you," he said to Trang Sen. "I knew the mob went past the school."

He accepted the glass of tea his mother offered. "It's all the Americans' fault."

"You always blame the Americans."

"They don't understand how this country works, so their so-called help only makes matters worse. They think Ky is so great, but he's just a handsome pilot. What does he know about running a country?"

It all seemed terribly complicated. She wondered if Billings understood. "I need you to explain these things, the way you did before. I try to think about them, but I'd much rather read Verlaine."

"Much better that you read neither," said her mother. "What has all this to do with us, simple farmers?"

Ba Cao got up and went into the kitchen with Long's tea glass. They could hear her moving about, refilling the kettle.

Long said quietly, "What is this Ong Ngoc tells me about an American friend?"

Trang Sen's voice froze in her throat. With great effort she tried to sound bewildered. "American friend? I . . . I don't know."

"He's talking about the American officer you've been so friendly with."

"I . . . it's really nothing. I . . . don't know what he meant. Sometimes I talk with the customers, that's all."

"It was more than that. Look at me."

Reluctantly she faced him, her face flushed.

"I don't want to hear again of the kind of conversation Ong Ngoc reported. No," he insisted, as she attempted to interrupt, "he knows what he saw and heard. That is a dangerous game, and you don't know what you're doing."

Trang Sen lowered her head as her mother emerged from the curtained doorway. She was ashamed, but she was also angry with Ong Ngoc.

Who does that nosy old tailor think he is, spying on me and reporting to Eldest Brother? And why should Eldest Brother believe everything that busybody says? He doesn't even know Billins, why should he be telling me not to talk with him? I'm not doing anything dangerous, I just like talking with Billins, that's all.

She shut her mind to the American's flattering statements and suggestions of being in love with her.

THE SEMI-DARKNESS OF the shop felt almost cool after the bright heat and the cacophony of cyclos and cars, the sidewalks glutted with people. To Trang Sen's surprise, Ong Ngoc was alone.

"Where is Ba Chau? And Ong Chau?"

"Ba Chau's pains have begun. Ong Chau has gone to fetch Midwife Than."

Trang Sen hurried up the stairs. Kim Hoa was lying on the bamboo platform, wiping the sweat from her face and trying to reassure Van Hai.

Trang Sen took the child and squatted down, rocking him. She looked anxiously at Kim Hoa. "When did it start?"

"About the time we were opening the shop this afternoon." Kim Hoa's words came in breathless spurts. "They're coming so fast. Not like before. Then they were easy, slow." She winced as her belly tightened in an insistent spasm.

Trang Sen reached out and smoothed the other's forehead. Kim Hoa closed her eyes and waited for the next onslaught.

It seemed a very long time before the midwife arrived. Van Hai fell asleep and Trang Sen laid him in the hammock. She sat beside Kim Hoa and held her hand tightly as the contractions intensified, then subsided. What if Ba Than didn't get there in time? She tried to remember Trang Mai's birth, when she had peeped through the curtained doorway, watching the bustling, anxious excitement of the village midwife.

At last she heard the hurried slap, slap of plastic sandals on the stairs and Ba Than emerged panting.

The old woman examined Kim Hoa with a practiced eye. "Not long now."

Kim Hoa produced a sharp-edged shard. "For cutting the cord. He wants it done the old way." She moaned softly, turning her head from side to side, clutched Trang Sen's hand in a crippling hold when the pressure grew unbearably strong, but she did not cry out.

The room slowly darkened as the afternoon lengthened. Suddenly Kim Hoa bit her lip hard and gasped. Ba Than wiped away the gush of water and helped her to a squatting position. Leaning heavily on Trang Sen and gripping her arm, Kim Hoa threw her strength into several hard exhalations that forced her belly muscles downward.

"Yes, yes, good. Just a little more and you'll be done."

Kim Hoa gave one final heave and Ba Than grasped the tiny shoulders. "Ah, a girl. But very strong and healthy." She cut the cord.

"One more push, then you can rest. Yes, there it comes." The bloody afterbirth slid out.

Dazed, Trang Sen helped Kim Hoa lie down. She looked at the tiny creature Ba Than was cleaning and wrapping in castoff clothing from its older brother.

"Here." The old woman thrust a handful of clean cloths into Trang Sen's hands. "No time to stand there gaping. Help clean her up, and get her settled with the baby."

Together they cleaned Kim Hoa and the platform.

Kim Hoa held the baby against her breast. "I'm glad it's a girl," she whispered to Trang Sen. "I was hoping it would be, but don't tell Ong Chau." She smiled weakly and closed her eyes.

Ong Chau was called and the baby presented to him, with apologies for its sex.

Van Hai, forgotten in the hammock, began to fret. Trang Sen fetched him and showed him his new sister, cradled in Kim Hoa's arms. He looked at her briefly, then, sensing his own displacement, "Hold, Ma-ma," he demanded, stretching his arms toward her. Kim Hoa nodded, and Trang Sen lifted him onto the platform.

"It's late. Ma-ma won't know where I am. I'll go now and be back tomorrow, as soon as school is over." Trang Sen nodded to Ong Chau and started to leave.

At the top of the stairs she hesitated and turned once more to look at the scene on the platform, wondering at the peace which succeeded Kim Hoa's ordeal, more precious because the mother and baby were both alive and fine, and might not have been.

She walked softly down the stairs, nodding slightly to Ong Ngoc. She no longer trusted him, spoke to him as little as possible.

"Is the baby doing well? And Ba Chau?"

"Both well. A girl." She bowed and hurried out.

The street was unnaturally silent, as if suddenly emptied of life and movement, though it was full of people. She wondered if there had been another riot. But this felt different, oddly unsettling.

As she came up to the bus stop, a mass of people was shoving in her direction from the other end of the block. There was a desperate frenzy about them. She heard snatches of sentences. Those on the outer fringes sometimes pulled away as if in fear, but others were kneeling, or prostrating themselves, on the street. She saw a Buddhist monk at the center of the mob, his saffron robes clinging limply to his body. Then she knew what it was.

Her chest closed up and she swallowed hard. She wanted to get away, but her legs wouldn't move. Almost as if by magic, the monk's robes burst into flame. The crowd drew quickly away, people stumbling over each other. An American television van careened around the corner and the crew poured out, hastily setting up their cameras. The smell of gasoline and burning flesh stung her lungs.

It was all over very quickly. Steeled for that moment, the monk had not uttered a sound. Now the charred remnant of his blackened body fell over, the flames still leaping weakly around it. Trang Sen stared at them hypnotically for a long moment, then was overwhelmed by nausea. Reflecting afterward, she thought the most horrible part was how clean it all was, no blood, no shrieking, no cry of pain. That made it worse, not better.

Now, though, she could only retch and heave, burying her face against a building so she wouldn't have to look at anything. She stood there for a long time, her shoulders shaking.

Then she thought of Kim Hoa, of the bloody birth. It was as if the baby and Kim Hoa had been burned alive. She stumbled back to the shop.

Ong Ngoc looked up from his noodles in surprise at her disheveled appearance. He intercepted her before she reached the stairs.

"Trang Sen, what . . ."

She pushed past him. "Kim Hoa. I must see her, see if she's all right. And the baby."

He caught her arm. "Of course they're all right. Just stop a minute. You don't want to alarm Ba Chau. What's the matter?"

His words brought her somewhat to her senses. She stood still and shook her head. "I . . . I . . . the . . . the monk . . . oh, it was so awful." She burst into tears and covered her face with her hands.

He led her to a chair. "Sh, sh," he urged her. "Remember the new baby."

She nodded, trying to control herself.

"Terrible, terrible," he sympathized. "So it's happening here again. But look, child, it's their fate to do this, it's nothing to do with you. You must forget it."

"Yes," she whispered, "forget." At last she said, more formally, "Thank you, Ong Ngoc."

"Yes, yes. Now you must go home. We'll find you a cyclo. You won't want to go back to the bus stop just yet. No, no, this is on me. Little enough I can do after all your brother's kindness to me, to help his sister get home."

She allowed him to lead her into the street. He called a cyclo over, instructed the driver and handed him some bills, saw her safely on her way. "Forget it," he advised her again.

But she could not. Long afterward it invaded her dreams, and was forever mixed up with Thi Ba's birth. Her entranced wonder at a baby coming alive was tainted, as if the birth-blood became blood spilled by the burning monk, who had died so cleanly.

U.S. troop strength up to 540,000,
its highest point, by the end of 1968

CHAPTER 6

YEAR OF THE MONKEY

> . . . Monkey who rules this year will urge us to
> gamble, speculate and exploit risky but ingenious
> options. . . . It is definitely not a year for the faint-
> hearted or slow-witted. The Monkey gives no
> concessions and asks none in return. . . .
> . . . Monkey's year will bring many new and
> unconventional ways of doing things.
>
> *The Handbook of Chinese Horoscopes*
> Theodora Lau

TRANG SEN PAID no attention to the crowds clogging the sidewalk and bumping into her. Since the day of the burning monk, she had pulled a veil over her eyes, willed herself to ignore the pain around her. The smell of gasoline sickened her.

Arthur Billings had gone back to America, temporarily, he said. She blushed with shame when she remembered their goodbye. At the same time, the memory filled her with a guilt-tinged urge to repeat it.

He had followed her from school, late one afternoon. "I came to tell you I have to go home. I'm leaving tomorrow morning."

He led her through a narrow street to his military compound, past the guard hut, to a bench, away from the dusty space just inside the gate, secluded behind some hibiscus bushes. He sat disturbingly close to her, and she edged away. Then he put his arm around her and before she could pull away (and she hadn't been sure she wanted to), held her tightly and kissed her straight and hard on the mouth.

She protested. But she couldn't stop herself from returning his kisses, surprising herself with her own passion.

He laughed. "Well, is that no or yes?"

She *had* pulled away then, and refused to promise to wait for him, or to tell him where he could write her.

Now she was waiting for him after all, regretted not telling him her name.

Sister Louise was urging her to accept a scholarship from her own convent school outside Paris. It wasn't a university, but when they learned what she could do, the sisters there would help her move on. She didn't want to leave. But when she thought of Eldest Brother, her passionate longing for Billings was frozen out of her heart, and she didn't want to stay either. She was glad not to see Long very often, relieved that he was too busy to pay much attention to her, though she nevertheless still yearned for the closeness of that first year she was in Saigon.

Tonight, for the first time in weeks, he was sharing their evening meal. So she was hurrying home.

She reached the bus stop as her bus was pulling away. She flung herself onto the lower step, grabbing the handrail to regain her balance. It was crammed, those who couldn't get in hanging onto the window panels and the back of the bus. She claimed a tiny space for herself on the step.

Ba Cao was already busy in the kitchen when she got home. Trang Sen could smell the frying peppers as soon as she reached the gate.

"I'm glad you're home, child. Take the buckets and get some water. Second Daughter knocked over the jar."

Trang Sen opened her mouth to protest, but instead went outside and hoisted the bamboo pole, a bucket on either end, across her shoulder.

Long arrived as she let herself out the front gate, and walked with her to the tap. "Did you run out of water?" They usually got their day's supply in the early morning, when the pressure was more dependable.

"Your baby sister spilled it."

"And you think she's the one who should go get more." He sighed. "You're probably right."

She looked at him in surprise.

"I have to admit she doesn't do the things most children take on. She could become a far worse problem than Fourth Brother if we aren't careful. Or than you," he added with a smile.

Thinking guiltily of Arthur Billings, she didn't answer. Instead, she told him about Sister Louise's proposal.

"Do you want to go?"

"I don't know."

Now he was surprised.

"I . . . I suppose it's scary, to think about leaving here, going so far away."

He was silent for a few moments. Then, "You should go," he said. "Not many have such a chance."

"I thought you wanted me to stay here."

He shook his head. "There's no reason for that anymore. It might even be that Second Sister will have to grow up if there's no one else to help Ma-ma."

"But Ma-ma can't even manage the money."

"She might learn that, too, or Second Sister might learn."

She lowered the buckets and stood waiting for the trickle of water to fill one, then the other.

He was going on. "Do you remember what I said, two years ago? I'd like to know you're safe in France, that at least one good thing is preserved from what is to come."

"Do you think . . . ?" She couldn't finish the sentence.

"It's going to get worse. To the Americans things look good now. They pay no attention to things like this" — he flung his arm out at the street crammed with refugee shacks and families living under the eaves of buildings — "and they don't go to the market, so they don't know food is scarce, that some things you can't get at all anymore. It has to get worse. The only solution is to make our peace with Ho Chi Minh."

Trang Sen looked around in fear. "You shouldn't say such things here."

He laughed. "So my little sister has finally learned something about politics. She knows our noble government has spies."

"Please. Don't talk so loud."

But he kept on. "I see many more years of war, suffering, killing. Like that monk you saw. Better to get away from here."

She supposed Ong Ngoc had told him about the monk too. *No wonder I understand about spies,* she reflected. Aloud, she said, "I didn't think you knew about the monk."

"I watched you afterward. I didn't like what I saw. There's a hardness about you now that troubles me."

"A hardness? I only don't want to see such a thing again."

"No, nor any of the other pain. There, you see, my French education has ruined me. People here say the only thing to do is forget, and pay no attention."

"That's what Ong Ngoc said."

"But it isn't what I would say. So I want you to go where such choices don't have to be made, at least by nineteen-year-olds."

"You came back."

"Sometimes I wish I'd stayed."

"Do you want me to do that?"

"I don't know. I only want to think one thing is safe, can be salvaged from all this, one thing I care about. I think about it all the time. If you stay here, what are we to do with you? Marry you to some handsome officer? You're too honest, you know too much ever to be content with such a life. An American husband? Even worse. Then you would forget who you are. No, it's best that you go away."

She caught her breath when he mentioned an American husband, suddenly afraid her meetings with Billings had not been a secret after all. She wanted to comfort him, to promise she would always obey him. But her throat tightened with anger at the way he was planning her life. *How does he know what's good for me? If I want to marry an American, what would be so wrong about that? I wish Billins would come back.*

As they entered the gate, Long turned to her. "Tell Sister Louise I approve of her arrangement."

AT THE CORNER of the school wall, she was suddenly face to face with Billings.

He took a deep breath. "I was afraid, so afraid I wouldn't find you, that I was gone too long."

She stood still, overcome by an aching urge for him to kiss her again. She let him take her once more to the secluded bench.

He held her tightly, at last releasing her and shaking his head as if emerging from underwater.

She stood with her head down. "I thought you weren't coming back."

"But I told you . . . well, it doesn't matter." He sat down and pulled her close beside him.

They sat for some minutes. "Your school course will soon be over, I'm remembering."

"Yes."

"And then?"

"I'll be going to France. The Sisters have arranged it."

"But you . . . you can't. I . . . I thought your family . . ." He put his head in his hands and violently ran his fingers through his hair. When he looked at her again, his hair stood up stiffly, so that he seemed strange and unfamiliar.

"All these months, I thought of you all the time. It was only you who kept me going, the memory of your beautiful face, your gentleness, the way your eyes flash when you're angry. Your eyes, I remembered your eyes most of all, like pools of dark water. I could have stayed, they offered me that, but I wanted to come back. Because of you."

She could hardly breathe. *Could those things be true? Even for him to think them! It's like a book.* But she was also afraid.

"And what of you? I can't tell what you're thinking. Am I saying the wrong things again? I thought you loved me, but maybe I was wrong. Too many things can happen in six months. I stayed away too long." He put his head in his hands again.

Timidly she touched his arm. "No, not too long. But what do you want? I shouldn't let you touch me, or say the things you say to me. I'm not a tea-girl" — she overrode his protest — "no, my brother would never let me go outside again if he knew. Even Ba Chau would be very angry with me. I think we must forget about each other. I will go away to France and it will be over." She finished in a rush, trying to convince herself that could be true.

"What's the harm? Many Americans have Vietnamese girl friends, not all tea-girls."

"That can never be me. My brother would be very angry."

"When two people love each other, it's right for them to be together. That's what I want for us."

He held her tight again for a few moments. "Do one thing. Don't decide yet to go to France. Give me a chance to show you how much I love you. Promise me." He kissed her gently and let her go. "I can teach you to love me."

SHE WAS SPINNING with contradictions. Part of her sang, *He's back, he loves me, he's back.* Her physical longing for him left a tight knot in her chest and throat. She was angry at Billings for going away, and for presenting her with impossible choices; angry at Long, for the plans he kept making for her. At the thought of Billings's kisses, she blushed with embarrassment and guilt. But she touched her lips, remembered his face against her hair, and smiled.

Billings waited for her, at the places he knew he could find her. Sometimes she returned his kisses, sometimes resisted. Her dream of rescue and darkness came back, haunting her. She wished he had never come back. And she dreaded encounters with Long. *What if he finds out?*

The holiday marking the start of the year of the monkey promised a brief reprieve. Kim Hoa and her family, as well as Long, would join them for the feast.

She was at the market by dawn. But it was surrounded by soldiers. "Can't come here today. Big changes coming. Go back home and wait."

Inside, they were bullying vendors and making a mess of their goods.

She turned and ran home, sprinting through the gate and not stopping until she was inside the house. She looked quickly around, as if expecting to see a soldier right there in the room.

"Daughter, what is it?" Fear in Ba Cao's voice.

"Soldiers." She breathed hard for a few moments, then went on. "They're beating people, wouldn't let us go into the market."

Ba Cao began to wail. "No one to protect us! What will become of us?" She grabbed Trang Mai. "My poor baby."

Trang Mai added her screams to the tumult.

With an effort Trang Sen controlled herself. "We just wait here, that's all. That's what the soldiers said. They won't come to the house, I think." She wasn't sure that was true, but it reassured her mother and sister.

All that day they stayed there. From time to time they heard gunfire from the direction of the market, or rockets farther away. Darkness came, and nothing changed.

Dawn the next day — loud shouts and pounding on the door awakened them. Trang Sen opened the door a crack.

Two soldiers stood there, pressed uniforms at odds with their unkempt hair and beards.

"This whole part of town has been liberated. You're under our control now."

"Liberated? Who are you?" As she asked the question, she suddenly knew. Not government soldiers. The Front.

"Don't ask questions! Do as we say! How many people here?"

"Only my mother and sister and I."

"No soldiers? No brothers, no husband?"

"Yes, no one else."

"You stay here. No one leaves."

They went away. Trang Sen leaned against the wall.

"Daughter," whispered her mother, "what are we to do?"

Her answer was almost inaudible. "They're Front soldiers. Something terrible is happening."

All day the sound of soldiers tromping through the alleys, knocking loudly and insistently on the tightly shuttered doors, alternated with a deadly silence.

Then, late that afternoon, gunfire began again, and the rumbling of tanks, coming closer and closer. They heard people running, falling, screaming, crying. As night fell, the frightful sounds receded, farther and farther away.

Over Ba Cao's frantic objections, Trang Sen went to the end of the alley and peeped out. Sprawled across street and sidewalk were the bodies of soldiers and refugees, some dead and some apparently alive but with all degrees of wounds. Many were children. All were covered with blood, their own or that of others. Overwhelmed by nausea, she turned and ran back.

"What is it?" Her mother opened the door only wide enough to let her through.

"The soldiers are gone. Many dead, some not. All . . . all out there, in a heap. All bloody."

"Don't think about it, child . . . the soldiers, are they really gone?"

"They're not there now. Except the dead ones."

Soon they heard more rumbling wheels. A blaring loudspeaker thundered, "The city has been saved from the Communist enemy! All citizens to remain inside your houses until further notice!"

They were running out of food and water. Ba Cao added a little rice to most of what water remained, saving out enough for a vegetable broth.

"I'm still hungry," Trang Mai wailed.

"Hush crying," her mother scolded. "We're lucky to have anything to eat at all."

All that night they heard trucks, and the keening of those who were discovering family members dead, wounded, lost. Muffled gunfire sounded, far away.

At dawn they were allowed out. The street was eerily clean, sand poured over pools of dried blood. Refugees were already trying to rebuild shelters. Sickened at the memory of yesterday's death scene, Trang Sen hurried past.

The market was almost empty, only a few vendors drifting in to set up shop. She joined the long line at the public tap. The pressure was almost non-existent, even so early — evidently everyone in the city was doing the same thing.

Her mother was in the garden, Trang Mai playing with pebbles on the path when she got back. *Almost as if nothing has happened*, she thought.

Late that night, Ba Cao and Trang Mai asleep, she sat staring at her French book, scanning the pages without knowing what she was reading. Her mind would not cooperate. All that lay behind seemed to have vanished, her school life a dream from which she had awakened into blood and death.

The gate latch clicked. She blew out the candle and crept to the window. It was Long.

The terror of the past few days came flooding back. "You're all right, you're all right." She clutched his arm, half sobbing, half laughing. "Were you . . . where . . . are you . . . ? We didn't know what was happening, then they came to the house. And the bodies, all the blood — so awful."

"Yes, yes, I know."

She started into the house, but he stopped her. "No, first I must tell you something." She turned back, frightened again. *Has something happened to Billins?* In the next moment she remembered Eldest Brother wouldn't know.

"The school, no one thought it was a target . . . a firebomb. No one was prepared. They're all dead, all the nuns except Sister Nguyen. The girls are safe, because of the holiday. But everything burned, there was no way to stop it, with all the fighting."

She felt as if turned to cold stone. "Sister Louise . . . ?"

"She too, dead."

She put her face in her hands, beyond tears. "She was angry with me. She thought I didn't want to go, I couldn't explain. Now she'll never . . ." She bit her lip and looked away.

He touched her arm gently. "I wish I could comfort you. But there is no comfort. No one knows how many are dead, the soldiers carted away some who were surely alive. They're still fighting in Cholon. It's the same all over, Danang, Hue — we've had no news from Hue."

"Kim Hoa . . . ?"

He shook his head. "I don't know. There's been no time, no way to find out. I only know about the school because it's so close to the compound."

"Are we going to lose?" she whispered.

"What is lose? The city is safe, we've pushed them back, killed many. Whether that's good news, I don't know."

She thought of Billings, and tears came to her eyes then. *What if he's dead? The school, how could the school be bombed? And Sister Louise, never to see her again.* She rubbed her sleeve across her face.

Long touched her arm again. "I'd change it all if I could."

Belatedly, she noticed his exhaustion. "You too, it must have been terrible."

"Let's not talk about it. I must see Ma-ma, then get back. They'll be needing me."

She DREAMED OF blood and pain, fire and explosions. In the morning her face was wet with tears, but awake she could not, would not, cry. She ate little and grew thin, her hair lost its luster, her eyes their brightness. In the peasant clothing she now wore, she looked like one of the refugees.

Kim Hoa, despite her own problems, worried about her. "You aren't the only one to suffer. I have lost my husband. But we must live."

Because they ran a tailor shop for the Americans, Ong Chau and Ong Ngoc had been taken away, beaten and left for dead. Front soldiers looted and trashed the shop. Kim Hoa huddled in a corner of the bed platform upstairs, hiding under a quilt with the children held tightly against her to stifle their cries. Ong Ngoc survived and struggled back to the shop. Kim Hoa took care of his wounds, then went looking for her husband. She found him curled in a heap against a building and dragged him home. He died that first night.

Ong Ngoc was ill for a long time. Spiritless, he took no initiative in refurbishing the shop. Kim Hoa, following some dim instinct of survival, did it all, deciding on her own to use some of their profits to rebuild.

Trang Sen's hand shook as she responded to Kim Hoa. "They . . . they're all gone, everything, gone."

"The school, the Sisters, Sister Louise . . . they're gone, yes. But the world goes on."

"It's as if I have died too. All my dreams . . ." She put her face in her hands.

"Then you must begin new dreams. You have always found dreams. What of the school in France?"

"I don't know. I never knew the name. All was to be arranged by Sister Louise."

LONG WALKED QUICKLY down the plank walk to the house, the hard-soled shoes that were part of his uniform thudding. He bowed to his mother, who was sitting next to the oil lamp mending a pair of black trousers.

"Ah, my son, for too long we haven't seen you."

He looked at Trang Sen, crouched in a far corner of the bed platform, her arms folded across her knees, her hands clenching them tightly.

"It is as if she sees nothing, hears nothing. She eats nothing — you see, she has become so thin. I try to talk with her but it's no good." Ba Cao shook her head.

He went over and knelt beside Trang Sen.

She looked up, then laid her head down on her arms.

"I'm trying to find Sister Nguyen. It may be she can tell us the name of the school in Paris. If not, I can write a friend there, and ask him to forward a letter to the order."

Her whisper was almost inaudible. "I wanted to see you. Then you didn't come."

"I'm sorry. My life also has been filled with confusion." It seemed he was about to say something else, then changed his mind. "Will you help me?" he asked instead. "You may be able to find Sister Nguyen more easily than I."

"Sister Nguyen doesn't like me."

"She would help you now, I think."

She didn't answer.

He finally said, "You must at least do this — read French each day, and help Cousin Hoa." He held out a book. "I've brought you something you'll like — Sartre. He's totally different from your favorite romantics. You should begin to know the twentieth century. It will help you in France."

When she didn't take it, he laid it beside her.

It was the first Ba Cao had heard of Trang Sen's going to France. She followed Long to the door.

"It's best for her, Ma-ma. She's too much of a rebel. There, in France, she can find her own way."

"That child has had her head turned too much already by all the studying, and those nuns too. She needs a husband to set her straight. More school won't do it."

"No, Ma-ma, that way will never work for First Sister. And where are we to find a husband for her now?"

Ba Cao shrugged. "I knew this would happen, didn't I say so when you first talked of sending her to school?"

Trang Sen lay staring into the darkness long after her mother and Trang Mai were asleep. She heard the hammock creak when Trang Mai turned over.

She wouldn't sleep, she thought. Then the nightmares wouldn't come.

She was running through the city, dashing from the shadow of one building to the next, as she had done that night she went to find Eldest Brother. There was a great darkness behind her — as she moved away from each building, it disappeared into the black depth. She heard Sister Louise calling out of the darkness. She was afraid to turn around, the blackness might suck her into it. But she could not ignore that call.

At last she turned and ran toward the voice. She heard it clearly now, though the darkness kept growing blacker. "Ma chère."

Suddenly there was a burst of fire. The darkness and the voice were engulfed in flame.

She awoke sweating and breathless, still in the power of the dream. Trang Mai and her mother did not move.

As if obeying a command, she sat up, slid off the platform, and tiptoed out. She ran as if the darkness of her dream was pursuing her. But, in contrast to the dream, she knew where she must go. When she could run no longer, she leaned panting for a moment against a building. A child, sheltered by a rough lean-to, stared up at her. She went on, walking rapidly.

She stood on the corner at the end of the block where the school had been. When she went around that corner, she would see it. She wanted to go the other way, but as if some other will was forcing her forward, she took a deep breath and made the last turn.

Most of the wall was intact, though the gate was gone. She could see the ruined buildings, partially standing. Spellbound in sorrow, she walked through the space where the door had been, into the courtyard. Unaccountably, a bougainvillea still bloomed there, its dark branches etched in shadow on a broken wall. She caught her breath against the sudden pain its simple beauty kindled.

The ruined compound had been taken over by refugees. They lay hunched on sleeping mats, a thin brown arm or leg flung out. Some had built flimsy shelters. From the other side of a pile of rubble she heard a child crying.

She stood for a long time, her eyes closed. Half dreaming, she thought Sister Louise brushed by her, the long white habit swishing softly. Almost, she felt a hand of blessing on her brow. As if that imagined gesture was permission, or perhaps command, she began to weep. She groped her way through the gaping entrance and leaned against the broken wall.

At last she raised her head and rubbed her sleeve across her face. It was growing lighter at the eastern edges of the sky. She took several long breaths and shook her head, like a swimmer rising out of the sea. She would read the book, she would try to find Sister Nguyen. But first . . . she wanted Kim Hoa, Kim Hoa so anxious for her, with so many problems of her own.

Oblivious of the hour, she headed for the tailor shop. The locked door and dark emptiness within jolted her back to reality. She squatted in front of the shop, leaning against the display window, waiting until someone woke up. Street vendors rumbled past and set up their cooking stalls. Assaulted by hunger, she tried to remember how long it had been since she had eaten, really eaten. A very long time.

She thought of something else she had forgotten — Arthur Billings. *Where is he? Has he been looking for me? Where would he look?* She could find him, at the American compound. But she wasn't sure she wanted to. She felt cleansed, purified not only of grief but of passion.

She heard movement upstairs, and Kim Hoa calling to the children. She stood up and knocked loudly on the door, then went to the edge of the sidewalk and called up at the windows. Van Hai's tousled head appeared, Kim Hoa behind him looking astonished.

The heads disappeared and she heard Kim Hoa coming rapidly down the stairs.

Kim Hoa unlocked the door and grabbed Trang Sen's arm. "What's happened? . . . but you seem all right."

"Yes, yes, I'm fine. But, oh, Kim Hoa, so much has happened to you, I never thought."

"I've been so worried."

"I'll help you now, it will be like before. Only now" — her voice became unsteady in spite of herself — "there'll be more time. No classes."

"Where have you been, so early?"

Her answer was vague. "I had to walk."

They went upstairs, Kim Hoa chattering in relief. Trang Sen ate greedy bowls of rice porridge, devoured the condiments Kim Hoa set out.

"Are you going to make up for all your weeks of starving in one meal?"

Trang Sen laughed. "I thought I might try, at least." She put the bowl down. "Well, what's to be done? Where shall I start — arranging the shelves — or whatever you say?"

"It is possible you might want to change clothes first. Those look as if you'd slept in them for days."

"Oh." Trang Sen looked down at her wrinkled trousers. She suddenly felt very tired. "Perhaps I'll rest first."

She lay down on the platform and fell immediately into a dreamless sleep.

She awoke toward evening, amazed at the dusky light. She sat up and rubbed her face, her sleep-clouded eyes slowly coming into focus. Thi Ba was solemnly watching her.

Trang Sen smiled. "Where is your Ma-ma, little one?"

"Downstairs. Auntie hold?"

Trang Sen held out her arms and the child ran into them. *This is peace,* she thought, *this is good. If only I could be like Kim Hoa, so simple, so calm.*

Kim Hoa's head appeared at the top of the stairs. "I thought I heard you awake."

"Yes. It's so late. Ma-ma doesn't know where I am."

"I sent someone to tell her, I said you would stay here tonight if you like."

"I could sleep and sleep. But I'm also hungry again." Trang Sen was apologetic.

"I expected that. I bought all the market would sell me. But Cousin Long is waiting for you. He didn't want to wake you."

"Eldest Brother? How did he know I was here?"

Kim Hoa hesitated. "He didn't. He came to see me. I went to him yesterday and told him I was worried about you." She smiled uncertainly. "I hope you aren't angry."

"No, only . . . was I really so alarming?"

"It doesn't matter now."

Kim Hoa went to get Long.

Trang Sen smoothed her hair and straightened her rumpled tunic. She felt like a sobbing child again, reluctant to be discovered by him.

He greeted her as if she had been ill a long time. "Are you really all right?"

She nodded. "Yes, I'm not sure why, but it's as if I've come back to the living world. I want to read the book you brought, and I'll do what you said, help Kim Hoa and try to find Sister Nguyen."

But Paris seemed very far away.

MOST DAYS SHE spent at the tailor shop. There were more Americans than ever now, bringing more and more business. When Trang Sen was there, Ong Ngoc perked up, the only time he seemed interested in what was happening around him. Kim Hoa noticed and smiled.

In the evenings Trang Sen read, as she had for so many years in the village. After she finished the Sartre, Long gave her other modern writers. Detecting a worrisome passiveness about her and not knowing what else to do, he came to see them more often, and emptied his bookshelf for her.

They never found Sister Nguyen. Trang Sen had gone to Thanh Thuy to see if she could help. She wore the uniform ao dai, embarrassed to appear at the gate of such an elegant house in her peasant clothing. Thanh Thuy was pleased to see her, insisted that she have some tea. Unexpectedly, Trang Sen was also glad to see Thanh Thuy. But her classmate knew nothing of Sister Nguyen.

Long wrote his friend in Paris.

To her, all their effort was part of that shadowy, inaccessible world behind her. She would do these things for Long, out of a dim sense of loyalty and duty, but she didn't believe anything would come of them.

Billings too seemed part of the unreachable past. She couldn't remember the passion of his kisses. She was neither surprised nor disappointed that he had not tried to find her.

Late on a rainy evening she walked to the bus stop. Ong Ngoc, once more his old self, had wangled a large amount of cloth from the American military exchange, and it had to be put away. He did this occasionally, with the help of a friend who worked there and could divert a shipment on the sly from time to time.

She slogged wearily through the streets flowing with water from the overtaxed sewers, her trousers pushed up to her knees. The flood caught the trash from the streets and carried it along as well. Cast off watermelon rinds, orange peels, old plastic bags, caught at her ankles. The air was acrid from the exhaust fumes that hung damply and almost visibly around her. She fought to keep the umbrella over her head, but was wet in spite of her efforts.

A hand closed over hers on the umbrella handle, bringing her to a stop. "Thank God I've found you." Arthur Billings tried to kiss her.

She resisted. But now that he was standing beside her, some of the old feeling emerged, a hint of the passion she had forgotten. She reached up and pushed a wet strand of hair out of her face.

"Ah, you're beautiful. Even now, bedraggled, in your peasant clothes. Especially now. But here, we can at least get out of the rain."

They went to Tudo Street, to a tiny bar squeezed between two glittering nightclubs, their neon signs cutting sharply through the rainy night and music blaring from inside. He guided her toward a small booth far in the back, a diminutive lamp on the wall its only light. Sliding in beside her, he took their dripping umbrellas and laid them on the floor.

She sat with head down, looking at her locked hands. The unruly tress had strayed again. Gently he pushed it back and laid his hand against her cheek, turning her face toward him. "I've missed you so much. I've been so terribly afraid I'd lost you for good this time." He tried again to kiss her. She neither resisted nor responded.

He drew back. "What is it? Are you angry with me?"

She turned her head away. "Everything changed. You too, I thought."

"I was up at Danang when the attack started. Then we were so busy, other matters came up, I was back and forth, sometimes here, sometimes in Danang. When I finally had a moment to look for you, the school was gone. I . . . I couldn't believe it. For a while I went to the market every day. But no luck. Then I thought of the tailor shop. I watched it for a long time, waiting for you. I didn't like to go in and ask. You should have asked for me at the compound."

"I thought you were gone."

"My poor baby. You've been through a kind of hell, haven't you? And I wasn't even there to help." He put his arm around her.

She leaned against him. "It was so awful, that day they came . . ." Until now, that memory had been wiped out by her sorrow over the school. She began to cry.

"It's all right, I'll take care of you. I won't let us be separated again. I'll be here for you all the time."

She raised her head and looked at him, tears still flooding her eyes. "I won't run away from you anymore. Only . . . only . . ." She stopped, thinking of Eldest Brother.

"Only?" He crooked his finger and touched the tears.

"My brother . . . he'll never . . ."

"I'll explain everything to him."

She shook her head.

He laughed. "My powers of persuasion are considerable."

How could she tell him how Eldest Brother felt about Americans? But it was impossible to worry when he was so sure. It was good to be with someone who was sure. She was tired of Eldest Brother's doubts, his bitterness and anger. That disloyal thought brought a jolt of guilt.

"So what are you thinking, beautiful?"

She shook her head, but smiled at him.

"It's time you told me your name."

To tell him her name — a barrier she would never be able to get back across. "Trinh Trang Sen." She said it all in one breath.

"There, now was that so hard? . . . Trang Sen . . . white lotus, is that it?"

She nodded.

"A beautiful name, like you. There are no lotuses in America. Our water lilies, they lack that delicate, almost untouchable beauty. Since I came here, I've always thought lotuses were the loveliest things."

"They used to grow in the stream in front of our house. Really, it was more a canal, the water was very still, except in the floods."

But he wanted something else. "Your brother's name?"

"No, no, I can't."

"I promise, I won't try to find him, without telling you."

She whispered, "Trinh Van Long."

Billings whistled softly. "Not the Major Long on General Le's staff?"

Her nod was almost imperceptible.

"Everybody knows he's the real brains in Le's outfit. You aren't just an ordinary peasant girl, are you?"

Something about that made her momentarily angry. "I didn't know he was so famous. He . . . he never talks about his work."

"No, he wouldn't. But I can tell you, we'd have a much harder time of it if Major Long wasn't there. So you're his sister!" He pulled back and looked at her. "Come to think of it, I can see the resemblance."

She felt very proud of Eldest Brother. But if he was so important, why was he so angry? She wondered what he thought of Billings.

Billings was saying, "It may be that if I talked with him" — she looked at him in alarm — "only if you agree. But he seems a reasonable man."

They stayed there until very late. She told him of her village, how they had come to Saigon after her father was killed. When she told him about that, he muttered something in English under his breath.

She didn't tell him they were still trying to find a way for her to study in Paris. She didn't want to think about that.

The restaurant was closing.

"Come with me tonight."

Embarrassed, she looked away. "No, oh, no, I could never do that." But she wasn't angry.

Every afternoon he waited for her in front of the Rex Hotel, half a block from the shop, and they were together until a dinner or party forced him to leave her.

"What do you do at these affairs?" she asked him.

His answer was vague. He didn't want to talk about his work, about the war, or about any of the things Long tried to explain to her. "Don't worry your little head about such things."

They ate together on the rare nights he was free. On those occasions they parted when Trang Sen felt she could find no lie to explain to her mother why she had stayed away any later. Her mother thought she was having her evening meals with Kim Hoa.

He took her to small restaurants in the narrow lanes and alleys off Tudo Street, some Vietnamese, others American or French. They went to Cholon for Chinese. Sometimes they simply sat together on their secluded bench.

She was not entirely comfortable about going to Tudo Street, with its bars and tea-girls, but she lacked the will to argue when he took her there.

He was teaching her English. Her aptness seemed to surprise him, which annoyed her. She told him, with hurt pride, that she had been at the top of her class, had learned as much French in six months as the others had in three years. He nodded absently.

She no longer cared to study anything but English.

He kept trying to persuade her to let him rent a hotel room for them overnight, or to come with him to Vung Tau for one of his free weekends.

"I'm not a tea-girl," she reminded him angrily. But the sexual stirrings she felt when she was with him were painfully insistent.

She was afraid of what would happen when Long heard from his Paris friend. She would never leave Billings now.

Long thought she continued to study French, as she regularly asked him for more books. He was relieved that she seemed to be her dreaming, hopeful self once more.

Only Kim Hoa suspected that there might be more to the dramatic change than simply time healing Trang Sen's grief. At first she thought Ong Ngoc's obviously growing attraction was mutual, but soon realized Trang Sen paid little attention to him. Though Billings was never mentioned, Kim Hoa guessed he had not disappeared from Trang Sen's life when he no longer came to the tailor shop. It would be just like Trang Sen, she thought, to marry an American.

Billings was waiting for her as usual by the entrance to the Rex. "I've a surprise for you."

They took a cyclo to a hotel, not far from the U.S. embassy. The lobby was full of Americans. Off to one side was a small theater.

"It's time you saw a movie. I bet you've never seen one."

She shook her head.

"You'll like this one. It's just the sort of thing to strike your romantic imagination."

Beside the door was a billboard announcing the current attraction. She tried to make out the title with her limited English. "Loof . . . iss-a . . ."

He laughed. "The first word is love. You remember, I taught you that. *Love Is a Many-Splendoured Thing.*"

"What does it mean?"

"You'll understand when you see it. I suppose you could say it means love is very precious."

"A love story."

"Yes, and a true one. It really happened."

She had seen a few very serious, very documentary, films at the convent, but this was like seeing her own dreams unfolding. The lovers' meeting in Macao was somewhat unnerving — it was too similar to what Billings kept trying to persuade her to do. But she liked the fortune teller part.

By the time Mark and Suyin said goodbye, standing on the hill, the wind blowing Suyin's dress, tears were streaming down Trang Sen's face. Billings squeezed her hand, and she held it tightly. She almost screamed out when the bomb dropped and the ink bowl shattered, was inconsolable when Suyin received the news of Mark's death.

Billings put his arm around her and she hid her eyes against his chest. "It's all right, it's all over now, baby."

She raised her head and gazed at the empty screen, as if the characters might reappear. "So sad." She burst into tears once more.

He kissed her. "Let's go," he whispered. "It's a thing that happened years ago, nothing to do with us. Don't cry, sweetheart."

They sat together on a bench beside the river. He began kissing her. Shakily and tearfully at first, she responded. Her own desire seemed to melt into the story of Suyin and Mark, their story became her own dream. She gave in at last to the feelings she had held in check for so long, and kissed him without restraint.

"Ah, honey," he whispered, "we've waited too long, too long."

Resolutely, he drew away from her. "Not like this, not here." He stood up, pulled her up beside him.

She looked at him, her eyes dark and luminous.

"I know a place, not far from here. It's time we went there."

She let him lead her, clinging tightly to him.

Always afterward, that night was a blur. In a dream she followed him to the room in the tiny hotel, with its strange Western-style bed. She kissed him frantically as he fumbled with her clothing. Gently, so gently, he laid her on the bed. Almost he sought to overcome her passion with his calmness, then entered her. She didn't remember any pain, but, still under the spell of the movie, she began to weep.

Billings kissed the tears on her cheeks and eyelids, until their climax engulfed them.

Afterward, propped on his elbow, he observed her. She stared at the ceiling, her dark eyes blank.

"What are you thinking?"

She shook her head. "I'm no better than a tea-girl."

"You mustn't think that. You're beautiful, and I love you very much."

She turned her head to look at him. "Will you marry me, Ar-toor, take me to America?"

"Tonight let's just be happy together. You don't have to worry."

"I love you, Ar-toor. But . . ." she shuddered to think of Eldest Brother.

"No thinking tonight. Tomorrow we think." He kissed her forehead, eyelids, mouth.

She turned to him and said no more.

There were two lovers, Kim and Kieu. To pay her father's debts Kieu unknowingly sold herself to a brothel. She lived long years in moral turpitude, at last throwing herself into a river. Miraculously saved, she was reunited with Kim.

Kim, trying to persuade her to marry him, said

> . . . Among those duties falling to her lot,
> a woman's chastity means many things . . .
> in crisis, must one rigid rule apply?
> True daughter, you upheld a woman's role:
> what dust or dirt could ever sully you?

But Kieu replied

> . . . If you want to get what they all want,
> glean scent from dirt, or pluck a wilting flower,
> then we'll flaunt filth, put on a foul display,
> and only hate, not love, will then remain. . . .
> What little chastity I may have saved,
> am I to fling it under trampling feet?

They agreed to marry and live together as friends, not lovers.

from *The Tale of Kieu*
Nguyen Du

MESMERIZED BY HER constant, almost unbearable desire for Billings, with difficulty she maintained a charade of normality before her family and Kim Hoa.

One morning as she entered the shop, Kim Hoa pelted her with questions. "Where have you been? Cousin Long is looking for you. He's very upset. Aunt thought you were here."

Trang Sen's chest felt as if it was squeezed in a vise. "I . . . I . . ." she searched frantically for an explanation. "I saw Thanh Thuy yesterday, she asked me to come home with her, we hadn't seen each other in so long, we talked very late. I went home after that." She said it all in a rush.

"How strange. Cousin Long was here again a few minutes ago. He says you never were home last night."

"I . . . I left very early this morning. I walked here. It took a very long time."

Kim Hoa turned away from her. "Cousin Long will be back in an hour."

What to tell him? Perhaps that she had stayed the night with Thanh Thuy. Yes. She would have to be sure Kim Hoa didn't hear her. She wished she could run away. She felt sick, her throat was dry, her forehead hot.

Too soon, he came through the door. She turned an ashen face toward him.

"You're all right. I was so worried."

His distress and trust were too much. She burst into tears.

"What is it, what's happened?"

"I . . . I'm so sorry."

Ong Ngoc was staring at them, almost dropped the bolt of cloth he was holding.

"We can't talk here." Long led her up to Kim Hoa's apartment.

"What is it?" he repeated.

She told him the lie about Thanh Thuy, almost choking on the words. She began to cry again. "I never thought how it would worry you."

He looked at her anxiously. "Never mind. Just don't go off like that again. I didn't know you and Thanh Thuy were such friends. It's all right. I know her father."

Now she was afraid he would say something to Thanh Thuy's father.

"I came to tell you I heard from my friend in Paris."

"Oh." She caught her breath. "Did he . . . ?"

"He contacted the order, sent my letter on to the school. He sent me their answer. Here, you can read it yourself."

Her hand shook as she took it from him, and he looked at her sharply again.

The nuns wanted her to come immediately, included a money order for the plane fare.

Long was watching her eagerly. "So you see, out of all the sadness and death, something good also remains. I talked with Ma-ma last night. While she's not happy about it, she'll permit you to go. And I'll be glad to know you're safe."

Still she said nothing.

"Aren't you happy? It's what you've always wanted."

She tried to smile. "So many things have happened, I never thought it could be."

"Yes, you're very fortunate, in spite of everything."

She nodded, almost absently.

"Are you sure you're all right?"

"I'm sorry I worried you."

"You've always been worth my worry." He smiled. "I'll take the money order and see about a reservation. Be kind to Ma-ma. Your going off alone to France is more than she can imagine."

He left her then. She stood frozen in despair. She couldn't go. He would be so angry.

Kim Hoa came up the stairs. "What is it? Is Cousin Long angry with you?"

Trang Sen handed her the letter.

Kim Hoa shook her head. "You know I can't read the French."

"It says the Sisters are expecting me at the school, they want me to come now." Her voice broke off in a sob.

"But that's good, it's what you've wanted. What's wrong?"

Kim Hoa, always so wise, so calm, Kim Hoa would help her. "I . . . I . . . . If I tell you, will you promise not to tell?"

"Have I ever told on you?" Kim Hoa was silent a moment, then added, "I've guessed something was going on. Something has happened to you, changed you."

"Then you knew?"

"I know nothing, I only see what's before me and try to guess."

"It is Billins," and she told Kim Hoa everything.

"And that's where you were last night. Oh, Trang Sen, do you know what you're doing?"

"He wants us to have a house, he wants to talk with Eldest Brother, to marry me. But Eldest Brother . . . Eldest Brother hates the Americans, no, he doesn't hate them, but he doesn't want them here, and he wants me to go France. What am I going to do?"

"Will you leave him now?"

"I . . . I can't. If I did, I'd be no better than a tea-girl."

Kim Hoa looked away from her. "Always I thought you'd go to France, become famous some day. It was your fate, I thought. And I was glad you were different from the rest of us, all so ordinary. Now . . ."

"Don't be angry with me."

"I'm not angry. Only . . . I've heard stories about the Americans, what they think of their girlfriends here."

"What can I do?" The tears started once more. "I can't go to France, I can't."

Kim Hoa didn't answer.

"I . . . have to see Billins."

He was very upset. "You should have told me this might happen, we should have talked with your brother long ago."

"I don't want to talk with him at all."

"Then what do you suggest we do?" he asked her icily. "Do you want to go to France?"

"No." Her voice caught. "But he'll be so angry. With you too."

He laughed. "I can take care of big brothers."

"What will you do?"

"Nothing terrible. Appeal to his reason. Major Long is a reasonable man."

How to make him understand? "You can't do it yourself. It will only make him angry. You need a middleman."

He looked at her in confusion. She had used the technical Vietnamese term. "A . . . a negotiator, to talk between two people, so they won't have to face each other."

"Why shouldn't we face each other?"

"He'll be angry. This way . . ."

"How can I find this . . . this, ah, negotiator? If I decide I want one."

"They're in all the markets. But it's best to have one who knows both sides. I know!" A glimmer of hope broke through. "Kim Hoa . . . she's the perfect one."

"Ba Chau? What could she do?"

"If anyone can persuade Eldest Brother, she can. Oh, please say yes, let's go talk to her right now." She stood up and pulled at his hand.

"Wait a minute. Tell me more about how this works."

Impatiently she explained how the middleman would work out the terms of the marriage agreement, the payment from the groom, an auspicious date for the wedding.

"You're talking about a marriage contract?"

"Yes, yes, come on." She tugged at his hand again.

"Sit down," he said. "There's something you and I need to talk about."

His expression wiped out her eagerness. Silently, she sat down beside him.

Turning his face away from her, he took her hand, holding it gently. "I can't marry you."

"But, but, you said . . ."

"I never said that. You're the only one who ever said that."

"But you said you loved me. I thought . . ."

"I do love you, more than anything in the world."

"Then why . . . ?"

"It isn't possible for me to marry you. I'm already married."

She withdrew her hand. She was silent for so long that he put his arm around her. "All the things I said are true."

She pulled away. "Don't touch me," then, almost to herself, "Kim Hoa was right."

"How so?"

"She told me what you Americans think of your girlfriends, how you treat us. I'm just a tea-girl, that's all."

"No, no. I love you."

"What are you going to do with me?"

"Do with you?"

"Will you take me to America?"

"I can't do that, there are rules."

"And when you go back?"

"I've asked to stay, because of you, only because of you."

He put his arms around her again. She didn't resist, passively allowed him to hold her and kiss her. She felt as if part of her was standing aside, looking at herself and him. She had no feeling, no will, to return his kisses or reject them.

He pulled back from her. "You're being very foolish. This sort of thing happens all the time. Men have two loves, the one who is the wife is often the least of the two. So it is with us."

She listened to his words, or another listened to his words. *He deceived me, made me believe he would marry me, whether he used that word or not. Eldest Brother, what will Eldest Brother say? This very moment buying my ticket to Paris, so proud of me. He'll never trust me again.* She wanted it to be yesterday, before all this happened. She wanted it to be long ago, before she knew Billings.

Never to have known him? No, oh no, not that, I don't want that. I love him, love the way he holds me, his pale tan skin, odd habits, things I never knew before.

"I have deceived him." She said it aloud, but to herself, not Billings.

"What, my love?"

"Eldest Brother."

"Don't worry, I can talk with him."

"*You*, talk with him?" She was suddenly angry. "And what will you say? Do you think he will be pleased to know you've turned his sister into a prostitute? Do you think he will thank you? What do you think we are, you Americans?"

He got up and went to the window, stood with his back to her, then, glancing at his watch, said reluctantly, "I can't stay with you now. Will you wait for me at the tailor shop? We'll think of a way."

She shook her head. "There is no way."

"Wait here, if you'd rather. I'll tell the clerk to extend our time."

"No, I want to leave here."

She dragged her feet to the only sanctuary she knew, Kim Hoa. Ong Ngoc looked at her curiously as she drifted past him and up the stairs.

Kim Hoa was feeding Thi Ba. "You've seen Billins."

"He said . . . he said he has a wife in America."

Kim Hoa put down the bowl and stared at Trang Sen.

"He says I was the one talking about marrying, never him."

Thi Ba stretched out her arms to her mother. "Rice, rice."

Kim Hoa picked up the bowl.

Trang Sen stared at the child opening her mouth wide when her mother approached her with the spoon. Like a baby bird.

Kim Hoa put away the empty bowl and turned to Trang Sen again.

"He says he can make Eldest Brother understand. But how can Eldest Brother understand?"

"He mustn't talk with Cousin Long."

Trang Sen lowered her head. In a whisper she said, "I don't want to leave him. I want to stay here with him." She shuddered. "Perhaps, perhaps I should be like Kieu, throw myself in the river. Then Eldest Brother would know I wasn't really bad." She was silent, imagining it. "I would be afraid. But I'm afraid of Eldest Brother too. I can't bear for him to hate me."

Still Kim Hoa said nothing.

"Billins said to wait for him here. Will . . . will you be kind to him?"

"I'll do as you like."

Trang Sen's thoughts went round and round in an endless desperate circle: *I'll give up Billins, go to France, and Eldest Brother will never know. Never to see Billins again? I'll tell Eldest Brother I shouldn't leave for France immediately, that I'd like to find a job, a real job. I'll tell him I feel responsible to help support the family. Will he agree, now that he wants me to leave? I'll tell Eldest Brother everything, face his anger. And have him know how I've betrayed him?*

BILLINS LOOKED AROUND the shop expectantly.

Kim Hoa intercepted Ong Ngoc as he started toward him. "Ong Billins." She bowed.

Billins looked at the mask of her face. "Trang Sen," he blurted, "where is she?"

"Co Sen is upstairs. She would like to see you if you wish."

"Yes, yes, up this way?"

He hurried up the stairs, his shoes clattering. He looked around the room, lit dimly by a small electric bulb. Trang Sen had risen when she heard his steps. The pale light cast a faint halo around her dark hair. In her white ao dai she looked so vulnerable that his breath caught in his throat. Something about her prevented him from going to her.

"I never meant to hurt you."

"We have done what we have done."

"And now?"

"Now we accept our fate. For me, that is to follow this path I have chosen, not knowing what the path was. For you, someday I think your fate must be to choose."

Though she was saying she would stay with him, that invisible barrier was still thrown up between them. And her talk of fate, her words, which seemed almost to be a look at both their futures, froze out all joy.

"You may find a place for me, for us. Now I must go to my brother, endure his anger."

"I can help you . . ."

"No!" She put out her hand as if to prevent him. "You must not talk with him, ever."

"But . . ."

"No."

It was unbearable that she should stand before him, so remote, so unfeeling. He walked over to her, tried to put his arm around her.

She drew back. "No." But her tone was gentler than before. "It is like a vow I have made. It is the only way I can do it, to face him. After that, it won't matter anymore."

"Won't matter?"

"Whatever we do. It will all be over then."

Leaving, he went past Kim Hoa and Ong Ngoc without acknowledging either. Ong Ngoc raised his eyebrows. Presently he told Kim Hoa to mind the shop and went out, almost stealthily.

Very late, Trang Sen went to Long's compound and asked at the guardhouse for him. Sooner than she wished, she saw him crossing the bare courtyard. His face had the tight look that meant he was very angry.

"What is it?"

"You can tell me, perhaps. Something about that American, I understand."

"That . . . that's what I came to tell you. But how did you know?"

She told him of Billings then, but not his name.

"That's where you were last night."

She nodded, avoiding his eyes.

"Why do you come here? What has this to do with me?"

She was silent.

"You needn't have come at all."

She was on the verge of tears, but she would not let him see her cry.

"I am still the same Trang Sen."

"No, you will never be again." He too was controlling himself. "Let me buy your ticket, send you on to Paris. Then it will be as if this never happened." There was a plea in his voice.

"I can't," she whispered. "I have to stay here with him. I . . . I want to stay."

She watched until he disappeared into the darkness of the building, remembering that other night when she had come here. She knew now that he had been right then, that he had always been right. *Well,* she thought, *I'm accepting these consequences too.* She might call him back, tell him she would not see Billings again, would go to France. But she couldn't. Her choice had been made, perhaps as long ago as that day she saw Billings in the marketplace, or even before that, when she saw the American by the river.

CHAPTER 7

ARTHUR BILLINGS

TRANG SEN BOWED slightly to the doorman, her arms loaded with groceries. At the apartment door, she fumbled awkwardly for her key. *What an inconvenient way to live*, she thought for the thousandth time.

They had been here three months, but every time she came in she felt she was in someone else's house. The fat upholstered chairs and tall table still seemed incurably alien, the soft bed made her feel as if she were sinking into insubstantial cloud.

Billings laughed at her ideas. But he was proud of her, introduced her to his friends, took her with him to their parties. She discovered that many of the foreigners, not only Americans, had "steady" Vietnamese girlfriends.

"What is 'steady'?" she asked.

"They stick with one girl, take care of her, don't go looking around Tudo Street," he explained.

Most of these girlfriends, though, were tea-girls, and Trang Sen felt isolated — and embarrassed when she allowed herself to acknowledge that the Americans she was meeting probably assumed she was also a tea-girl. Sometimes she couldn't face going anywhere with Billings.

Except for Kim Hoa, she had no connections to her former life. Her mother had denounced her in a bitter tirade, ending at last with, "Never

113

come back here, never! Second Daughter must not see your filthy ways!"

Now, though, she wasn't thinking about any of that. Passing in front of the bedroom mirror, she pirouetted a little, admiring herself in the pale pink ao dai. Billings had commissioned Kim Hoa to make her a closetful of ao dais, in pastel, sherbet-like colors. Before, she had never thought of wearing anything but the white ao dai of the school, or black peasant pajamas.

Billings had invited guests that evening, in honor of a colonel visiting from America. He wanted a Vietnamese feast, but he also wanted everything done properly. He spent days teaching her how to set the table and serve the meal. She was very nervous, afraid a fork or plate would be out of place. Though why it mattered, she didn't know.

He sniffed appreciatively at the spicy odor of chili peppers, onion and ginger that greeted him as he opened the door. Peering into a large pot, "What is it?" he asked.

"A cabbage soup, in ginger broth. And here, Ar-thurr, let me show you the crabs." She lifted the lid of the bamboo steamer to reveal a confusion of orange-red legs and bodies, ready to be cut up and stir-fried in soy sauce, onions and ginger. Lettuce was laid out on a platter, for wrapping around strips of beef fried in a dry pan with black pepper, chilies and garlic. "And there's the nam — I used pork for that, since we were having the beef. Do you think they'll like it?"

He smiled at her and she forgot about the dinner.

"And here I am, so interested in the food that I haven't told you how much I missed you all day — every minute, every second." He kissed her, then led her into the living room. "I have something for you."

Inside the oblong box was a mass of flowered silk, shimmering with blues, greens, and bright shades of crimson and violet. Taking it out, she discovered a western-style dress, its lustrous folds falling gently from her hands. "It's the most beautiful dress I've ever seen. But . . . but I've never worn a western dress. Do you think . . . ?"

"It'll be perfect. Try it on. I want you to wear it tonight."

The lowcut rounded neckline, flowing sleeves and softly draped skirt that skimmed her knees suited her figure, the vibrant colors accented her dark hair and eyes.

"Is it all right?"

"All right? We may have to lock you up, to prevent someone stealing you away from me. After they've all finished fighting over you, that is."

She blushed. "Don't say such things, Ar-thurr." But she was pleased, and thought herself that the dress looked very nice.

The guests arrived and Trang Sen was introduced to the visiting colonel. She bowed in Vietnamese fashion, said in halting English, "I am very pleased to meet you."

At the table Blake Decker sat on one side of her. Since arriving at the embassy a few weeks earlier, he and Billings had become friends. She also liked him. He was different from Billings — much younger, nearer her age. He was quite tall, with thick dark hair that always seemed slightly out of control. A bushy mustache heightened the impression of unruliness.

"How are you tonight, Co Sen?" He smiled at her.

He always used that formal way of addressing her. And she knew she could depend on him not to say anything that would embarrass her, such as a reference to her new dress. Perhaps that was why she liked him; he seemed to understand her ways better than the others. The rest of Billings's friends called her Trang Sen. She always had to suppress a momentary surge of anger at their disrespect.

Now she bowed slightly to acknowledge him. "How are you? Are you busy at work?"

"Always. And never time to do the real job."

"What is that?"

"To talk with people on the street, away from this part of town where the foreigners live — just start conversations with ordinary people, find out what they think about the war."

She remembered she had first met Billings in the market. "Do they teach Americans to do such things?"

He laughed. "No, it's just an idea of mine." He changed the subject. "How is your English?"

She shook her head. "Seems not too good," she said slowly, in that language. "I read, not bad, but talk much harder. Harder than French, I think," she continued, switching to Vietnamese.

"You're doing well. All you need is more practice. We should be speaking English, nothing but English."

She smiled. "It's easier this way."

His attention was diverted by the conversation at the other end of the table, a rather heated discussion she was unable to follow. She had understood enough over the months, though, to begin to sympathize with Eldest Brother's feelings about the Americans. Sometimes they seemed not to like anyone here. They complained that the generals cared only for money, that the Vietnamese army was afraid to fight. She thought of her lost brothers, held in such contempt.

She fetched more food, then sat silent for some time, looking absently at each speaker. Billings caught her eye and smiled at her. The colonel noticed, she saw, and his attention was momentarily diverted from the discussion.

Blake turned back to her.

"What are they talking about?"

"The American election. Vice-President Humphrey has just been nominated, and there were some violent demonstrations. The colonel and a couple of others get very angry at the demonstrators. But some of us feel they're making a point." He smiled and shook his head. "Very complicated. Do you know much about our politics?"

"No. But I would like to understand."

"You should read the English-language newspaper, or one of the weekly news magazines. Now there's an idea — you find out about America and improve your English at the same time."

"Perhaps Ar-thurr could bring something home for me to read."

"Or you could go to the American cultural center. Has Art told you about it?"

"No. What is it?"

"An excellent place, they have a library, with all kinds of books. They also have books that are easy to read, to help you learn. He really should take you there."

Billings had risen. She too stood up and led the way into the living room. She served coffee while Billings brought out brandy and liqueurs. She cleared the table and started on the stacks of dishes in the kitchen.

Blake came in. "I have to leave, Co Sen. I came to say good night."

"Oh, yes." She dried her hands. "So soon? Can't you stay? It's very early."

"Not this time. I'll come back soon. Don't forget to ask Art about the library."

"Yes, I won't forget." She followed him into the living room. The party was breaking up.

The colonel glanced in her direction, then turned to Billings. "I compliment you on your wife. She's charming."

"I'm very lucky."

Trang Sen understood the exchange. Did he pretend to others that she was his wife?

She walked over to them and smiled at the colonel. "Please to come again soon," she said in English.

"Thank you, little lady, I'll try to do that."

Billings closed the door on the last guest with an impatient gesture. He put his arms around her and gave her a long kiss. "I thought they'd never leave," he whispered. "You look so lovely tonight, so lovely." He laughed suddenly. "That colonel. I thought he was going to eat you alive."

She was more interested in what the colonel had said. "Do people here know you have an American wife?"

She felt his body tense up. "What made you ask that?"

"Is it so strange to wonder? You treat me as if I'm a second wife, but you tell me in America they have no such things."

"It's no one's business. There's no need for explanation. Half the Americans here are doing the same thing, I wager."

He moved away from her and poured himself a brandy. She followed him to the sofa and curled up next to him, put her arms around his neck and began kissing him. "I love you."

He put his glass down. His hand skimmed over the silky smoothness of her arms and back, rounded to the curve of her breast.

"I'll never be able to get out of this dress," she whispered. "What strange ways Americans have of fastening clothes."

"I'll help you," he said. "With pleasure."

IN HER AMERICAN life, as Trang Sen thought of it, the war and all that came with it seemed a dream. In their cushioned world, the Americans were untouched by the increasing squalor and disintegration of the city. They got whatever they needed from the military exchange; so the shortages in the markets didn't touch them. Occasionally a stray bomb or rocket landed in the foreign section, the work of a Front member indistinguishable from the black-pajamaed refugees. It was usually her own people who were hurt.

When she was with Kim Hoa, the dream was shattered and she was seized with an urgency to make sense of all the pieces of her life. Then she missed Long with a pain that was almost physical. Only he, she felt, could help her sort it all out.

Billings liked having Kim Hoa and her children around. It made him feel he was part of a real Vietnamese family. Perhaps because Kim Hoa spoke no English and seemed interested only in her children and the tailor shop, he thought she was more "Vietnamese" than Trang Sen, whom he considered westernized. The five of them spent holiday afternoons together, visiting the zoo or driving a short way up toward Bien Hoa.

They took a somewhat longer trip, west of the city along the road leading to the military camp near the old Trinh village. Billings wanted to see the part of the country Trang Sen was from.

Trang Sen and Kim Hoa began telling stories of Trang Sen's childhood exploits.

Billings laughed. "I'm going to borrow a couple of buffalo and see if you can still handle them," he threatened.

"Of course I can." She turned to Kim Hoa. "You could plow with them too, if you had to, couldn't you?"

"Yes, I think so. But I was never so good at it as Trang Sen," she said to Billings. "She was the best in the village."

"Come on. She couldn't have been more than a little kid when all this was going on. Are you telling me she was better than the grown men?"

"Yes. Everybody knew it."

Billings held Trang Sen's hand up and examined it. "I don't believe it. This pretty little hand was never callused by a plow, or dirtied in the paddy fields. It was meant to arrange flowers, to float lotuses in bowls of colored water, to embroider silk cushions."

"No, no." Trang Sen was choking with laughter. "That's Kim Hoa you're talking about. I could never do those things. I was always too bored to learn. Besides, who would ever float lotuses like that?"

"Joking aside, you aren't strong enough to do such work. It wouldn't have been right for your family to expect it."

He squeezed her hand and she withdrew it, serious now. "There was no one else to do it. Besides, that was what I wanted to do, not all the boring women's jobs. But I didn't know how hard it would be."

Glancing at her quickly, Billings also turned serious. "I know how hard it is. I did the same kind of work myself, when I was a kid on my folks' farm.

But we didn't have water buffalo, we had . . . what do you call them?" He hesitated, then, "A . . . a mule," he said in English. "What would be Vietnamese for that?"

"Mmyewl." Trang Sen mimicked the sound. "What is myewl?"

Switching back to Vietnamese, he explained the animal's genetic background. The two women looked at him in disbelief. "Why would anyone want such a thing? Why not just use a horse? Or a buffalo. They're much better."

The countryside had a sere, burnt-out look. Charred tree trunks stood up from the jungle growth seeking to reestablish itself. On either side of the road were flattened fields, the stubble black from repeated fires.

Trang Sen looked at Billings. "The . . . the fighting . . . ?"

"Partly. Also, to prevent ambushes, we cut down the forest and burn these stretches from time to time to keep them from growing up again."

She shook her head, thinking, *There's nothing left. If we were to go to the village, there would be nothing, perhaps not even in the new place.*

"What of Uncle?" she asked, turning to Kim Hoa. She hadn't thought to ask in a long time.

"First Sister — her husband and his parents were all killed, and Pa-pa and Ma-ma went to live with her. You remember, she lives farther over toward the mountains. Our village is gone."

"But the people, what became of the people?"

"Probably some went to other villages, like my parents. Most may be in Saigon. I hear stories, Ong Ngoc seems to know a lot about what's happening."

They toured the base, which interested Trang Sen since it had been the place her brothers had gone. She tried to imagine what it must have been like for them, the strange impersonal barracks and the mess hall with the endless long tables, the buildings nothing more than tents erected on concrete slabs.

They were quite late getting back. Billings stopped in front of the tailor shop and got out to help Kim Hoa with the children. He lifted Van Hai gently, shifting him expertly to one arm in order to open the door of the shop, stood aside to let Kim Hoa pass and followed her in. Trang Sen watched his back disappear into the dimness. *So good with the children,* she thought. Watching him with Van Hai and Thi Ba, she thought he probably had children. He wouldn't tell her anything about his family, changed the subject if she tried to ask him.

When he returned she slid close to him, tenderness awakened by his gentleness. "I'm glad you like the children."

"They're a nice age, still young and wanting to be held and played with. Mine . . . " he stopped.

"What?"

"Nothing. I wasn't saying anything."

SHE LOOKED UP from the magazine with a frown as the doorknob rattled. At Blake's urging, Billings had taken her to the cultural center. Since then, she had been reading the way someone dying of thirst dreams of drinking water.

Billings came in, with Blake behind him.

She got up quickly. "I didn't know it was so late. Are you staying for supper, Ong Blake?"

"Trang Sen, you've forgotten." Billings was impatient. "We're going to Cholon for Chinese food."

"I'm sorry. I only forgot at the moment. We can go now."

He put his arm around her, to her embarrassment because of Blake's being there. "We thought of a drink first."

She prepared the ice-cold martinis Billings insisted on every evening.

"How is your reading, Co Sen?" asked Blake.

She glanced a little anxiously at Billings. He was not altogether pleased with her new obsession.

"Very interesting. American politics is complicated." She thought a moment, then asked, "Why do the Americans hate the war so much?"

Blake began a lengthy explanation of the protest movement, prompted into more and more detail by her questions.

"Then why are the Americans still here?"

"To take care of pretty young things like you." Billings tweaked her ear. "Enough of this serious talk. You and Blake could go on all night."

"I just want to know." She pouted.

Blake defended her. "It's good for her to understand, Art. And she's gotten really good at reading English."

Billings nodded absently, set down his glass. "Enough of this. We drink and Trang Sen reads. It all amounts to the same thing. What we need is some good food."

•

He rose and pulled her up after him. "We have a surprise for you tonight. The mysterious Blake Decker has consented to introduce you to his girlfriend."

"Oh." Trang Sen looked at Blake. "Who is she? Is she Vietnamese?"

He laughed. "No. In fact, she's British."

"What he's not telling you is that she's a lady diplomat."

"Do they have such things?"

"Yes," answered Blake. "We have them also, but not many."

"We'd better go, or this one will think we've stood her up. She's meeting us at the restaurant."

The driver inched the cab along, dodging trucks and buses and clearing a path among the bicycles, pedestrians, and cyclos by endlessly blowing his horn. At last he pulled up in front of a wide doorway flanked by garish red columns decorated with gilt and blue Chinese characters.

Seated at a table just inside the door, a western woman was sipping beer, absently making figure eights on the table with the water that dripped from the cool bottle.

Her eyes turned to Trang Sen in an openly curious stare. Trang Sen couldn't tell whether it was friendly or hostile.

Blake introduced them. "Co Sen, Susan Brownwell."

Trang Sen repeated the name carefully and bowed in greeting. She more than returned Susan's curiosity. Except for the nuns, she had never met a European woman. In the general confusion of getting seated, ordering beer, and apologies from Blake and Billings for being late, Trang Sen watched her covertly. She was very fair, with somewhat large, chunky hands. Trang Sen thought she was rather large all over. Her hair was long and pale, with streaks that were lighter blond than the rest. She wore it clipped behind her ears. Stray pieces kept escaping and curling damply around her face.

When they were done with the complicated process of ordering the meal, Susan turned to Trang Sen and smiled.

"No beer for you?" She pointed to Trang Sen's tea cup.

"No," answered Trang Sen, almost apologetically. "I don't like it."

"You're wise. It's a bad habit. But all Britishers drink beer you know. Of course, tea is very British also. We drink it with sugar and milk."

Trang Sen said nothing.

"Blake tells me you've been learning English, and that you were in a convent school for a while."

"Yes. It was bombed at Tet and after that I didn't go to school anymore."

"I see." Susan added matter-of-factly, "I'm sorry. Many terrible things happen here."

Again, Trang Sen wasn't sure what those brusque words meant.

Blake interjected, "I was telling Susan about some of the Vietnamese stories and legends, Co Sen. She's really interested in them, especially the ones about the women who saved their country."

"Ah, the Trung sisters. Do you know that story?"

"Not really. Would you tell it to me?"

Trang Sen told her, her eyes lighting with enthusiasm as she talked of her heroines — the Trung sisters, then Trieu Au and the story of Kieu. Suddenly she stopped, embarrassed. She rarely spoke so much in Billings's presence. "There are books," she finished, blushing. "Would you like to read about them?"

"If the books aren't too complicated." Susan smiled. "I'm not so good at languages as you."

"Oh, no, you speak my language very well."

Susan laughed. "Not so well. But I'd like to try to read them. I like to hear you tell them, too."

The conversation drifted off into a discussion by the other three, in English, of what Nixon might do. Trang Sen followed it with difficulty, but reflected that she had definitely improved.

"I think they could decide to use tactical nukes on Hanoi," said Blake. "It's frightening."

"Oh, no," said Billings. "That's just your radical campus attitude coming out. No chance of that."

"I hope you're right," he answered gloomily.

Trang Sen made a mental note to look up "nuke."

Blake looked her way and smiled. "Can you understand what we're saying, Co Sen?"

"A little."

"What do you think we need to do to win the war?"

She was caught by surprise. She remembered some of the things Long had said to her. "Perhaps my people need to work it out with each other."

"Where would that leave you?" protested Billings. "Do you want to be a communist?"

She shook her head doubtfully. "For my people, I think it might not be too different."

"Nonsense. Don't forget who killed your father — and bombed the school."

"I know." She was reluctant to carry the discussion farther.

"I think I see her point, Art," said Blake.

"You would," answered Billings. "It's that Berkeley training again."

They all laughed, Trang Sen not quite certain what the joke was.

"No, but seriously," continued Blake, "we may be preventing a solution rather than helping it along."

"Preventing a communist takeover is what you mean," insisted Billings.

They lapsed into English again. Susan remained silent. She was watching Trang Sen, who had withdrawn into her own thoughts.

"Do you read much about the war, Co Sen?"

"I've started reading the American magazines, *Time* and *Newsweek*. The election and all the angry students — very interesting. Not like here. Before . . ." she shrugged. How could she tell her about Eldest Brother, about all that had happened?

She refused to be drawn out, and she and Susan sat listening to the men's conversation.

The arrival of the waiter, offering additional beer, broke up the discussion. The talk moved into a less serious track. Again Trang Sen was left to observe the others. Somewhat enviously, she noted the ease with which Susan participated in the banter. *Not very pretty*, she thought. Susan's face was rather square, and she wore no makeup. Trang Sen was fascinated by the lightness of the other woman's hair and her casual cotton dress, busy with a pattern of tiny pale flowers and bright green leaves.

They said goodbye outside the restaurant, Billings suggesting that he and Trang Sen walk part of the way home. He put his arm around her shoulder. She was more willing to lean against him, now that Susan and Blake were gone. But always in the back of her mind was the niggling anxiety that she would be taken for a tea-girl.

"Arthur, does Ong Blake like her?"

"I'm not sure. What do you think?"

She shook her head. "I don't know. She seems . . . she seems, well, almost like a man."

He laughed. "Why do you think that?"

"The way she talks with you, and she's so big."

"She's not really big. A normal size for a Brit or an American. You're just accustomed to the size of Vietnamese. I think your size is nicer." He squeezed her closer.

"Are all of them like that?"

"Oh, I don't know. Depends on what you mean by 'that'. Actually, Susan is quieter than most, a little hesitant to leap into things that don't concern her. But I'll tell you this: western women don't sit in a corner and wait to be asked what they think. They tell you. And you don't always want to know," he added, chuckling.

BILLINGS WAS BUSIER. Many days he left in the early morning, and didn't return until midnight or later. Blake was equally busy and she saw little of him. Susan, who lived not far away, stopped for tea sometimes.

Trang Sen's obvious intelligence prompted her on one of these occasions to say, "You should go back to school, you know."

"Oh, no, I can't do that anymore. Where would I go? And Arthur —" Trang Sen stopped.

"Doesn't want you to be any different from the way you are now," Susan finished the sentence for her.

"He's very good to me."

"Of course he is, but he wouldn't want you to do anything that might change you, make you more independent."

Trang Sen didn't answer.

Trang Sen also spent more time with Kim Hoa, especially the long evenings when Billings wasn't home. The only drawback to going there was Ong Ngoc, but he was away more and more, leaving the shop for Kim Hoa to run and never saying where he was going or for how long.

"Kim Hoa," she said one evening, "what is it like to be pregnant? How does one know?" As ordinary as the condition had been in the village, and despite the fact that she had been present at Thi Ba's birth, she knew little about the early stages. There had been no reason for her mother to instruct her, since she was not being prepared for marriage.

"Are you . . . ?"

"I'm not sure. Only I should have had the bleeding twice and it hasn't happened."

"You are surely pregnant." Kim Hoa looked at Trang Sen anxiously. "Do you want to be?"

"I don't know. Well, yes, I think so. I see Billings with the children, and it seems it would be nice if we had a baby."

"But what will happen when . . . when he goes away?"

"He says he won't go away."

"How can he stay here forever? He must surely go back to America some day."

"He says he'll take care of me and he's asked to stay."

Kim Hoa thought since Trang Sen had been with Billings she refused to face facts. Before, she had faced them, however unpleasant, and refused to be bound by them, always seeking a way around them. Now, she simply pretended they weren't there. Like this.

"Have you told Billins?"

Trang Sen shook her head.

"You should tell him soon, in case . . ."

"In case what?"

"Well, if it isn't convenient for him, he perhaps will want you to get rid of it. Women in the village know what to do. Many times they don't even tell their husbands. I thought of that the second time. But I wanted a girl, and hoped all the way through I would have one."

"Do you know what to do?"

"I know a woman here who does. You must let me know if you don't want it. But you must do that soon."

Trang Sen spent the next few days dreamily imagining what it would be like to have a baby. She felt her body, examined her stomach for signs that it might be enlarging. A boy, she was sure it would be.

Pregnancy made her want Billings more. The very fact that he didn't know about it added to her pleasure, a delicious secret she was holding inside. She would roll over toward him as he slipped into bed, insinuating her body against him with insistent relish. He was delighted.

Finally one night, "Arthur," she asked, "would you like a baby?"

He rubbed his lips against her hair. "You are a baby," he murmured.

"No, no, I mean our baby."

He was wide awake. "Are you trying to tell me something?"

She nodded.

"When did this happen, how long have you known, why didn't you tell me? Are you sure?"

"I'm sure." She didn't know whether his excitement was due to pleasure or distress. "Do . . . do you want it? Kim Hoa said I should ask you."

"Do I want it? Of course I want it. Oh, honey, it will be such a beautiful baby, a girl, beautiful like you." He was almost shouting his elation.

It was her turn to be cautious. "But how will you take care of us, when you have to go back to America?"

"Ah, that won't be for a long time. They need us too much here, and not so many are willing to volunteer for a war. As long as I keep volunteering . . ."

"And when the war ends?"

"That will be a long time. We don't need to worry about that."

Trang Sen shook her head vigorously. This child, this child would be born of blood and pain and suffering — not only her own, but that of too many others.

Billings was watching her. "What is it, sweetheart?"

"Arthur, I think . . . I don't want to have this baby. Kim Hoa said . . ."

He frowned. "Hold on. A baby isn't something you choose to have or not have. You're all right, aren't you, you're not having any problems? We need to get you to a doctor."

"I'm all right. I don't want a doctor. But . . ."

"What kind of ideas has Kim Hoa been putting into your head?"

"She said there were ways to get rid of it if we didn't want it."

He grasped her shoulders and held her away from him. "Let's get one thing straight right now. You won't ever do such a thing with my baby. It's wrong, and I won't have it. Do you understand?"

When she didn't answer immediately, "Do you understand?" he repeated. "We won't even talk about that. I don't ever want to hear you mention it again. Why did you go to Kim Hoa instead of me anyway? You should have told me right away."

Sudden nausea almost choked her. "Arthur, I . . . I . . . what have I done wrong? I didn't mean to . . . I wanted to be sure . . . but, oh, Arthur, what are we going to do? What will the baby do? I don't want the war to go on!" She wrenched away from him and flung herself face down on the bed.

He bent over her. "Control yourself. All this emotion isn't good for the baby. Everything will be all right, I promise you."

At last she peeked tentatively at him, still bending over her. His anxious face provoked a new storm, though now she clung to him.

SHE COULDN'T FEEL the same about the baby after that, all the pleasure of it wiped out by the terrible awareness that there wouldn't be this baby at all if the war weren't still going on. She was ashamed for people to see her increasingly obvious condition, as if it were a sign of the dreadful wrong entangled in her relationship with Billings. *I'm no better than the girls of Tu Do Street*, she thought. She refused to go with Billings when he went out with his friends and their Vietnamese girls. She didn't want to see anyone, even Blake. She was glad Susan was away in London, reluctant for her to know of her pregnancy.

She retrieved the Sartre book from her small collection of treasures, not to read, but for the pain it evoked by reminding her of Long. She thought of going to look for him, of standing near the entrance to his compound and waiting for him. She could stand there for days, she thought, like a statue. She went to Kim Hoa for comfort, though she didn't share her turmoil with her.

To get to Kim Hoa, she must find her way through the refugees, the wounded and the sick, the starving and the miserable. She couldn't bear to walk, to touch the misery around her. She thought she would splinter like untempered glass if she got too close. She hired a cyclo and closed her eyes as it crawled along.

Billings ignored her despondency, assuming it was part of the emotional ups and downs of pregnant women. He couldn't understand her casual approach to her condition and her refusal to see a doctor. They argued over her insistence that the wisdom of Kim Hoa, and a Vietnamese midwife when the time came, were all she needed. So far she had prevailed, partly because he fell back from the outbursts which marked the conclusion of every argument.

Nevertheless, Trang Sen clung to him as if to fend off the time of certain separation. Often there were tears in her eyes at the end of their love-making. He too felt a tinge of sorrow that took the edge off his pleasure. But his ability to live in their illusory world had not been shattered as hers had been. He looked forward to the birth of the child with unmixed anticipation.

Susan appeared at the apartment late one afternoon. She glanced quickly at Trang Sen's expanding belly before giving her a hug.

Trang Sen realized suddenly that she had missed Susan and was glad to see her, pregnancy and shame or not.

They sat together on the couch, Trang Sen's legs tucked under her in Vietnamese fashion. Prodded by a battery of questions, Susan chatted about London, the British spring, her visit to her family.

"We're from the Lake District. Do you know Wordsworth, the poet?"

"No. I only studied French literature and history, no English."

"No matter. Someday, when you're tired of American politics, I'll give you some things to read." She looked at Trang Sen acutely. "Well, should I congratulate you?"

"Thank you." Trang Sen lowered her head in a slight bow.

"Are you pleased?"

"Yes, yes, of course. Arthur will be a good father."

"And you?"

"I will be glad."

"I saw Blake last night."

"I don't see him so much these days. I think he must be very busy."

"Yes." Susan added, "He's quite worried about you."

"Me? Why should he be worried about me?"

"He's worried about you and the baby."

"There's no need." Trang Sen shook her head energetically. "I'm very healthy. Perhaps our people are different," she added, smiling. "Arthur keeps wanting me to see a doctor. But I don't need to do that. A midwife can help when the time comes. And Kim Hoa will be with me, the way I was with her. You'll see, it will all be fine. Ong Blake need not worry."

"I don't think he's worried about that part of it, actually. He's thinking about the future, what may become of you when Art goes home. He won't be here forever, you know."

Trang Sen wasn't willing to share her own feelings. "Arthur says he'll always volunteer to stay. He says they'll surely let him."

"But what happens when he finally has to leave?"

Trang Sen didn't answer.

Susan kept at it. "One thing would solve the whole problem. Has he ever talked of marrying you?"

Trang Sen blushed. As always, she was unprepared for the blunt frontal attack. "We . . . we like things the way they are."

"But they can't stay the way they are any longer, now that there's going to be a child."

"Arthur will take care of us."

"I don't really understand," Susan mused in English, more to herself than to Trang Sen, "why he hasn't married you before now. He clearly adores you, and it's not like the blokes who've casually picked up tea-girls to live with."

Trang Sen sat with her head bowed, her face hot with mortification.

"Well, I'm upsetting you, talking about this. Perhaps Blake should talk with Art. But you shouldn't be so agreeable. Men are funny, at least western men, about a thing like this. They'll always take the easiest path. Sometimes you have to insist on something more dependable."

Susan must think she didn't know how to fight for what she wanted. "We've talked about it," Trang Sen finally whispered. "But . . . but we can't . . ."

"Of course you can. What reason can he possibly give for not marrying you, especially now? Why, I don't think under American law, the baby will even be an American citizen. Something has to be done about this. Art simply isn't thinking ahead."

"No, no, you see —" Trang Sen stopped. If Billings hadn't told them of his marriage, how could she? "I'm sorry, no way to explain." She blushed more deeply.

"There now, I'm the one to be sorry. I should never have brought it up. It's a thing Blake should discuss with Art. I haven't meant to upset you."

"No, please, Ong Blake mustn't mention this to Arthur. He . . . he . . . I'm fine and everything will be all right, really. Please . . ."

"Don't worry about it. I can't stop Blake if he wants to talk with Art, but I promise to tell him how you feel about it, okay?" She used the English word, which was fast becoming part of the Vietnamese language.

Trang Sen clutched Susan's arm. "Please tell him not to. It . . . it's much better not to say anything."

"I'll do my best." She changed the subject. "If Art won't be here for dinner, you and I can go out. Would you like that?" At Trang Sen's doubtful look, she smiled. "I promise not to bring up the subject of the baby. I want to know what you've been reading."

They went to a nearby noodle shop. "Something simple will do nicely," Susan said.

Trang Sen found herself telling Susan of her life in the village, and later at the school.

"But how did you happen to come to the school? That in itself is amazing." Trang Sen had omitted any mention of Eldest Brother.

"My . . . my brother helped me."

"Which brother? Surely not the one who was killed so quickly. And the others . . ."

"No, my oldest brother. He went to study in France, but then he came back."

"Where is he now, what happened to him?"

"I don't know," lied Trang Sen. "He . . . I don't see him anymore."

Susan thought she could piece together the untold part of this story. She didn't want to hear the rest of it. "So tell me about the school."

Relieved, Trang Sen continued her account.

"How did you meet Art? He doesn't seem to fit into any of this."

"Very accidental, perhaps fate." Trang Sen told of their encounter in the market and later at the tailor shop.

"Quite accidental. And your mother and sister? Do you visit them often?"

Trang Sen shook her head. "Only Ba Chau."

"Ba Chau?"

"My cousin, at the tailor shop."

"Oh, yes."

Susan looked at her watch. "I never realized how late it is. All the things that have happened to you are so fascinating — and unusual."

"Not so unusual, except the school part. Otherwise very ordinary."

"To me they're unusual. No one I know has had such experiences, and you're so young, too. Well, we must go, but I'll see you again soon."

"I'm glad you've come back," Trang Sen said shyly.

BILLINGS ANNOUNCED HIS arrival by slamming the door violently. He collided with Trang Sen as she rushed out of the kitchen at the sound.

"Arthur, what —"

"What, indeed! What have you been telling Susan?"

"Telling Co Susan? Nothing, only we were talking about before I met you. Shouldn't I?"

"That's not what I mean. I don't like them prying into my business, pumping you for information because they think they can get more out of you. Tell me now, what did you say to her?" He caught her shoulders and held her angrily.

"Arthur, I didn't say anything to her. Don't hurt me."

"You must have. How else could they have known? Let me tell you something, you little —" He stopped at what he was about to call her and shook her instead.

"Arthur, I don't know what I've done. You're hurting me."

"I'll tell you what you've done. You've been out airing my private life to anyone who might listen."

Trang Sen shook her head. *Blake must have said something*, she thought, *but how could he have known?*

Billings released her and stomped into the bedroom. She curled into a corner of the sofa and stared at the bedroom door. She could hear him moving around.

He emerged in white shorts and carrying a tennis racquet, glanced in her direction and left without saying anything.

She had never seen him so angry before, she had never seen anyone so angry. This was completely unlike Eldest Brother's tight-lipped fury, which she had only encountered once, that last night. *And that*, she reflected, *was only to be expected*. Nor was it like her frequent clashes with her mother, which passed as quickly as a sudden rainstorm. This anger frightened her. *He shook me, it was as if he never loved me at all. What am I going to do? What if he never comes back?*

He found her there asleep, curled into a little ball as if she herself were the fetus. Her hands, half clenched, looked peculiarly defenseless and defiant at the same time. He went to her and gently lifted her. "Let's get you to bed, baby."

She stirred sleepily against him. "Arthur, please don't hurt me. I love you, Arthur."

"I won't hurt you."

"I'm glad," she mumbled, "I was so afraid."

It was weeks before she could trust him. She was very careful not to evoke his violence again. After a time, when there was no repeat performance, she almost forgot. But not quite.

For several months Blake didn't come to the apartment. And Trang Sen was reluctant to bring up any personal topic when she was with Susan. Susan seemed to avoid this also.

Not wishing to be embarrassed by ignorance in her conversations with Susan, Trang Sen haunted the library once more.

She was standing at the magazine rack when she heard Blake's voice behind her.

"Ong Blake, I'm so glad. It is so long not to see you."

"Too long. How are you, Co Sen?"

His question was not the usual formal one. Instead, it reminded her of what Susan had told her. She lowered her head, blushing, and gave the polite answer.

He smiled and shifted to the impersonal level. Finally, though, he said, "I've been wanting to see you. Will you come with me for tea?"

He guided them to a small shop, found a table and sat down across from her. The preliminaries with the waiter taken care of, he sat looking away from her for several minutes. At last, not turning his head, he said, "I think perhaps you'd rather I not mention this, but it seems important to tell you I didn't know about the situation between you and Art until a few months ago."

Trang Sen blushed. But he was saying these things so gently that she was able to respond. "I know."

"I found out by accident. Some military biographies came across my desk, just routine stuff, and his was one of them. I'm really sorry about the way things are. It puts you in a difficult position."

"Everything will be all right. Arthur will take care of me." But her mouth trembled. Staring at her hands, she added, "I'm sorry we don't see you any more. It's my fault Arthur is angry with you."

"I was just in a rage that day. I couldn't believe he had gotten you into this."

"You should be friends again. He likes you very much, really. He was angry with me, too." She stopped and bit her lip.

"With you? Why was he angry with you?"

"Nothing, really."

But he was not to be put off.

At last she admitted, "He . . . he thought I told you, or told Co Susan."

"So he blamed you?" Blake's voice was glacier-cold.

"Please don't be angry again. Arthur is really very good to me."

"You're too nice a girl, you've got too much promise, to be in this situation. Surely he didn't think you were a tea-girl."

She shook her head. "No, oh, no." But she couldn't go on. All the others, Billings's friends, her own family, all but Kim Hoa, accused her, silently or directly, of being just that. Even Billings sometimes, she suspected, saw no difference. One person at least, besides Kim Hoa, no, two, Susan also, saw that she was different. Her eyes filled with tears, and she looked away from Blake. "Thank you," she said in a low voice.

"Thank me? For what?"

"For thinking I'm not a tea-girl." Her voice was lower still.

"Well, of course not," he said, thinking of all his friends who did think that. He continued, "I just wanted to say, I know Art will take care of you, but if there ever comes a time when he can't, for whatever reason, I want you to promise to let me know. Will you promise?"

"Arthur will take care of me."

"I know, but if he should just temporarily not be able to. Will you promise?"

"Yes." But she felt disloyal to Billings.

Blake added, "I'll say the same thing to Art, that he can count on me to help you."

"Thank you, Ong Blake." She bowed.

He sat uncertainly, pulling on his mustache the way he did when he wasn't sure what to say or do next. At last, "I'm glad I saw you," he said. "I've thought of coming by the apartment, but we've been so abominably busy."

She smiled. "You must find time. I'll ask Arthur. Perhaps you and Co Susan could come for dinner?"

"Perhaps. But you mustn't be working too hard."

"No, no, it won't hurt me." She looked anxious. "Will you tell Arthur you saw me?"

"I think not," he said, quite casually. "I'll go to him soon, though, and mend the fences. And tell him I'll stand by you."

"If you think it's good."

"I'm sure it is."

He paid the bill and they stood a moment on the sidewalk. "We'll see you soon, I think," then, "just don't have that baby before we get there."

"No," she said, "I'll try."

CHAPTER 8

SPIES AND BABIES

October 1, 2005

Dear Kenneth,

Again, my apologies for taking so long between letters. The summer went by too fast, and in the past month I've been so focused on our current disasters that I haven't been able to get my head around those of thirty-plus years ago. That, and gearing up for the start of classes.

I've been thinking quite a bit about your questions after my last letter. No need to apologize for your curiosity — it's quite understandable. Let me get one thing out of the way first off — your question about my feelings for your mom. This is a hard subject to talk about with you — it almost feels like a breach of her confidence. But I guess I can't laugh it off any longer, the way I used to do when you were a kid and kept pestering me to marry her. So I'll be very brief, and you'll just have to be satisfied with what I say.

There may have been a time — no more than a moment — when our friendship could have become something else. Perhaps if I hadn't gone off to Thailand when I did . . . But I don't know. By then we had become more like brother and sister. And that's the way it's stayed, only getting deeper with the years. I'm not sure your mother ever wanted

•

another serious involvement after what happened with your father. My sense is her dreams always centered almost completely around what used to be called the life of the mind. As for me, I'm happy with the way things have turned out. Do I love her? Yes, very much. And that's all I'm prepared to say about it.

Well, to get back to the war. There was a huge rise in unemployment all over South Vietnam in the early 1970s as more and more Americans were pulled out — not only people working directly for us, but taxi drivers, prostitutes, anybody whose business depended on the Americans being there. Your Aunt Hoa ran up against this fall-out at the tailor shop. Negotiations in Paris were going nowhere because the South Vietnamese knew any agreement acceptable to the other side would be the beginning of the end for them. But Nixon was determined to end the protests and demonstrations that kept bedeviling him at every turn. So Kissinger began secret talks with North Vietnamese General Le Duc Tho.

A U.S.-sponsored coup in Cambodia replaced Prince Sihanouk, who had tried to stay at least ostensibly neutral, with a general named Lon Nol, who was willing for us to expand the ground war into Cambodian territory for the first time. So really, the war actually got worse after 1970. The only "improvement" was that U.S. troops were going home.

Thinking about Cambodia leads me to a little aside. In retrospect, through the whole war most Americans were abysmally ignorant of the culture and geography of the places we were helping to wreck. What made me think about that is, nothing has changed. I've just graded the geography quiz I give early every semester. The grades are dreadful, as always. But at least I can say, with some pride, that by the end of term, most of the students do much better. (If nothing else, the improvement gives me a sense that I've managed to pound something into their heads.)

Anyway, the Kissinger-Le Duc Tho talks continued into 1972, right along with the fighting. The two of them managed to come up with a ceasefire proposal which South Vietnamese President Thieu, not surprisingly, opposed. So the talks came to a standstill. But after what came to be called the "Christmas bombing" of Hanoi, the North Vietnamese agreed to start talking again. A ceasefire agreement was finally signed on January 27, 1973, and the last of our troops left by the end of March.

Sounds like progress, right? Except there was one big problem — the fighting never really stopped. A second attempt at an agreement in the summer simply repeated what had been agreed to in January, and didn't *stop the fighting either. With gallows humor, the guys at the embassy called this "son of ceasefire."*

I wasn't in Vietnam when most of what I've just been talking about was happening. I had been transferred to Washington in 1971, and worked on the Vietnam desk for two years. I don't mind telling you, watching all this from the U.S. side of the Pacific, I was worried sick about you and your mom, especially after your dad came back home.

In Washington, the whole Watergate affair began to unravel, and of course Nixon was forced to resign in August 1974. I can honestly say, though, that I don't think we would have done anything differently if the administration's attention had been wholly focused on Vietnam.

Well, as I was finishing that last sentence the phone rang. It was my dean, about a thorny little problem over a grade I've given one of my students. Hammering that out ate into my letter-writing time, so you're going to have to hang on for the rest of what I have to say. I really must do a bit of preparation for tomorrow's classes before going to dinner with some friends tonight. I'll try to get back to you before too many more days have passed.

Uncle Blake

BILLINGS NAMED THE baby Kenneth. She called him Second Son, to fool the gods. He looked mostly like her own people. His eyes were dark like hers, though the wisps of hair were pale brown and his skin was rather white. He was healthy, if small. Billings said if he was fatter he would be more content.

Impatiently, Trang Sen placed him in the crib. Specially made, to Billings's exact specifications. He had insisted on it, to her mystification. What difference did it make where a baby slept? She could never remember how to slide the side up and down. Giving up in disgust, she leaned almost double over the railing.

Billings had also ordered clothes and toys from America. But she dressed the child according to her own customs, swathed him in layers of wrapping to protect him from possible chill.

An ecstatic new father, Billings called from work several times a day to check on his new son, often appeared unexpectedly in the middle of the morning or at lunch for a brief glimpse. *He likes the baby better than he does me*, Trang Sen thought resentfully. Sometimes she wanted to hit him, or throw something at him, hard. He would come in, caress the child, hold him for a while. But if the baby disturbed him, he grew angry with Trang Sen. If the baby was hungry she must feed him, if he was dirty she must wash him, if he cried she must find a way to stop him. And he cried and cried.

She longed for her family, and for the village, where there was always someone to help — an older sister, aunt, grandmother. Her loneliness and isolation glossed her memories with a contentment she had never felt when she was living there. She daydreamed of the village women coming to admire her new son, of her mother doting on the first grandchild, even of Trang Mai transformed into a very satisfactory young aunt, always offering to care for her new nephew. It was a hopeless dream, more poignant because now she could never go back, with her half-American child like a brand.

She seemed unable to hold her own about anything anymore. Even the birth had been out of her control. One moment Kim Hoa and the midwife were on their way. The next moment Billings was bundling her into the car, in spite of her protests. "You don't understand," he kept saying. "You could die. That woman doesn't know the first thing about cleanliness."

No, she didn't understand. Why couldn't she be home, Kim Hoa there to hold onto when the pains were strong, the way she had been for Kim Hoa? Why this frantic ride through the dark streets, her belly cramped against her knees, when she wanted to be lying down, letting the waves of pain wash over her?

There was worse to come. The awful glaring light in the hospital, an American nurse covering her with sheets. She was cold, lying on a narrow metal slab, as if she had indeed died, in some strange bloodless world that had no connection to her.

The pressure got stronger and stronger, she thought it would finally tear her apart. There was no one to hold onto, no one who seemed to care. She called out for her mother, wept in despair and anger in this sterile, unfeeling place. *How could Arthur think this was better?* She hated him.

Finally, when the pain was worst of all and she only wanted them all to leave her alone to die, they wheeled her hurriedly into another white room with the same glaring lights. An American doctor was drawing on a pair of rubber gloves, and the nurses made her push her body down to the lower edge of the metal stretcher. In a haze she understood that the baby was coming at last. She tried to squat, her body screaming with all the strength of its contractions to be upright. But they forced her feet into some metal things, so icy cold that she cried out in shock.

And that was the way the baby came, the doctor using some kind of strange instrument to cut her, so that she had a wound there afterward. The baby too seemed a strange, alien thing, part of the horror of the glaring lights and cold metal, not part of her at all.

And now he had to be cared for. *How can he cry so much? Why did I think I wanted a baby? I wish I hadn't told Arthur anything about it, had done what Kim Hoa said. Now it's too late.*

She was very gentle as she lowered him onto the mattress. She didn't want to wake him.

She heard a soft tap on the door, tiptoed hurriedly over, and opened it gingerly, to avoid its creaking. "Asleep," she mouthed to Kim Hoa, who nodded and slipped silently into the room. She went into the kitchen, Trang Sen following.

"Some soup." Kim Hoa placed it on the counter, shoving aside the piled-up dirty dishes to make a space for it. The state of the kitchen was another source of tension between Trang Sen and Billings. She lacked the energy to keep it in the spotless order he liked.

"When was the last time you were out of this place?"

Trang Sen shrugged. "I don't know."

Kim Hoa shook her head. "Always the same. Even having a baby, you have to be different from everyone else. It's not such a big thing. You feed him and you take care of him. If you want to go somewhere, you take him. Why make such a problem of it?"

"He . . . he's just always there, I guess."

"Come visit tomorrow. Van Hai and Thi Ba want to get acquainted with their new cousin. They talk of nothing else."

Trang Sen smiled a little.

"So you'll come then. Tomorrow." Without giving Trang Sen an opportunity to argue, Kim Hoa was out the door.

Billings brought some people home for a drink.

She sat quietly in a corner of the living room after serving them. Billings hadn't asked about the baby. In fact, he was so preoccupied over something she hadn't yet been able to discover that he hardly seemed to notice where he was.

The men were talking excitedly, interrupting each other, sometimes laughing, occasionally swearing in exasperation. She could only catch snatches of what they were saying, slowly pieced together what had happened.

"... a spy ring ... all the way to the President."

"My God, you don't think ..."

"How the hell are we supposed to do anything for these people?"

Right under their noses. Her people weren't so stupid. She found herself thinking it was a good joke on the Americans, and on Billings as well. She stifled a desire to laugh out loud.

But as they talked on, a cold fear, indefinable, clutched her. A figure seemed to be huddled against a wall. She seemed to know that figure, but it was so indistinct, she wasn't sure.

She heard the baby cry. She went to the bedroom, lifted him and held him against her. His warm body comforted her, his impatient crying spoke of life. She held him to her gratefully. Almost, he was dispelling that coldness, yet the fear would not go away.

Was it a memory, possibly from that awful time of Tet? Or would she find that lifeless figure, crumpled at the bottom of a wall, in some desolate future? If only she could name it, warn it. She shuddered and held the baby closer.

Sensing sympathy in her, perhaps for the first time, the child became quiet and lay breathing softly against her shoulder. She was moved by his vulnerability, and began at last to understand a mother's feeling toward her children, so helpless, so weak.

She sat down with him on the edge of the bed, rocking back and forth, until he fell asleep. She laid him carefully in the crib, stood watching him, reluctant to leave the comforting darkness of the bedroom. But she wanted to hear what the men were saying. Giving the baby a final pat, she slipped quietly out.

Billings held up his empty glass and she refilled the drinks. The clinking of the ice in the glasses was slightly off-key, like the sound of a cracked bell.

"And guess what this horse's ass of a gook did next? He actually took the papers, was on his way out the door ..."

"I've got a better one than that. Last week ..."

"Trinh Van Long is the only one worth his salt ..."

They were talking about Eldest Brother! Her mind alert, she lowered her head to hide her sudden interest. She didn't know what "worth his salt" meant, but it was clear they were praising him. She thought of the spy again, and remembered some of the things Eldest Brother had said to her, his indecision when he first returned from France, his anger at each new set of leaders in Saigon. She told herself it was far-fetched, but she couldn't prevent the return of that cold fear, the image of that crumpled shape. She could hardly sit still, yet she wanted to hear everything they said.

Their conversation, though, wandered to another subject. Finally, they got up to leave. She watched them go with relief. Never had she felt so alienated from them, and from Billings.

He walked to the window, opened it, and pushed back the shutters. A faint breeze stirred the blossoms of a frangipani tree in the courtyard. Their scent drifted into the room.

Trang Sen began clearing away glasses and emptying ash trays. "Are you hungry?"

He looked around startled, as if he had forgotten she was there. "What? Oh, yes, yes, of course."

She prepared a steak for him, Kim Hoa's soup for herself. They ate in silence. The subject of the spy ring seemed to her to hang between them, though Billings gave no indication that he thought she might have been listening to the conversation.

The baby woke up again. She brought him in and sat with him against her shoulder.

Billings looked at him speculatively. "He seems calmer tonight."

She nodded. "Not so much trouble now."

Finishing his meal, he reached for his son. She could never get over her amazement at the competent way he handled the baby. The child relaxed against his father's arm.

A wave of tenderness swept over her, dispelling some of her anger and alienation. She got up and stood behind Billings, leaning down and putting her arms around his shoulders. "You're a good father," she murmured, "good to Second Son and me. I'm glad you like the baby."

It was true, at least right now. For the first time they all seemed to be a family, not three separate beings vying for each other's attention.

Billings was both pleased and surprised. "He's a beautiful baby, beautiful like his mother." He chuckled. "Perhaps with some of his mother's temperament too." He skimmed his lips across her hair.

She went to stand by the window, her back to him. She caught the shutter, which had begun to rattle as the breeze became stronger. "It's going to rain again."

He came over, kissed her softly on the neck. "I'll put this little fellow to bed."

He returned and stood beside her, turning her toward him.

She responded to his kisses, reluctantly at first. The unknown shape against the wall kept intruding.

She dreamed the old dream of sinking into increasing darkness, awoke cold and frightened. She lay stiffly for a while, then sought the comforting warmth of Billings's sleeping back. But she could not go back to sleep and was glad when Second Son's insistent cry impelled her once more into her waking life. A baby has its uses, she began to understand.

She left the apartment early, carrying Second Son on her hip, her arm cradling his back and head, village-fashion. She headed for the central market, walking down the shady, tree-lined street toward Le Loi Avenue, which would take her across to the big yellow building with its clock tower in the middle and long wings stretching out on either side.

The crowds were noisy, the traffic a confusion of auto horns, bicycle bells and the angry shouts of frustrated drivers. A welcome relief after her morbid dreams and imaginings.

She decided to go on to the tailor shop after finishing at the market. It felt good to jostle against the crowd, pit her wits against the chaos of motor vehicles. She smiled at the refugee children who filled the sidewalks, imagined Second Son in a few years, fat, happy, running and playing. Not like these children, so thin and sad.

Kim Hoa was delighted to see her. Van Hai and Thi Ba pulled at her ao dai for attention, reached up to touch the baby. She placed him in the hammock strung across the back of the shop, leaving the children to stand watch.

Ong Ngoc was nowhere to be seen, to Trang Sen's relief. She dreaded more and more the scrutiny of his lidded eyes, like those of a carrion bird, sitting on a dead branch calculating its descent on a still-warm body.

"Ong Ngoc is still away?"

Kim Hoa nodded. "Away more and more these days. Very strange. Usually he comes back with more cloth, but we don't need any now. With so many Americans going home, we aren't so busy."

Trang Sen had begun to suspect Ong Ngoc of being up to something sinister. She didn't know what she meant by that, but she didn't trust him and she often wondered how such a person could be Eldest Brother's friend.

Kim Hoa turned back to her sewing, expertly stitching the seams of a pair of trousers. Trang Sen watched absently.

Back in the apartment, she prepared a Vietnamese meal, for the first time in weeks. By the time Billings came home, the odors of ginger and garlic were almost visible in their strength.

"Smells like a Vietnamese restaurant in here. What are you cooking?"

"Nothing special, just a chicken with garlic and pepper and a little fish sauce, and shredded roots to put in the rice paper with that sweet and sour pepper sauce. Would you like it?"

"Of course. I always like it."

At the table, she brought up the spy ring. She wanted to find out more about it, but she didn't want to reveal how much of last night's conversation she had understood.

"I went by the cultural center library today," she lied. "Some of the people who work there were talking about spies in the government. Do you know anything about that?"

"Oh, yes." He reached for the vegetables, wrapped a small handful in the rice paper.

She waited, but he said nothing more.

"They didn't think it was so surprising, they think there are probably others doing the same thing. Only these got caught."

Now he was alert. "How do they know, where do they get their information?" He added, almost coldly, "How do you know anything about this?"

"I don't. They don't know anything either. They're just guessing."

She wanted to shrink back from him when he looked at her. His eyes glinted sharply behind his glasses. "This is important. If you know anything, tell me. If you hear anyone who knows anything, tell me that. Understand?"

His cold, clinical voice was unnerving. *Is this the way he is at work?*

"No one knows anything," she said again.

From being innocent even of a suspicion of espionage, the Americans seemed to be suspecting everyone. Again she wanted to laugh.

SUSAN CALLED ONE morning, arranged to come by that afternoon. That was a change — she no longer visited without calling first. Trang Sen rather liked the unexpectedness of the old way. It had made Susan seem less foreign.

She answered the door holding Second Son against her shoulder.

Susan glanced quickly at her. "You're much peppier than you have been, I can tell already," she said with her usual bluntness. "Even your voice this morning sounded as if your old spirit had come back. I don't mind saying I've been a bit worried about you. I was afraid the baby had been too much for you, and with everything you went through before he was born . . ."

Her voice trailed off. She turned her attention to Second Son.

"Come in, come in. I have some tea for us. The baby will be asleep soon."

"Oh, no matter. I came to see him too, you know. Might I hold him, do you think?"

"Of course. He must get to know his English auntie."

She handed him to Susan, who received him gingerly. The child frowned at first, then snuggled contentedly against her.

Susan followed Trang Sen to the kitchen, watched her as she poured boiling water over the teapot to warm it, then threw in a handful of tea leaves and filled the ceramic pot with the hot water. Heedless of its dripping wetness, she carried it to the living room and set it steaming on the table. They settled themselves on the couch with the baby asleep between them.

Trang Sen brought up the subject of the spy ring.

Susan shook her head. "Really too bad. The American embassy is going crazy. But Blake says we should have suspected such doings all along."

"Ong Blake said that?"

"Umh-hmh. What do you think?"

Trang Sen took some minutes to answer. "Ong Blake may be right. Why does he say that?"

"I'm not too sure. He's been so busy we haven't had much time to talk. Why do you think he's right?"

"An old custom of my people. You protect yourself by having more than one way to escape. Like the headmen in the villages. They help the government soldiers in the daytime and the Front at night. That way, whatever happens, they'll be safe."

"So you think it's just that these people got caught?"

"Maybe." Trang Sen hesitated, remembering Billings's reaction. "But I don't know. Only a guess."

•

Susan nodded. "Perhaps that's what Blake meant. After all, if it goes on in the villages, why do we think it stops there? Yes, it must be that way. What does Art think?"

Trang Sen lowered her head. "I . . . I don't know," then, almost inaudibly, "I think he wants their names."

"Whose names?"

"The ones who are spying."

"Does he think you know? He can't possibly think that." Susan shook her head.

"He wasn't angry, he just seemed very strange."

"All this craziness gets to everybody. They're all overworked."

"He's very happy about the baby." Trang Sen laughed. "He keeps calling to see if he's okay. A very anxious father."

Susan laughed too. "I suppose it may seem the one sane thing in this insane world. But you, are you happy? I've not been so sure."

Trang Sen's eyes darkened. "I'm glad to have the baby, glad Arthur likes him."

Susan pulled a book out of her bag and offered it to Trang Sen. "It's time we started our study routine again. I think you'll like this. It's one of my favorites, the most real description of the way women live that I've ever come across. And it's also a very honest, wise commentary on communism."

Trang Sen looked at the cover. *The Golden Notebook*. Doris Lessing. But it's so long. Do you think I can read this?"

"I'm sure of it. Besides, I can help you over the rough spots. I want to talk with you about her ideas." Susan picked up her teacup and sat holding it. "I've been thinking. It's also time you began learning to write in English. That's very important, because someday you may go to the States. Or to England. Who knows?"

Susan's words stabbed Trang Sen with the memory of that other time, when Eldest Brother had suggested the same thing about France, in almost the same words. For a moment she was again in the little French restaurant, chasing skittering snails across the plate. That long-ago world, full of promise, was gone. But she smiled at the memory of the snails.

"You would like that, then?" Susan misinterpreted the smile.

"What? Oh, yes. You're very kind to help me so much."

"It's an excuse to be with you." Susan looked at the sleeping baby between them. "And to watch Kenneth grow."

"Second Son," corrected Trang Sen.

"Yes, Second Son."

TRANG SEN LOOKED down at the baby sitting on a blanket next to her chair, contentedly sucking on a toy and prattling to himself. Sometimes she thought, with a sharp pain, that he resembled Eldest Brother. He had the dark liquid eyes that were both hers and Long's. The lightness of his skin and, strangely out of place, the light brown cast of his hair, did nothing to dispel her impression. She was inordinately proud of him, noticed every new thing he learned. *So quickly*, she thought.

She squatted down beside him and tickled his foot. He had only recently begun to respond to being tickled. He pulled his foot away and laughed, squeezing his eyes shut.

"Ah, little Second Son, you're a funny one." She picked up a rattle and shook it gently. He crowed with delight, reached to take it from her.

She gave him the rattle and went back to *The Golden Notebook*. Working her way through the English sentence structure, Trang Sen reflected, not for the first time, that English was not nearly so lovely as French. But she liked the challenge of something new and unfamiliar.

Second Son interrupted her with a piercing shriek. Surprised, she slid off the chair and knelt beside him again.

She was still trying, not too successfully, to soothe him when Billings barged into the room. Not greeting either of them, he said, "Can't you get him to stop that?"

"I'm trying. He just suddenly decided to be unhappy." She smiled and shook her head.

Billings went into the kitchen, began rattling glasses and ice cubes. He reemerged, glass in hand, and poured himself a drink, then sat down and stared gloomily at them. Soon he got up and began pacing up and down the room.

Second Son stopped crying and reached up to his father. Trang Sen held him toward Billings. "He wants you to hold him."

"What?" He brushed them away impatiently. "Put him in the crib or something. I have to talk with you."

"He won't stay, he'll just cry. It's better if you hold him."

"Take him to the bedroom, I tell you."

It finally penetrated that something was very wrong. She took Second

Son to his crib, handed him a bottle of sugar water, and closed the door on his screams.

In the living room, Billings had sat down again. He brushed his hand across his face, then took off his glasses and polished them on his shirt.

She gently touched his arm. "Please tell me. Whatever it is, it will be all right."

He shook his head. "They're sending me back home."

"Oh."

"In two weeks."

"So soon . . ." She tried to put the next thought away, but she had to ask. "Will . . . will you be coming back?"

"I don't know. They can't tell me about that."

"What will you do with us?" she finally managed to ask.

"I promised to take care of you, and I will. You won't want for anything."

"Only for you."

He pulled her onto his lap and held her tightly.

Her mind was swirling with questions, but she only leaned more closely against him. She had come to take for granted the warmth of his body, even when she was angry with him.

He freed one hand to reach up and take his glasses off, rubbed his sleeve across his eyes and took a deep breath. Turning her face to his, he kissed her gently. "I'll get back somehow, somehow. Even if they won't let me."

"Don't you want to go back, to see the . . . the others?"

She had often wondered what was happening to his American wife, where she lived, what his children — if he had any — thought of their absent father. What did he tell them of his life here? More than once, she went through the desk in the corner of their bedroom, looking for letters, which she would have read shamelessly; but she had found nothing.

He was silent so long she thought she had made him angry again. But when she looked somewhat fearfully at him, he caressed her cheek.

"I love my children" — *so he does have children* — "but — it's hard to explain — this is like being in another world. When I'm in Vietnam it's hard to believe that world is real, and I forget. I don't suppose that makes any sense."

Is it the same about his life here when he's there?

"And things are complicated, so many problems they expect me to solve. My older ones will soon be teenagers, a most difficult time."

"Maybe," she suggested, her heart constricted in a tight little circle, "maybe it's time you went back and saw to them."

"Never time for that, as long as you're here. You and Kenneth."

It was like knocking down a wall. Once it was down, she couldn't resist exploring all there was. "But your wife."

He laughed shortly. "Yes, my wife. Who knows what she'll want, what little world she'll have built for herself. The most difficult teenager of them all."

And now the final question. "Don't you love her? I thought Americans married for love."

His laugh was bitter. "Americans marry for many reasons. Sometimes love is the least. What if I told you I married her because I slept with her, years ago when we were very young. And we both made a big thing of that, too big, I think."

"No love?"

"I suppose I loved her once. I can't remember anymore. You're the one I love."

A kind of triumph immersed her. *It must be true, all those things he said in the beginning, how he loves me. But then* . . . "Why don't you stay here? Or take me with you?"

He pulled away from her. "I can't. You don't understand. You mustn't ask that of me."

Her elation evaporated, as quickly as it had come. No, she didn't understand. And fear that he would forget them in America settled like a lump at the base of her windpipe.

"I've been thinking," he was saying. "You can't stay here. These places are government contract, not permitted to rent to Vietnamese. We'll find you a nice little Vietnamese-style house — you'd like that, wouldn't you?"

She nodded absently.

"I've asked Jim Hawkins to see to you."

"No. I don't want him. I want Ong Blake to take care of us. Ong Blake and Co Susan. He promised he would. Didn't he tell you?"

Billings ran his arm across his face again. "Please don't be difficult about this, Trang Sen. I have to do what I think is best."

"But didn't he tell you?"

"Yes, yes, he told me. But that was months ago. This other arrangement will be easier."

She shook her head vigorously. "No. Not Ong Jim. I don't like him. I don't like the way he looks at me."

"I've got to get money to you, and that's the best way."

"You can send it to Ong Blake."

He shook his head. "This is hard enough on both of us. Don't make it harder by being unreasonable."

"Not unreasonable. Ong Jim will make it harder for me."

He sighed. "Later," he pleaded. "I've had too many things to think about today."

She looked around the room. To leave this place would be very strange. She never had felt it was her place, but she had forgotten what it was like to live anywhere else. Above all, she had forgotten what it was like to live without Billings. Memories flooded back, of those months when he had gone away before, of that time after Tet when she had lacked energy even to try to find him, of the way he rescued her from the darkness and sadness all around her.

"I don't want you to go." She wept against his shoulder.

HE WAS CAUGHT up in a round of farewell dinners and parties. She began to think it would be a relief to be past this strange time when he was both there and not there.

Blake and Susan came one afternoon.

She made tea for them, brought Second Son, fresh from his afternoon nap, and revelled in their admiration of him. He was particularly taken with Blake's bushy mustache, pulled at it with astonishing, and what must have been to Blake painful, strength.

Extracting the small hand from its grip once more, Blake asked, "What are your plans after Art leaves, Co Sen? He says he'll find you a place to live, but we're wondering if you've thought what you might do."

"No . . . it doesn't matter. Perhaps I'll help Ba Chau again. I did that before."

"They're looking for people at the culture center library. Working there would give you some good experience."

"A library."

"You'll need something interesting to do when Art leaves," added Susan. "And I can tell you like the idea. I saw your eyes light up at the thought of all those books." She smiled at Trang Sen.

"I don't know."

"Don't you think it would be better than working in the tailor shop?" asked Blake.

An image of Ong Ngoc, his lidded eyes veiling his thoughts, emerged in her mind. "Yes. It would be better."

"I called today. You must go talk with them, and there are papers to fill out. We can help you with those."

After they left, she sat for a long time, thinking. It was still hard to imagine a life after Billings was gone, but Susan was right — she did like the idea of the library.

Billings returned late that night, slipped quietly into bed beside her. She moved against him, and half in a dream, sleepily murmured, "You've come back. You weren't gone so long after all."

He put his arms around her. "I hope, I hope," he whispered. "Trang Sen, Trang Sen, I don't want to leave you."

"Don't leave." She was still not fully awake.

He didn't answer, but held her tightly. "After tomorrow, the rest of the time is for you. Only four days, but better than none."

They embarked on an increasingly frantic search for a house or apartment. He had thought it would be easy, but he was particular, kept looking for a place that met his American standards.

Trang Sen argued with him. Over and over, he rejected places that she found acceptable.

"This will be fine, much better than the village. And not so different from the house my brother got for us." The one they were arguing over appealed especially to her, as it reminded her of that house. Filled with a sudden nostalgia, she didn't think about the strangeness of a woman and child living alone.

They were standing in a large oblong room, a bit larger actually than the one in her family's house. The walls were unpainted wood, darkened by time and the constant humidity. The bed platform ran across the entire width on one side. Next to it was the door to the tiny kitchen, empty except for a narrow wooden counter across the back wall. A door led to the small back yard. Beyond the fence, a row of stilt houses fronted the Thi Nghe River. The front yard was shaded by two tall palm trees. The outside walls were wood on three sides, but the front was stucco, its yellow paint faded and peeling. A cream-colored bougainvillaea splashed over one side of it.

"I want this one. I like it," she said again.

He shook his head, smiling in exasperation. "Stubborn Trang Sen, always so difficult, even now."

"We've surely looked at twenty houses. You like none of them. But you said we can't stay where we are. I like this house. It's nice. It's near the water tap, and not so far from the market. Life will be easy here. There are children for Second Son to play with, I can walk to Ba Chau's. I like it," she repeated.

The landlord had been standing discreetly aside. Now he stepped forward. "The Ba is right. You see, a very good house, very solid, no roof leaks when it rains. Very convenient too. The major would like it?"

Billings hesitated. "Perhaps you're right," he conceded to Trang Sen. "Still, if we could find one with running water, it would be better."

"We've looked and looked. There aren't any."

"And you wouldn't mind this?"

She nodded vigorously. "It's perfect. The water is no problem. Only with you was there water inside the house."

He smiled. He thought she was becoming more Vietnamese again. That made their parting even more poignant to him. He fought back the tears that came so easily. "All right," he said huskily, "we'll take it."

He paid extra for a five-year lease, promised to pay the full five years' rent, whether they stayed or not. It was worth it, he thought, to be sure Trang Sen would be settled for that long. If he didn't come back.

Trang Sen was exploring, talking softly to Second Son as she did so. Billings came over to her. "It's done. We can start moving you in this afternoon, getting the furniture together and deciding what you'll need and what I'll take back with me." The tears were close to the surface again, and he turned away from her.

He insisted on thoroughly cleaning the apartment, even washing the walls, and enlisted her help. This made no sense at all to her. *Why clean a place for strangers? And is it really so dirty?* She couldn't bear the sight of the empty rooms. Cleaning them was even more painful, as if they were washing away all traces of their existence.

They had dinner with Blake and Susan the night before Billings left. The four of them laughed and drank too much beer. Even Trang Sen, who never drank more than a few sips, got slightly drunk. That caused the others to laugh even more. Billings guided her stumbling home, one arm around her and the other holding Second Son.

Inside the apartment, she fell against him giggling, kissed him passionately and wetly on the mouth. He laid the baby in the crib, one of the few pieces of furniture remaining, and took her in his arms. At last, for one final time, he could love her without the tears welling in his eyes. He laughed and brushed her hair from where it had fallen across her face, kissing her eyes, her forehead, her neck. Frantically, she covered him with wet kisses. In the midst of their lovemaking he whispered, "I'll always remember this, no matter what happens, I'll always remember."

"I love you, Arthur," she said. And she was no longer tipsy, but the beautiful, serious Trang Sen he had loved in the beginning.

"I love you," he answered with a long shuddering tremor.

BILLINGS TOOK THE two of them to the house and insisted on bringing in the first supply of water himself.

He seemed a stranger in his dress uniform. She had seen it often before, but always when he wore it she felt shy of him. Now the memory of her abandoned lovemaking the night before made her doubly shy. She avoided his eyes, slipped silently to his side to help him empty the buckets into the big urns.

He looked around. "Do you need anything else?"

"Only you," she whispered.

He put his arms around her. "I don't want you to come with me. I . . . I couldn't bear that." He kissed her, then went to the crib where Second Son was napping, picked him up and held him gently, kissed him softly on his forehead. The child stirred, but did not wake up.

He laid him down and touched Trang Sen's arm.

"My God," he said suddenly, "I almost forgot. The money . . . I'm leaving you enough now for two months." He handed her an envelope bulging with bills, secured with a rubber band. "Jim will come by every month. So you should always have one month ahead. And if anything comes up, you run out, tell Jim."

She took the money, angrily feeling that she had been tricked again.

He squeezed her arm and kissed her once more, then turned quickly and left, not looking back. She stood looking at the blank whiteness of the open door, as blank herself, as if her life had been drained from her body, leaving nothing but a dry white shell.

Mechanically, she began arranging the room, moving the same

object over and over. Second Son woke and she went to him. The crib she would get rid of. She had always hated it. The baby could sleep with her on the bed platform, and when he was older, in the hammock. Then she felt guilty for her disloyalty.

She picked the child up and crooned in a low toneless sing-song. He laughed happily and pushed his hand hard against her face. The pain broke through the arid void and brought tears to her eyes. She blinked them back and caught Second Son's hand.

"Don't hurt me," she whispered. "We're all that's left, you and I. We mustn't hurt each other."

His mood changing quickly, he leaned his head against her shoulder, looking up at her soberly.

She made a space for him on the bed platform, arranged a blanket and set him down, ringing the space with bedding. "No more cribs for Second Son."

She went back to the task of settling in, talking to him while she moved around the room. Some of the neighbor children came by and peeked around the door. One said, "The American brought you here. Where is he?"

"Gone now," she answered.

They ran off.

By late afternoon, everything was arranged. She looked with satisfaction at the pile of quilts neatly stacked in a corner of the bed platform, the clothes hanging on hooks, the rice pot and big iron pan in the kitchen. She felt strangely clean, not only of emotion, but of her double life, as if she had put her Americanized self in the corner with the other American things, to await . . . what? The return of Billings? Or their eventual disposal, when they were clearly no longer useful?

She ate supper, fed Second Son, then settled down to *The Golden Notebook*.

She finally focused on what a strange thing it was, to be alone. No one ever thought of being alone. There was always one's family. With marriage, one only exchanged one set of people for another. *I like this*, she thought, savoring the silence of the room, contrasted to the loud sounds of the city around them. Tomorrow, perhaps, would come the pain of missing Billings. Today there was deadness, almost welcome after the turmoil of the past days.

She stayed in her silent world for two days, only briefly exchanging greetings with her neighbors around the water tap. They left her to herself, having decided she was a tea-girl who had made good. She forgot about the job Blake had suggested. She almost forgot about Blake and Susan, part of her other life.

However, they appeared at the door, quite real. They looked curiously at the neatly arranged room.

"Co Sen, are you comfortable here?" Blake sounded doubtful.

"It's so different from the apartment," put in Susan.

"Yes, yes, quite comfortable. It's much better than most houses."

Susan glanced at a pile of appliances in one corner. "What are those?"

"Arthur left them. There's no way to use them, no electricity."

"Maybe we could rig up a line." Blake went to the door and peered out, assessing the distance to the nearest electric pole.

"No, no, no need. I don't want it. I was always without it before Arthur . . . before we lived in the apartment."

Susan inspected the kitchen. "Can we get you anything? This looks pretty primitive."

"No, no, it's fine. It's what I'm accustomed to. But sit down," she added, remembering to be polite. "I'll get you some tea."

She motioned to the bed platform and they sat gingerly on the edge. She wanted to laugh. But she only went into the kitchen to fetch the tea.

She returned, put down the tea things and sat down Vietnamese-style, her legs tucked under her.

It was Susan who began to laugh. "We have to learn your habits in this house, Co Sen. I don't know whether I can be comfortable in that position or not." She set her teacup down, straightened her skirt and sat back on her haunches. She shook her head, still laughing. "Impossible. British legs must be made differently."

Trang Sen laughed. "No, that can't be. Oh, wait." She jumped up, dragged two folding chairs from behind a curtain. Blake got up to help.

"Much more comfortable," Susan observed. "But I really think we must learn your ways. You've adjusted so well to ours."

Blake pulled some papers from his shirt pocket. "From the library. They want you to bring them, filled out. We can help you with them now."

Trang Sen looked hesitant.

"Don't you want to do this?"

"I . . . I think so. But my English is so bad. And I don't know about Second Son. I'd have to leave him with Ba Chau."

"Well, I think you should talk with her about it." Susan, always so direct.

"And as for your English, Co Sen," added Blake, "this is not polite talk. Your English is excellent. They'll be delighted to have someone who speaks so well."

She was not totally convinced, but they were being so kind that she did what they wanted.

Kim Hoa was enthusiastic. "Of course you must do it. I've worried about what you would do now. You won't ever be satisfied if it isn't something to do with books."

"But I can't take Second Son with me."

"Leave him here. Thi Ba and Van Hai will love playing with him. We'll take good care of him."

"SON VERY WELL, I busy. Miss you much since going away. . . ." She laboriously erased a misspelled word.

She didn't know how many letters she had written Billings, none of them mailed. He had been gone a month and she had heard nothing from him. At times she had difficulty conjuring up an image of his face.

Jim Hawkins had come once with money. In spite of her longing, pride prevented her from asking him for news of Billings, and he offered none. He looked around curiously, commented on the house, and asked if her money was holding out. She nodded, but made no effort to prolong the conversation. When he left, he tried to squeeze her arm. She pulled it away.

At the library she was learning the intricacies of the catalog and check-out systems, how to log in the magazines and newspapers which arrived daily. There was surprisingly little contact with the books themselves. Even shelving them was a mechanical process. Occasionally, surreptitiously, with a tinge of guilt, she stole a few moments to look inside the covers of one, read a few snatches.

She was amazed at her salary. Even without the money Billings sent, she could support herself and Second Son, with some left over.

Living with Billings, she had been shielded from the realities of Vietnamese Saigon. Now she realized that refugees seemingly occupied every patch of ground, crowded together in flimsy makeshift lean-tos. The lucky ones who had houses lived mostly on land partially reclaimed from boggy marsh areas, subject to persistent flooding, like those between her house and the river. And the prices in the market — several American dollars for a handful of rice. Only American salaries made it possible to buy enough food. She wondered if Eldest Brother's salary was still adequate for her mother's needs. *I'll have to find out, see if they need anything.*

She took Second Son to the tailor shop early every morning, sharing a bowl of rice soup with Kim Hoa. In the evening she usually stopped at the market and bought a few vegetables, sometimes a small fish, for supper for her, Kim Hoa and the children.

Blake interrupted her thoughts, calling from the doorway. She hastily slipped the unfinished letter between the pages of her book and went to let him in.

"How is Co Susan?" she asked.

"Busy. She wanted to come with me, but couldn't. Has she told you her news?"

"I've heard nothing new. I haven't seen her much. No time in the afternoon, and evenings seem not convenient for her."

Blake nodded. "It's the life of a diplomat. Always a party."

"Yes, like Arthur."

"Well, she'll be leaving soon, another assignment."

"Leaving and not coming back? Not like last time, just temporary?"

"No. She's going to Sweden. A good job, but very cold there."

"Sweden." Trang Sen tried to conjure up a map of Europe from the memory of her convent school geography lessons. "Yes, I remember."

She thought of something else. What of Blake and Susan? She was too shy to ask. "Everything is changing," she observed soberly. "People go away and never see each other again."

"Yes, but you never know. I keep running into people I've known before. It's not such a big world after all."

"I'll miss Co Susan. She's been very kind to me."

"You've been a good friend to her. I rather suspect this isn't the end of her interest in Vietnam. You've told her so much about this place, and your people."

That reminded her of something she had been meaning to ask him about, an article she had found in the library. "Ong Blake, do you know M. Mus, who writes so much about my people?"

"I've read some of his stuff. Don't tell me you've read that."

"I read an article about his ideas. It's not wrong, is it?"

"No, no, of course not," he assured her. "What do you think of him?"

"I don't know. He seems to think village people can be very rebellious. I never thought of it, but I suppose I'm like that." She smiled. "My mother always told me my headstrong ways would get me into trouble. Perhaps they have," she reflected, then moved away from that idea and added, "But Ba Chau isn't the same at all. She doesn't fight against anything. And my brothers don't either, except . . . except for . . ." She stopped, thinking of Eldest Brother, then of her father, refusing to give up his plow. "Maybe we are, after all. Maybe I'm more like everybody else than I thought."

"Your people seem so capable of enduring terrible hardships. You also."

She looked at him in surprise. "Me? What hardship?"

"You see, you don't even know it. An American child could hardly have survived the things you've experienced."

She shrugged. "Things happen, you go on. Is that what you mean?"

He nodded, overwhelmed by her unconscious courage.

"Is M. Mus right about the history too?"

"From what I know, it's a pretty accurate account. But you should know that better than I."

"No, it seems I only know the brave stories. I know more about French history."

"It's the way of a Western education, to do that to you. It could make me very angry. This is the sort of thing they're protesting about in America."

"Are they? They care about our education? I thought they only wanted the American soldiers back."

"That's only part of it. I can't say they're specifically concerned about the Vietnamese educational system, but part of what at least some of them are trying to get at is what they call the 'cultural imperialism' of the West and especially America."

"And you think that's what the convent school was like?"

"Probably. That doesn't mean it's not a good education. But they should have taught you your own history, from your viewpoint, not theirs. Instead they . . ." He hesitated, searching for the word. "They co-opted the Vietnamese nuns," he finished in English.

His explanation recalled that long-ago conversation with Eldest Brother. She nodded. "Yes, I think they did that."

She sat beside the sleeping Second Son for a long time that night. For the first time in years, her mind was totally alive. She thought of Billings, and of their life together. She longed for him with a pain that was sharply physical. But this renewed vitality of her mind, could it have happened if he was still here? She didn't think so.

Then was she glad he had left? The thought brought tears to her eyes. She longed to see his face, to feel him beside her, watch him sipping the inevitable martini or forever wiping his glasses on his shirt. Yet this life without him seemed clear and clean, the life with him a dark whirlpool. Even writing the letters seemed to draw her once more toward the vortex.

SHE DREADED SUSAN'S departure. Almost, her friend had taken the place of the teachers at the convent school, though not Sister Louise.

Susan's last weeks, like those of Billings, were a chaotic mixture of obligations and farewell parties. She came to see Trang Sen not long after Blake's visit, apologetic that she had not come earlier.

"No matter." Trang Sen pushed down the seat of the folding chair and hastily wiped the dust off with her hand. "Ong Blake told me you would be leaving. I thought it was like Arthur, so busy."

"Very busy. But I've wanted to see you, take advantage of the little time left."

"I hope you like your new job," said Trang Sen politely. She didn't quite know what to do with this departing Susan, felt as if their friendship was over. "Ong Blake says it's a good thing."

"Yes, quite good, really." Susan was thoughtful. "I don't mind telling you, though, it's difficult to leave Saigon. That's largely due to you, you know."

"To me?"

"You've been a good friend. You've told me so much about your life and your people, and I understand you wouldn't do that with many strangers."

Trang Sen was embarrassed.

"I don't like leaving you, either," Susan went on. "I think perhaps I've been of some help to you at times. I worry about you. This isn't a good place for a woman and child. I wish Art could have taken you to America."

"The war will be over some day." Trang Sen heard echoes of that statement down all the years since her brothers were taken away.

"Let us hope so." Susan looked around her. "Are you sure you're comfortable here? I don't like to think of you in this house. And I'm afraid it could be dangerous for you, here alone."

"It's really what I want, much better than our house in the village."

Susan sighed. "There hasn't been time for me to get accustomed to your living here. I'll miss you."

"I too. You've been a good teacher for me."

"You've been more than that to me. You've been a good friend," Susan repeated.

"You too," Trang Sen agreed, then lowered her head shyly.

"Would you write me? I'd like it very much if you did. I don't want to lose track of you."

"Will you write to Ong Blake?" Trang Sen asked suddenly, then blushed. Susan laughed.

"I'm sorry."

"You needn't be. I think we're only friends, a very good friend. He's an unusual person, very sensitive. I've not known anyone quite like him before."

Her answer left Trang Sen as curious as ever.

KIM HOA VISITED Trang Sen's mother often, taking the place of the banished daughter to some extent. Trang Sen was never mentioned on these visits. But Trang Sen wanted to give her mother money, and asked Kim Hoa to take it to her.

On her next visit Kim Hoa sat nervously chatting, wondering how her aunt would respond. At last she tentatively began, "Cousin Sen feels much concern for you."

Ba Cao stiffened, appeared to concentrate on Thi Ba, sitting in her lap.

"She's very sorry for the trouble she caused you."

"That child was always trouble. Better that she's away from us."

"She's always asking after you. She wants to know whether you need anything."

"We won't take help from the American."

Kim Hoa went on, undeterred. "The American is gone, returned to America. Cousin Sen has a good job, at an American library, the Americans pay high salaries. Everything is so expensive, she wants to know if Cousin Long's salary is enough, if she could perhaps make things easier for all of you."

"The American got her this job?"

"She got it herself, because her English is so good. She is very talented." Ba Cao laughed harshly.

Kim Hoa ignored her aunt's response. "She asked me to apologize for her mistakes in the past. She would like to make up for them now."

In spite of herself, Ba Cao was curious. "She has a child?"

"A fine son, a very good baby, very bright. Would you like to see him?"

Ba Cao shook her head. "No need to see, a child of her disgrace." But she went on, "Does it look like the American?"

Kim Hoa sidestepped the question. "A beautiful child." She pulled a wad of bills from her jacket, offered them to Ba Cao. "Cousin Sen wishes you to have this, to give you this much each month."

Ba Cao wouldn't take the money from her.

"It's her own money."

Ba Cao still refused to take it. Kim Hoa put it on the platform beside her. "It's here, when you want it. I can't take it back. Cousin Sen would be very angry with me if she knew I had failed to give it to you."

"You're a good niece. For your sake I'll take it." Ba Cao stuffed the bills inside her jacket.

The next time Kim Hoa visited, she took Second Son with her. Trang Sen had taught him to say "grandma." For days he had been repeating it over and over, delighted with the sound.

Ba Cao stiffened as they came in. For a moment Kim Hoa thought she would refuse to greet them. Kim Hoa pointed to her. "Grandma," she said to Second Son.

He grinned and stretched his hand toward his grandmother. "Ga-ma," he said. "Ga-ma."

Ba Cao was pleased in spite of herself. "Such a smart child."

"Please hold him for me."

Ba Cao stretched her arms for him and he went to her willingly, still chattering his new word. She examined his hair, his face, and his sturdy little body. "A healthy child," she pronounced. "His lightness is not so ugly."

"Cousin Sen sends greetings. She would like to come visit if you would permit it."

Ba Cao was absorbed in her grandson. "Such a fine baby. My only grandchild."

Second Son responded with a broad smile. "Ga-ma," he said, patting her cheek.

She laughed, then turned to Kim Hoa. At last she said, "There's surely no harm in First Daughter coming. It is well that she wishes to be dutiful."

So, with much anxiety, Trang Sen visited her mother. She carefully rehearsed what she would say. But when she saw Ba Cao standing at the door, she forgot her prepared speech. "I have caused you much trouble,

Ma-ma."

Ba Cao looked at her daughter. She was definitely a woman now, but still so beautiful, the source of all the trouble.

Ma-ma is getting old, Trang Sen thought. *Was her hair always so grey, and surely she's thinner?*

"Are you well, Ma-ma?"

"Well, my daughter. I only grow old. It is good that you bring a grandson to see an old woman." She reached for the child and Trang Sen handed him to her.

They sat over tea, both silent in the shyness of their reunion.

"You are beautiful, my daughter," said Ba Cao at last.

Trang Sen lowered her head modestly.

"I still fear for you."

"Yes, Ma-ma." Trang Sen was filled with longing and a kind of aching anxiety toward her mother. "Does Eldest Brother look after you, Ma-ma, does Second Sister help you?"

"They are good children. Eldest Son comes when he can, always provides money. Second Daughter is growing up, she carries the water now, learns to cook a little. We are not so busy anymore." Tho, Ba Cao said, stationed in the Delta, visited briefly from time to time.

Going home, Trang Sen thought, *All things are changing, we must think of new ways, leave the old behind, over and over. Second Sister must grow up, we must cease to hate each other, Ma-ma must grow old, there's nothing to be done. Only Eldest Brother won't change — he'll never forgive me.*

And in fact she only saw her mother that one time. Though Second Son was always welcomed by his grandmother, Long forbade any further contact with Trang Sen.

JIM HAWKINS HAD come once more, and Second Son was making his first unsuccessful attempts to walk. Susan left, and Trang Sen missed her. Despite geography lessons, Sister Louise's and Eldest Brother's talk of France, and her long-ago dreams of going there, that world which had reclaimed both Susan and Billings seemed to her a limitless void into which they had disappeared forever, as completely and finally absent as Sister Louise. If they returned, they would be returning from nothingness into the real. She cherished Blake's visits, partly as a link to that dreamlike past with

Billings, and with Susan.

During the long evenings alone, she developed the habit of talking with Second Son, explaining to him what she was reading and thinking.

"And President Nixon make decision to go to Cambodia," she told him in English. "This cause much confusion in America. He hopes by that means to speed victory here."

Second Son, sitting on her lap and slowly drifting toward sleep, looked solemnly at her.

She didn't hear the footsteps. Jim Hawkins suddenly appeared in the door, grinning widely.

She got up quickly, blushing a little, and laid the child down. "Ong Jim." She bowed.

Still grinning, he ignored her greeting. "Art's little girl friend must be lonely, talking of such complicated matters to her little baby."

She blushed more deeply.

He watched her for a few moments, then held out an envelope. "Your loyal lover is still true to his word. I'm to ask you if you need anything."

She took the envelope and shook her head.

"He asked me to take care of you, you know."

"I don't need anything," she whispered. "We are fine, Second Son and I." But she was suddenly overwhelmed by a longing for Billings, for word of him if nothing else. "Do you hear from him? Is he all right?"

"Ah, so she misses him, she's found no one to take his place."

His insinuation infuriated her.

He looked at her, calculating, took a step toward her. She moved toward Second Son, leaned over and tucked a quilt around him.

"He's fine, he says, happy to be home. He says to tell you he'll write you soon, but you never know. Things happen."

"He says he'll write?" Her eyes softened.

"Did he ever tell you how beautiful you are?" He came closer, grabbing her arm before she could move away. "I'm sure he'd understand if you should be lonely. After all, he has ways to take care of his own loneliness."

She twisted against his viselike grip.

He tightened his hold. "All those months you were with him," he whispered harshly, "I was very jealous. Curse his luck to find someone so beautiful, then cut out all the rest of us."

Managing at last to free her arm, she pushed hard against his chin, forcing his head back.

He released her and looked speculatively at her. "So the little doll can also be a fighting bitch. You know," he was grinning again, "I think you're even more beautiful this way."

"Out!" she hissed. "Out now! Don't ever come back, ever!" She spat at him.

He laughed and stepped toward her again. "Very beautiful, and such a good act she puts on."

"Don't touch me! Never come here again!"

"But what about the money?" He was still edging toward her.

"I don't want it, you can keep it!" She threw the envelope down.

He tried to put his arms around her. She slapped him hard on the side of his face.

He reeled back, rubbing the reddening cheek. "Stronger than I thought. Where did you get such a punch, honey? And you so little and delicate too."

"Get out!"

"This time I'll go. But I'll be back. You can count on that. A pretty little thing so lonely she reads the newspaper to her baby will be glad to see me one day. And you'll keep wanting the money. I know you people, milking us for all we're worth."

"Go! I don't hear your filthy insults!"

"So I'm going, I'm going. See you again, sweetheart. Your Art asked me to take care of you, and I intend to do that."

She heard his footsteps receding down the path. She stood at the door, her face buried in her hands. He was worse than she thought. She closed the door and fastened the flimsy latch.

She spent a sleepless night, trembling at every sound.

She was afraid to tell even Kim Hoa. She had imagined she could tell Blake anything. But what would either of them think?

She couldn't sleep at night, lay listening for footsteps. Kim Hoa, looking at her red-rimmed eyes, tried to find out what was wrong.

At last, exhausted, Trang Sen, haltingly and deeply embarrassed, told her what had happened.

Kim Hoa was silent for so long that Trang Sen whispered, "Do you think this proves I'm just a tea-girl?"

"Of course not. You didn't do anything." Kim Hoa shook her head.

"Billins should never have made this arrangement. This man is no good."

"I don't ever want to see him again. How can I keep him from coming back?"

"But you do want the money."

"I don't care about the money."

"You must care about the money. Billins is sending it for his child. The money is important."

"But I don't ever want him to come back there."

"Could you write Billins?"

She shook her head. "I don't know how."

"Perhaps Ong Blake could help?"

"What if he thinks it's my fault?"

"He's the only one who can help." In one of her rare moments of assertiveness, Kim Hoa stood up. "Yes, that's what must be done. Ong Blake will surely know what to do."

It was a relief to have someone tell her what she should do. She was so tired, so tired fearing he would come back.

But only she could get a message to Blake. The imposing bastion that was the embassy, surrounded by its high wall and guarded by American Marines, completely intimidated her. Much as she hated the telephone, she decided to call him.

She had to ask permission to use the phone. Hesitantly, she approached the door of her American supervisor. "Please excuse, I need to call my friend at embassy."

The young woman looked up. "We don't usually allow calls from here, you know."

Trang Sen lowered her head. "So sorry." She turned to leave.

"Wait a moment. If it's important, and doesn't happen often, I think it will be all right."

"Yes, not often."

"What is your friend's name?"

"Ong Blake," she began, then, "Deck-er, it is Deck-er."

"Yes, yes, I know him." She thumbed through a directory, picked up the receiver and began to dial. She motioned Trang Sen to a desk outside her office. "It's ringing. Pick up outside."

Trang Sen hurried out and picked up the receiver as the call was answered. "Please to call Mr. Deck-er," she said, at last remembering the

American form of address.

"And who is calling?"

"It is Co Sen."

"Does Mr. Decker know you?"

"Yes," she answered, her voice almost inaudible.

"One moment."

After what seemed a very long time, Blake's voice came on the line.

"Co Sen? Are you all right?"

"Yes, Ong Blake. Only a small problem. Can you help me?"

"Of course. Would you like me to come by tonight? Let's see, yes, I can do that. Is that soon enough?"

"Yes. Thank you, Ong Blake."

"Until tonight then."

By the time he arrived, Trang Sen had almost lost the courage to tell him. She went nervously back and forth to the kitchen, preparing tea. That done, she was silent for so long that Blake finally asked, "What is it, Co Sen? Something I can help with?"

"Yes." But she couldn't continue.

"Do you think you can tell me about it?"

"It's very terrible. I'm so frightened." She was near tears.

He looked at her seriously, and at last she was able to tell him what had happened.

"The filthy bastard," he muttered in English. "I'd like to tear him apart."

"What can I do, Ong Blake? I don't want the money, but Ba Chau says I should take it for Second Son."

"Of course you should take it. It isn't Hawkins's money, it's Art's, and it's for you and the boy. But you aren't going to be treated like this. We've got to tell Art."

"Can you write him?"

"I can find out how. Hasn't he written you?"

"No, no letter, only the money."

He wanted to pat her hand. Instead he nodded matter-of-factly. "Yes, that's one step. But we've got to do something about you too." He looked around. "You shouldn't be here by yourself. Anything could happen."

"It's all right. I'm not afraid. Only of him."

"That's enough." He shook his head. "I don't like it. Respectable women don't live by themselves. We should have thought of that before. As for

Art," he went on, "suppose you write him, explain what's happened. I'll find a way to mail your letter to him. I'll also send him a cable, asking him to make other arrangements about the money, and tell him a letter from you is on the way." He pulled on his mustache. "Yes, I think that's the way."

She agreed somewhat reluctantly to write the letter. What if Billings thought it was her fault?

"Should I write in Vietnamese?" she asked as she prepared to begin. "My English is no good."

"Vietnamese will be fine."

He waited while she wrote the letter, rubbing the ends of his mustache. He would also write Billings, he decided. He would confront Jim Hawkins too. Damn the bastard, he thought again. She didn't need this problem added to all the others, some of which he could only imagine.

He looked at her, her head bent over the letter. In the States, he thought, she'd just be finishing college about now, or starting her first real job. And here she was, in the middle of a war, saddled with a kid, going from one damnable mess to the next. And apologizing when she complained.

She added a final word to the letter and looked up. "How long will it take to get there?"

"Hard to say. A couple of weeks, maybe longer. Then again, maybe he'll get it next week."

He put the folded letter in his pocket, looked around anxiously again. "I don't like your staying here even one night."

"It's all right. I'm not so afraid now."

He walked over and examined the latch. "Not much use."

He pulled a card from his pocket, began writing something on it. "This has my phone numbers on it, and I've just added the address of my apartment. I should have given it to you weeks ago. If you need me for anything, let me know. I should have prevented this."

"No, not your fault. Ong Jim is a bad man. Who would have known?"

"I should have." He didn't share his sudden anger at Billings, who, it seemed to him, should have known also.

He handed her the card, which she accepted with both hands, as if it were a gift.

THE PROMISE OF hearing from Billings almost overrode everything else. After what seemed weeks, but was really only a few days, Blake received a reply to his cable. "You can read it." He handed it to her. "For now I'm to get the money from Hawkins. He'll work out something more permanent later."

"Why not just send it to you?"

"I think it's easier and faster for him to use the military system. He can't get it to me that way."

She was avidly reading the telegram, as if it was a love letter in Billings's own handwriting. "He says he'll write."

Blake looked away from the longing on her face.

She could think of nothing but the promised letter.

Blake came one evening with a new lock and tools to install it. "At least someone will have to think twice about getting in here. It isn't just Hawkins, you know. Anybody, seeing you here alone with the baby, might try something."

At last Blake brought the anticipated letter. Tactfully, he refused to stay even for tea.

"I'll try to come back tomorrow. Art has some suggestions we'll want to do something about. He wrote me too."

She didn't hear him, only stood looking at the letter. "Until tomorrow," he repeated.

She looked up then. "Yes. Goodbye, Ong Blake."

She walked over to the bed platform, holding the letter almost reverently in her hands, sat looking at it for a long time. At last she slid a fingernail under the flap and slit open the envelope, taking care not to tear it.

She read the letter three times. "My most lovely White Lotus," it began. He said he had been very busy since returning, didn't mention his family. "I miss you terribly," he wrote. His words were strangely unsatisfying, dead black things marked down on a piece of paper. "I think of you all the time, long to be with you, to watch Kenneth grow. Write and tell me all about him. By now he's surely walking. Take good care of him until I can come back to you." About Jim Hawkins, he said, "You were right. I can see that now."

The fact of the letter itself did more to bridge the distance than what he had written in it. She wished she had waited longer to open it. "Please write soon. I want to know all about you. How are you keeping busy?" Of course, she remembered, he didn't know about her job. "I live for the time I can be with you again. Take good care of Kenneth until I can come back to you. Until then, my little Lotus. I love you."

Does he really miss me? She remembered what he had said about forgetting his family in America. Her suspicion that it also worked the other way lay like a heavy rock on her chest. Yet his last sentence made her smile softly. "Little Lotus" — incongruously, the words evoked an image of Second Brother, the only other who had ever called her that.

She folded the letter back into its envelope and tucked it into the packet holding all her unmailed letters. "Please write soon," he had said, and he gave her an address. She pulled out paper and a pen and settled herself into a long letter, telling him all the things she had stored up. "I work in the cultural center library now. Second Son stays with Ba Chau while I work. He loves playing with Van Hai and Thi Ba." She couldn't bring herself to write of her longing for him. At the end she told him a small lie, hoping to keep alive his desire to return — "Second Son calls for his Pa-pa all the time. Hurry and come back to us." Laboriously, she added in English, "Excuse that I write in my own language," and put down her pen. She would get Blake to address the envelope. She was afraid her own writing would be indecipherable in that strange far-off America.

BLAKE INSISTED THAT she not keep living there alone. "Could you live with Ba Chau?"

The idea of being under Ong Ngoc's constant watch made her shudder. She shook her head.

"Or return to your family?"

To that suggestion she didn't respond.

For the moment he had no other ideas. But he turned around after saying goodnight, came back into the room and sat down again. "I'm afraid I don't make a very good Vietnamese."

"You make a very good American."

He smiled. "Maybe not even that. If I'm going to help you," he went on, "I need to know how things stand with your family, whether it's possible for you to live with them."

She blushed.

"I know I shouldn't ask that."

She made a great effort to overcome her embarrassment. "I'll try to answer."

"They were very angry?"

"My mother said I must never come back." Her voice was so low he could hardly understand her. "How do you say it in English? Disowned?"

"That bad. Do your brothers know?"

"No," then, truthfully, "yes, one knows, my oldest brother. But what difference does it make now? There is Second Son for all to see, with his strange lightness. Surely not a child of our people."

He persisted. "And your brother who knows? Did he also disown you?"

"He was angriest of all. He . . . he said I'm not his sister."

He filled in the missing piece. "And this was the one who helped you go to school?"

She nodded.

"You care very much for him, don't you?"

She nodded again. "He helped me study, gave me books to read. And he was helping me go to France."

"You were going to France?" This was the first he had heard of such a plan.

"Yes, to a convent school there."

He didn't want to hear the rest. It was Billings who had changed that plan. The bastard, he thought. More calmly, he reflected that it had been her choice too. But she was just a kid, he argued with himself. Art took unfair advantage.

"You should have gone."

Tears filled her eyes. "I couldn't. I wanted to be with Arthur. And I'm not sorry," she added defiantly.

He was silent. At last, bringing them back to the present difficulty, he said, "And now you think your brother won't forgive you. Perhaps you're wrong."

"No."

"Is he here in Saigon?"

She nodded.

"I'd like to talk with him, try to convince him it's not what he thinks."

"He would only be angry, the way he feels about . . ." she stopped.

Blake guessed the reason. "The Americans?"

"He doesn't hate them. He explained that to me."

"Well, it's a wonder he doesn't."

He stood pulling at his mustache for a long time. At last, reflecting that he had already said so much she might never want to talk with him again, he ventured, "There's one more thing. What of Art? You plan to keep writing him?" He patted the letter in his shirt pocket.

"Yes," she whispered.

"Co Sen, I will act as your brother and give you advice. It's better for you to forget about Art." He stopped, not adding that Billings had created enough problems for her already.

He went away, his concern unrelieved. He thought of sabotaging the communication channel, but decided that deceiving her would only lead to more complications. He suspected Billings would be just as happy not writing. Sending the money was a duty. Beyond that he might forget her, back with his family. Blake hoped that would happen.

He kept worrying about her, went to consult Kim Hoa.

"I too worry about her."

"Could someone go there to live with her?" A thought suddenly occurred to him. "You and the children."

"I never thought of that." Kim Hoa considered the idea. "Yes, it could be done. Ong Ngoc would have to agree to it, we'd have to find someone to stay here at night, but that could be done. Yes, I think that would work."

"Can it be settled, then?"

"I must first talk with Ong Ngoc. But I think it can be settled."

Trang Sen was pleased. She could stay in the house. She'd never see Jim Hawkins again. And she didn't have to see Ong Ngoc every day either. Billings would write and Blake would mail her replies.

CHAPTER 9

TRINH VAN LONG

SHE WAS SITTING on a bench outside the library, the letter Blake had brought in her hand. She stared at a patch of shade on the white-hot concrete. He was coming back, in two months. How could she wait so long? And yet, and yet — now that she was used to this life, this job, the comfortable presence of Kim Hoa, how could she go back to that other life? Between the letters, she sometimes almost forgot him. Now, she was almost angry with him. But that filled her with remorse. *I want him to come back, to me and Second Son.* And thinking of making love again filled her with a pleasant, achy anticipation.

She said nothing to Kim Hoa or Blake and didn't answer the letter.

Blake's appearance in the library at closing time a few weeks later jarred her out of her silence.

"A cable from Art, wondering why you haven't written. He's anxious about you."

She blushed. "I'm sorry, Ong Blake. So much trouble for you."

"I must admit, I was surprised when I didn't get a call asking me to mail a letter for you." He smiled. "You always answer the same day you hear from him."

She looked away. "He's coming back."

He took in his breath, but answered casually. "It's the way of soldiers and diplomats, full of surprises, never knowing where they'll be next."

She nodded.

He pulled on his mustache, hesitated, then, at last, "Are you glad?" he asked gently.

"Yes."

"It changes things, though, maybe complicates them."

She didn't answer.

He looked around at the deserted library, the caretaker standing at the door waiting for them to leave.

"Will you go for a bowl of noodles with me?"

"Yes. Thank you, Ong Blake."

Seated in the dark interior of the small restaurant, Blake ordered a beer, took a long drink and rubbed the back of his hand across his mustache. "That's better."

She still said nothing.

"You don't have to go back to him," he finally suggested.

"I want to . . . it's all I've wanted."

"And now you're not so sure."

"I'm *glad* he's coming back. But I wish . . ." She hesitated. "I wish things were different."

He didn't answer immediately, then finally asked, "Do you want me to tell him you're all right?"

She shook her head. "I'll write him. Tonight."

Their noodles arrived.

Blake said, "I have some news too. I'll be leaving soon. Back to Washington for a tour."

"Oh." She felt as if he had put a heavy weight on her chest. She depended on his being here. "Everything changes. I hope you will be very happy with a new job," she added formally.

"Yes, well, thank you. Actually, I'd rather stay here. I never wanted to work in Washington, I went into the Service to work overseas."

"I thought you'd want to go home."

He smiled and shook his head. "I guess I'm just a footloose bachelor, no roots."

"When do you go?"

"In two months. I'm due for some vacation first, won't actually start work until late fall."

"Will you see your family?"

"What there is of it. My mother's dead. I'll spend some time with my father, maybe see my sister. She's much older than I."

"You should see her. Does she have children, nieces and nephews for you?"

"One niece, let me see, she would be about ten now, I think. It's not like here. We all go our own ways, sometimes brothers and sisters don't see each other for years. No close family ties, not like you and Ba Chau, for instance."

"Why not?"

"We move around, it's a big country, so distance can be a problem. If you don't particularly get along, you just don't keep in touch."

"And your sister? Is it that way with her?"

"In a way. By the time I was old enough to pay much attention, she had gone away to college, then got married."

"Like my brother. Only he came back."

"Yes. Well, that probably wouldn't happen with an American family. We all try to take care of ourselves." He added, "Your way is better, I think. Much more human."

"Perhaps you should have a family, since each one must have his own," she suggested, then blushed, thinking of Susan.

He laughed. "Maybe so. Others have given me the same advice."

She wondered if he wrote to Susan, but said nothing.

"So what will you do? Go back to Art?"

Her eyes clouded. "Yes."

"You know he'll just leave again, don't you?"

She avoided his eyes.

"Nothing will change, Co Sen. It's important for you to know that."

"A son should have a father. Too many now without one. Like Van Hai."

"Ba Chau does very well. And so do you."

"He wants to come back. Maybe this time he can stay longer."

"When they need him somewhere else, he'll have to leave again. Next time he may not come back." He pulled on his mustache, then, "Have you told Ba Chau?" he asked. He held out a small hope that Kim Hoa could persuade her where he could not.

She shook her head. "She won't like it."

"You should listen to what she says."

Trang Sen didn't answer.

"I worry about you. It's not a good place for you to be, this city. Anything could happen any time. These peace talks are a sham, a cover for us to get out with the shred of dignity we have left. After that, all bets are off."

She looked at him in surprise. In the long months since Billings and Susan left, he had never commented on the war. "It may be better if the Americans leave," she suggested.

"For you, with a brown-haired kid? What do you think they'll do about that?"

She shrank from his harshness. "They are my people," she whispered.

"And for that, it may be worse. It's all politics, Co Sen, politics and ideology. You can't get away from it. When it comes down to it, they won't care who you are. You'll be part of the enemy. And your family too."

For a moment she couldn't breathe. She remembered Eldest Brother's fear that he had been the cause of their father's death. "Then," she said, almost inaudibly, "it's best for me not to be with my family, not to harm them."

"I want two promises from you. I want you to promise not to forget what I just said, no matter how good it all looks, and especially if Art isn't here any longer. Just hold on to that one little piece of reality, even when you sink into that fantasy land you and Art are so good at creating."

He held up his hand to stop her protest. "There's one more promise. When it gets really bad, let me know — write, cable, send a message, whatever." He fished in his pocket and brought out a small address book, opened it to a blank page at the back and wrote something on it. "This number and address, no matter where I am, they'll know how to find me. Promise me you'll use it if you ever even *think* you need me." He tore off the page and handed it to her. "Keep it. Tell Art if you like, but don't ever lose it."

His anxiety inflamed her own fear. For a moment the transience and tenuousness of all she was part of overwhelmed her, seemed the only sure reality. Tears filled her eyes. "Thank you, Ong Blake." She took the paper. "You are always very good to me."

"Will you promise those two things?"

"I promise."

●

SHE STRUGGLED OVER the letter to Billings, unable to evoke the enthusiasm she wanted to feel. At last she folded it and sealed it into the envelope.

Kim Hoa was watching her. "A letter to Billins?"

"He's coming back." Trang Sen said it in a low voice, almost guiltily.

"I've thought of this. I knew it would happen. The children and I can move back to the shop. Ong Ngoc will be pleased, I think. The boys he hires to watch the place are worse thieves than those they're guarding against. He's taken to sleeping there himself at night."

Trang Sen said nothing. As always, Kim Hoa was making things easy for her.

For the time being, they continued their familiar routine, Kim Hoa taking the three children to the shop with her every day, Trang Sen manipulating things so she paid for most of the food. Whatever else happened, she resolved to make sure both Kim Hoa and her mother had enough money.

Blake had said she and Billings lived in a fantasy land. Now, she reflected, smiling at the irony, this was the fantasy, this make-believe world without him, so soon to end, in which she walked as if it would go on forever. Blake had said she could decide what she wanted. She repeated, as a mantra, Arthur will be here on such and such a day, so many weeks, so many days, from now. And all she felt was numbness. Perhaps she only wanted something that would last. When that thought occurred to her, it was Kim Hoa, not Billings, who came to mind.

She had what she thought of as her spy dream, again saw the crumpled figure huddled at the foot of a wall. She cried out in her sleep and was awakened by the gentle hand of Kim Hoa. In the darkness of the room, it all seemed real. As she clung to Kim Hoa desperately, Kim Hoa said nothing, only smoothed the damp hair away from Trang Sen's face, murmured soothing sounds, as if to a child waking up from a nightmare.

SHE SAW HIM from the end of the block, standing at the edge of the street in front of the house. She stood still for a moment, feeling as if she were suffocating. But only for a moment. Then she hurried toward him, until at last he saw her too. He ran to meet her, caught her in a crushing embrace.

"I miss you so much. How tell you?"

She trembled in his arms. "I too, Arthur. I've missed you too."

He held her away from him. "Still same, always beautiful."

But he seemed changed to her, and not only because of his uncharacteristically halting Vietnamese. His hair was shorter and thinner, there were lines on his face which she hadn't remembered. And so pale, as if no sun had warmed him in all the long months. Oblivious of the people on the street, she burrowed into his shoulder, so as not to look at him. The warmth of his body was home.

He began kissing her. Then, remembering where they were, she pushed him away.

"Not here, not here," she whispered.

"Then where? Ba Chau is in the house, with all the children."

"Did you see Second Son? Did he remember you? Isn't he beautiful? Are you pleased with him?"

He laughed. "I'm pleased. After much effort by Ba Chau, he called me Pa-pa. But I hardly think he remembered. How could he?"

"Ah, he's very smart. You don't know."

He laughed again.

"But let's go in. I've brought things for dinner."

"Well, I wasn't so much interested in food as . . . Isn't there someplace we can go, someplace private? Are they there all the time?"

She blushed. "I didn't know when you were coming, what you would want." She felt she should apologize. "I . . . I didn't like to ask them to leave. Ba Chau says she can move back to the tailor shop. But it seemed best to wait, to know what you wanted."

"Well, look, take the things in, leave them for Ba Chau and the children, and you and I can find a place to eat, whatever."

"Leave Second Son, too? Don't you want to be with him?"

"Tomorrow. Tonight I want just you."

She felt as if she had lost all capacity to think or make decisions, could only drift along with his wishes. She went in, made an excuse to Kim Hoa, and rejoined him.

Billings guided her along the narrow street to its intersection with Phan Than Gian Road and hailed a cab. He put his arm around her. "For our reunion, we'll go back to the Paradise," he said, "where it all started. When we want, we can get some dinner in one of the restaurants we used to like. Like old times."

She didn't say she hated that hotel, the memory connected with it of Eldest Brother's anger at her, that last night there. She followed him in, her head lowered as he engaged a room, was handed the key.

She had forgotten his tenderness, the gentleness that tempered his passion, the comfort of his arms when their lovemaking was over.

"I missed you," she said, now honestly. "So much, I couldn't remember you. But no more." She clung to him in sudden panic. "Don't ever go away again. Please don't ever go away."

He said nothing, but held her tightly. "So tell me what you've been doing," he said finally, "tell me about Kenneth."

She talked and talked, all the things she had longed for so many months to tell him. He let the talk flow over him, comforting him.

"Arthur," she asked at last, embarrassed, "will . . . will we be together, like before?"

"Absolutely. It may take a little time to work out. But they have to give me a place to live, and that means you'll have one too."

"What about our house? If I'm not there, Kim Hoa would rather be at the shop."

"You'll have to stay there until they find me an apartment. I'll be with you whenever I can. Do you think Ba Chau would move now?"

"Whenever I ask her."

"Good. That way you and I will have a little privacy."

"What about the house, later? You promised that man, about the rent."

He shrugged. "I'll just pay the rent. What difference does it make?"

"But so expensive. Ong Blake said it would be easy to rent it, not tell the landlord."

"I'll worry about that later. You don't have to think about it."

Turning to another matter, "You don't need the library job anymore," he said, "now that I'm back."

"But I like it."

"You'll be busy with Kenneth, taking care of our apartment and so forth. The apartment will be bigger this time, a separate room for Kenneth, maybe more. I got some good news, just before I left Washington" — her heart jumped, not knowing what to expect — "I've been promoted to a full colonel."

"Oh." She was disappointed. "That is good for you, for your job?"

"At least it means more of the comforts of life, like a bigger apartment."

She wondered why they needed a bigger apartment. The other one had been fine.

"So you see why you'll be too busy to keep working at the library."

"Second Son can stay with Ba Chau, the way he's doing now."

"I want you to look after him yourself. And you don't need the money."

"I've been giving Ba Chau some, and my mother. You don't know, things are so expensive. Only an American salary is enough."

"Well, I can work something out. I should be able to help your relatives a bit. Be glad to, should have done it before."

She was silent, remembering her mother's refusal to accept money she thought came from Billings.

He nuzzled her shoulder. "Tonight, let's just enjoy each other. We'll work everything out later."

She snuggled against him. But there was still ambivalence. All his plans made her even more reluctant to let go of the easy comfort she had settled into with Kim Hoa and the children. Though if it was all to change, she wanted to get it over with quickly.

"I talked with Ong Ngoc," Kim Hoa said the next evening. "He wants us to go back to the old way. He says nothing has worked right since I left. I didn't tell him anything about Billins," Kim Hoa hastily added, as she saw Trang Sen's look of apprehension.

Trang Sen made a polite protest. "Oh, no, you can stay here as long as you like. Billings has a place to live, he doesn't need this."

"Ong Ngoc wants us there as soon as possible. I thought I might go today."

Trang Sen nodded, but her reluctance was real. With a heavy heart, she helped Kim Hoa pack up their things. "I wish it didn't have to end."

Kim Hoa shrugged. "We must walk our own paths. But we'll always help each other."

Trang Sen went with them, helped Kim Hoa settle in.

"Auntie," clamored Van Hai and Thi Ba, "Little Cousin can stay with us tonight, please, please?"

Kim Hoa smiled and nodded, so she left Second Son to spend the night there.

She had expected to see Billings at some point. But Blake, not Billings, was waiting when she returned to the house.

"Ong Blake. Have you seen him, Arthur?"

"We ended up at the same party tonight, he suggested I come by afterward." He looked at her sympathetically. "No trouble for you, not inconvenient?"

"Never any trouble." She followed his glance around the bare room. "Ba Chau has gone back to the shop. I've just been helping her."

He made no comment.

"Would you like some tea? Now that Arthur's back, perhaps you want beer. I'll ask him to get some."

"Tea will be fine." He smiled. "My taste doesn't change because Art has returned."

She returned his smile. "No, I just remembered, you always drank beer before."

Billings came in while she was making the tea. He stood indecisively in the middle of the chairless room, mopped his face.

Trang Sen hurried in, arranged a pile of quilts on the bed platform. "Sit here, Arthur." She looked at him anxiously. "You perhaps must be somewhat Vietnamese while we are in this house."

"That I may never be able to do," he said as he tried to find a comfortable position. He looked around. "I forgot there was no electricity. What we need right now is an air conditioner. It's going to take me a while to get used to the heat again."

"We could hook up a wire, no doubt," suggested Blake. "I thought of doing that after you left, but Co Sen said she didn't need it. I think we'd better not try that in the dark, though."

Billings nodded. "We won't be here long anyway. They're getting a place ready for me now." He looked around once more, then turned to Trang Sen. "Ba Chau has left? Where's Kenneth?"

"Yes. Second Son is staying there tonight. He didn't want to leave Van Hai and Thi Ba."

"Good."

Blake watched him with interest. "Ba Chau has been a big help to Co Sen while you were away, Art. It was good for them to be together."

Billings nodded absently. "Yes, I'm sure it was. Ba Chau's a good girl." Glancing at Trang Sen and smiling at her, he added, "I learned long ago that Trang Sen can't get along without her."

The two men began discussing the progress of the peace talks. *Like it used to be,* thought Trang Sen. *Only Susan should have been part of this. Soon Blake will be gone too.*

After Blake left, Billings looked around the room. "I should have left some furniture for you," he said.

She shook her head. "I didn't need it. The hammock and the bed, the little tables, quite enough."

"Then I should have left some for me," he amended. "What happened to the crib?"

She had meant to bring it out before he got back tonight. "There." She pointed to it, collapsed, leaning against the wall in a corner of the room.

"You haven't been using it?"

"Second Son is so big now, he does very well on the bed. It's quite safe, with quilts piled around him."

He looked skeptical.

"And what do you and I do about sleeping?"

"There are quilts, but the mats are cooler. Or you could sleep in the hammock."

He whistled in disbelief. "I can't believe you've been living like this."

The comment irritated her. "It's always been the same. Only with you it was different."

"Well, it won't be long before we can move to the apartment. Meanwhile . . ." He began to undress. She brought out a bamboo mat and unrolled it on the bed platform.

"I hope you'll be comfortable," she said with concern. "The hammock is really cooler."

"Next to you is comfortable." He lay down gingerly and reached for her, chuckling. "I'll pretend we're making love on a dock."

HER VOICE DRONED on, lulling Second Son. Absently, she patted his back as he lay beside her on the sofa. She read him whatever she happened to be in the midst of, usually some American news item or magazine article. She did it to hear the sound of her own voice in the solitary silence of the apartment, so big it almost echoed.

She felt him relax into sleep. Giving him one last pat, she laid aside her book and carried him to the bedroom. She could never get over her anxiety at leaving him by himself. It seemed a strange thing, to shut him away from his family every night. But Billings said everyone did this in America.

All she had to do was care for the apartment and Second Son. She was bored and lonely, missed the library. She often spent evenings at the tailor shop, preparing dinner while Kim Hoa worked downstairs, and staying until the three children fell asleep. It was good for Second Son, she thought, to spend time with his cousins. He still missed them during the long days.

Billings was increasingly frantic about his work, was seldom home except to sleep. When he was there, he was caught up in apparently endless paperwork. She heard him muttering from time to time — ". . . hands are tied"; "what do they expect when we have no troops"; "these bloody bastards can't fight."

"Arthur, you work too much, you mustn't worry," she said to him once.

He lashed out at her. "It's none of your business, you're to pay no attention, you hear?"

She had crept away and after that said nothing to him, only welcomed him into her arms when late at night he lay down beside her. Sometimes it seemed that his passion would use up his last remaining energy, for his lovemaking approached a frenzy which approximated the way he was going at his work. She matched his passion, but something in her pulled back, as if she heard a warning bell. Afterward, she would lie awake, cold undefined fear washing over her.

She was pregnant. She was sure, no need to ask Kim Hoa this time. The life within her brought with it a sickness and lassitude that made the simplest tasks unendurably difficult, caring for Second Son an almost impossible burden. She didn't tell Billings, remembering his reaction before. She couldn't bear such enthusiasm. And he would surely make her go to an American doctor. She shrank from the remembered nightmare of the hospital. In his absorption he didn't notice the change in her, the dimming of her vitality.

Kim Hoa prescribed soothing tonics, insisted that Trang Sen eat certain foods, which, she said, would unite her body forces with those of the growing child and restore her energy. Again, though, she asked, "Do you want the baby? Does Billins know?"

Trang Sen shrugged to the first question, shook her head to the second. She was too tired to consider such complicated matters.

It had finally begun to rain after the long dry season, but the showers hadn't lightened the atmosphere, the damp heat which had hung heavy in the clouds for weeks and seemed to sap what was left of her energy. She curled listlessly on Kim Hoa's bed platform, trying to shut out the noise of the children playing around her.

Kim Hoa looked at her anxiously. "You'll harm the child. Aren't you resting enough? Do you sleep at night?"

"Yes." Trang Sen sat up, passed her hand over her face. "I feel so tired."

"Why don't you leave Second Son here tonight, spend one night without having to think about him?"

Trang Sen nodded. She rubbed her face again, shrank from the sudden laughter of Thi Ba. "Maybe I'll go now."

"Yes. The children are too noisy."

She hired a cyclo, watched the passing crowds absently. Why was this baby so difficult, so different from Second Son? She hadn't answered Kim Hoa's question about whether she wanted to keep it. Maybe she didn't.

She entered the building the back way and let herself into the darkened apartment, went to the bedroom and lay down.

She wasn't sure how long she had slept when she was awakened by voices, Billings with some of his friends. She heard him rustling around in the kitchen, clinking ice into glasses. She started to get up to help, but then thought she would lie there for a while.

Listening, she surmised they were now sitting down with their drinks. Then she heard someone ask about her.

"No problem," she heard Billings answer. "She's taken the boy and gone to visit her cousin. She does that most evenings if she thinks I'm not coming home."

Why would it matter whether I'm here? She thought of going out then, announcing her presence. But some faint intuition, or perhaps curiosity, held her back. She lay there, straining to hear them. What were they saying? Something about a spy, but she couldn't catch where. *In President Thieu's cabinet again?* she speculated. Then she heard quite clearly, "Trinh Van Long."

She caught her breath, put her hand hastily over her mouth as if to prevent herself from crying out. For a moment all was blackness. That image of the dark figure against a wall flashed through her mind.

When she focused again on their discussion, she heard someone say, ". . . won't let this one go scot-free like the last time. Best thing to do is go tonight, right now, get their security forces going. I guess we could even do it ourselves, since he's been dealing with our stuff."

"And right under our noses. In that office he has access to everything." The speaker laughed mirthlessly. "He was one of the damned little bastards we trusted."

Then it has to be him. They're surely describing Eldest Brother. A desperate, momentary hope that she had misheard the name was extinguished. She lay quite still, her mind working frantically. *I must warn him, I have to get to him, they mustn't know I'm here.*

What if Arthur comes into the bedroom? She froze at the thought. Slowly, inch by inch, so as not to cause the bed to creak, she worked her way to the edge, carefully lowered herself to the floor and crouched on the bed's far side.

Would they never leave? She heard Billings get up, then more clinking of ice cubes. She forced her whirling brain to focus on what they were saying. They were going to the Vietnamese security force. "But," insisted one voice, "whatever those guys agree to, we've got to take care of this tonight, even if we have to do it ourselves." Another voice, "Right you are. We can't take a chance on somebody tipping the bastard off. He's too valuable a customer for that, he knows too much."

At last she heard them filing out. The door closed and the key turned in the lock. She lay quite still for several more minutes, until she was certain they were really gone. Then she got up and, in the dark, fumbled through the closet for her most elegant ao dai. She would have to convince the guard to call him; her best bet, she thought, was to look as important as possible.

The doorman. She didn't think he had seen her come in, and she would go out the back way again. *But just in case . . . what? Money, I'll have to bribe him.* Shakily, she pulled some bills from her purse. *The guard too. I'll have to bribe the guard.*

She left the apartment by the back entrance and walked to the street, glancing back as she reached the sidewalk. Absorbed in his paper, the doorman wasn't looking her way. She hurried on.

She could walk. It wasn't far to Long's barracks. But someone might recognize her, one of Billings's colleagues. She hailed a cab, gave the driver the address, and sat back in the shadows, her heart beating rapidly. *Will he come to me? I'll have to make him think it's Trang Mai, that some emergency has come up with Ma-ma. What if he isn't there? He has to be there, I have to tell him. If not . . . if not, I'll have to find him, that's all.*

The cab drew up to the gate, she paid the fare and got out. The guard shifted his rifle as she approached.

"Please, I need your help. A big emergency. I must find my brother. He lives here, I think, Major Trinh Van Long?"

"We have a colonel by that name." The guard looked at her suspiciously. She smiled, nervously. "It is he. I am so stupid to forget."

"And who are you?"

"I am his sister. Please, it is very urgent. Could you call him for me?" *Hurry, hurry. Even now it may be too late.*

"What kind of emergency, miss?"

"My . . . my mother, she . . . she's very ill. Very sudden. I don't know what to do." There was a note of panic in her voice, a hint of tears in her eyes. She held out the major portion of her money, retaining only enough for another cab fare. "My mother said to give you this. She said you would help us."

"Yes, miss, of course." He took the bills and quickly put them in his pocket. "And who should I say is here?"

"His sister. Tell him . . . tell him it is Trang Mai. Ask him to come quickly," she added urgently.

The man nodded and walked toward the barracks. Trang Sen moved into the shadow of the guard house, faced partially away from the gate and stood waiting, her head lowered. *What if he won't talk to me? But he has to, for his life.*

Her head swirled. No, she mustn't faint, not now, not here. By a sheer force of will she overcame the momentary weakness.

She heard the footsteps returning, Eldest Brother speaking to the guard in a low voice.

He came to her side. "Second Sister?" he asked doubtfully.

She half turned toward him. He stiffened, averted his face.

"Please," she begged him, "I must talk with you. I . . . I know how you feel. I wouldn't have come, disobeyed you. But it's important. Life and death."

"We have nothing to say to each other."

"No, no, you must listen to me. Only this one time. We must hurry." She caught his arm, to prevent him from leaving.

"Then say whatever it is quickly." He pulled away from her. "I have no interest in prolonging this."

She must not notice the scorn in his voice, the rejection in that gesture. She must only warn him, nothing else was important.

She looked around desperately. "Not here, where someone might see us. Will you walk with me, somewhere . . ." — she glanced toward the guard, who had moved away from them — ". . . where no one can hear us."

A look, perhaps of comprehension, flashed across his face. He guided her into the shadow of the wall, propelled her around the corner to the side of the compound. "This will do. What is it?"

"They . . . they're after you, they've found out," she whispered quickly. "They're coming, tonight, soon . . . before," she laughed shakily, "before someone can warn you. You must leave, now." She finished on a breathless note and stood with her head down, isolated from him.

"How do you know?"

"I heard them, they didn't know I was there, they said your name. I . . . I would have known anyway, I think. I dreamed it, long ago. Only I didn't know what it was."

He looked at her sharply. "How much do you know?" he asked in an urgent whisper.

"Nothing, nothing." An image of the tailor's lidded eyes flashed through her mind, and, with sudden understanding, she said, "Only Ong Ngoc . . ."

He clapped his hand over her mouth. "You must not speak of him, never ask, you must never try to find out. Do you understand? It would be very dangerous for everyone."

She nodded. He released her and for the first time noticed her paleness, the thinness of her face. "Are you all right?"

Tears filled her eyes. "Yes," she said, almost inaudibly.

"My loyal little sister," he said, echoing his words of long ago, "always helping me." He touched her arm in the familiar gesture. "Can you, for a moment, tell me how it is with you?"

She could stand there forever, telling him at last all the things she had stored up for so many months and years, asking him all the questions. But he must go, even now they might be on their way.

"No," she said through tears, "no, there is no time. Perhaps . . . perhaps someday. But now you must go, hurry, there's no time." She tried to push him away from her.

There were tears in his eyes now. "My best little sister, through so many years," he said, adding, in a broken voice, "Take care of them, Ma-ma and Second Sister. There's no one else to do it now."

"I will. Just go."

He touched her arm again. "Yourself too. Take care of yourself."

She nodded. "Go," she choked out.

He looked at her again through the blur of his tears, grasped her by the shoulders and kissed her on both cheeks, European fashion. "The French manner," he said with a faint smile, then, "I'll never forget."

He disappeared into the darkness. She strained to see him, blinded by the bitter saltiness that streaked down her face. She longed to run after him, knowing she would destroy him if she did.

Voices at the guardhouse reminded her of her own danger. She thought quickly. The guard, if he remembered a name, would remember Trang Mai. *Ma-ma and Second Sister! They could be in danger. What can I do?*

First, she must not be found here. She ran soundlessly the length of the wall and turned away from the compound, scuttling through an alley and onto Tran Quoc Tuan Boulevard. She walked quickly toward Petrus Ky. At the intersection she could find a cab. *Where to go? To Kim Hoa? How much to tell her? Anything she knows could be dangerous. What should I do?*

The cab screeched to a halt at her signal and she climbed in. The driver looked at her expectantly. "Where to, miss?"

Where, where? Whatever else, she had to get Second Son, be home when Billings returned. She gave the address of the tailor shop and leaned back against the seat, fighting nausea. She swallowed hard, breathing long deep breaths. She couldn't give in now, not yet, there was still much to do, she had to think clearly. *I don't want to tell Kim Hoa. But I have to. Kim Hoa will help me, together we can decide what to tell Ma-ma. They'll surely question her, discover she's not sick at all. Why didn't I tell the guard some other lie?*

The cab made a U-turn and pulled up in front of the shop. To her surprise, Kim Hoa and Ong Ngoc were just closing up. *It's not so late then. I thought it had been hours, but it isn't late at all. There's still time to think of a plan.*

She paid the driver and almost stumbled toward the shop. Kim Hoa and Ong Ngoc looked at her in surprise.

"Trang Sen, what's happened?"

"It's all right, everything will be all right now. I came for Second Son, I must take him back."

Ong Ngoc looked at her sharply. She turned away. She would never be able to trust him, in spite of, or maybe because of, that sudden insight.

"Really nothing," she repeated, "only . . ." — she cast about for a plausible excuse — ". . . only Billings doesn't want me to leave Second Son here. I'll get him." She turned and rushed upstairs.

Kim Hoa found her curled miserably on the bed platform, Second Son clasped to her.

"He's gone," she answered Trang Sen's questioning look. "But he's very suspicious. What's wrong? Some terrible thing has happened, hasn't it?"

Trang Sen nodded. Her mouth was suddenly very dry. She wet her lips. "I shouldn't tell you," she whispered, "but, oh, Kim Hoa, I don't know what to do." She looked around furtively. "Are you sure he's gone, can anyone hear?"

"I'm sure. I saw him leave."

In a voice so low Kim Hoa had to strain to hear, Trang Sen told her what had happened. "Now, I've gotten Ma-ma and Second Sister in trouble. And you, too, maybe, just from knowing. I shouldn't have told you. Oh, why didn't I think of something else to tell the guard?" Her voice rose hysterically.

"Trang Sen, listen. You've done the most important thing. He's gotten away. Of course you should tell me. And Aunt and Cousin Mai, they'll help. Only calm down and let's think what they can say. The police will surely come to question them."

That confirmation of her fears almost led to a new fit of despair, but Trang Sen controlled herself. "There's no time. I don't know when they'll look for him, but soon, tonight, maybe right now. And the guard will tell them. I too, I have to get back with Second Son so Billings won't suspect anything."

They decided to tell Ba Cao the truth. But Trang Mai didn't have to know anything. That way her denial would be genuine. They thought Ba Cao could speculate that the young woman must have been a girlfriend, who lured him out by pretending to be his sister. She could further suggest that she knew of a problem between this woman, whose name she had never learned, and her son.

"Does Billins know he's your brother?"

"I told him once, long ago." It seemed the ultimate betrayal.

"Then he will almost surely question you. What will you say?"

Trang Sen's face hardened, a veil of blankness shrouded her eyes. "I'll swear I was here tonight as usual, that I know nothing. I'll tell him how terrible it is, how much I hate my brother for doing this."

Kim Hoa left to warn Ba Cao and Trang Sen returned to the apartment with Second Son. Entering once more through the back door, she put the child to bed and got in bed herself. *It's lucky*, she thought, *I wore the fancy ao dai*. It would make her mother's story more believable.

She lay stiffly, staring at the ceiling. She must pretend to be asleep. She thought she would never sleep again. Anger overwhelmed her. *How could Arthur do this?* Another thought. *Will he tell the others he's my brother? Am*

I in danger? And Second Son? She panicked at that, but could think of nothing else to do but lie there and wait for him to come back.

She remembered with revulsion the baby she was carrying. At last she gave in to nausea and rushed to the bathroom. She squatted heaving over the toilet and afterward clung to it as the white tiles whirled around her. They reminded her of the hospital, that terrible time when Second Son was born. She wouldn't have this baby, fathered by this man who would condemn her brother to his death. He would pay for it with his child, though he would never know. *It will be my revenge,* she thought, *my sacrifice for Eldest Brother, almost like Kieu throwing herself into the river. I'll sacrifice this part of myself.*

But to do that, she must play the role of normalcy carefully, Billings must suspect nothing. She arose slowly, so as not to bring on another attack of dizziness, cleaned the traces of her sickness, and washed her face. Then she lay back down to wait for him.

It was almost morning when she heard the sound of the key turning in the lock. She pretended to be asleep, with effort forced herself to breathe regularly, though her heart was pounding. He closed the door softly and tiptoed shoeless into the bedroom. He stripped to his undershorts, sighed wearily as he sat down on the edge of the bed, then lay down beside her. He turned to her, put his arm around her.

"Arthur," she mumbled. "So late, I thought you weren't coming back."

"A terrible night. And you and I must talk about it, but not now. In the morning."

He held her to him. "Whatever happens, as long as I have you. I don't ever want to lose you . . ." He fell asleep.

She forced her body to remain relaxed in his arms, but her mind was rigid with apprehension. *Does he suspect something? Surely if he does, he wouldn't have come back, wouldn't have said that about losing me. Or would he?* She was relieved when Second Son's cry gave her an excuse to leave him there.

Billings got up as usual, despite his long night. He watched her pour coffee for him, and as she was turning to go back into the kitchen, caught her arm. "Sit down. I must tell you, ask you, about last night."

She looked at him in simulated puzzlement, put the pot away and joined him at the table.

"Your brother —" he started to say.

She clutched at him. "What? Has anything happened to him? You didn't tell him . . ."

He shook his head. In his weariness, he began speaking English. "I don't know what's happened to him, or where he is. I wish to hell I did." He looked sharply at her. "I'm going to assume you know nothing about this, and I'm not telling anyone he's your brother. I'm the only one who knows that."

"But what is it?" she asked again, seemingly more anxious, but actually relieved.

"He's a spy."

She drew in her breath.

"We didn't know until yesterday, went to get him last night, but the son of a bitch was gone. Someone must have tipped him off."

She showed no anger at the epithet, feigned distress and surprise. "Are you sure? I . . . I can't believe it."

He muttered, more to himself than to her, "It couldn't be worse. He knows everything . . . *everything* . . . about what we're doing."

She said nothing.

"I have to ask you this," he finally said, switching back to Vietnamese. "If you promise me your answer is the truth, I'll believe that and we'll say no more about it." He took a deep breath. "Did you have any idea what he was doing, even any suspicion of such a thing, any involvement in it yourself?"

"He would not speak to me since I . . . since we . . ."

"I must insist that you look at me and give me your answer clearly," he interrupted her.

She recognized that clinical tone she hated so much. But she raised her head and looked directly at him. "I know nothing."

He relaxed, slumped back in his chair and wiped his face, took off his glasses and rubbed them vigorously across his shirt. "Thank God. I didn't really suspect you, but I was so afraid. I . . . I couldn't bear to lose you."

Even now she loved him, part of her wanted to hold him in her arms, reassure him. But another part hated him, would never forgive him.

He was standing up. "It'll be another long day, mopping up after last night. We'll never find the bastard now. He's probably holed up in some jungle in his black pajamas, like all the rest of them."

Her chest was constricted with hope and anguish. But he was pulling her up, holding her tightly. "Wait for me tonight," he whispered. "I need you so much, love you so much."

"I too, Arthur," she managed to respond. "I'll wait."

She hoped Billings was right about Eldest Brother, but the thought that he was with the Front in the jungle wasn't much comfort. She would never see him again.

She forced herself not to go to the tailor shop until afternoon. She still didn't trust Ong Ngoc, regardless of who he was. The tailor, with his drooping eyelids, appeared not to notice her. Kim Hoa nodded slightly and reassured her with a faint smile. *At least*, Trang Sen reflected, *I didn't put Kim Hoa in more danger by saying something about Ong Ngoc.*

Kim Hoa had gone back at noon to check on Ba Cao and Trang Mai. The police had come early that morning. Trang Mai of course totally denied going anywhere the night before. Her mother had rolled her eyes mournfully, declaring she had warned her son about this girl friend, who now had caused this trouble. The police eventually went away, warning her that she should report to them immediately if Long came there.

So Ba Cao and Trang Mai were safe. Things were turning out as well as could be expected — Billings suspected nothing about her, and Long, Trang Sen hoped, was also safe.

SHE LAY AWAKE for hours, or, in a fitful sleep, dreamed of death and darkness, awoke with a memory of Long calling her. Between her insomnia and the illness of her pregnancy, she lived in a nightmare of exhaustion. Kim Hoa had given her some medicine to cause her to bleed and expel the child. She hoped it would happen soon. She now spent most days, as well as the evenings, at the tailor shop. The empty apartment, her solitary thoughts, were unbearable.

She had just arrived there and released Second Son to join his cousins when she was racked by a sharp cramp. She tried to hold onto the wall as the room swam around her, then she sank to the floor. Her last thought was that it was she herself huddled against the dark wall of her dream.

When she came to, she was upstairs on the bed platform, Kim Hoa gently rubbing her forehead. "How did I get here?" she whispered weakly.

"Ong Ngoc carried you. He's really quite concerned about you."

Trang Sen didn't respond to that, but, as another cramp seized her, "Oh, Kim Hoa, I'm so sick," she gasped. She rolled over on her side and hugged her stomach. She felt a warm trickle between her legs, accompanied by a cramp even worse than the previous one. In spite of Kim Hoa's resistance, she forced herself to sit up.

"The . . . the baby, something is happening." She bent double at the onset of yet another severe cramp, looked at the blood stain where she had been lying. She clutched her belly in reaction to the onslaught of pain.

"Lie down. No need to fight it. You'll only make the cramps worse. It'll all be over soon."

But it wasn't over soon. By late afternoon she was still bleeding profusely. In desperation Kim Hoa sent for a midwife. The blood-stanching herbs the old woman applied didn't work either.

"Sometimes nothing helps. It may be wise to call her husband." The midwife shuffled out, not wanting to sully her own reputation by being present when it was clear that her efforts had failed.

Kim Hoa bent over Trang Sen. "How can I find Billins? He has to help us."

"I don't want him to know, he'll be angry about the baby."

"I won't tell him about the medicine, but we can't make the bleeding stop."

"I'm afraid of the hospital. He'll make me go to the hospital."

"Don't think about that now, just tell me." Kim Hoa was almost shouting in her desperation.

Too tired to argue, Trang Sen whispered instructions. "There's a telephone number, but you can also ask the guards at the gate. Or at the apartment. They'll help you."

She closed her eyes and sank into a sleep that bordered on unconsciousness, awoke to see the blurry outlines of Billings's anxious face. "No hospital, Arthur," she mumbled.

"Hush, don't try to talk. We've got to get you some help." He reached for her hand and held it in both his own. Its cold dampness deepened his alarm.

She was dimly aware of someone — it must have been Billings — carrying her out of the shop, helping her into the car. She had no memory of anything after that until she awoke in a narrow white bed.

The pains were gone, but something, what was it, something — or someone — made her want to weep. Eldest Brother and Billings, that was it. She would always be tired now, because of them. It seemed that the pain had been connected with them also, but she couldn't remember how.

Slowly she opened her eyes. Billings was sitting in a chair close to her bed. She thought she was supposed to hate him, but she was too weary.

"Arthur," she said groggily, tried to reach her hand toward him, only to discover that it was hampered by tubes and needles. She looked up at the jar of blood slowly trickling through the tube. Wildly, she thought they were giving her back her own blood. "Mine?" she asked in wonder.

"No," he said, very seriously. "But like yours. You lost so much, they are building it back."

She closed her eyes and slept again. When she awoke the next time, his head was resting on his folded arms on the edge of the bed. She lifted her encumbered hand then and clumsily touched his hair.

When he looked up, there were tears in his eyes. "Oh, Trang Sen," he whispered. "I love you so much. I was so afraid I had lost you. If I had known . . ." A sob caught in his throat.

There was something, she tried to remember, some awful thing. Eldest Brother, he would have killed him. But he loved her.

"Are you angry at me about the baby, Arthur?"

"No, not angry, just sorry. You should have told me, it might be that this could have been prevented."

She shook her head. "No good from the beginning. Something was wrong. It was making me too sick."

"Nothing matters, only that you're all right. I couldn't bear it if something happened to you." He buried his head in his arms again, so she might not see his tears.

It was all too complicated to sort out, and she was so tired. She couldn't hate him, when he loved her so much.

SHE COULDN'T REMEMBER what she had done before that terrible night. Her whole life seemed composed of those weeks afterward — the pretense she maintained before Billings and her secret anger; her anxiety for Eldest Brother; the pregnancy that made her so ill. She lay on the couch, day after day, staring listlessly at the blank whiteness of the wall.

Caught between the increasing demands of his work and his desire to be near her, Billings was almost mad with anxiety. He was desperate to help her, to divert her, once more to evoke her gentle smile, the sparkling liveliness in her dark eyes. But he didn't know what to do. He tried to hire someone to care for her and Second Son, cook and look after the apartment.

That plan sparked her into momentary life. She was afraid a servant would treat her like a prostitute. In her pride and shame she couldn't explain this to Billings, and he was mystified and frustrated by her stubbornness.

At last he went to Kim Hoa for advice.

"She doesn't need a servant," asserted Kim Hoa with rare directness, shaking her head vigorously. "She needs to be interested in living again. A servant would just give her an excuse to go on lying on the couch."

"Then what can I do?" Billings ran his hands through his hair in despair.

Seeing that gesture, Kim Hoa felt pity for him. "It won't happen very quickly, Ong Billins, only slowly, bit by bit. We must be very patient."

"But what can I do?" he asked again.

"Once, long ago, after the school was gone, and Sister Louise dead, she came here and helped. After a while she came back to herself. Reading too, reading always helps her."

"I tried that, I bring her books from the library. She just stacks them in a corner."

"Perhaps she could come here with me for a few days? Another place might be good for her."

"You're already taking care of Kenneth." He didn't want to admit to himself that Kim Hoa might succeed where he was failing.

"We are cousins," Kim Hoa said. "We always take care of each other."

But he went away undecided. He didn't want to give up Trang Sen, even temporarily. At last, though, when she showed no sign of recovering, he decided to try Kim Hoa's suggestion.

He was somewhat doubtful about Trang Sen's reaction to the idea. To his surprise, he thought he saw a slight sparkle in her eyes.

"Yes, maybe it would be best. But, Arthur," she added, remembering his objection to her working in the tailor shop, "you don't want me to help them."

"Just for a short time, I think you could do that. It's only temporary, you know," he added quickly.

Knowing she would be away from this place, with its memory of that awful night, revived her. But she tried to hide that from Billings, fearful it would make him change his mind.

"When should I go, Arthur?"

"When would you like to go?"

She shrugged. "No need to wait, I think."

He had an uneasy feeling that she wanted to leave. "I could take you over there tonight."

She made a bundle of the few things she would need. As he waited for her, it was his turn to sit and stare at the unrelieved bareness of the wall.

She came in, ready to go. He got up, held her unresponsive body against him momentarily. "I love you so much," he whispered, then, "Are you sure you want to do this?" he asked.

Something like pity for him surfaced, and a memory that she loved him. "Just for a while. Then I'll come back. It will be better then," she added, more to herself than to him.

He took her bundle and guided her to the car. They were both silent as he steered and honked through the clogged streets.

Second Son greeted them both ecstatically, throwing himself first into Trang Sen's arms, then his father's. Trang Sen smiled a little and returned his hug.

Billings held his son tightly, then, "Come back soon," he said, struggling to maintain control.

Trang Sen watched until she could no longer distinguish his car in the congestion of cyclos, cabs, lambrettas, moving at snail's pace along Nguyen Hui Boulevard. It reminded her of the days when she was still at the school, when they met secretly, when her heart had skipped to see his light brown hair appear in the midst of a throng of people coming toward her. How innocent it all seemed now, and how inaccessible. If only she could love him again in the simple, unthinking way she had then, when it was all a lovely game.

Reluctantly she acknowledged Second Son's tug at the skirt of her ao dai. That time would never return. There was this child, and the other, lost one, and so many things lost, her love now complicated, and an unbridgeable gulf between her and Billings.

She shook her head as if to rid it of her rambling thoughts, and forced a smile for Second Son. Bending down, she took him in her arms, listening to his chatter as she walked toward the back of the shop.

She nodded her usual silent greeting to Ong Ngoc, who looked at her speculatively. He seemed to treat her with something like respect these days, but she thought that might be her imagination.

Kim Hoa and the children surrounded her then, and she was comforted by their eagerness. Maybe she *could* feel better here. She thought with something like anticipation of the simple task of sorting bolts of cloth and stacking them neatly on the shelves, of the brightness of their clean, unfaded colors.

THE DAYS SETTLED into a routine. Assisting with the customers, Trang Sen was forced to talk cheerfully, to assume a liveliness she was far from feeling. One day she realized that she often went for hours without thinking of the terrible events of the past weeks. And when she thought of them, they seemed like a dream, not a reality she had to relive over and over again. Billings also seemed part of that dream. Perhaps he too would become just a memory. She had insisted he not come to the shop, partly because of her own ambivalent feelings and partly because of her continuing mistrust of Ong Ngoc.

Eventually, she began to miss him, at first in the hopeless, nostalgic way of missing someone who will never come back. She remembered his anxious face, seen through the haze of near-unconsciousness, when he came to take her to the hospital. And after that, his tearful vigil at her bedside.

"You almost died," he told her afterward. It hadn't seemed that way to her, only that she was very tired and wanted to sleep. She had come to think of dying as being blown to bits by bombs, or torn apart by bullets, not such a calm falling into oblivion.

Arthur . . . She gave in to a reverie of remembering. And awoke to a desire to be with him which had the strength of a sharp, physical pain.

"I'm going back," she told Kim Hoa.

The other nodded.

"Shouldn't I?" Trang Sen asked, almost like the submissive child she had never been.

Kim Hoa smiled and shrugged. "Only you can know. But I worry for you, seeing your pain."

Trang Sen looked beyond her, her eyes opaque. "It's also pain to be away from him. Only . . . only . . ." She couldn't bring herself to mention Eldest Brother.

"One could say he was doing what he had to do, and you and Cousin Long did the same. One could even say if someone else had done it, you would never have known, and would have had no chance to help."

Trang Sen stared at Kim Hoa in amazement. "I never thought of that. Of course, it's true. He . . . he gave me the opportunity."

"You should go and be with him. Who knows what will happen later?"

But Trang Sen was somewhat shy about simply reappearing in the apartment. "I'll call him first," she said.

Shakily, she dialed his office, asked for him in her careful English.

His voice too was somewhat shaky when he came on the line. "Trang Sen, nothing wrong, I hope? You and Kenneth are all right?"

"Yes, yes. Arthur." She hurried on before she lost her nerve, "I . . . I want to come back."

He took a deep breath. "Yes, yes, of course. When . . . when, do you think? Now, today?"

She laughed with relief. "Yes, Arthur, when it is convenient."

"It's always convenient. To see you, to be with you again, always convenient. Look, I should be finished here about seven. I'll come by for you then."

"We can go there, Second Son and I."

"No, no, I want to take you. I . . . I couldn't bear to think of you going home without me. Wait for me."

"Yes, Arthur, we'll wait."

"Until tonight then. And Trang Sen?"

"Yes, Arthur?"

"I've missed you so much."

She carefully replaced the receiver and looked up to see Ong Ngoc hastily avert his eyes. *What was that about?* she wondered. *Does he report on me to someone, or,* she suddenly thought with a chill, *on Arthur?* She thought she had been right to insist that Billings stay away.

As she gathered their belongings, it seemed to her they were returning to another world, where everything — the habits, the food, the clothing — was different. It was hardly more than a few blocks.

At seven, she stationed herself outside the door, scanning the street anxiously for Billings's car. At last, after more than an hour, he pulled up to the curb. Suddenly shy, she made a tentative step forward, then stood still and waited for him to come to her.

"Arthur," she greeted him, bowing a little.

He had been prepared to take her in his arms, but her formality reminded him of her reticence and he briefly touched her hand instead. Flustered, he said, "So sorry I'm late. A damned meeting at the last minute. I could have murdered them all." He looked around. "Where's Kenneth? I can't tell you how much I've missed that little fellow."

"I'll get him."

"We should go, I think," she suggested after father and son had greeted each other exuberantly. She glanced imperceptibly in Ong Ngoc's direction, but the tailor appeared to be absorbed in his accounts.

Billings steered them to the car, threw her bundle in the back seat, and went around to the driver's side. He climbed in beside her and put his hand briefly on her knee, glancing toward the shop. Kim Hoa and the children were waving goodby. He waved back, then started the car and edged out into the traffic. Second Son chattered away, covering up his mother's shyness.

At the apartment Trang Sen unlocked the door when Billings handed her the key, stood for a moment inside, as if in a strange and unfamiliar place. Then his arms were around her.

"Thank God you've come back. I was afraid, so afraid. I thought you were angry with me, about the baby."

"I don't want to talk about it, Arthur. I don't ever want to talk about it."

"As long as you're here, as long as you love me, that's all I care about."

Her eyes brimming, she said shakily, "I missed you very much. This morning I knew I had to come back. Oh, Arthur, I do love you." She buried her face in his shoulder and tightened her arms around him.

After a while he raised her head and kissed her long and gently on the lips. "Take your time, honey, take your time. I don't understand all of what's been going on with you lately, but I guess . . ." he stopped, about to mention the baby. "It's enough for me that you're back and want to be here," he said again.

Second Son pulled at his father's leg. "Hold me, Pa-pa."

Billings picked him up and carried him to his room. Trang Sen walked slowly into the kitchen, ran her hand along the white tile counter, went on toward their bedroom. As she passed the door to Second Son's room, she heard father and son deeply engrossed in a conversation about what it had been like to live at the tailor shop, about Second Son's envy of Van Hai's school paraphernalia and the privilege of spending most of the day at school.

"I can go to school someday, can't I?"

"You bet you can," answered Billings. "And it won't be long now, you're getting to be such a big boy."

"Yes, very big. Almost as big as Van Hai." He thought a moment. "Thi Ba is bigger, though. I guess she'll go to school first."

Trang Sen smiled and walked on past the door. She went into their bedroom and looked around. She couldn't avoid the memory of that night she had crouched beside the bed, fearful of being discovered. But she could think about it now with something like detachment. Perhaps it was her fate to overhear and warn Eldest Brother. A good fate after all. So much had been lost, but so much saved as well. She wanted to love Billings now. This was what was left.

He interrupted her reverie by putting his arm around her waist. "Are you happy to be back?"

She nodded.

"But I almost forgot." Taking her hand, he pulled her toward the living room. "When I knew you were coming, I ran over at lunchtime and put a bottle of champagne in the fridge. It should be just right about now."

"No, you sit here and wait," he added as she was going to follow him into the kitchen. "You're the honored guest tonight. Only please God don't be a guest. Let this be home you've returned to."

She heard him whistling as he opened and shut the refrigerator door and clinked glasses around. He reappeared with a frosty bottle and two glasses on a tray.

She shut her eyes as he uncorked the bottle. He laughed.

Handing her a glass, he took his own and touched it to hers.

"To our love," he said. "May it last forever."

"Forever," she repeated and touched her glass to her lips gingerly.

"Come on, drink up."

So she drank until she was in a state of lyrical oblivion, leaning on him and laughing, kissing him and kissing him. He too laughed, holding her gently, feeling that any excess of passion would shatter her fragility, aware of a melancholy that had never been there before and that made her more vulnerable.

And indeed there was an undercurrent of sorrow in her love which would always be there now. She could relegate Eldest Brother's narrow escape and her part in it to her store of memories, along with Second and Third Brothers, her father, Sister Louise and the convent school, her estranged mother — all the things and dreams and people lost. And she did love Arthur Billings again. But always, at those times when she felt that love most deeply, there was a well of tears for all the pain that loving him had brought her.

CHAPTER 10

BLAKE

BILLINGS HAD BROUGHT a stack of Kris Kristofferson records with him when he returned to Saigon. He played them constantly. She also liked the songs. Their melancholy sense of loss haunted her.

> *Don't look so sad, I know it's over*
> *But life goes on and this old world will keep on turning*
> *Let's just be glad we had some time to spend together*
> *There's no need to watch the bridges that we're burning*
> *Lay your head upon my pillow*
> *Hold your warm and tender body close to mine*
> *Hear the whisper of the raindrops blowing soft against*
>   *the window*
> *And make believe you love me one more time*
> *For the good times . . .*
> *Don't say a word about tomorrow or forever*
> *There'll be time enough for sadness when you leave me*
>
>   *. . .*

He had to leave again. Because of the peace agreement, he

explained. There was no need any longer for so many Americans, now that the war had ended.

But everything was the same, food scarce, prices higher than ever, Eldest Brother gone. "It isn't over," she said. "It is only over for the Americans."

He turned away from her, clenching his fists. "Yes," he whispered. "You're right." He took her in his arms then, held her tightly. "I'm so afraid for you."

Cold fear choked her. "Take me with you."

"I can't. You know I can't." He paused. "I'll send you money when I can," he promised. "There'll be guys coming out from time to time who can bring it. If things turn bad, then I don't know. I'll do what I can."

She would go to the tailor shop, stay with Kim Hoa, she told him. He hadn't argued.

"He's gone away forever now," she told Kim Hoa.

Kim Hoa, to cheer her, disagreed.

Trang Sen shook her head. "I know. It's because of what will happen here. Someday soon all the rest of the Americans will leave, for good. It will be necessary."

"You think too much of politics. It's better not to pay attention, like me, an ordinary person."

She tried to take Kim Hoa's advice.

The shop was strangely quiet, with so many Americans gone. Kim Hoa was practical. "We must get more of our own people as customers."

She set Trang Sen to making signs and posters, urged Ong Ngoc to paste them up near the government and military buildings.

The project brought in some business. Ong Ngoc, who had been reluctant at first, seemed eventually to see the value of the effort. Trang Sen thought his changed attitude must reflect new orders. She wondered if he had contact with Eldest Brother, even if Eldest Brother might be giving the orders. The tailor was away more and more often, for longer periods each time. She tried to guess what he might be doing.

BA CAO AND Trang Mai were totally dependent on Trang Sen. Ba Cao, still obeying her eldest son's injunction, persisted in refusing to see her daughter. She doted on her grandson, though, continually begged Kim Hoa to bring him for a visit, even leave him for her to care for. But Trang

Sen refused to be separated from him, even for a few days. She would have liked for them all to be together, commissioned Kim Hoa to urge her mother to join them at the tailor shop. Ba Cao in her turn refused to move.

Kim Hoa returned from her weekly visit to report that her aunt was ill.

"What is it? How ill?"

Kim Hoa shook her head. "She says it's nothing, but she didn't get up to greet me, and was too tired to play with Second Son."

"How does she look? Does she have medicine?"

"Not so good," answered Kim Hoa to the first question. "I've thought she was looking very old for some time now, very thin and her skin seems almost grey. Cousin Mai says for many weeks she has gotten up from the bed only for my visit."

"I must go to her. We must get her some medicine." Trang Sen turned as if to leave immediately.

"Wait," advised Kim Hoa. "Aunt says you aren't to come. I promised to go there again tomorrow, we can see about some medicine and I'll take it to her."

They visited an apothecary shop and obtained the services of an old-style doctor. He shook his head doubtfully after examining Ba Cao and prescribed a regimen of herbal medicines.

"It's difficult to say," he told Kim Hoa. "She's very weak and it is a fierce illness. If I had seen her sooner . . ." He shook his head again.

Trang Sen was frantic. "I have to see her."

"We don't want to upset her. Let me try once more to persuade her."

Trang Sen waited impatiently for Kim Hoa to return the next day. She shook her head. "Aunt says there's no need. Perhaps for a little while we must obey her wish."

"Is Second Sister seeing that she takes the medicine? Is there enough food? Does Ma-ma eat to regain her strength? Do they need money?"

"All is as well as can be. I'll go every day, prepare the medicine and instruct Cousin Mai."

Trang Sen, Kim Hoa and the children were eating lunch when the bell signaled a customer had come in. Trang Sen put down her bowl. "I'll see who it is." She put her hand out to prevent Kim Hoa. "No, no, no need for you to disturb yourself."

His back was to her as she emerged from behind the curtain. She didn't recognize him at first. Then she remembered the owner of that unruly dark hair. "Ong Blake?" she said doubtfully as he turned around, then "You've come back," she finished joyfully.

"Co Sen." He bowed slightly, formal as always.

"When did you get here? How did you know how to find me?" and, in a rush of hopefulness, "Have you seen Arthur?"

He grinned at the flood of questions. "I've seen him. I have a letter for you. Like old times, but this time I brought it all the way myself."

She examined it eagerly, but put it in her pocket. "Later, I can read it later. But how is he? Did you see him often?"

"Not so often. We were both very busy, not much time. But we had a long visit before I left. I can't stay now," he added. "I only came to let you know I'm back." He looked away, continued, "I wanted to make sure you're all right."

She bowed. "I am very grateful. And thank you for bringing the letter."

"May I come for a longer visit, tomorrow? Could we have dinner?"

"Of course, Ong Blake," she said, less stilted. "I'd like that."

She stood feeling the letter in her pocket. She would wait to read it, savor the pleasure of it tucked safely there unopened.

Kim Hoa looked at her in surprise when she returned to the little back room. "Who was it? Has Billins . . . ?"

"Ong Blake is back. He came to find me. And there's a letter from Billins."

"The way you looked, I thought . . ." Kim Hoa left the sentence unfinished.

BILLINGS'S LETTER WAS far from reassuring. It was filled with concern about what was happening in Saigon, Second Son's welfare, their safety. "You can write me," he continued, "and Blake will find a way to get the letter to me. I think it's better not to trust the mail, even the military system."

The letter wasn't very long. "Depend on Blake," he added in closing. "Do whatever he says." Billings had enclosed several hundred U.S. dollars, which she could exchange at the premium rate. "I don't know when I'll be able to send more money." He also included a few Vietnamese bills. "I found them in my shirt pocket." *They won't be much good now*, she thought ruefully. Prices had gone up almost daily since he left.

She showed Kim Hoa the American money. "We can buy more expensive medicine for Ma-ma."

Kim Hoa was amazed. "So much. A very rich man, Billins."

"He says not. He says he may not be able to send more. We must use this carefully."

She waited impatiently to see Blake again. Perhaps he could reassure her, banish that vague fear which now lay always at the back of her mind.

He arrived punctually but somewhat breathless. "I have to become accustomed again to all the crowds. And the crazy driving." He looked around. "Where's Second Son?"

"I'll get him." Trang Sen disappeared behind the curtain and returned holding the boy's hand. He clung to her shyly.

"Do you remember Uncle Blake?"

The boy shook his head and retreated behind her leg.

Blake squatted down and held out his hand. "It's been a long time. You were just a little fellow when I went away. Now you've grown to be quite a young man, I see. I have a message from your Pa-pa," he added.

Second Son peeked out. "Do you?" he mumbled into Trang Sen's skirt.

"Yes, indeed. If you'll shake my hand like the big boy you are, I'll tell you about it. He sent you something too."

Second Son emerged from behind his mother and shook Blake's outstretched hand.

"Greet Uncle the way I taught you."

Second Son made the formal bow of greeting, then sidled confidingly against Blake's knee.

"Did you see Pa-pa? Is he coming back?"

"Not now. But he asked me to help your Ma-ma look after you. Would you like that?"

Second Son nodded. "What did you bring?"

Blake handed him a package.

Second Son tore it open to find a yo-yo, a package of balloons and a tin of Play-doh. He pulled the yo-yo's string and it clattered to the floor.

"Here, let me show you how to work that." Blake took the yo-yo, rewound the string, and sent it into several arabesque-like arcs.

Second Son's eyes widened with delight. "Can I do that?"

"Sure. But you'll have to practice." Blake showed him how to hold the yo-yo and let it out on the string, then bring it back. "There are other things, too. They'll be here soon."

Second Son nodded, still fascinated by the yo-yo.

"Say goodbye to Uncle and ask him to come see you again soon. Then go show your new toys to Van Hai and Thi Ba."

"He could go with us," suggested Blake.

"No need. He's quite happy here."

He guided her out the door. "I'm getting back into my Vietnamese mode. Shall we try my favorite restaurant? Is it as good as ever?"

"I'm not sure, Ong Blake. I haven't been there in a long time."

"Well, let's go see."

"I have news of Susan," he said when they were seated and the food ordered.

"Oh. I've wondered about her. After a few letters, we never wrote anymore. How is she?"

"She's fine, the same as ever. She's back in London now. She asked about you. If you'd like to send a message, she'd be glad to hear from you."

"Yes. I can tell her about Second Son. She'll want to know how he's grown."

"She'll want to know about you, too. I want to know that too."

"I'm fine. I help Ba Chau."

He opened his mouth to say something, then didn't. "How much do you know about what's happening here?" he asked instead.

"Not much. Even the American radio doesn't say much. But I think it's no good. The prices, so high, and very difficult to find food. Many people are poor since the Americans left."

"You're right, it's no good. Did Art say anything about the peace agreement?"

"Only a little. But the war isn't over. How can it be peace? Everything is the same except for the Americans."

"It isn't peace." He was angry. "It's a big farce. One of these days the north is going to send in its regulars and this place will fall apart. It's already falling apart."

"I'm scared, Ong Blake."

He was silent for a few minutes. Then he said, "I promised Art, and you too, that I'd take care of you. I wasn't too eager to come back here, knowing this place is heading for disaster. But I'm glad I'm here, to help

•

you when the time comes."

Remembering Tet, she said, "There'll be nothing you can do. I know what it was like before. Not even Eldest Brother could get to us."

"This time we'll get you out of here, that's all."

"Out? Where out?"

"To America. Where else can you go?"

"But Arthur said —"

"He couldn't take you," he finished the sentence for her. "When the crisis comes, there'll be no choice. I'll get you out, I promise."

She didn't answer. He looked at her anxious face and added, "But who knows? We may be wrong. And for now you're safe and with Ba Chau. Let's not be so gloomy."

He talked then about Billings. He tried to be cheerful, but it wasn't easy.

She told him of her mother's illness.

"What medicine is she taking?"

"Some medicine known to my people. A doctor prescribed it." She used the word for the traditional herbal doctor.

"But shouldn't she see a Western-trained doctor? Perhaps other treatments would help. Has she improved?"

"Ba Chau says she seems to grow weaker."

"We should get her to a real doctor."

"He'll send her to a hospital. She won't go to a hospital."

"But, Co Sen, if it will make her better —"

"A hospital is a terrible place. You don't know."

Blake couldn't convince her to take his advice.

As they prepared to leave the restaurant, he wrote down two phone numbers for her. "Call me if you need anything at all."

He CAME BY the shop frequently. Often he stayed only a few minutes. Sometimes he joined them for a meal, sharing whatever they were eating. When he saw how simple their meals were, he began bringing them meat or a fish, fresh fruit, imported chocolates. "It's my pleasure," he said when they protested, "to repay your kindness."

Ong Ngoc watched him, but so imperceptibly that only Trang Sen noticed. Could Blake be in danger? Are we in danger because he comes here? She wished Blake wouldn't come so often. But she would not hurt his feelings by suggesting that, and she couldn't explain the problem to him. Besides, she wanted to see him.

Kim Hoa visited Trang Sen's mother daily now, seeing to her medicine. She returned from one of these visits to report that Ba Cao was much worse. "The change was quite sudden. Yesterday I thought she was a little better. She asked for you to come."

"Yes, yes, I'll go now."

Trang Sen hurried out of the shop, hailed a cyclo, fidgeted impatiently as it wound its way through the crowded streets. At last they arrived at the familiar market entrance. *Here*, she thought with a stab of nostalgia, *is where I saw Arthur for the first time*. So many other things had happened near this market, at this bus stop.

"I'll get out here." She would walk through the market, call up the memories of those years she lived with her mother and Trang Mai. It seemed a necessary preparation.

She paid her fare and battled her way between the crowded stalls. The discordant sounds of shrill bargaining, the inevitable odors of half-day-old fish entrails and decaying vegetables, decomposing quickly in the fierce dry-season sun, assaulted her. The ubiquitous plastic implements which had replaced the older style tin and iron goods, bolts of black cloth for pants and tunics, all so familiar, really no different from those in the big Central Market on the square across from the Rex Hotel. But here, senses sharpened by her impending encounter, each item, each odor, each sound, penetrated and caused a separate pang of familiarity. Only once before, she remembered, had everything stood out in such sharp detail — the night she had stood in the ruined entrance-way of the school, felt Sister Louise brush past her. Then, the sharpness had been of the contrast between the shadows and the moonlight. Now the harsh midday sun limned unbearably bright colors, seemed to heighten the cacophony of noise and intensify the pungent odors.

Leaving the bright confusion behind her, she approached the familiar alley with dread. Now that the moment had arrived, she wanted to avoid seeing her mother, let Kim Hoa continue to look after her and bring her news, stay one step removed.

Trang Mai was standing at the gate. Trang Sen hardly recognized her. Since she had last seen her, her sister had grown into a slender young girl, the pleasing slimness of her figure apparent beneath the unflattering black pajamas.

"Oh, Sister, I'm so glad you're here. What are we to do?"

Things were serious indeed, thought Trang Sen, for Trang Mai to greet her with such warmth. She laid her hand on her sister's arm and tried to smile. "How is Ma-ma?"

Trang Mai shook her head, tears brimming in her eyes. "She gets worse and worse, no matter what I do. I don't know how to help her."

For the first time, perhaps ever, Trang Sen felt sympathy for her sister. She too, so young, too young, to bear the burdens thrust on them all by this endless war, to be alone and watch her mother slowly sink toward death.

"It's all right. You've done well, to care for her. I'm here now. We'll be together from now on."

Giving Trang Mai a final pat, she went past her through the doorway, standing still for a moment until her eyes adjusted to the dimness.

Ba Cao lay on the bed platform, her head falling back on a thin pillow intended to prop her up. With anguish and pity Trang Sen noted how emaciated she had become, heard the rattle of her shallow breathing.

"Ma-ma." She touched the bony arm.

Ba Cao opened her eyes, tried to sit up.

"No, no, lie back and rest. Can I bring you something? Have you taken the medicine?"

"Medicine no use. Not much time. So tired."

"Don't talk, Ma-ma, just rest. I'll sit here beside you."

Ba Cao closed her eyes. Trang Mai crept in and squatted on the floor beside her sister.

"Will she get better?"

Trang Sen shook her head.

After what seemed a very long time, Ba Cao opened her eyes again. "First Daughter? It wasn't a dream then."

"I'm here, Ma-ma."

"Second Daughter, is she here too?"

"Yes, Ma-ma." Trang Mai's voice was choked with tears.

"The coffin, there's been no time to get a coffin."

"We'll see about it, Ma-ma. But you won't need it, you'll have many long years to look at it and admire it."

Ba Cao ignored Trang Sen's reassurance. "The ancestors' burial ground. What are we to do? Can you take me there?"

"We'll see about that, Ma-ma. Don't worry. We'll take care of all that. But there's no need. You must rest and get well."

Ba Cao shook her head weakly. "No, no, promise me you'll do those things."

"I promise, Ma-ma."

"There is more, more important things."

"Yes, Ma-ma?"

"Second Daughter, take care of Second Daughter."

"I'll take care of her."

"Don't . . . don't let her . . . meet Americans."

"No, Ma-ma, I won't let her become like me."

"You're a good daughter, only so stubborn."

"Yes, Ma-ma."

"Your brothers, find your brothers, find Eldest Son, then he can take care of you. Your father always said he was a dutiful son."

"I'll try, Ma-ma. Don't worry about anything. Just rest."

"Yes, rest. So tired." Ba Cao's head sagged over the edge of the pillow. She closed her eyes.

Trang Mai was weeping, but Trang Sen's feelings were beyond tears. Could this be death, this quiet drifting away? Could death come as one lay on one's bed, no bullet or bomb to hasten it? It seemed unreal, but something infinitely to be longed for, to be beyond the violence and blood and fire of the war, to die in one's bed, however painful that death might be. Could she hope for herself this weariness, sinking into nothingness, which, she suddenly remembered, she too had felt that time she lost the child? Or was all to be consumed in a bright flaming moment of war? For her, and especially for Second Son? No! She would save him, so at the last he could feel the sweet calm of lying down to sleep forever, someday when he was very old.

Trang Mai's sobs brought her back to this reality, this deathbed. She put her arm around her sister. "Hush," she crooned, as she might comfort Second Son, "it's all right, it's going to be all right. You'll see. We mustn't disturb Ma-ma's rest."

Trang Mai sobbed against her sister's shoulder, but at last, with one final heave, she was quiet. Trang Sen patted her gently, repeating in that crooning voice, "It's all right."

Her sister raised her tear-stained face. "What are we to do, Sister, what are we to do?"

"Don't worry. I'll take care of you."

"I don't want her to die!" Trang Mai almost broke into another wail.

"Hush, don't disturb her."

They sat together for a long while, transfixed by the faint movement of Ba Cao's shallow breathing. At last Trang Sen dragged her mind back to practical matters. A coffin, they must buy a coffin. And find out what one did about burial in this city. There was no possibility of taking her back to the village.

"Can you stay with her a little while," she asked Trang Mai, "let me take care of some things?"

Trang Mai pulled away from her. In the old, petulant voice, "You promised not to leave me," she said.

Trang Sen thought a moment. "Then you must do something for me. Go to Cousin Hoa and ask her to come here."

"Should I get the doctor?"

Trang Sen shook her head. "We must prepare for Ma-ma's burial. It's too late for a doctor now. Be brave and do these things I ask."

Trang Mai's face trembled, and Trang Sen prepared herself for another outburst of tears. But instead the girl turned and ran out the door, her hand pressed to her mouth. Trang Sen looked after her, wondering if she was going for Kim Hoa, or was simply wandering tearfully up and down the alley.

Ba Cao opened her eyes. "First Daughter, are you still there, my child?"

"Yes, Ma-ma."

"Second Daughter . . . ?"

"She'll be back soon."

"Some tea . . . mouth so dry."

Trang Sen prepared a diluted version of the medicinal tea and brought it to her mother.

"Drink this, Ma-ma." She lifted her mother's head and held the cup to her lips.

Ba Cao sipped a small amount, swallowed it with difficulty and fell back against Trang Sen's arm. "So weak," she whispered.

"Drink it slowly, a little at a time."

Ba Cao nodded, closing her eyes. When she opened them again, she pushed the tea away. "Must talk. So many things to arrange."

"No need, Ma-ma."

Ba Cao shook her head. "Second Daughter not here?"

"No, Ma-ma, not now."

"The child . . . must be taught, I . . . was too . . . too easy with her. My mistake . . ."

"It's all right, Ma-ma, don't worry about her. I'll take care of her, Kim Hoa and I."

"Yes, my niece, she's . . . a good girl, very dutiful. She'll help."

"She'll be here soon. And Second Sister too."

"Yes . . . they should be here . . ." Ba Cao closed her eyes, then opened them and raised her head a little. "More tea." She reached for the cup.

Trang Sen held it to her lips again.

She swallowed a small amount, then looked at her daughter. "Something . . . I must say to you, too . . . important." She took a breath and continued, "You . . . you're always my favorite, like me when I was young, I thought. I . . . was afraid for you, knew you could make big mistake, and when you did I was very angry, wanted it to be as if you were dead . . ."

"Ma-ma! Don't —"

Her mother held up her hand. "No, must finish . . . you still my favorite, I couldn't change that, couldn't forget. I want you . . . want you to have the mirror. Nothing else left now." She pointed toward a box in the far corner of the bed platform. "In there."

Trang Sen opened the box and took out the metal mirror, its sheen dulled from neglect. She handed it to her mother.

Ba Cao attempted to polish it with the edge of the quilt. "My mother gave it to me, a special gift, for my marriage. Yours now, I give it to you the same way. You have your child now, and your American. It all went wrong. But you're my favorite child, still. You must have it."

Trang Sen took the mirror. Looking at it through a film of tears, she remembered that moment long ago when her mother, her own eyes brimming, had sent her off to Saigon, that brief moment when it seemed her mother loved her. "I never understood, Ma-ma. Eldest Brother, he tried to explain it to me, but I never knew. I only thought . . ." She couldn't go on. At last she said, "I'll keep it, Ma-ma, my treasure always. And I'll try to honor you."

"You will honor me, child. Always my daughter." She dropped her head back on the pillow and closed her eyes. "Rest now . . . more later."

It was too much to think about, this sudden revelation. And there was so much to do, to manage this dying. For a moment she felt unequal to the decisions that lay before her. She longed for Eldest Brother. But Eldest Brother wasn't here. Everything was up to her. She straightened her shoulders, reached out to smooth the faded quilt.

Her mother stirred, opened her eyes, and seemed to start to speak. Then she closed her eyes again with an almost imperceptible sigh. Trang Sen sat beside her until she heard the gate creak, the sound of voices as Trang Mai and the others came up the walk. She rose and went to the door.

"We must be quiet," she told the children. "Grandmother is very tired."

To Kim Hoa she said, "There is much to do, so many arrangements. What happens in this city?"

"When my husband died we went to the temple. They helped us."

"Can you stay here with Ma-ma? Younger Sister and I will see about a coffin. She's very anxious about a coffin."

"She'll be at peace when she sees it."

Trang Mai readily went with Trang Sen, eager for another excuse to avoid the deathbed vigil. They selected the most expensive coffin Trang Sen dared to buy, and arranged to have it delivered. It would be there by the time they themselves returned, the shop-keeper promised.

And as they turned into the alley, they saw the shining oblong box being carried up the walk, Kim Hoa standing at the door to direct its placement.

The commotion awakened Ba Cao. "First Daughter," she called weakly.

"Yes, Ma-ma, I'm here."

Her mother raised her head. "Is it . . . is it the coffin?"

"Yes, Ma-ma."

"A beautiful coffin, I can see. You did well, my child. A good daughter." She closed her eyes, this time with a contented sigh.

"Sit here with her," Trang Sen suggested to Trang Mai.

"I don't want to see her die."

"It's right for us, her children, to be here. I'm also beside her. Sit with me." Trang Sen was firm, and Trang Mai, with a petulant shrug, obeyed. It isn't going to be easy, caring for this sister, thought Trang Sen.

Their mother awoke one last time, looked at her younger daughter, and said in a whisper, "Take care of her."

Trang Sen squeezed her hand in reassurance. The bony fingers closed around hers in a feeble squeeze, then fell open. The shallow breathing stopped and Ba Cao's body was still.

Trang Mai began to wail. Kim Hoa brought the children to honor their grandmother and aunt.

Second Son, sobbing, took refuge in Trang Sen's arms.

"It's all right, it was her fate to die. We must do her honor now by mourning her."

THE NIGHT AFTER the third-day ceremony, a shabby facsimile of the village pattern, attended only by the outsiders Blake and Ong Ngoc, Trang Sen was awake long after the others were sleeping. She got up, retrieved the metal mirror, and sat looking at it in the moonlight. Her tears dropped on it, and she rubbed it with the edge of her tunic. She looked at her face in its dimness, remembering the times as a child when she had examined her reflection, had envied her mother the beautiful mirror. She had always been so angry with her mother. And yet, her mother had made the astounding statement that Trang Sen was her favorite. Even now, she could only remember that one time when it seemed to be so. One day, perhaps, she could return her mother's love. But now, she could only marvel at the revelation of it. She looked once more at the mirror. *I must polish it*, she thought, *make it beautiful and shiny again. I will always keep it so.*

Chapter 11

Fall of a City

... fragile images, often carried next to the heart, or
placed by the side of the bed, are used to refer to that
which historical time has no right to destroy.

Another Way of Telling
John Berger and Jean Mohr

B<small>E READY TO</small> leave at a moment's notice," Blake said, "you and
Second Son."

"What about Ba Chau and the children, and Sister?" she asked.

He shook his head doubtfully. "I can't promise anything."

She almost stomped her foot in her determination. "I won't leave
without them, never!"

At last he promised to do what he could for them also.

Still, there was no change she could pin down, only one sign, which
she took to be ominous — Ong Ngoc disappeared. The tailor had been
gone for weeks. Trang Sen, always watchful of his movements, was sure
there was something different about his absence this time.

Kim Hoa began to worry. "Do you think something has happened to
him?"

"Check the money. Is it all there? Is any of it there?"

Kim Hoa dragged the heavy metal box out and snapped the lock open. "He . . . he's taken all of his part. I divide it every month and put it in here, but his is gone." She looked at Trang Sen. "What do you think it means?"

"He's not coming back. I think it means the shop is yours now. We're probably lucky he didn't take your money, too. I never trusted him."

She remembered the way he sat hunched in the big swivel chair behind his desk, watching everything she did. And telling Eldest Brother about Billings. She started to say something else, then changed her mind. Even now, especially now, it was safer for Kim Hoa to know nothing of Ong Ngoc's duplicity. She was relieved he was gone, relieved not to be under the scrutiny of those furtive eyes. *But,* she thought, *perhaps he's still watching us from somewhere, hidden.* The thought made her shiver, in spite of the sticky heat.

November 11, 2005

Dear Kenneth,

I was surprised to get an email from Randy this week. I hadn't heard from him in a long time, and I didn't know he even knew where I was after I retired from the Service. He said he hadn't heard from you in ages, wondered how you were doing. He sounded a bit sad about losing touch. I told him I'd pass a message along to you. I'll leave it to you whether to write or not.

Well, back to our little project, and the part I hate to remember, the bitter finale of that terribly mistaken war.

By the end of 1974 South Vietnam was falling apart by the minute, and North Vietnam started its big push. A siege-type battle against Phuoc Binh in the Central Highlands was a preview of things to come. South Vietnamese pilots were afraid to drop low enough for accurate bombing or supply drops, so the place was left pretty much to its own defense. The town fell in early January 1975, and after that the North Vietnamese literally tore through the Highlands. By the end of March, the South Vietnamese army was in a full-scale, disorganized retreat toward the coast. Danang fell on March 30.

As you may remember vaguely, I had returned to Saigon in the summer of 1973. From where I sat in the embassy, the eventual outcome was obvious. But our ambassador kept insisting the situation wasn't as bad as it looked. No one could convince him otherwise. I don't know how we could have found a less likely leader for that crucial time. His refusal to face facts meant we essentially abandoned to their fate the Vietnamese who were likely to be persecuted or killed for their involvement with the U.S. Those of us who cared did our best to help as many as we could find ways to escape. Obviously you and your mom and her family were at the top of my list.

A lot of us at the embassy spent those weeks and months on the verge of tears. The stories coming back from Danang and other places along the coast made me physically sick. Evacuation procedures, if they could be graced with that term, were inept to the point of criminality. Ships were crammed with evacuees for days. It was a common thing for Vietnamese soldiers to literally trample women and children to get hold of scarce rations. Panicked Vietnamese tried to force their way on to evacuation planes, some even clinging to the landing gear as the planes were taking off. The desperation was overwhelming.

In the last weeks before the end, President Ford approved a plan to airlift Vietnamese children to the safety of the States. On April 4 one of those flights — with about 250 kids and 60 or so adults — crashed in a rice field next to the airport. About half those on board were killed. To me, that plane going down was one of the worst of all the heartbreaking disasters of that last month. I was out there at the airport when it happened, and for years, a certain smell of gasoline would bring it all back — the burning plane, the rice field on fire, the nauseating stench of seared flesh. If you've never smelled or seen a burning human body, I hope that you never will, Kenneth.

On April 21 the North Vietnamese broke through the last defense line around Saigon. So finally — finally! — Ambassador Martin authorized an evacuation, and we got over 30,000 Vietnamese out of the country. But because he had waited so long the situation was really nasty, with people fighting each other for a chance to leave and American officials resorting to force to try to keep some kind of order.

Martin himself left on April 29. The North Vietnamese had postponed their total takeover for ten days to give the Americans a chance to get out. In the last eighteen hours, after the ambassador left, American helicopters evacuated over 1,000 Americans — journalists, volunteer organization workers and the like — and over 6,000 Vietnamese. Another 75,000 Vietnamese were rescued at sea. God knows how many drowned.

I was assigned to help manage the airlift, so I was one of the last to get out. I don't remember much about those last hours, except that I was overwhelmed with a terrible sense of betrayal. Whatever the rights and

*wrongs of that war, the way we handled the ending of it was beyond
criminal.*

*Well, I finally climbed into a helicopter myself, and I'll never forget
looking down and seeing hundreds of people still outside the embassy
gate, struggling to get in, to get away. We landed on an American
aircraft carrier waiting in the South China Sea. The ship was up to the
gills with Americans and Vietnamese. It was another strange, chaotic
time, on that ship. We sailed to Taiwan, where I was transferred to a
military transport plane that flew me to Washington.*

*Of course, you and your mother were gone before those nightmarish
last few days. I kept hanging on to the knowledge that at least I'd
been able to help a few people who really mattered to me — your mom
and you and what was left of your mother's family. That was about the
only thing that gave me any comfort.*

*So that brings you up to the time you remember pretty well, those
first months and years in the U.S. I'm not going into what happened
between your mom and dad. I know you've talked with Art from time
to time, and hope you've been able to resolve some of the issues that have
bothered you so much. I'll just say one thing, and leave it at that — I was
increasingly bothered by the way he handled his relationship both with
your mother and with you, from the time early on that I learned he had a
family in the States. But out of what I'd call — to put it politely — his
thoughtlessness, came not only my friendship with your mother, but you.
And I'll never be able to feel anything but joy that you're in this world.*

*Enough already. I've made my reservations for Christmas with your
mom. I'm glad you and the family are going to be in Washington too. It will
be good to see you guys. It's been much too long since I caught up with those
growing kids.*

*I'm hoping your mom and I can find time for a little side trip
to New York — as you so well know, my favorite place to be at
Christmastime.*

Until the holiday . . .

Uncle Blake

BLAKE TOLD THEM what was happening outside the city, the safe area
drawing closer and closer to Saigon. As it had been for years, Saigon was
bursting at the seams with refugees. Petty thievery was rampant, as prices
skyrocketed and the markets became ever emptier. For Trang Sen and her

family, the out-of-control inflation was manageable only because Billings continued to send money. Without it, Kim Hoa's savings from the shop would have been quickly depleted. Only U.S. dollars seemed as good as ever.

Where the children were concerned, Trang Sen gave in to anxiety. Every day she waited nervously for Van Hai and Thi Ba to return from school. She insisted that Trang Mai go with them in the morning and return to fetch them home in the afternoon. Only when they were all together in one place could she relax a bit. She was glad Second Son was not yet old enough to go to school.

There was little to do in the shop. "Why not just close it down?" she suggested.

Kim Hoa wouldn't hear of it. "Business will get better again. It always does. Maybe things aren't so gloomy as you think."

Blake came by frequently, his urgency increasing as the days passed. "We've got to find a way to get you out. There's not much time."

Trang Sen went over to the bed platform, pulled a wooden box from the far corner. "I have money, Ong Blake. After you came back, I saved it, because of what you said. It's enough, perhaps, for plane tickets."

He pushed it away. "You'll need it later. But plane tickets are the least of the problems right now. You have no passport, no permits, no permission to leave, or to go to the States."

"But Arthur . . . "

"He's working on it. It isn't easy. Hundreds, thousands, are in the same fix, a half-American child not recognized by America, no legal status."

THE CITY AT last began to feel the effects of the debacle outside it. Remnants of the routed units roamed the streets, harassing civilians, stealing from them, demanding first choice of whatever the depleted markets had to offer. Trang Sen wondered if Fourth Brother was one of them. Had he too become a thief and murderer? Was he dead? *Better dead*, she thought, *than to lose all self-respect, like these*. Their impersonal desperation was far more threatening than the crime born of hunger that had become so common. These angry, shamed men would stop at nothing.

They decided not to send the children to school any longer; they themselves left the shop only when necessary, always with each other or Trang Mai. Kim Hoa gave in and ceased opening the shop daily. "It's only inviting thieves, or worse, to come in," she acknowledged.

Finally, Saigon was sealed off, guards posted at all the incoming roads. A curfew was imposed. The city became strangely calm and silent at night.

Beyond the silence of the darkened nighttime streets, they heard the explosion of distant shells. Trang Sen imagined they came closer as the days went by. She and Kim Hoa laid elaborate plans for meeting places if an attack came and they were separated.

Blake looked wearier and more haggard each time they saw him.

"You're working too hard, Ong Blake."

"No help for it. I only wish it was doing some good."

Though he kept warning them to be ready to leave momentarily, he hadn't yet found a way to get them out. "The Americans," he said, "are going to send in planes to evacuate relatives." But they weren't relatives. "There's a new program starting, to get children out for adoption in the States —"

"Ong Blake! I'd never let anyone have Second Son!"

"No, no, of course not. I only thought, perhaps I could find a way to get the little ones on it, send them to Art, or to someone he suggested. It would just be a scheme to get them out, you see. They'd be quite safe, and waiting for you when you got there."

Trang Sen stared at him skeptically.

"It's only an idea. It might be easier if we don't try to get all of you out together. Don't worry, we'll find a way."

He seemed unconvinced of his own reassuring words. They did little to dispel Trang Sen's growing nervousness.

BLAKE CAME IN, his unruly hair looking even more uncombed than usual, his tie undone and his shirt rumpled and damp. He leaned against the counter, started to speak, then shook his head.

"Ong Blake, what's happened?" *Are they fighting in the city?*

"We've blown it, this time we've really blown it," he muttered in English. "Can't we do anything right, even get a bunch of kids out?"

"What is it?"

"The . . . the plane, with babies . . . crashed." He rubbed his hand roughly across his face. "I was out there, I saw it. It went down in a rice paddy. You could hear the kids screaming, people were trying to get the ones out who were still alive." He choked on the words and covered his face, his shoulders shaking.

Second Son might have been on that plane. Trang Sen felt sick.

"Not your fault," she said at last. It was like Eldest Brother, that long-ago night when he had wept over his inability to stop the terrible course of events. As she had done that other time, she placed her hand on Blake's arm.

"Ong Blake, it wasn't your fault. You could do nothing to stop it." Her voice hardened. "It is the war. All goes wrong in the war, it is my people's fate."

He said nothing, only closed his hand over hers, resting lightly on his arm. He squeezed it briefly, then put it away from him.

They were both silent.

"I think," she said at last, "I don't want Second Son to go on such a plane. I must be with him. Then, if —" She couldn't finish the sentence.

She dreamed of a plane-shaped bomb, hurtling toward the earth, its payload children, all with the face of Second Son. It blasted in a thousand fiery directions, flaming bodies flying everywhere, making the night sky as bright as a red-dawned day. Waking, she crept to where Second Son lay sleeping, placed her hand against his cheek to assure herself he was safe and whole. She left it there until he stirred restlessly.

The dream reawakened in her the panicky fear she had felt during the Tet attack. She walked within that memory waiting for a terrible climax, which would be the horror going on and on, never stopping. She longed to be gone, away from this awful place, to America, where there were no bombs, no rockets, never the sound of shells exploding in the night. But she was afraid of the plane too.

She couldn't eat or sleep. "When will you get us out?" she continually asked Blake.

He shook his head. "You mustn't worry like this, Co Sen. You'll make yourself ill. Then you'll be no help to anyone."

Her lips trembled. "I can't help it. I'm so afraid."

ONE MORNING, VERY early, they were startled by a pounding on the door. Peeping between the slats of the green shutters, Trang Sen saw Blake standing in front of the shop. She hurried down.

"I've made an arrangement for Ba Chau and the children. They'll have to wait for permission to get into the States, no one knows how long, but at least they'll be out of here."

"The children . . ." She scarcely heard the rest of what he said.

"Not Second Son. I knew you'd never consent to that." He looked past her, up the stairs. "Where is she? They'll have to hurry. These people won't wait for anyone."

"I'll get her. What should they take?"

"Not much. But money, she'll need all the money she can get her hands on. Now!" He almost pushed her toward the staircase.

She ran up the stairs and returned with Kim Hoa, who, uncharacteristically, looked nervous and frightened.

"I've gotten space for you on a military plane to Guam, carrying people who've worked for the Americans. I told them you worked for me in the embassy. You've got no papers for the States, but I can get you on the plane. They won't send you back. I'm afraid the set-up there will be pretty bad and you may have to wait quite a while. But it's the best I can do. At least you'll be safe from the war, and you'll eventually get to the States."

Kim Hoa looked dubious. "Would it be better to stay here?"

"No!" Trang Sen almost shouted. "You don't remember what it was like, have you even forgotten what happened to Ong Chau? How can you forget that?"

"I . . . I was thinking perhaps someone might help us. Like . . ."

"No!" Trang Sen hastily intervened, wouldn't let her say Long's name. "We can depend on no one, we must take care of ourselves."

Blake looked from one to the other curiously.

"I'll go then, if you think we must. But I know no English, I'm not clever and educated like you. What will I do there?"

"We'll be together, as always."

Kim Hoa turned to Blake. "What must I do?"

"Only one bundle or suitcase, just the clothes you'll need. Money is more important. If you'll give me whatever you have, I'll go exchange it, give you a chance to get ready, and come back for you."

Kim Hoa pulled out the metal box and handed him its contents. "There's more. But Trang Sen . . . Trang Sen needs it too."

"Art will take care of Co Sen. There may be no way to get money to you. Take all of it."

She began to extract money from several hiding places, while he watched in fascination. Handing Trang Sen a wad, "This I leave with you," she said.

•

Trang Sen protested but finally gave in and took the money.

"This is all," Kim Hoa handed one last bulging envelope to Blake.

He hurried out. Kim Hoa got the children up, and they were waiting when he returned.

"I'll go with you to the plane," said Trang Sen.

Blake shook his head. "You don't know what it's like — mobs of people, all trying to get on without permission. An ugly sight. Better say goodby here."

Trang Mai, who had moved about as if sleepwalking through all of this, began to wail. "I don't want to go! You promised Ma-ma you'd take care of me, Sister. Please don't send me away." She wound her arms around Trang Sen and clung to her tightly.

"Hush, hush. We'll only be separated for a little while. We must do what Ong Blake advises. Be a good girl and go with Cousin Hoa. She needs your help with the little ones. You'll help her, won't you?"

"I don't want to leave you. I'm so afraid."

"Do as we say, and you'll be safe."

"Are you sure?" She turned to Blake. "Is Sister really sure to leave, will we all be together again, safe from the war?"

"Yes. Afterward you'll be much better, no war, no guns, no bombs exploding."

She stood for several moments, the tears still rolling down her cheeks. At last she wiped her eyes. "You're going to make me go, aren't you?"

No one answered. She picked up her small bundle and went to stand beside Kim Hoa. "I'll go with you."

"You're a good girl, to obey when you're so frightened."

Kim Hoa turned to Trang Sen. "Go well and safely."

Trang Sen bowed her head slightly, then grasped Kim Hoa's hand. "You also," she whispered, "you also."

Blake took Thi Ba's hand and motioned the others out ahead of him. He turned to Trang Sen. "Don't leave the shop unless it's absolutely necessary. Keep the door locked. No matter what happens, wait here for me."

Trang Sen nodded, swallowing hard against her fear.

Blake looked over his shoulder at her as he followed the others out. "Now. Lock the door right now."

She nodded, closed the door, turned the key in the lock and slowly went back upstairs. She looked around the room, so desolate with the others gone. It seemed unnaturally, ominously, quiet. She squatted beside Second Son, still sleeping peacefully. Always able to sleep through anything, he had barely stirred during all the commotion.

Blake came back to report that Kim Hoa and the others were safely off. "Now we have to figure out what to do about you."

"Will I go to . . . what did you call that place? . . . Kwan?"

"Guam. I don't know. We may be able to get you directly to the States."

"But we won't be together after all. What will become of them?"

"You'll all be together, I promise. Perhaps not right now."

She had to be satisfied with that.

He went with her to the market, urged her to buy enough for several days. She selected a few chicken wings and some dried shrimp. There was little choice, only rather bedraggled heads of cabbage and bunches of limp mustard greens, a few bananas and mangosteens.

"I don't want you going out by yourself," he said. "Our side is looting, killing, raping."

Back at the shop, he added, "I'll come whenever I can. Meantime, keep the door locked and stay inside." He paused. "I know this is difficult, almost like a prison. Will you be all right?"

She thought of something else. "What if someone tries to break in?"

"I thought of that. We need to move everything out of sight, make it look deserted. That won't be much help if they decide to use it as shelter, but at least it won't attract thieves."

With Kim Hoa gone, she gave way to the eerie feeling that she was waiting for that terrible new year time to reoccur. Instead of moving forward, it seemed to her that time was moving backward, to repeat that awful culmination. But this time there would be no end, no denouement, only shooting, killing, and the agonized screams of the dying, going on and on forever.

She couldn't keep her mind on anything. Mostly she paced aimlessly around the room, Second Son watching her anxiously. Picking up his mother's mood, and perhaps something of the danger lurking behind the unnatural silence of the nighttime streets, he became quiet and withdrawn. Often the two of them sat huddled together in a corner of the bed platform.

Only his needs roused her. Without him, she would have forgotten to eat or sleep. As it was, she could choke down only a few mouthfuls.

SHE COULD STAND it no longer, staring into the empty space that seemed to reflect the images in her own mind. Blake hadn't been there for several days. She had to go where warm, flesh-and-blood people would push against her, convincing her of a present reality. She took Second Son's hand and went out.

The sharpness of the bright sun startled her, the sudden heat took her breath away. She stood blinking, almost turned around to retreat into the dusky shadows of the room that was her prison. But instead she plunged into the swarm of people and vehicles, pushing and shoving along with everyone else. Scantily dressed children eeled through the forest of black-clad legs. She held Second Son's hand more tightly.

In front of the Rex, desperate women dressed Western-style had surrounded two Americans, waving dollars and shrilly begging for plane tickets. Across the street near the Central Market, a tight knot of people were forcing their way toward a vendor. He waved a pair of high-heeled shoes, then lifted up a man's wool suit, shouting prices. "Stereo sold already. Don't wait to buy. Good clothes, liquor, soon nothing left. Hurry, hurry!" He had evidently robbed some American's house.

Even now, she thought, *even now. What do they want with these things, when it will soon be all over and no Americans left?* As she stood dreamlike watching them, the greedy vendor and his greedy customers, she was suddenly aware of a purposeful hand on her elbow. She turned quickly and found herself face to face with Ong Ngoc.

"You!" She almost cried out in fear and surprise. She looked around desperately for some place to run.

"Hush," he said quietly. "I'm not going to hurt you." He forced an opening through the crowd and turned his head. "Come with me."

As if bewitched, she obeyed, lacking the will to resist him. He led her into a small alley, away from the deafening mob. "A message." He forced a small folded piece of paper into her hand. "Destroy it when you've read it."

She took the note from him, quickly put it in her jacket.

"I am instructed," he said formally, "to be sure you are all right. Please assure me, so I can fulfill my obligation."

"Yes, yes. I'm all right, I'm fine. He . . . he mustn't worry."

The lidded eyes slid almost closed. "You must leave. The note advises you."

Before she could say anything else, he turned and slipped quickly through the alley.

She watched until he turned the corner at the far end, closed her hand around the note, and fought her way through the crowd-crammed sidewalk back to the shop.

Mechanically, she fastened the door behind them, released Second Son, and followed him upstairs. She squatted down on the bed platform and pulled the note out. Slowly, almost reluctantly, she unfolded it.

"*Ma chère soeur*," it began, "I can say little, even in this language which too many understand. Perhaps the faithfulness of my friend in bringing it to you, at great danger to himself, will prompt you to think of him more kindly.

"I have known more than you think of the events of these three years. With you, I mourn the passing of our mother. You have been true to your promise to care for our sister. For our brother, there is little anyone can do. He must find his own way, as must you and I.

"Our long and righteous struggle is nearly over. I am sure you rejoice with me that it is so. There will be great danger for those who pinned their fortunes on the Americans. If they value their lives, they will get out. There will be no place for them in the new Vietnam. No one on our side will wish to help them in any way. I think you can see what I mean.

"I can write no more. Your loyalty to our family and to me is always remembered. Go well and safely, my little sister."

The last sentence was in Vietnamese.

She stared at the note. How cold it was in its formality, how stilted the political phrases. This was not her brother, there must be some mistake. Yet she saw that he could not have written any other way. The danger was too great, for all of them, Ong Ngoc included.

Eldest Brother was indeed telling her to go away. If there had been any lingering doubt about what she should do, it was dispelled.

She read the note again. Ong Ngoc had said destroy it. If she found herself trapped here, no way to escape, she would do that. For the moment, she couldn't. She had so little from him, only her memories, and the Sartre book. She picked out the small volume from her meager collection of treasures, reread the note, then folded it carefully and placed it between the pages.

She descended once more into her nightmare world. There was no Eldest Brother to care about her, Kim Hoa was gone, Arthur would never again come back to cheer her. All, all were gone. She alone remained.

Blake, too, it seemed, had disappeared forever. She hadn't seen him in days. She began to worry that something had happened to him.

Listening to the gunfire through the quiet night, she was now certain that the sound was getting closer. What would she do if Blake never came back? How could she hide Second Son? She wished Kim Hoa hadn't left. They should have stayed together. Together they would have been able to think of a plan. But when the soldiers came, no plan did any good. She knew that from the other time.

She huddled close to Second Son. He sat most of the day next to her, the mirror image of her own listlessness. At night they slept beside each other, shuddering at the sound of exploding shells.

IN THE DEADLY silence of an early morning she heard a knock on the door. She picked up Second Son and went downstairs. Beyond caution, she turned the lock and opened the door wide.

"Ong Blake. I've been so scared."

"I'm sorry, so sorry. There's been no time. I've worried and worried about you, I couldn't get here. But I've found a way for you to leave."

"I'm afraid."

He put his hands on her shoulders, held her in a tight grip. "I know, I know. Be brave just a little longer. It will all be over soon." He released her, began to rattle off instructions. "I've gotten you on a Pan Am flight, maybe the last one. It connects with one to Washington. I've talked to Art. He'll be there, waiting for you."

There was a flicker of interest in her eyes. "You've talked with Arthur?"

"Yes, he'll meet your plane, is finding you a place to live. But there isn't much time." He patted his bulging pocket. "These are your plane tickets, and the passports and visas you'll need to get into the States. They're forged papers, for you and Second Son. They'll get you in, and Art will take care of things after that. We've told them you're a nurse, accompanying this child, who is to be adopted. There's money too," he went on. "Do you have the dollars we changed before?"

Numbly, she nodded.

"We must go to the airport now, the plane leaves in two hours. Get the money and anything else you need. Hurry!"

His urgency impelled her. She ran upstairs, Second Son following. He clung to her leg.

"Are you leaving me, Ma-ma?" He wailed in anticipation of impending abandonment.

She knelt and put her arms around him. "No, no, of course not. We're both going, going to Pa-pa."

"Let's stay here, Ma-ma, you and I," he begged.

"Hush. We can't do that. We're going to a new country, to America, on a plane. You'll be with me all the time. Be a good boy now."

He watched her silently as she got the money and put together a small bundle of clothing for him. Some long-forgotten pride led her to change from the black pajamas into a pastel ao dai. Billings would be waiting for her.

Blake took Second Son from her as she came down the stairs. "Is he all right? I heard you up there."

She nodded. "Only afraid."

He guided her out the door.

"Wait," she said as he closed it behind them, "I forgot."

"There's no time now, we have to go."

"No, no, I can't leave without them."

Pulling away from him, she ran back upstairs, Second Son crying after her. She hastily opened the wooden box and took out her mother's mirror and the Sartre book with Long's note inside. *How could I have almost forgotten them?* She looked around the room, whose very walls must bear the imprint of so much of her life — the terrible encounter with Long, the birth of Thi Ba which had affected her so profoundly, her own bare escape from death.

No time now to think about those things. At last fully aware of Blake's urgency, she hurried down the stairs. Blake impatiently propelled her through the door and into the car. He handed Second Son to her, then climbed in under the wheel.

"I'm sorry," she said. "I . . . I couldn't leave these."

He took in the mirror and book, but made no comment.

She stared at the streets, coming alive now as the curfew ended. Motorcycles were being revved up, a vendor uncovered his stand of odds and ends and his meager supply of French loaves, so different from the abundant stacks of a few years past. As they passed the Rex Hotel, cyclo drivers who had slept curled on the seats of their vehicles were stretching awake, some spooning a hasty breakfast of rice soup, others relieving themselves at the edge of the sidewalk.

"I need to explain some things." Blake anxiously noted her white face.

"Tell me what to do."

"Whoever asks, you're taking Second Son to a family in New Jersey. Can you remember that?"

She nodded.

"The name and address are written in your papers. You, too, you are to be his nurse. They've hired you for that. You mustn't tell them you're his mother. That would ruin everything."

"Wouldn't it be better to be his mother?"

"No, no, it's our laws. They wouldn't let you in."

It made no sense, but she hardly knew how to form a question about it, here on the edge of chaos. *What kind of country is this America, that won't let mothers come with their children?*

"The plane stops twice, so you mustn't be frightened. They'll tell you what to do. In San Francisco, you'll have to go through immigration. Just do as they tell you, show them your papers, stick to your story. They won't be expecting you to know any English. Don't say much."

There was only one thing she cared about, Billings would be waiting for her. What happened in between didn't matter, was something to be endured. "Will Arthur surely be there?"

Blake looked at her, his hands clenched on the steering wheel. "Yes. You . . . you understand, don't you, it won't be the same. He . . . will have other . . . ah, people to care for."

In the turmoil of the moment, she had forgotten that. For an instant she felt like she was suffocating. "Yes," she said in a small voice.

He glanced down at Second Son. "Is he likely to give you away?"

She forced herself not to think about what Blake had just said. Turning to Second Son, she said, "We're going to have to pretend. I'm not to be your Ma-ma, you must call me Auntie. Can you do that?"

Second Son's face puckered. "I don't want to pretend!" He started to cry. "I just want you to be my Ma-ma!"

"I'll always be your Ma-ma. Just for a little while, we don't want anyone to know that."

"But they'll take me away from you!"

Blake broke in. "It's just a game for you to play. Wouldn't you like that?"

Second Son gulped back his wail. "I . . . I guess so."

"Good for you. Let's start the game now. Look at your Ma-ma and say 'Auntie'."

"Auntie," said Second Son, then, "like Auntie Hoa."

"Exactly. She's now your Auntie Sen. Now don't forget."

Second Son giggled. "Auntie Sen. It sounds funny."

Trang Sen looked gratefully at Blake. "And you're Little Brother Ko," she said to Second Son.

They were passing the American field hospital where Second Son was born, where Billings took her that other time when she was bleeding away his child. *I'll never be here again, never see these places, these people.* She tried to imagine never returning, struggled not to feel as if, when she stepped on the plane, she would be stepping into nothingness. She could imagine not being here, but she couldn't imagine being anywhere else.

At the airport, it seemed that all of Saigon was trying to leave with her. People were pushing, shouting, waving fistfuls of bills, demanding tickets. Slump-shouldered porters were scurrying around or dragging enormous wagon-loads of luggage. Passengers clutching tickets were trying vainly to check baggage. An unruly mob surrounded the check-in agent.

Blake showed a side she'd never seen in him before. Unlike his gentle, polite self, he pushed people aside, forced his way up to the check-in counter. "Confirmed tickets!" he shouted, slapping them down in front of the harried agent. The man glanced at them, handed them back, and pointed toward the emigration desk.

Someone tried to snatch the tickets from him. He gave the thrusting arm a sharp shove and pushed Trang Sen and Second Son in front of him toward emigration.

Blake talked their way through the complicated procedures, pointing to the New Jersey address, confirming the adoption arrangement. Second Son, who had said nothing since they arrived at the airport, clung to Trang Sen in fright.

At last they were waved toward the door to the tarmac. Blake handed Trang Sen the packet of papers. "Your tickets, here on top. You must show them to get on the bus, and then inside the plane. Hold onto them. You saw what that fellow tried back there."

She took them, but made no move to leave his side.

"You must go to the plane now, Co Sen."

"Come with me," she whispered.

He put his hand on her arm. "I can't. Go now, and if they'll let me, I'll check to see that you're settled in." He cast about for a way to restore her courage. "Don't be afraid, you've been through much worse than this, even living in Saigon." He tried to make her smile. "Just think of it as one of your adventures."

She looked at him solemnly. "Always before I was on the ground. And I knew where I was going."

"I know. When all this is over, there are so many things I want to show you, so you'll like America. But you must go to the plane now."

He nudged her toward the door. Reluctantly she joined the unruly passengers, almost all of them Vietnamese, shoving for a spot on the bus that would take them to the huge plane waiting in the middle of the tarmac. Guards were using their bulky rifles to push back anyone who didn't show a ticket.

Squeezed into the mass of people on the bus, she once more felt as if she were going to suffocate. Children wailed and adults fell against her as the bus pulled, none too gently, away from the terminal. An American woman crushed next to her, blond hair an unruly frizzle, cursed loudly in English. Trang Sen clutched Second Son and her small bundle of possessions against her body and desperately steadied herself as the vehicle lurched to a stop beside the plane.

The passengers disgorged and formed a haphazard line, prodded into a semblance of order by another group of armed guards. The hot sun beat on her bare head as she stood waiting to board the massive 747. *Can anything that big possibly stay in the air?* she wondered nervously. Mingled with that apprehension, she became aware of the humid air she was inhaling, savored the familiarity of the combined odors of acrid woodsmoke, the sicky-sweet and always present opium, and the equally pervasive decaying sewage.

She took a deep breath, as if to hold this air in her lungs, this moment in her memory. Second Son began to fret in the heat, and she picked him up and again shielded him with her body. "Little Ko," she whispered, "remember the game."

Finally she was climbing the metal steps, pushed onward by those behind her. A disheveled American flight attendant looked briefly at her ticket and motioned her through the door. Trang Sen looked around in confusion. So many people, perhaps she would have to stand up the whole way. But another attendant was beckoning her toward the back of the plane and she struggled down the crowded aisle. She was guided to an empty seat. In a daze she climbed over the young Vietnamese woman in the aisle seat and sat down, clasping Second Son tightly.

Blake found her there, her legs tucked under her, staring at the noisy mob of passengers who were scrambling for seats and vying for space in the overhead luggage racks.

"You'll remember what I told you?"

She nodded.

"You mustn't be frightened. You only have to do as they say, and tell them what I told you to say."

"I understand." His anxiety touched her deeply. She reached her hand across her seat companion and he grasped it tightly.

"I wish I could do more for you, go with you to help you. You *will* be all right?"

"Yes." She tried to smile. "You've been a good friend, Ong Blake."

"So little I could do."

A flight attendant was coming down the aisle, rubbing her arm across her hot forehead. "Sir, you have to leave now. We're closing the doors."

Blake squeezed Trang Sen's hand. She pulled it away, bowed her head in a vestige of the formal leave-taking. "Go well and safely, Ong Blake."

"You too, you too." He turned and walked quickly up the aisle. When he reached the first class partition, he looked back and raised his hand against his forehead, as if to tip his hat. Then he was gone. From the window, she could see him walking, head bowed, toward the terminal.

The metal steps were rolled away and she heard a pneumatic wheezing as the plane door closed. With a frightful noise, the engines revved up and they were taxiing down the runway, going faster and faster. Everything became a blur. Suddenly the plane lifted into the air and there was a sickening thud. She trembled, not knowing it was the wheels retracting. As the landscape rocked back and forth, she closed her eyes and clutched Second Son more closely. When she opened them again, she saw nothing but sky, washed to pale blue by the bright sun.

She looked down at Second Son. As the plane's noises settled into one constant hum, he relaxed against her. How long, she wondered, did it take to get to America? She had forgotten to ask.

Chapter 12

Journeys

SHE WAS COLD. She and Second Son sat wrapped around with two of the meager airline blankets.

Her seatmate, at first aloof, was ultimately charmed by Trang Sen's quiet, undemanding endurance. She fumbled in her bag, brought out a western-style sweater and offered it to Trang Sen. "Take it. I have another if I need it."

Trang Sen accepted it gratefully.

"Where are you going in the States?" the woman asked.

"New Jer-sey," answered Trang Sen, pronouncing it carefully.

"Do you have relatives there, you and the boy?"

"He does," she answered briefly. She turned her face toward the window to discourage further conversation.

She never imagined it could take so long to get anywhere. The passengers grew more and more clamorous, the stewardesses less and less accommodating, the plane dirtier. She wrinkled her nose against the stench from the toilets.

When they landed in Guam, she stumbled gratefully toward the door. Guam, where Kim Hoa was. She had a fleeting thought of staying there. But how would she find the others? She gave up the idea and returned to the plane when called to reboard.

Settled once more in the seat that was becoming like a cocoon, she nestled Second Son against her shoulder and sank into a deep, dreamless sleep, for the first time in weeks. She awoke refreshed in spite of being cold once more, anxiously felt Second Son's arms and legs. He was warmer than she. She pulled the borrowed sweater more tightly around her and looked out the window. The clouds were like what she imagined snow-covered mountains to be. The sun was turning them pale gold at the edges. It was hard to believe they were suspended between sun and sea, with nothing but air to hold them up. She shivered at the thought, discovered she was exhilarated, no longer fearful.

Blake's elaborate deception of her identity no longer seemed so urgent. She turned to her neighbor, who was staring past her out the window.

"Do you know where we are?"

The young woman smiled. "I'm not sure exactly, over the Pacific Ocean, somewhere between Guam and California."

"Have you been to America before?"

"My husband is an American. He was transferred back to the States, to California, four years ago. I hadn't been back home until now. I came to take my mother to live with us, but she wouldn't come." She sighed. "Now, I don't know . . . a wasted trip. My husband didn't want me to do this anyway. He thought it was too dangerous. I suppose it was, but when you're in the middle of it, you don't think about it."

Trang Sen nodded. "Only I was scared," she admitted. "I kept remembering the year of the monkey."

Second Son woke up. Trang Sen pointed out the window, showed him the clouds, and explained that the ocean was beneath them.

His eyes grew wide. "Will we come down to the earth again, Ma-ma?"

"Hush," she whispered.

Her seatmate placed a gentle hand on her arm. "It's all right. I guessed already that you are his mother. I'll say nothing to anyone. I can give you some advice, though. You only have to be very careful in San Francisco, when the immigration people will ask you questions. After that, they won't bother you anymore this trip. Later, there may be difficulty, but you perhaps have a plan for that. And, then, what can they do anyway? They can't send you back."

HER HEART POUNDED as she stood in line at the immigration booth.

When her turn came, the man verified her name and where she was going, began asking questions about the adoption arrangements. Trang Sen smiled and shrugged helplessly. "So sorry, not understand."

It was not totally untrue. He was talking so fast, and it had been so long since she had heard people speaking English that she could only catch part of what he was saying. At last he gave up, stamped her papers and motioned her through.

She stood dazed for a moment, looking around at the sterile walls, the knots of bewildered people, bundles and bags piled on the floor beside them. *America*, she thought.

After some false starts, she found her way to her gate. Hurrying down the endless, crowded passageways, she discovered that her knees were weak and shaky. Was she going to be ill, on her first day in America? She shifted Second Son to her other hip and plodded on, feeling small and incapable next to the tall Americans who kept rushing past her. On the plane at last, she sank gratefully into her seat.

This time, except for the two of them, the passengers were all Americans. In her weariness, the strident sounds of their chatter grated on her. The big man sitting next to her seemed to spill over into her seat, hogging the armrest and apparently oblivious of her and Second Son. Soon after they were in the air a meal was served. She examined the foil-wrapped contents on the tray, was repulsed by the strong smell of beefy gravy and the soggy noodles. Shaking her head, she pushed the tray aside, but gave Second Son a roll to nibble on.

She was restless with the enforced waiting and impatient with Second Son, who was weary and irritable.

"Will we be there, soon, Ma-ma?" he kept asking.

"Soon, soon."

"When, Ma-ma, when?"

At last he fell asleep. In all the long hours she had been moving steadily toward him, she had hardly thought of Billings. But now that she was really in America, he filled her mind. *Will I remember what he looks like, will he be pleased with Second Son?* She sank into a half sleeping, half waking fantasy. Staring blankly at the clouds, she saw Billings running toward her, could almost feel his arms around her. Nothing mattered, not the war, not Blake, not Kim Hoa and the others, only to be with him.

The flight attendant's announcement awoke her. She didn't understand the words, garbled by the loudspeaker, but she saw that the other passengers were getting their things together. They must be in Washington. Billings was waiting for her right now. Self-consciously, she smoothed the skirt of her ao dai. She looked at it ruefully. After all the hours on the plane, it was hopelessly rumpled.

Awakening Second Son, she straightened his clothes and ran her fingers across his hair. "You'll soon see Pa-pa," she whispered.

The plane slowly taxied to the gate, the doors were opened, and the passengers moved at a snail's pace up the aisle. *Hurry, hurry,* she thought, *he'll think we're not here after all. What if I can't find him?* Somewhere, somewhere, Blake had given her a phone number. *Where did I put it? What will I do, all alone with Second Son?*

She emerged into the waiting lounge, her head down. She couldn't bear to look for him.

He ran to them, and caught them both in a massive hug.

Glancing around with embarrassment, she pulled away from him.

He laughed. "No need for that here."

He took Second Son from her, indicated her small bag. "How much luggage?"

"Only this."

Outside the airport she shivered as the sharp wind hit her. "So cold."

"Yes, April isn't a very warm month here." He put his arm around her.

As she had in the San Francisco airport, she felt assaulted — by all the people, the rushing traffic, the bright sun which seemed to hold no warmth. "The Americans are so tall." Again, she felt very small.

He settled them in the car and climbed in on the driver's side. "Are you terribly tired?"

"Yes, no, I don't know. So long on the plane. I don't know how many hours."

"Almost twenty-four, a whole day and night. Let's see, Wednesday afternoon here, it will be Thursday morning, very early, in Saigon now."

"How can that be? We left Wednesday morning, and all those hours went by."

"A very complicated thing called the International Dateline."

He told her he had rented them an apartment, bought some food. "But we can stop for something to eat now." He looked down at her rumpled ao dai. "What about clothes?"

"Only this. It doesn't matter."

"No, we must get you some warm clothes. That should be the first thing."

He started the car, eased it into the line to the collection gate. "A bad time to be at the airport. The beginning of rush hour."

"Rush hour." She tried to make sense of the Vietnamese words. "Oh, I see, many cars on the street. But, Arthur, it's all so quiet, no blowing of the horns."

He laughed. "Yes, a big difference from Saigon, wouldn't you say?"

She laughed too, not quite sure why it was funny.

The next few hours were a confused jumble. He took her to a store called Penney's, larger than she had ever seen. They went first to find clothes for her, afterward for Second Son. Billings bought her slacks, tops, a jacket, and a pair of loafers.

She wiggled her toes gingerly inside the shoes. "They hurt, Arthur. My toes are all pushed together."

"They're the right size. You'll get accustomed to them, and you need them for the warmth." He suggested she wear one of the new outfits.

She had to admit she was more comfortable in the jacket and the warmer slacks.

The sun had turned to a bright orange ball, low in the sky, when they came out of the store. In its fading light the brick buildings were deep vermilion. *Everything here is sharp and hard*, she thought, *all angles. The people too, and what they wear.* She looked at Billings's profile, at his hands moving from the steering wheel to the gear shift and turn signal lever. He too seemed angular. She suddenly felt as if she was sitting beside a stranger.

He glanced at her. "I think we'll try a Chinese restaurant. There's nothing Vietnamese around here, or I'd take you there. Chinese will be best, don't you think? Not so strange for your first real meal in America."

She nodded, not knowing what the choices were.

He parked in front of a small restaurant not far from Penney's. The cars zipped past. Standing on the edge of the sidewalk, she clung tightly to Second Son's hand.

The restaurant was dim, lit by small lamps covered with red Chinese lanterns above each table. It smelled of stale sesame oil and dried shrimp. She wrinkled her nose appreciatively.

"It's a good place, Arthur, a good place to bring us." She wrapped her hands gratefully around the warm teacup. She was hungry. "Lots of rice," she told him. "Ask for lots of rice."

He laughed and communicated this in English to the waiter, who smiled. She then realized the waiter too was speaking English, but it was impossible to understand.

"The English here sounds very strange," she observed after the waiter left. "I can't understand any of it."

"You will. It just takes time."

"Is this near where we're to live?"

"Not too far, maybe a couple of miles."

She asked about Kim Hoa.

"So far I've had no luck. I finally located the camp where they say she's living, but her name isn't on any of the lists."

"Second Sister is with her. I promised Ma-ma . . ."

"I know, I know. I'll find them and get them here, one way or the other. Right now, you've no idea how confused things are. Once this is all over, it'll be easier to locate people."

His promise didn't ease her anxiety.

He drove them to the apartment. The headlights streaking past were even more disconcerting than the daytime traffic. Though not chaotic like Saigon streets, these seemed more hazardous.

Billings opened the door and turned on a light. They entered a small living room, furnished with a sofa and a couple of chairs, one of which was upholstered, the other straight-backed. Two small end tables completed the furnishing. He led them through to the bedroom, off which opened a tiny bathroom. Next to the double bed was a narrow roll-away for Second Son. The only other furniture was a chest of drawers against the wall next to the closet door.

In the kitchen he opened cupboards and the refrigerator, stocked with a few necessities, to show her what was there — rice, chicken, fresh greens. She picked up a small bottle and examined the label, opened it and sniffed. Fish sauce, Thai style. Not the same, but it would do.

"I hope this will be okay," he said. "There wasn't much time to get the place set up."

"Are we going to stay here, Pa-pa?" asked Second Son.

"Yes, you and your Ma-ma."

•

"You, too?" he persisted.

Billings didn't answer.

Trang Sen realized that, aside from that first embrace, and his arm around her for warmth, he hadn't touched her. She felt cold inside. "Do you still love me, Arthur?"

"Of course."

"Will you stay here tonight?"

"Not tonight, I can't. She . . . they're expecting me back."

She stood in front of him, her head down, her hands twisted together. "You'd rather we stayed in Saigon."

"That's not true. I could never have let you stay there, with what was happening."

She was near tears. She looked at her unfamiliar clothes. "It's like these clothes and this place, America. All so new and strange. You too. You are strange. Here, I think you don't love us."

"It's only that I haven't had time to figure this all out."

She didn't answer.

He turned toward the door. Second Son ran to him. "Are you leaving us, Pa-pa?"

Billings knelt on one knee and put his arm around him. "I'll be back tomorrow, son."

Second Son wrapped his arms around his father. "I love you, Pa-pa."

Billings held him tightly, pressed his face against Second Son's head. "I love you too," he whispered, "I love you too."

At last he stood up. Not looking at Trang Sen, he hurried out.

She stared at the blank door, stumbled to the sofa and lay face down. Second Son came and nudged her gently, then moved away, saying nothing. When at last she raised up, he had fallen asleep on the floor. She picked him up and took him into the bedroom. The apartment felt cold. She decided to leave his clothes on for warmth and tucked a blanket tightly around him.

Sitting on the edge of the bed, she felt utterly spent. Her hands were shaking. She lay down, but instead of sleeping, her mind whirled with thoughts about this new Billings. *What am I to do?* A cold chill ran over her. *Have we come all this way, for him to abandon us?*

She finally slept, worn out both from the trip and Billings's apparent indifference. *She was running toward him, all excitement and anticipation, only to find an unknown person, his face all right angles, looking unsmiling at her, his hand out rigid and at right angles too, to repulse her.* In her dream she couldn't understand. *"You told me it's all right to embrace here in America,"* she pleaded. *"Not for you,"* he answered, *"never for you."* She awoke in the cold darkness and pulled the blanket more closely around her.

She couldn't sleep enough. Once, when Second Son woke up, she got up and fixed him something to eat. Then both slept again.

A knock on the door awakened her. She stumbled toward it, opened it to Billings. "Arthur," she mumbled. "I dreamed about you, dreamed you didn't come back."

He looked at her uncombed hair and disheveled clothes, her sleep-fogged eyes. "Trang Sen, I'm so glad you're here, so glad."

"What are we to do, Arthur?" she asked, still sleepily.

"Well, I thought we'd have some supper, then I'll drive you into Washington, show you a bit of the city. Would you like that?"

"But that's not what I meant . . ."

"You aren't to worry about anything. Let me do the worrying, okay?"

He went into the kitchen. She followed him and stood at the door watching him open and shut the cabinets. "Can you fix us something to eat?"

She nodded.

"I didn't know quite what to buy. We should do that tonight too, go to the Giant so you can pick out what you need. And we should get another key made, for me."

"The giant?"

"A supermarket, where you buy groceries."

It was a long time before she realized that "giant" wasn't what all the big supermarkets were called.

Second Son came in rubbing his eyes. Billings scooped him up in a tight hug.

"Will you stay with us, Pa-pa?"

"For a while, son. I thought we'd go riding after supper. What do you think?"

"Yes, Pa-pa. I like riding in the car."

He seemed more like the Billings she remembered as he played with Second Son and ate the Vietnamese dishes with obvious appreciation.

•

"I've missed the food."

She said nothing.

He reached his hand across the table and placed it over hers. "You too, I've missed you too."

The Giant was as confusing as Penney's had been.

"Think of it as a big indoor market," he suggested. "Only here, you pay for everything in one place."

"Perhaps there's a small store somewhere. It would be much better."

"There's one not far from the apartment, at the corner of Pershing and Glebe Road. We passed it last night. This has more different kinds of food."

He drove them into the city, around the Tidal Basin and past the Capitol, white marble gleaming. "Too bad you weren't here a week or so ago when the cherry trees were in bloom."

But she was trying to figure out the geography. "Arthur, aren't we living in Washington, in the apartment?"

"The apartment is in Virginia. When we crossed the river, we came into the city. It's like . . . like" — he tried to think of a comparison — "well, it's something like Saigon and Cholon."

He noticed Second Son nodding on her lap. "We'd better get this little fellow home."

He carried the boy in and put him to bed, tucking the blanket carefully around him.

In the living room, Trang Sen was staring absently out the window, her back to him, somewhat square and shapeless in her new jacket.

He put his arms around her from behind. "I hardly know you in your new clothes. Is it the same Trang Sen?"

"It is the same. Are you the same, Arthur? It seems it is you who have changed."

He turned her to face him, looked into the depthless brown eyes. "The same, always the same."

"Then why —" she began, but he stopped her with his lips.

"I love you," he whispered, "so much, so much."

"I too, Arthur, I too. Only —"

"Hush, no 'onlys'."

She gave in finally to his kisses, allowed him to lead her to the couch.

"Arthur, Arthur, what are we to do?" Even as she asked the question, she kissed him with increasing frenzy, pressed her body against his as he fumbled with her buttons and zippers.

In the calm aftermath of love, staring at his face, again she thought his features were sharper here. With her finger, she traced the outline of his jaw.

He opened his eyes, smiled at her. "Trang Sen, Trang Sen, so beautiful." He caught her hand in his and kissed her again, this time gently.

She sighed and leaned against him. "I missed you, Arthur."

"I missed you, so much. I always miss you."

"What are we to do, Arthur?"

He shook his head. "I'll work something out. I don't want you to think about it."

She wanted to ask how she could avoid thinking about it.

Suddenly he sat up, looked at his watch. "I didn't realize what time it was. I have to go."

She tried to pull him back down beside her. "Don't go yet."

He pushed her away, pulled on his clothes and ran a comb through his hair. Picking up his glasses, he rubbed them across his shirt.

She watched him, her heart constricting at the familiar gesture. "I love you, Arthur."

"Yes, yes, well, I'll come back when I can. Will you be okay for a few days?" He was standing at the door, his hand on the knob.

She got up and went over to him, tried to put her arms around him.

He stiffened. "I really must go, Trang Sen."

She backed away. In the next instant he was gone, leaving her once more staring at the closed door.

She went into the bedroom and lay down, weary with anxiety. *Why did we come here? We should have stayed in Saigon. But we couldn't stay there either. There's no place anywhere for us. Arthur doesn't want us, and nobody in Vietnam wants us. Eldest Brother said that.*

SHE WAS AFRAID to go out, afraid of the tall, seemingly unfriendly people, of her inability to speak English. She hovered between the reality of this new world and the shadows of the one she had left behind. Sometimes she woke in the night thinking she heard the sound of shells exploding. Then she remembered there were no shells here. She dreamed of her father, dead in the rice paddy, of that frightful time of Tet, of a gasoline-drenched saffron robe. She awoke sobbing, muffled a scream so Second Son wouldn't hear.

Billings came in, sat down without greeting her and passed his hand over his face. He took off his glasses, leaned his head back and closed his eyes.

"Arthur." She treated him gingerly, never knowing whether he was going to be his old loving self or the cold American stranger.

He rubbed his hand across his eyes again, then methodically polished his glasses on his shirt. He put them on, sat gravely looking at her. "It's over." He reached his hand to her.

She sat down beside him and he put his arms around her. "Thank God you got out, at least one thing salvaged."

His words awakened an echo from another time, Eldest Brother saying, *You perhaps can make the blood and pain worthwhile, you and others like you.* Now she had turned her back on Eldest Brother's dream and she was here, somehow imprisoned, in America.

"I shouldn't have come here. No one wants me here."

He held her more tightly. "I want you here, you're the one who's given meaning to my life these past few years, only you. I'll tell you something, all day, the reports kept coming in, some of us who had been over there were grabbing the stuff as it came off the wire. All day, I only wanted to be with you. I kept thinking of you, it was all I could think about. I thought the day would never end, so I could come to you. You don't know."

Hardly hearing what he said, she gave herself up to the images flashing through her mind, all pleasant, for the moment the pain and war blocked out. She was once again at the school, and there was Sister Louise; she stood beside the river bank, tongue-tied with shyness before a tall, light-skinned stranger; Eldest Brother sat across the table in a small French restaurant. All, all gone, forever. She began to cry.

Once started, she couldn't stop. "I . . . I want to go home."

"Home is here with me," he whispered.

"I never should have come. You don't want me here, I'll never see Kim Hoa again. We should have stayed, like she said."

He was dismayed by her apparently endless grief. "I do want you, I do want you. And I'll find Ba Chau. Try to stop crying, honey."

At last she quieted down. But, the tears still running down her face, "I should never have left," she repeated.

"Listen to me, Trang Sen. There was no place for you there. What would you have done, what would Kenneth have done? You had to leave."

"No place for us here either. No place anywhere." She began to cry again.

"Hush, hush, you're just exhausted. This whole thing has been too much for you. I never realized . . ."

She looked up at him, his face blurred by her tears. "Don't leave me, Arthur, please don't leave me." Then she buried her head against his shoulder.

"No, no, I won't. But I have to go away, only for a few minutes, make some phone calls." He put his hand under her chin and lifted her head to face him. "Will you be okay? I'll come right back, I promise." He touched her wet cheek, wiped away the tears with his finger.

When he had gone, she thought of Eldest Brother. He too had told her to leave. *He didn't want me, just as Arthur doesn't want me.* The tears welled up again.

Second Son, who had stood in the bedroom doorway watching, came to her and timidly touched her. "Don't cry again, Ma-ma, please don't cry. I don't like it when you cry." He crawled into her lap.

She rocked him back and forth. "Whatever happens, I have you. I didn't mean to upset you."

Billings returned, sat down beside them.

Second Son looked at him gravely. "Will you stay with us, Pa-pa? Will you help Ma-ma? She's very sad."

"Yes, son, I'll help."

SHE REMEMBERED BLAKE. "Arthur, what about Ong Blake? Is he all right? Where is he?"

"On his way home, with the rest of the Embassy. I haven't heard from him, but I'm sure he's all right."

She was ashamed that it had taken her so long to ask.

One morning she could no longer endure the closed up apartment, with no air coming in. She had to open a window, no matter how cold it was. To her surprise, the light breeze was quite warm.

"We must go out," she said to Second Son. "Summer has come perhaps."

They walked along the street, Second Son sometimes running ahead.

She avoided eye contact when anyone passed, or when they encountered an occasional workman. Here in America, someone was always digging in the street. She had noticed that before, in the car with Billings. She was surprised there were so few cars or people. She hadn't been out at this time of day, only in the late afternoon or evening with Billings. Then everyone was hurrying about, in cars or on foot. She liked this better.

Second Son was half a block away, squatting on the ground in front of a small animal that looked like a rat with a bushy tail. Horrified, she rushed to him, snatched him up. Startled, the animal scurried up a tree.

"A rat," she hissed. "You know you mustn't play with rats. Filthy!"

"It didn't look like a rat, Ma-ma."

"An American rat. The same thing, only with a different tail."

Now the quiet street, which had seemed almost friendly, became ominous. She noticed more of the animals. She almost ran back to the apartment, dragging a reluctant Second Son.

Billings laughed at her. "They're squirrels. Some get quite tame. I doubt even the tamest would let Ken touch it, though. There's nothing to worry about. Let him play with them."

"Sqwair-rrel." She curled her tongue around the strange sound. "Are you sure they're not rats?"

"I'm sure they're not dangerous. People even feed them."

The weather stayed warm. Unable to resist the soft breeze coming through the window she now kept open, she ventured out again. This time she went all the way to the intersection of Pershing and Glebe Road. She wandered along the sidewalk, looking in the windows of the little shops, too shy to go inside. All the stores in America aren't so big then, she thought. Outside the Buckingham Theater she and Second Son examined the posters.

"Are there stories inside, Ma-ma?"

"Yes, the pictures move." She remembered the first time Billings had taken her to a movie. So long ago.

Second Son tugged at her sleeve. "Can we see them, Ma-ma?"

"Not now, but sometime." Before Billings had gone away the first time, they had gone to movies from time to time and taken Second Son, then a small baby. "You went to movies," she told him, "when you were very little, too little to remember."

Across Glebe Road was the food market Billings had mentioned. Vegetables and fruits were displayed on the sidewalk in front. She looked dubiously at the cars rushing past. At last she grasped Second Son's hand tightly, waited for the light to change, and ran across.

She examined the fresh greens and brightly colored fruit. Recollecting exchange rates, she didn't think they were expensive. The clerk had come to the door and was looking at her. Hastily, she bowed, then felt foolish.

"Can I help you, lady?"

She froze, not sure she understood and unable to think of any English response. At last she said, "Very good fruit. I not buy today." Overcome with embarrassment, she hastily bowed again and backed out toward the street. She waited impatiently for the traffic to halt, resisting with difficulty the impulse to plunge between the moving cars.

Her heart was pounding by the time she reached the apartment. She closed the door and locked it, then stood leaning against it. She felt as if she had escaped some threat. *What is wrong with me*, she asked herself, near despair. *I can speak English, I've been around Americans, even worked for them. Why am I so afraid?*

Billings was no help. "Just pay attention to what they're saying, and think about what you want to say, then say it. That's all. You're making too big a thing of it."

Her eyes filled with tears of frustration. "Not so easy. What am I going to do? I can't talk with anybody here, only you."

"And that isn't enough?" He tweaked her ear.

She refused to be jollied out of her anxiety. "It's important."

She encountered some of the other Vietnamese tenants. The women looked with disapproval at Second Son's Caucasian features.

Second Son was lonely. He began to ask after Van Hai and Thi Ba. "When are they coming, Ma-ma? You said they would be here too."

"They will be, soon I hope. I miss them too."

Mostly to give him something to do, she began to teach him English. Billings approved and helped by talking with him and bringing simple books for her to read to him. "You'll be starting school in the fall," he told his son. "The teachers will expect you to speak English."

Trang Sen hadn't thought of that. She looked at Billings with a worried frown. "What will we do? Where is the school?"

"I'm not sure. I'll have to look into that."

SUDDENLY IT WAS very hot, the apartment stifling. She didn't mind the heat, but there was no way to get air into the small rooms. She left the door open until Billings discovered it one evening.

"You must never do that, understand?" His voice was so harsh it frightened her.

"I'm sorry," she mumbled, her head down.

"It's very dangerous. You don't know. Anyone could come in, rape you or murder you both. Don't ever stay in here with the door unlocked. And don't leave it unlocked when you go out either."

She didn't dare tell him she had been doing that too.

The next time he came, he brought her an electric fan.

The incessant droning of the fan, oscillating back and forth in its circumscribed orbit, mirrored her life. Second Son was learning English very quickly, but she was still unable to understand or respond to the simplest comments. That frightened her and made her feel more and more a stranger. Her only goal was waiting for Billings's next visit. He was tender and gentle with her, but continued to refuse to answer when she asked what she thought was a very simple question, like what he was going to do about them.

He told her Blake was back.

"Oh, why didn't he come with you?"

"I didn't think about asking him. I gave him the address, so he'll probably be by. He was very anxious to be sure you're all right."

"Tell him to come soon."

A few days later there was a knock on the door as she was fixing lunch. Unaccustomed to anyone stopping by other than Billings, who always let himself in, she opened the door a crack and cautiously peered out.

"Ong Blake!" She opened the door wide and bowed in greeting.

He took her hand, held it tightly in both his own. "Trang Sen, so good to see you."

She was a little startled, but, "Come in, come in," she said, withdrawing her hand.

Second Son, peeping around the kitchen door, ran to him. "Uncle Blake!" He stopped short, remembering his manners, and bowed the way he had been taught.

Blake squatted down and hugged the boy. "So tell me, do you like America?"

Second Son nodded, began babbling away.

Trang Sen laughed. "Ong Blake would perhaps like to sit down and have a cup of tea before hearing all that."

Blake shook his head. "No tea. It's much too hot. Some water and a little ice would be fine."

He followed her to the kitchen, stood in the door watching as she settled Second Son at the table with his bowl of noodles. "Do you want some noodles, Ong Blake? We have plenty."

"No, thanks. But look, no more of this Ong Blake. In this country you may as well get accustomed to our ways. We're very informal."

She blushed a little. "Yes, very strange." She added, "I always liked you best because you treated me properly. I thought most of Arthur's friends were rude. Now I think they just didn't understand, they didn't mean to be rude or disrespectful."

"Most of them didn't, with a few exceptions we won't try to recall."

Accepting the glass she handed him, he went over to the couch. She sat down in the chair and curled her legs under her.

"Still wearing the ao dai. You don't seem very Americanized."

"Only because it's hot. I wear the clothes Arthur bought me when I go out. People stare at me in the ao dai and I don't like that."

"So how's the English?" he asked, speaking it.

"Not good," she answered in Vietnamese. "I can't understand anything, and I can't remember how to say anything."

"This will never do. Does Art help you?"

"Oh, yes, he takes me to the market, helps me buy whatever we need."

"That wasn't what I meant. That in fact may not be helping you at all. Does he help with the English?"

She shook her head. "He helps Second Son. I've been teaching him, because he has to go to school, and Arthur helps him with sentences and brings books for me to read to him."

He set his glass down and slapped his hand against his knee. "All right. We'll start right now with a program guaranteed to have you speaking English like a native in one short week. Tell me about your plane trip, what you think about America. All in English, please."

She laughed. "In a week," she said, disbelieving, in Vietnamese.

"No, no." He raised his hand as if to stop her. "No more Vietnamese."

She struggled to find words to describe the experiences of the past few months. Second Son came in, listened in fascination.

"But Ong Blake . . . ah, Blake," she amended self-consciously, "you

●

too. How has it been with you? Very terrible, I think."

"Well, it's not something I'd want to go through again. The worst part was knowing how irresponsible we were." He looked down at his hands, clenched together. "You don't know. We did so little to help people who needed to get out. I'm ashamed to sit here and tell you how we blundered."

"But you helped all of us get out."

"I know, but that was a . . . a drop in the bucket. And for most of the people who were helped, it happened the same way — somebody who knew them pulled some strings, lied or cheated, to get them on a plane or boat. What I meant was, there was no program set up to evacuate as many as possible. That should have been done months earlier. As it was, it was a mess." He shook his head. "Well, it's all behind us now. I'm glad you're here, on this side of the Pacific. What's the news of Ba Chau?"

"Don't know. Arthur says it's very confusing to find them."

"I don't like to think of them being stuck in those camps all this time."

"I wish they were here. It would be better if Ba Chau was here."

"Has it been difficult, Trang Sen?"

"Arthur is very good to me."

"It's not enough, is it?"

She didn't answer.

He reached over and patted her hand. "One of these days it'll all be worked out. I promise not to ask any more questions you don't want to answer. Well," he continued, "the most important thing is to find Ba Chau and the children and bring them here. I should have some time to work on that while the Service decides what to do with me. Right now, though, why don't you come for a ride in my new car? First thing I did when I got here was buy a car." He laughed. "After that, I decided I really did need a place to live."

He drove them to a Baskin-Robbins, insisted that she do the ordering, which she managed more easily than she had expected to. Then he drove along the river, past the Pentagon — "Art works there, did he show you?" — stopped at a picnic area from which they could see the marble monuments on the other side of the river, chalky white in the hazy sun.

Blake's arrival encouraged her to concentrate on her English. She began to notice the comments and conversations of people on the street, in the apartment complex, in the stores. Shamelessly, she eavesdropped.

She picked up new words. When she didn't understand, she asked Billings or Blake. Forcing herself to overcome her fear, she went into Pershing Market, bought some things, and exchanged a few sentences with the clerk, the same one who had stood at the door watching her that other day. She realized he had difficulty understanding her. In a flash of insight, she understood that his problem was the same as hers. "Please to listen carefully," she advised him. "Sorry I'm not so easy to understand." She smiled at him. "I get better soon, okay?"

He accepted her advice good-humoredly. "You do that, little lady."

Blake took her to the county library on Quincy, a few blocks from the apartment. He helped her select books both for her and for Second Son.

He showed her the magazine rack in the Giant, bought her a copy of *Time*. He picked up a copy of *Glamour*. "Would you like this, to learn about American fashions?"

She blushed and looked down somewhat self-consciously at her clothes. "These are fine."

"No, no, I'm serious. You should learn about these things. It's like, like . . . wearing the fancy ao dai."

But she shook her head. "Not now."

He also showed her the bus stop on Glebe Road, got her a schedule and taught her how to read it. She began to take Second Son on bus excursions, riding to a stop and getting off, exploring whatever was there — a neighborhood of houses, an apartment complex, a shopping center. She learned how to transfer to a line that would take her into the city, where she discovered the museums. They spent hours exploring the wonders of the Smithsonian. That gave Blake another idea, and he took them to the zoo, which immediately became Second Son's favorite place.

He pestered his father to take him there again.

"We'll see, someday maybe, son."

"But why can't we go soon? If Uncle Blake could take me, why can't you?"

Billings lost his patience. "I don't want to hear any more about the zoo, do you understand?" He was almost shouting.

Second Son backed away in surprise and ran to his mother for comfort.

"Blake, Blake, Blake! That's all I hear around here. This has got to stop."

"What has to stop, Arthur? Was it wrong for us to go to the zoo?"

"No! Of course it wasn't wrong! But what is this with Blake?"

It dawned on her that he was jealous. "Nothing, Arthur. He takes us places because he isn't so busy right now."

"Well, it's too much."

Trang Sen was angry. "Do you think it was better when we were sitting here all day doing nothing? Is that what you want? What am I supposed to do? I hardly ever see you, you won't even talk to me about what you're going to do about us."

"That's none of your business."

"It *is* my business. I want to know what's going to happen to us!" She was shouting at him.

"I'm doing the best I can," he shouted back.

She didn't answer, but bit her lip and fought back tears of anger.

"I want you to stop seeing so much of Blake," he said, his voice lower but his lips tight with anger.

"I won't. He's a very kind friend. I won't tell him not to come here."

"Then I'll do it myself."

She looked at him contemptuously. "Would you really, when he's helped us so much?"

He didn't answer.

"What are we to do about Second Son starting school?" she asked, hoping the subject of Blake was closed.

He took a deep breath and let it out in a sigh. "I've been meaning to make some phone calls. I've intended to do that every day, for weeks. There never seems to be any time." He took his glasses off, polished them on his shirt, and rubbed his hand across his eyes.

"Are you very tired, Arthur?" she asked, solicitous.

"Very."

She sat down beside him and he leaned against her.

She massaged his forehead and eyelids. "You mustn't work so hard."

"It's not just work, there are too many things to think about. If you only knew what a haven you are for me."

IT WAS BLAKE who got Second Son enrolled at K.W. Barrett School. He met them at the apartment and walked over with them the first morning, to be sure they knew how to get back and forth, and helped them find the right classroom.

To Trang Sen's surprise, Billings didn't object, but rather seemed relieved. She was still careful about mentioning Blake too often, and tried to keep Second Son from talking about him when his father was there.

It was also Blake who finally located Kim Hoa and the children, although it was Billings who brought the good news.

"It will still take a while to get them here, but at least we can get started now."

She was jubilant. "How long, do you think?" She looked around the small room. "We have to make some changes, with so many people in here. Could we get some hammocks?"

"I hardly think so. This place is too small for all of you."

"Not any smaller than the little house in Saigon where we lived, or the room over the shop. This is bigger," she argued.

"No, she should have her own place."

"But we have no money. Who knows how much she has by now. How will we pay for it?"

"I've told you I'll take care of you. Maybe Ba Chau can find a way to make some money. I know any number of people who would like to find such a good tailor. But we're skipping rather far ahead. They're not here yet."

The weather turned cool again. She pulled out the warm slacks and jacket Billings had bought her the first day she was in America, put on the strange heavy shoes. Now, though, she rather liked the coolness. She left the windows open in the apartment, enjoying the nippy breeze after the stagnant summer air.

With Second Son in school every day, she had nothing to do. She spent hours walking along Glebe Road. She noticed a sign in the window of the Roy Rogers at the intersection with Route 50 — "Help Wanted." Impulsively, she went in and asked the girl at the cash register, "Please, there is need for someone to work?"

The girl didn't answer her, but turned her head and shouted toward the kitchen, "Joe, somebody out here askin' about the job!"

A young man appeared. He looked at her. "You the one wants a job?"

"Yes," she almost whispered.

"Well, let's see, I hafta ask you this. You got a work permit?"

"Permit?" She shook her head in confusion. "I have no permit."

"Sorry, then, I can't do nothin' for you."

She bowed slightly and turned to go.

"Hey, wait!"

She turned around.

"If you was willin' to work for, say, a dollar an hour, I could prob'ly arrange somethin'. That would be just a slight reduction in your salary for my trouble, you understand."

She nodded. It seemed fair enough.

"We got a lotta shifts here. Busy time is afternoon and evening. You can start by workin' then, anytime. Want to start today?"

"So sorry, I have to work in daytime, while my son is at school. Unless I could bring him?" She looked hopefully at the man.

"Nah, that won't do. We can't have a bunch o' kids runnin' around here. At least not unless they're payin' customers." He thought a moment. "Hold on a minute. Let me see what I can do." He disappeared into the kitchen.

She looked around the almost-deserted room, its benches and tables gleaming in the sun. It was all so sleek and modern, very American. She would like to work here.

Joe returned. "Okay, I shifted some others around. I can use you right now if you want to start."

He took her to a small dressing room behind the kitchen. "This here's your uniform." He handed her a broad-brimmed hat, a checked blouse and a very short skirt, and a fringed vest. "You gotta keep 'em clean, and if anything happens to 'em, you haveta pay for 'em. Understand?"

She nodded.

"Okay, we'll start you out front. You can check right now to see that everything's lookin' spick and span, and all the napkin and straw holders are full. When people leave, make sure they emptied their trash and put their trays up here." He had walked back to the front part of the restaurant as he talked, she following behind him. He patted a stack of empty trays. "If not, you do it. When the stack has about eight or ten on it, bring 'em to the back. I'll show you where."

Breathlessly, she followed him toward the kitchen again. *His English is very strange*, she thought, *not proper grammar. And what is "spick and span"?* She was sure he was telling her to keep the place clean, but that was one she would have to look up.

He was talking again, though. "After a week or so, I'll get you started on the cash register. We'll see how you do on this job first. By the way, what's your name?"

"Miss Sen, please to call me Miss Sen."

"We usually use first names around here, but I guess that'll be all right. Okay, you can go to the ladies room and put on your uniform and get started." He walked away, then turned back. "One other thing — I almost forgot. When folks come in, you say 'Howdy, pardner.' When they leave, say, 'Happy trails.' Got that?"

She nodded. But what did it mean?

Billings was not at all happy about her new job. "You can't do that."

"Why not?" She was less and less inclined to agree with his ideas about what she should and shouldn't do.

"Well, for one thing you don't need the money. I've told you I'll take care of you. And you need to be here for Ken."

"I explained to the boss that I could only work in the morning. He said that would be okay."

"The most important thing is, you don't have a work permit. It's illegal for you to be working at all. Did he ask about that?"

"He said he would pay me a lower salary, to repay him for his trouble about no permit."

"How much is he paying you?"

"One dollar each hour."

"What?! He's stealing from you. No wonder he was willing to hire you. At that price, who wouldn't be?"

"It seems quite a nice salary," she argued. "And a fair arrangement because of the matter of the permit."

"He's a crook, that's what he is, cheating you out of a decent wage. I've a good mind to report him."

"This has nothing to do with you. I want to work there, I have nothing to do while Second Son is at school. You don't want me to do anything but sit in this place and wait for you. And you hardly ever come. Leave me alone!" She jerked her arm away from his tentative effort to touch her.

"You're being unreasonable, Trang Sen. You don't understand the situation, and you're letting this fellow take advantage of you. I don't like it."

"I don't care what you like!" She stopped, amazed at how angry she was. *What is happening to me in this country?*

To her surprise and irritation, Blake, when he heard about it, agreed with Billings.

"That guy's cheating you. He could never get an American to work for such a salary. In fact, it's illegal for him to try. To say nothing of being illegal to hire you. And you could get into a lot of trouble too."

He thought of something else. "Do you have to wear that crazy cowgirl outfit?"

She showed him her uniform. "I say 'howdy pardner' when people come in and 'happy trails' when they leave. I don't know why we're supposed to do that."

He laughed and shook his head. Then he was serious again. "You can't keep working there."

"But I can't sit here always doing nothing."

"No. We've been thinking of so many other things, we hadn't focused on that. We need to regularize your status. I'll speak to Art about it."

"What is this . . . this reg . . . reg . . . whatever you said, what does that mean?"

"We need to make you legal, get you the proper papers — your green card — so you can begin the waiting period to become a citizen and be able to work in the meantime."

"I see, you mean the permit. The boss mentioned this permit."

Reluctantly, she agreed to quit the job, in exchange for Blake's promise to get to work on her green card.

"We have to educate you too, so you won't let somebody hire you for below standard pay." He carefully explained the minimum wage law.

"Ah, so he was indeed cheating me. But if it's good for me and good for him, why does it matter?"

"That's just not the way we do things here. Workers have rights, and employers are supposed to be fair, though, as you've discovered, it doesn't always happen that way."

"So different here." She smiled at him. "Workers have rights." *I have rights, too, maybe,* she thought. "So different," she repeated aloud.

Blake realized Trang Sen was often short of cash and persuaded Billings to set up a bank account for her. Instructed by the two of them, Trang Sen learned how to use it, to keep track of the balance, and where she could cash checks. Neither she nor Billings realized that Blake added money to the account from time to time, to supplement what Billings provided.

SECOND SON SEEMED to be doing well at school. She received an occasional note from his teacher praising his quick grasp of English and his rapid progress in general. But some days he came home gloomy and untalkative.

"When are Van Hai and Thi Ba coming, Ma-ma?" was his constant question. "You said they were coming soon."

Sometimes he asked, "Will they go to school with me when they get here?"

She assured him they would.

One day when he came in, he had been crying.

"What is it?"

He turned his head away and refused to answer. He went to his bed, lay down and burrowed his head underneath the pillow. He stayed there all afternoon, finally gave in to her coaxing to come and eat supper. But he ate little, moving his food around the plate in slow, dispirited circles.

Billings stopped in that evening and took his turn at trying to find out what was wrong.

"Are you sick, son? Does your tummy hurt?"

Second Son shook his head, tears standing in his eyes.

"Then can you tell me what's wrong so I can help fix it?"

Wordlessly, he climbed into Billings's lap and, with a huge, shuddering sigh, buried his head against his father's shoulder, crying silently. At last, though, "They don't like me," he mumbled, "none of them like me." He looked up at Billings. "Do I look funny, Pa-pa?"

Billings laughed somewhat nervously. "Of course you don't look funny. Did someone tell you that?"

"They laugh at me and tell me I look funny, and they pull my hair. And . . . and they call me" — he gulped down a rising sob — "they call me g . . . g . . . gook!" He ended on a rising wail and hid his head against his father's shoulder again.

Trang Sen rose to go to him. Billings shook his head at her, holding Second Son tightly. "Let him cry. I have a feeling this has been coming for a long time."

When Second Son grew calmer, Billings set him on his knee and wiped his face with his handkerchief. "Feel better?"

"I . . . I guess so. But why would they call me that, Pa-pa? What is 'gook'?"

"It's just one of those words people use to hurt somebody's feelings. I'll tell you what I think. I think they're jealous of you because you're smarter than they are. That's what I think. Don't worry when they tease you about the way you look. You look fine, a very handsome boy. My advice is, don't pay any attention to them. Try laughing when they say those things to you. Whatever you do, don't let them see you cry. Can you do that? "

" I . . . I can try, I guess."

"Sure you can. And I want you to promise me something. Whenever you feel bad about what they've said, you tell Ma-ma, so she can help you feel better. Will you promise?"

"Yes." Tears filled his eyes again. "I thought she'd be angry with me," he whispered.

Trang Sen came over then, patted his back. "Never angry with you. Only with them."

The problem seemed to be taken care of, at least for the time being. But it made Trang Sen feel once again that she didn't belong here. When she thought about the past six months, she saw only a series of mistakes. She seemed always to get it wrong, whatever it was, like the job, or locking the door. She knew how Second Son felt, ached for him, and for herself.

Billings, Billings didn't want her either. They seldom made love. When they did, she felt he was always pulling away, holding himself apart. Sometimes she wished he would stop coming altogether, yet she longed for him with a hopelessness that surpassed anything she had known during their separations in Vietnam. Sometimes she wanted to throw herself at him and beg him to stay, beg him to be as he used to be. Her pride prevented her from doing that, and, she thought, it wouldn't do any good anyway.

She kept remembering that early, best time of their love, when, looking back, she seemed hardly more than a child. His light brown head bobbing above the crowd, coming to her as she waited near the school. His tenderness, and the hope he had restored to her in that time after Tet. She could feel the warm dampness of that rainy night they had sat next to each other in the restaurant, he so gently pushing the hair out of her face.

All that was over. Now he only wanted to hide her, didn't want anyone to know about her. She wondered once again about that family he refused to discuss. When she forced him to talk about their own relationship, he assured her he loved her best of all. *But what good does that do, she asked herself angrily, when he's hardly ever here?*

IT WAS LATE November. Trang Sen was fascinated by the radical shifts in the weather. One day it would be bright and sunny, and no colder than it had been in April. The next day she would awaken to a cold, penetrating rain.

Kim Hoa and the children had their plane tickets and would be coming soon. They were in a better position than Trang Sen, as they were official refugees. They had permits — Kim Hoa would be able to work. Trang Sen finally gave in to Billings's insistence that they live in a separate apartment. Blake and Billings had found one in the next complex, almost identical to hers, but with a small dining area where they could put an extra bed. Because of that, Trang Mai would live there rather than with Trang Sen and Second Son.

With the help of the two men, Trang Sen selected the necessary furniture and bought winter clothes for all of them, guessing at the size of the children. She worried about them arriving in the cold.

Second Son was ecstatic. "I'll show Van Hai and Thi Ba where the school is, we can walk there together. I'll help them with their English," he said grandly.

Blake took them to Dulles to meet the plane. Trang Sen and Second Son waited impatiently at the gate. When Second Son saw them, he dashed under the rope and ran to them. Kim Hoa looked anxiously for Trang Sen. In that moment before their eyes met, Trang Sen, looking at her, was reminded of that other time when she had waited on the other side of the busy Saigon street, watching Kim Hoa vainly trying to cross. Now too Kim Hoa seemed unable to cope. And had she looked so old during the years after that? Trang Sen wasn't sure.

Sympathy stabbed her. *Kim Hoa isn't like me. She would have been content to spend the rest of her life in the village, obedient to her husband, asking no questions. Perhaps, if I hadn't complicated her life she would never have had to leave.* Trang Sen was momentarily immersed in guilt. The next moment, unable to contain either her joy at being reunited, or those conflicting feelings, she too plunged under the rope and pushed her way to them.

"Kim Hoa, so good to have you here at last."

There was Trang Mai, walking a little behind. "Second Sister." Trang Sen greeted her more formally. "It has been well with you, I hope."

"Oh, Sister, how can I tell you? The camp was terrible." The girl shuddered. "And we had to stay so long. You did nothing for us," she ended on a complaining note.

"I'm sorry. For a long time we couldn't find you. Everything was very confused, so many people. But here's Ong Blake," she said, as Blake joined them.

Blake bowed properly to Kim Hoa and took her bag from her.

Kim Hoa returned the bow. "Ong Blake. We meet at the end as at the beginning of our journey."

"So cold," she said, turning to Trang Sen. "Is it always so cold?"

"I bought warm clothes for all of you, I hope the right size for the children. It's the beginning of winter here, very cold for many months."

Kim Hoa shivered.

Second Son was busy telling Thi Ba and Van Hai about his school and describing his life in America. "Only Pa-pa doesn't come to see us very often," he added, his face clouding momentarily.

Kim Hoa raised her eyebrows at Trang Sen.

"We must talk later," whispered Trang Sen. She glanced at Blake walking ahead. He didn't seem to have heard Second Son's comment, she noted with relief.

At last they were squeezed into Blake's little car. He turned to Trang Sen. "What do you think?" he asked her in English. "Should we take them for something to eat or go to the apartment?"

"The apartment, I think. I can fix something while they rest."

He nodded and pulled the car into the exit line.

Trang Sen turned to Kim Hoa and explained about their apartment.

"Not with you? So expensive, two separate places."

"Billings is a very stubborn man. He insisted." Trang Sen laughed self-consciously.

"There are rules," explained Blake. "Only so many people allowed to one dwelling. The landlord could throw all of you out if you broke that rule."

"Oh," said Trang Sen, "I never knew that."

Kim Hoa looked at the wide highway, the hills with bare trees stretching into the distance. She flinched as the cars sped by them. "So fast," she said breathlessly. "A strange country, America, and such strange trees, with no leaves."

"That's only because of the winter," explained Trang Sen. "They return in the spring. You'll see."

Blake helped carry their things into the apartment. He smiled a little and said to Trang Sen, "I'll go now, leave you to your reunion. You have much to talk about."

"Please stay. I'll have supper ready soon."

"I think not." He lowered his voice and switched to English. "Ba Chau seems very confused by everything. And she's had a hard time of it in the camp, I suspect."

"Yes, she looks very old."

He placed his hand briefly on her arm. "You can get home okay?"

"Yes." She blushed slightly. She rather liked his American way of touching her, but it also embarrassed her. "But perhaps we'll stay here tonight. Would the landlord be angry?"

"No, no, only if it's a permanent thing and you have no place of your own."

He left then and Trang Sen followed the others into the bedroom. Second Son had already given Thi Ba and Van Hai their new clothes. Thi Ba strutted importantly around the room. "I'm an American now," she said.

"You should change too," said Trang Sen to Trang Mai and Kim Hoa. "You'll be much warmer." She opened a drawer and pulled out the things she had bought.

Trang Mai was almost as proud of her new outfit as Thi Ba. If it weren't for her almost permanent scowl, she would be very beautiful, thought Trang Sen. Her figure had filled out, in spite of the fact that she looked thinner, and her black hair fell in a glossy wave, though she had pinned it severely back from her face. *We could have trouble with her*, Trang Sen concluded silently, and wondered how she would keep her promise to their mother.

Trang Sen and Kim Hoa discussed that, among many other things, staying up long after the children had fallen asleep.

"She's very hard to manage," admitted Kim Hoa, pulling a blanket more tightly around her. "In the camp, I don't know. I tried to be sure I knew where she was, what she was doing. You don't know what it was like. Everyone was selling themselves one way or another, trying to get out. The women mostly tried to bribe the immigration people by sleeping with them." She laughed almost bitterly. "I don't think Cousin Mai went that far, or we'd have been out sooner."

"Was it so terrible, then? And you, what did you do, how did you manage?"

"Terrible in a strange way. Not like the war, where you thought you might be killed. But much selfishness and greed, among our people as well as the Americans. Only a few of us helped each other. How did I manage?" She shrugged. "I used the money to buy food, not American help the way others were doing. I didn't know where you were, so I had nowhere to go. After a while, I began to do things for others in the camp. Sometimes I helped as a midwife. I found a way to buy cloth and made American clothes to sell people before they left. So our own people paid me, not the Americans. You saw I made clothes for us as well. But I never thought about the cold, so they were all wrong."

"Only now. You'll see. They'll be very useful in the summer."

"There was a family," Kim Hoa continued in a faraway voice, almost as if she was talking to herself. "They were going to California, they wanted me to come with them, said we would open a shop, just like Saigon."

"Did you want to do that?"

"I don't know. I . . . I couldn't imagine any life outside the camp after a while. Then the officials came and said they were arranging for us to leave. They mentioned Ong Blake, but I couldn't understand what he was doing."

"It was the permit. One must have a sponsor, that was what it was."

"Why not you? I asked about you, but no one could tell me anything. Finally I decided it was best to come on, that Ong Blake would know where you were."

"I couldn't help because I have no permit. They're getting me a permit now."

"Why didn't Billins get you a permit? How did you get here?"

"They made up a story." Trang Sen told her how it had been.

"And Billins, how is he?"

Trang Sen frowned. "Very busy. He has many responsibilities."

Kim Hoa opened her mouth to ask another question, but changed her mind.

CHAPTER 13

CHANGES

KIM HOA, IT seemed, would never adjust to the climate. She caught cold and sat huddled in blankets, looking desolately out at the cold grey sky as the winter deepened. Trang Sen tried to cheer her up, made strengthening broths and medicinal teas for her. At last, Blake persuaded her Kim Hoa must see a doctor. But the doctor said it was nothing more than a cold, made more severe and lingering because of the sudden change of weather.

It snowed, and the children were beside themselves. Even Trang Mai was shaken from her usual sullen mood and joined in the fun with the sled Billings had given Second Son for Christmas. Kim Hoa shivered as they stomped noisily into the apartment, bringing a rush of cold air and clumps of snow clinging to their clothes and shoes. Trang Sen came in behind them, her cheeks red with cold, her eyes bright.

"Oh, Kim Hoa, you must get well. So much fun, you can't imagine. It's like flying."

Kim Hoa shuddered and pulled the blanket more tightly around her. "Not for me. Too cold. How can you bear it?"

"You don't feel it so much after a while. If you'd only try, just once."

"How long does the winter last?"

"I don't know. It was cold even when I came here, but no snow."

She turned away and bent down to remove her wet shoes. Kim Hoa worried her. She almost wished the doctor had found something wrong with her he could cure. *She has helped me so many times*, Trang Sen reflected, *always seemed to know what to do. Now it's my turn, and I don't know at all*. She slumped her shoulders, her happy mood gone.

Only the little ones were content and adjusting well. There had been no more reports from Second Son of teasing by his classmates, and he had been much happier since his cousins arrived. Van Hai and Thi Ba were slowly but steadily improving with their English and seemed to enjoy the novelty if not the lessons of the new American school.

As for Trang Mai, Trang Sen despaired of keeping her promise to see that she grew up properly. Trang Mai had quickly gravitated to a group of Vietnamese teenagers attending Washington and Lee High School. They apparently spent most of their time thinking up ways to avoid classes and slip around the rules. There were one or two other girls among them, but most were boys. Trang Sen remembered Fourth Brother and his difficulties after they moved to Saigon. Something similar seemed to be happening with Trang Mai.

Billings laughed at her anxiety. "And what about you? When did you ever do anything the proper way?"

Trang Sen flushed. "I promised Ma-ma I wouldn't let the same thing happen to Second Sister," she replied through clenched teeth.

"Has it been so bad, then?" He leaned over and kissed her.

She pulled away from him. "It isn't funny. You come here when you want to, you never think about whether I need you, then you laugh at me when I worry about my family. There's no one else to take care of her. I don't know what to do."

"Hold on a minute. No need to get so excited. I just think you're taking this far too seriously. She's a normal teen-age girl, that's all. You don't think they're doing anything illegal, do you? Like drugs?"

"I don't know, I don't think so. But those kids are no good, I can tell that." She said at last aloud the thing she dreaded most — "What will I do if she has a baby?"

"Would that be so bad?"

"Of course it would!"

"You had a baby. Is your life ruined?"

"That . . . that was different, I . . ." she stopped. *How was it different?* She remembered all those times she secretly met Billings, Sister Louise's anguished disappointment when she neglected her lessons, Eldest Brother's anger. *Was this the way they felt about me?*

Billings was laughing at her. She turned on him in rage. "Out! Get out right now! I don't care if you ever come back!"

He stood up, still laughing. "What's the matter with you?"

She began beating on his chest with her fists. In mock horror, he fended her off.

She tried to wrench her hands from his grip. "Get out of here!" she shouted again. "Now!"

His bantering changed to anger, his face went cold and hard. He let go of her arms and turned around in a sudden motion. Impelled by the force of her own body, she fell down.

"Arthur." She looked up at him, blood running from her nose.

He left, slamming the door behind him.

She stared at the door, holding her hand up to her streaming nose. She became aware of a tentative hand on her shoulder.

"Ma-ma sick?" asked Second Son anxiously.

"No." She shook her head, got slowly to her feet and went into the bathroom for a cloth to stanch the bleeding. *What is happening to me?* Her own violence frightened her.

She returned to the living room and sat down with the cloth pressed against her face. Second Son was huddled in the chair across the room, looking at her fearfully.

"Come here," she said in a muffled voice. "You will soon see that I'm all right. Just a bleeding nose."

She held out her free arm and he tiptoed to her, allowed her to put her arm around him. He leaned against her, saying nothing for a long time. Then, almost in a whisper, he asked, "Did Pa-pa hurt you?"

"No, I fell. He didn't do it."

"But I heard you, you were angry and he was laughing." He hesitated. "He'll come back, won't he, Ma-ma?"

She pulled the cloth away, bent down and kissed him. "Yes, he'll come back. Don't worry."

And what will that solve? she asked herself. It was always the same — he came unannounced, left without any regard for what they wanted or needed. Even the rare times he stayed overnight were unsatisfactory, perhaps more unsatisfactory than his briefer visits. In the midst of their lovemaking, she often found herself overcome by anger and resentment. She would lie stiffly in his arms, unmoved by either his passion or his tenderness.

She was torn with curiosity about his family. His Christmas present to her had been a telephone, and she had learned to use the phone book, though it was still a laborious process. She looked up his name. He lived quite far away in Virginia, in a place called Dale City. She developed elaborate plans for going there, called for bus schedules, worked out the best routes. It would take, she calculated, with two changes and waiting between buses, almost three hours each way. A day's undertaking.

When she got there she would walk up to the door and ring the bell. "Hello, I'm Trang Sen," she would say when the wife answered. It was always the wife who answered, never Billings. She would laugh to see his face when she walked in.

She knew she could never do that. Perhaps she would simply walk past the house, try from the outside to get some idea of what his life must be like there. *But what if he saw me?* She blushed at the thought.

It was all an impossible scheme. She would never do it. But she was determined to find out more about that life which prevented him from coming to them. She hated that life, hated his children and his wife. Sometimes she hated him most of all.

She began to ask him questions. When he refused to answer, she simply kept asking.

"Arthur, tell me about your children. How many are there? Are they good children? Do they love you very much?"

He shrugged. "About like all children."

She persisted. "How many? Two, three, five?"

"What difference does it make?"

"I want to know."

At last, tired of her wheedling, "Three, then," he answered. "Are you satisfied?"

"How old are they, are any of them grown?" She thought they must be Trang Mai's age or older.

"Eighteen, seventeen, and eight."

Eight. She hadn't expected one so young. That one would have been

•

born while he was in Saigon, almost, she calculated quickly, the same time he had begun to tell her he loved her. A cold wave washed over her. From the depths of that coldness she felt a degree of sympathy for that other woman who loved him. In those years Billings had been hers far more than he had belonged to this American family. Had he not cared, even for his newly born child?

She got up and went into the kitchen, made a great production of fixing dinner. She was tired of this questioning game. For the moment, she knew more than she wanted to know. She went to the door and stood looking at him. He was reading a magazine, as if their conversation had never taken place.

He was waiting for Second Son, who was at Kim Hoa's. Trang Sen had called when Billings arrived and asked Trang Mai to bring him home.

"Are you eating with us?" She didn't care whether he stayed or not.

He looked up. "What? Oh, I suppose so. It won't be long, will it?"

Her anger blazed up. "Oh no, never long. I wouldn't want you to stay too long." She turned back into the kitchen and banged pans and utensils around. She wanted him to come in, say something so she could scream at him. But she knew he wouldn't. He never did. He just sat there as if nothing was happening. She wanted to hit him, beat her fists against him until he fought back.

BLAKE HAD A permanent assignment. He was still in Washington, but they saw him less often. Trang Sen missed his frequent visits, realized how much she depended on him, for advice as well as trips to the Giant or an occasional movie.

He arrived one evening directly after a particularly infuriating encounter with Billings. She opened the door a crack, half expecting, half hoping Billings had come back, though he wouldn't have knocked. Seeing Blake, she self-consciously ran her hand across her hair to smooth it, tugged at her rumpled blouse.

"I thought perhaps the children would enjoy a trip to Baskin-Robbins, or McDonald's if you haven't eaten. I was going to ask if you and Kim Hoa would like to come along too. But if this is a bad time . . ." He noticed her red eyes and looked away.

"Not a bad time," she answered, then, trying to smile, added, "never a bad time for one of your suggestions." In spite of her efforts, her eyes filled with tears. "I'll get Second Son." She turned quickly and ran into the bedroom.

Blake pulled at his mustache. He heard Trang Sen's exchange with Second Son indistinctly through the closed bedroom door.

". . . don't want ice cream," the child suddenly burst out. "I want Pa-pa to come back," he ended in a wail.

Trang Sen said something in a low voice.

"I don't care if Uncle Blake is here! I don't want anybody but Pa-pa! Why are you always angry with him?"

"Hush!" hissed Trang Sen, then, to her dismay, she slapped him.

"Ma-ma, you hurt me!" Second Son, shrieking, fumbled with the door knob, finally got the door open and ran to Blake.

Blake bent down and put his arms around him. When Second Son calmed down he said, "You don't have to go if you don't want to. It might be fun, though. Why don't you think about it while I talk with your Ma-ma?"

Second Son nodded.

Blake tapped on the half-closed bedroom door. "Co Sen? May I come in?"

She was lying across the bed, overcome with shame and remorse. *How could I have hit him? This isn't his fault, none of it is his fault. It's all, all mine, all of it.* She was doubly ashamed for Blake to have heard.

She sat up quickly, and for the second time in half an hour attempted to smooth her disheveled hair and clothing.

Blake hesitantly pushed the door a little farther open and saw her sitting there. She turned her head away. "I'm sorry, Ong Blake," she whispered.

"No need for that. Do you want to comb your hair, maybe wash your face?"

She nodded, tears welling in her eyes again, slid past him into the bathroom and shut the door behind her.

He turned back to the living room. Second Son, his momentary storm over, was looking at a book. Blake sat down beside the boy and asked, "Can you read it to me?"

Trang Sen emerged from the bathroom to find them there, Blake's arm around Second Son.

"Let's go for ice cream," she said, her voice almost normal.

Second Son looked up at her, then suddenly, "Okay," he agreed.

They drove to the other apartment, collected the children and persuaded Kim Hoa to come with them.

"It will be good for you," Trang Sen argued. "It's not so cold tonight, you'll be surprised. Perhaps even spring is coming."

At last Kim Hoa agreed. The enthusiasm of the children infected both their mothers. Trang Sen seemed almost cheerful by the time Blake pulled up once more in front of her apartment building.

He carried a sleepy Second Son to the door, and, uninvited, came in rather than handing him over to Trang Sen. He took him into the bedroom, set him on the side of his bed, pulled off his jacket and shoes, and settled him under the blanket.

Returning to the living room, he commented, "He'll be okay in his clothes for now. He's so tired, he'd sleep standing up if we leaned him against a wall."

Trang Sen didn't answer.

Blake pulled at his mustache. "We have to talk about this, Trang Sen. I'm sorry, I've told you before, I don't make a very good Vietnamese. I can't go away and say nothing about what happened tonight."

"Nothing to talk about."

He ignored her plea. "I think I can guess what's happening here. In fact, I'm not guessing. I'm simply observing the obvious."

Trang Sen looked up at him, her eyes opaque. "Please, Ong Blake."

"No, it's time we talked. Art isn't treating you right. What can you do about it?"

"Nothing to do," she whispered.

"How often do you see him?"

"Every week, most of the time."

"And, is it enough?"

Almost imperceptibly, she shook her head.

"You can't go on this way, taking it out on Second Son, the way you did tonight."

"I know." She lowered her head, her face red with shame.

"It's perfectly normal, Trang Sen, to be angry. Anyone in your situation would be. And people have done worse things than you did tonight. Far worse."

She was silent. He pulled at his mustache again. "Do you think it might be better to end the thing completely?"

She looked up in surprise. "End it? End what?"

"I'm sorry. I meant the relationship. What did you think I meant?"

"I don't know."

"Well, what do you think?"

"I . . . I can't," she whispered, looking at her hands twisted together in her lap.

"Would it be so difficult?"

She remembered how many times she had wished Billings would never come back. *Would it matter now? Would anything matter? But never to see him again, could I bear that? And what of Second Son?*

"What would I do? What would Second Son do?"

"I'm not sure. I'm not claiming to have any answers. But I don't think you can go on this way. Art needs to make a choice. He's apparently not willing to do that so you must make one."

"A choice? What kind of choice?"

"Between you and his other family."

She hadn't thought of that possibility since that terrible night he told her he couldn't marry her. "You . . . you mean marry me?"

"Yes. He should have done that long ago, or left you alone. Long ago."

"But he couldn't."

"You mean he didn't want to. It was very convenient for him. He had it both ways, a family here and one there. We have an expression for that — have his cake and eat it too. Perfect for him, wretched for everyone else. And the ones who suffered for it were on both sides of the Pacific."

Blake's vehemence startled her. "I thought you were his friend."

"Not such a friend that I couldn't see what he was doing to you — and to Second Son too."

She had to ask. "Do you . . . have you seen his wife?"

He shook his head. "Never. I mostly knew him in Saigon, not here. It was because of you that I saw him here."

"Such a good friend." She smiled at him then.

"I would like to have spared you this. I saw it coming, before you ever left Saigon, but there was nothing I could do. At least you can let me give you advice now. And that advice is to get him out of your life."

"I . . . I . . . Second Son would be unhappy."

"He's unhappy now."

"Only sometimes."

"When you and Art fight, like tonight."

"Arthur doesn't fight."

"When you fight, then. But I'm thinking about you. Second Son will be happy if you're happy. He's gotten along without his father before. And it seems to me Art isn't much of a father to him these days."

It was true. Even if there was no fight, Second Son was more often frustrated than satisfied with Billings's brief visits. She said, "I don't know."

"Well, think about it. Meantime, at least do this — use that new green card and let me help you find a job. That might make things look different."

"But Arthur . . ."

"It doesn't matter what Art wants. What do *you* want?"

She shifted her eyes away. "I hadn't thought about it since Kim Hoa and the others came."

"Kim Hoa too. It's time you both were doing something to bring in some money. It would make her feel more at home, and you would be a bit more independent."

He was right about Kim Hoa, Trang Sen thought. Perhaps he was right about her too. She thought of the shiny interior of the Roy Rogers at Route 50. "I could talk to the boss at Roy Rogers again. He would pay me properly now."

"He tried to cheat you once. Don't go back. There are other places. Do you want to work in that kind of place — a fast-food joint I mean? And in a cowgirl outfit?"

She shrugged. "It would be fine, a good place to be, and good money."

He smiled. "It's not good money. With your intelligence and education, you should have a better job than that."

"What is a better job?"

"I'm not sure at the moment. Let me think about it, ask around a bit. You might also go to the refugee center, you and Kim Hoa, see what they can suggest." A center had recently opened in Clarendon to help Vietnamese immigrants.

"Yes, we can do that. Kim Hoa will be glad of something to do."

"And think about what I said about you and Art."

THE SEARCH FOR a job led to another argument with Billings. The next time he was there, classified sections of the *Star* and *Post* were scattered around the living room.

"What's this?" He picked up a page and looked at the circled items. "I don't want you to work. You don't need to work."

Trang Sen was immediately angry. If she had any doubt about finding a job, it was now wiped out. "I don't care what you want."

"You need to be here for Ken."

"I'll be here when he needs me, just like always. Besides, Kim Hoa and Trang Mai help me now. He can go there if I'm not here."

"Do you really think Trang Mai can be trusted?"

"Do you think I can? You told me she was no different from me."

"That's not what I mean. You've made up your mind to misunderstand me."

"You've made up your mind to keep me in a prison."

"Don't be ridiculous. This is a hell of a lot better than the dumps you were living in in Vietnam."

"At least you weren't there telling me never to go out and do anything."

"Anyway, we're talking about now, not then. Now, I don't want you to get a job."

"I'll do anything I want to. You're never here anyway. What difference does it make to you?"

"I've told you I'll take care of you."

"Which means you come here once a week, sometimes not then. Do you want me to thank you for that?"

"I'm doing the best I can."

"Maybe that's not good enough. You used to tell me you loved us."

"I still love you."

"If you did, you'd stay with us." She thought of Blake's words, that Billings should make a choice.

"I've told you over and over, I can't do that."

"Why not?"

"I have other obligations. You know that."

"So you love them more than you do us."

"I didn't say that."

"You don't have to. You're there and we're here. I wait for you day after day, I never know when you're coming, what you'll want. You don't like it if I'm at Kim Hoa's when you come. Sometimes you stay with us, sometimes you help us, sometimes you don't do anything. What am I supposed to do?"

"I thought you understood. Now you're turning on me."

"You're the one turning on me. You insult my country, tell me I should be satisfied with nothing, and then want me to be grateful to you. What do you think I am, a cheap tea-girl?"

"And what do *you* think you are, you and your sister?"

"Get out! I don't have to listen to your insults!" She reached for something, anything, to hit him or throw at him. Her hand closed around a glass on the end table. "Out! Right now!" She lifted it over her head.

Instead of making him angrier, her furor amused him. "Oho, now you're going to attack me. What a brave girl."

"I hate you! Get out!"

Still laughing, he covered his head with his arms and moved toward the door. "Anything you say, dragon lady. The next thing, fire'll come shooting out of your mouth. Please don't burn me!" He brought his hands together in mock petition, then quickly retreated out the door as the glass crashed on the wall next to him.

Trang Sen heard his laugh echoing in the stairwell. She stood with her hands over her face, trembling with anger and horrified that she had actually thrown something at him. *What if I had hurt him? I'm glad Second Son wasn't here. He would have been so frightened.* She went to the kitchen and returned with the broom. Shakily, she swept the broken glass onto a piece of newspaper, crumpled it up and put it in the wastebasket.

She sat down and covered her face with her hands. *What am I going to do? And what's happened to Arthur? He never used to laugh at me or scorn me so. He hates me. They would all be better off without me, even Second Son. I hate it here; the Americans are so cold and heartless. Arthur too, he doesn't love me. Maybe he never did.*

She imagined what it would be like to take her own life. She would throw herself in the river, like Kieu. She could see her lifeless body, dragged from the Potomac, could see the strangers hovering around it.

Then she thought, *If I did that, he would know it was because of him.* Anger displaced the despair. She sat up straight and lifted her head. *I won't give him that satisfaction.* She would go on living, prove that what he was — or wasn't — doing couldn't destroy her. *That's a kind of revenge,* she thought, *like when I bled his child away, in revenge for Eldest Brother. Only this time the revenge is to live.*

BUT SHE WAS still torn. For a while she tried to please him. She made elaborate Vietnamese meals, all the dishes she knew he liked. When he came she changed into an ao dai, knowing he liked that too. But their arguments grew more frequent, not less. She found herself wishing again he would never come back. When she got to that point, he invariably grew tender and loving again, the three of them would have a pleasant evening together, and she would think once more that what they had in Saigon could be restored. Then the cycle started over.

A phone call came from Trang Mai's school. "Is this Mrs. . . . ah . . . Trinh?"

"This is Trinh Trang Sen, yes."

"Hold on, please. The principal wants to talk with you."

She waited nervously.

A male voice came on the line. "We've run into a bit of a problem with your daughter, Trang Mai."

"My younger sister, yes, what's happened?"

"Well, Mrs. Trinh, there's no easy way to say this. One of the teachers caught her and two of her friends smoking pot in the girls' restroom. We've suspended all three of them, of course. I'm afraid I must ask you to come here and fetch her. We also need to talk with you about what we do next. You say you're her sister. Are you her guardian, where are your parents?"

Trang Sen was horrified. "Yes, yes, I'm responsible, our parents died in Vietnam. I'm so ashamed, it's all my fault, I should have known what she was doing, watched her more carefully." Information had been sent from the refugee center explaining that marijuana was illegal and that what had been such a common thing in Vietnam was looked at very differently here.

"Can you come to the school now? Both I and her guidance counselor would like to talk with you."

"Yes, yes, I'll come now."

"Very well."

Trang Sen hung up the phone. She started to call Kim Hoa, then remembered that Kim Hoa was at work. Through the refugee center, she had found a job with a housecleaning service called Maid for You.

Oh, what am I going to do, I knew Trang Mai would get into some kind of trouble. What will they do to her? She put on her jacket and rushed out.

By the time she arrived at the school, she was in a frenzy of anxiety. She stood on the steps and took several deep breaths, then stepped into the wide corridor and tried to walk slowly to the principal's office. It seemed very important to be calm.

"I'm Trinh Trang Sen," she said to the secretary. "Mr. Stevenson called me about my sister Trang Mai."

"Oh, yes, he's waiting for you. I'll call Mrs. Anthony, they both want to see you."

Trang Sen sat down in the chair the secretary pointed to and tried to keep from rubbing her hands nervously together.

A rather thin, severe-looking woman came in and walked over to her. "Mrs. Trinh? I'm Mrs. Anthony."

Trang Sen hastily stood up. "Yes, so sorry to cause you trouble."

Seated in the principal's office, Trang Sen repeated her apology.

"We don't have many options in a case like this, Mrs. Trinh. Marijuana is illegal, you know. I'm afraid we're going to have to report this to the police."

Trang Sen felt sick. "What . . . what will happen to her?"

"Since it's a first offense, and not a hard drug, and since she's a minor, she'll be in your custody. And of course the suspension from school, for the rest of the year. But I must impress upon you that if she's caught doing this again, the consequences will be far worse. Do you understand?"

"Yes, I'm sorry."

"It's a bit late for that, Mrs. Trinh."

Trang Sen said nothing.

"We've had trouble with Trang Mai before this, Mrs. Trinh," added Mrs. Anthony, "nothing illegal, of course, cutting classes and a general lack of discipline or interest in her school work. She needs a great deal of supervision. Can you give that to her?" The guidance counselor sounded doubtful.

"I try, we do try, she's . . . not easy to manage." Trang Sen was reluctant to discuss Trang Mai's problems with these strangers. "Should I take her home now? What happens next?"

"If you can guarantee she'll be supervised at all times, she can go with you. But you must be sure she has no access to drugs, and that she doesn't break any other laws."

"Yes."

"The police will be in touch with you. And, Mrs. Trinh, we're here to help you when Trang Mai comes back to school next fall."

The principal picked up the receiver and buzzed the secretary. "Bring

Trang Mai in."

The girl looked defiant. The principal repeated what he had explained to Trang Sen and told them they could go.

In mutual isolation they went home. As often as Trang Sen had scolded and struggled with Trang Mai, she had no idea what to do or say about this. To be in trouble with the police was so devastating, so shaming and frightening, her most overwhelming desire was to hide. Looking at Trang Mai walking beside her in sulky silence, she detected no remorse. Why was she not ashamed, or at least apologetic? Trang Sen was at a loss to understand her.

"You'll have to come home with me, it's almost time for Second Son to get home, then we'll go to Cousin Hoa's," she said as they approached Fifth Street.

Trang Mai shrugged her shoulders. Trang Sen took that as agreement.

The thought of telling even Kim Hoa what had happened was mortifying. After Second Son arrived from school, the three of them walked over to the other apartment.

Kim Hoa was surprised to see Trang Mai home early.

"Tell her what you've done," Trang Sen said to her.

Again that defiant look. "Just a silly cigarette. Why such a fuss?"

"It wasn't just a cigarette, it was marijuana." Anger was overcoming Trang Sen's sense of shame. She explained what had happened.

"The police!" Kim Hoa gasped. "What are we going to do?"

"I don't know."

They talked around and around in the same circle, coming to no conclusion. When, later, Trang Sen told Billings, he shrugged. "As you say, she's your responsibility. You figure it out."

"What should I say to the police? I'm afraid."

"I guess that depends on what they say to you."

He refused to be any help. His unconcern reinforced the anger with him that was always ready to break out.

Blake was more helpful when she finally brought herself to tell him. "Don't worry about the police. They'll make a record of it for their files, and that will be the end of it unless she does something else. They aren't like the police in Vietnam. They won't drag her away or follow her around or anything like that."

"But it's so terrible."

He was reassuring. "It's not such a big thing, Trang Sen. I'd say at least ninety per cent of my college class smoked pot, and probably a lot of them still do. You could argue that the law is out of step with what people are doing. But Trang Mai's attitude and the pattern she's gotten into are a problem."

"I don't know what to do about her."

"One thing you don't want is for her to get mixed up with those kids again. They're obviously no good for each other. Could she get a job with those people Kim Hoa works for? She's sixteen now, maybe she's better off working, as school doesn't seem to do anything but give her an opportunity to get into trouble. And she'd be where Kim Hoa could keep an eye on her."

Trang Sen considered his suggestion. "Maybe so. I'll ask Kim Hoa what she thinks."

"Don't take this too hard. It's not your fault, you know."

"But I promised I'd take care of her, keep her out of trouble."

"You've done the best you can. None of you have had an easy time of it. Maybe this is the only way Trang Mai can handle all the changes she's been through."

She was grateful for Blake's calm good sense, but she worried about Trang Mai constantly, even after her sister started working with Kim Hoa. And Billings's indifference to her anxiety changed the way she felt about him. Her search for a job had been half-hearted, impeded by his disapproval. Now she ignored that and began following up on every ad that seemed at all promising. She discovered it was easy to get hired as a waitress. She worked at a Thai restaurant called Ghin Na Ree on George Mason Boulevard for a few weeks, then at a Mexican place near Bailey's Crossroads. Finally, she started a job at Tom Sarris's Orleans House in Rosslyn.

Blake had been right. Making money of her own, she felt less helpless, more in control.

Billings was not at all happy with the new situation. Through that spring of 1976 she seldom saw him, as she worked in the evenings, when Kim Hoa was home with the children. "At least change your schedule and do the lunch shift," he demanded.

She shook her head. She was less and less willing to accommodate him, and in spite of the fact that she was bored in her job, she had no intention of quitting simply because he wanted her to.

CHAPTER 14

NEW COUNTRY

> . . . The person who finds his homeland sweet is
> still a tender beginner; he to whom every soil is as his
> native one is already strong; but he is perfect to whom
> the entire world is as a foreign place. The tender soul
> has fixed his love on one spot in the world; the strong
> person has extended his love to all places; the perfect
> man has extinguished his.
>
> *Didascalicon*
> Hugo of St. Victor

IN THE SUMMER she began to read French again. With the children home all day, someone needed to stay with them, and it seemed best for Kim Hoa and Trang Mai to continue at Maid for You, to keep Trang Mai busy and under Kim Hoa's supervision.

Blake discovered her reading the Sartre she had brought from Vietnam. He was pleased. "That's a good thing to be doing. Though I can think of more cheerful authors than Sartre."

She smiled. "I wanted to read French, and this is the only thing I have. But isn't this lovely?" She read aloud Orestes' declaration to Zeus from *The Flies* — ". . . *je ne reviendrai pas sous ta loi: je suis condamné à n'avoir*

•

d'autre loi que la mienne. . . . Je ne peux suivre que mon chemin. Car je suis un homme, Jupiter, et chaque homme doit inventer son chemin."

"Lovely," he agreed, then added, "There's a book store in the District that specializes in foreign language books. I'll take a long lunch hour next week when the kids are in day camp and we can go see what they have."

"I'd like some other things to read. I keep remembering how I wanted to go to France and study French literature."

"You can still do that. There are schools right here you could look into."

"I don't know."

"Actually, I've had in my mind to say something to you about that. When you ended up working in restaurants this spring I realized you need to get a college education under your belt to get a decent job."

"I don't know," she said again. Though the refugee center might be able to help, finding out where she could go, what she would have to do to get in, how she would pay for it, all seemed too much to think about. For the moment, getting some books to read was enough.

They heard a key turn in the lock and Billings let himself in. Trang Sen thought he looked a bit surprised, perhaps not pleasantly, to see Blake there.

"Hello, Art, good to see you again. It's been a long time."

"Yes, well, so how've things been?"

"In fact, I came by to tell Trang Sen, I have a new assignment. I'll start Thai language training in the fall, go out to Bangkok next summer."

"Good for you — a promotion I take it?"

"Hopefully it will lead to that."

"Congratulations, Ong Blake." Trang Sen tried to sound pleased, but she could only think she'd miss him. More than Billings, she was deeply aware, it was Blake who had helped them most in the past year.

Billings, almost in an echo of her thought, was saying, "I guess I should thank you for all you've done for Trang Sen and Ken while you've been in Washington. That little fellow thinks the world of you. I suppose he's over at Ba Chau's, as usual?" he asked Trang Sen.

"I'll call and tell him to come home." She started for the telephone.

"Don't bother. I can't stay. I was working late, and thought I'd stop by for a minute and say hello. But I've really got to be going." He turned to Blake. "Good to see you again, old son." With that, he was out the door.

Blake raised his eyebrows. Before he thought, he asked, "Does he always breeze in and out of here like that?"

Trang Sen was on the verge of retreating behind her wall of politeness, then changed her mind. She shrugged. "He usually stays longer — sometimes eats with us, but not always."

"Neither you nor Second Son has said much about him in the past few months."

"When I was working, it was at the wrong time, he didn't come here so much. He tried to get me to change and work at lunchtime, but I didn't make as much money that way." She shrugged again.

He liked that shrug. However he might feel about Billings — and his long-smoldering anger was fast changing to something even less easily redeemed, a profound loss of respect — he was pleased to note this attitude that almost approached indifference.

"Well, what do you think? Shall we go get the kids and drive into the District? They're beginning to get the Mall ready for the Bicentennial doings. I thought we might go see what's going on."

"Yes, maybe Kim Hoa will go too, though she seems tired these days. That job she has isn't so easy."

THOUGH IT WAS only July, Blake had offered to take them to the Springfield K-Mart for school clothes. Kim Hoa was hesitant.

"I . . . I have to tell you something," she finally said to Trang Sen. "Do you remember the family I told you about in California?"

Trang Sen nodded.

"They wrote me. They . . . they still want me to open a shop with them. And . . ." she took a deep breath and finished, ". . . I'm going to do it."

"You mean they're coming here? Kim Hoa, that's wonderful!"

"No." Kim Hoa looked down at her hands. "I'm going there."

"Oh, Kim Hoa."

"You could come too. I told them about you and Second Son. They say the weather is really nice — rain sometimes, but not so cold, and no snow. Please come too. Billins . . ."

Trang Sen shook her head. "I . . . I don't want to leave here." She wasn't altogether sure why. Though part of the reason, still, was Billings, it was more than that. She couldn't put her finger on it. "I like it here," she explained lamely.

"I knew you wouldn't come. You . . . you seem to belong here. That's why it was so hard to tell you. But I don't, not at all. And there, I can do what I like, the tailoring. And it won't matter so much if my English isn't too good. And the children can be in the shop, like Saigon."

"When?" Trang Sen was trying desperately to grasp what was happening. In her world Kim Hoa was always there, it was like a piece of herself being torn away. *The children, how will Second Son manage without the children? How will I manage without Kim Hoa?*

"Next month, in time for the children to start school. They already have a place for the shop, they need me to help get started."

Trang Sen wanted to beg her not to go. At the same time, she realized Kim Hoa was right — this was not the place for her. She remembered how miserable Kim Hoa had been in the winter, how sick. And she thought of the Maid for You job, Kim Hoa's weariness. California, a little shop, would be better. She tried to be cheerful. "We can come to see you, Second Son and I."

Then she thought of Trang Mai. *What am I going to do about Trang Mai, with Kim Hoa not here to help?*

But Trang Mai, when she heard of the plan, wanted to go with Kim Hoa. "Sister, please let me. It would be so nice, not like here. And Cousin Hoa would like it, wouldn't you?" she finished her plea, turning to Kim Hoa.

Kim Hoa looked at Trang Sen and nodded.

"We'll see," said Trang Sen. To let her go seemed the final betrayal of her promise to her mother.

Discussing it later, though, she and Kim Hoa agreed that completely disconnecting Trang Mai from the places and people that were part of her delinquency might be the best solution of all. Trang Sen still felt somewhat guilty.

Kim Hoa, always wise, said, "Too much has happened, all that time in Guam, such a new place, America, we have to find new ways. If she's safe, that's keeping your promise. Maybe how we do it doesn't matter."

And Trang Sen remembered Tho, his apparent relief at being drafted, to get out of ways he had fallen into, which he didn't know how to control. *Maybe it's the same for Trang Mai.* In her mind, before she ever said it aloud, *Go well and safely, my sister*, she thought, like a blessing.

Reluctantly she helped Kim Hoa get ready to leave. Blake took them to a travel agency to buy the tickets, helped them negotiate with the landlord about giving up the apartment.

Billings didn't involve himself in any of this. They often didn't see him for three weeks or more, and his rare visits were brief — twenty, thirty minutes at most. His glimpses of his son were even rarer, for if Second Son happened to be at Kim Hoa's when he arrived, he left without seeing the boy. Trang Sen's reaction went from recurring disappointment to anger. Often she went for days without thinking about him at all. She had begun to feel that if this was the best he could do she preferred that he not come by at all.

"Can we go with them, Ma-ma?" was Second Son's repeated question through all the preparations for his cousins' departure.

He asked it for the thousandth time as Trang Sen tied his shoes. Blake had dropped by, and listened silently to their exchange.

"Don't you want to stay here, where Pa-pa is?"

"Why can't Pa-pa come too, and live with us?"

Trang Sen shook her head.

As Second Son ran off to play with Thi Ba and Van Hai, Blake asked Trang Sen, "When was the last time Art was here?"

"Two, maybe three weeks ago."

"Do you mind if I give you some advice?" He went on, not waiting for her to answer, "When you say things like that to Second Son, you're reminding him to want something he isn't getting, and apparently isn't likely to be getting, from his dad. Seems to me it would be better not to get his hopes up, at least the way things are right now."

"I don't know why I said that to him, just a way to get him to stop asking about going with them, I guess."

"Why do you want to stay? Is it Art?"

She shook her head. "It started as that, but I don't know, I like it here. I like the snow and cold, the way the weather changes. I like being so close to where so many important people live. And what would I do in California? I don't want to work in the tailor shop. I'd just have to start all over, learning the place, how to live there. I don't want to start over again." She smiled. "No good reason, I guess. But I don't want to go there."

He smiled then. "I'm glad. I'd miss you, and Second Son, too."

"But you'll be leaving too."

"Not for a year. A lot can happen in a year."

SCHOOL STARTED, AND Trang Sen began another job, at the Bella Vista, an Italian restaurant in a rather frayed-at-the-collar apartment complex in Rosslyn. Blake said the restaurant was good even if the apartments needed a face-lift. With Kim Hoa gone, she worked the lunch shift, to be home when Second Son returned in the afternoons. Blake was now studying Thai at the Foreign Service Institute a block or so away. He, and sometimes one or two of his classmates, came to the Bella Vista for lunch most days. Seeing him so often eased her over those first days and weeks after Kim Hoa's departure. Trang Sen missed her terribly.

Second Son's teacher sent a note asking her to come in for a conference. "I like to get acquainted with the children's parents," the note explained. Trang Sen's only interaction of any substance with school staff had been over Trang Mai's miscreance. In spite of the note's reassuring tone, she was very nervous as she walked the few blocks to the school.

She found the room Penny Gilmartin told her and knocked softly on the half-open door.

It was a tiny office. Mrs. Gilmartin turned her chair sideways from the desk and motioned Trang Sen to a folding chair.

"Would you like some coffee or tea?" She indicated the small table under the window behind her, with its bubbling chrome coffee pot. "There's both. That's hot water in the pot."

Trang Sen shook her head, then remembered to say "thank you."

Mrs. Gilmartin stirred her own cup and took a sip. "Kenneth is doing very well. He's a bright youngster. I'm especially pleased with his reading ability. I'd say he's reading at fourth grade level now."

Trang Sen inclined her head in gratitude, Vietnamese fashion.

"I'm so interested in these children like Kenneth who've come to this country. Some of them are doing so well. I sometimes wonder how my children would get along if they suddenly found themselves in a totally different culture, to say nothing of a strange language."

"Can be very difficult," said Trang Sen, thinking of Trang Mai.

"The adults, too," continued Mrs. Gilmartin. "Like you. You seem to have adjusted as well. Your English is excellent."

"I started studying it in Saigon, and then I worked for the American library there."

Encouraged by the teacher's apparent interest, Trang Sen found herself telling her quite a lot about her life in Vietnam. The question Mrs. Gilmartin didn't ask was about Second Son's father, and Trang Sen was grateful.

"I can see where Kenneth gets his intelligence. You should think about going back to school."

"A friend told me that too, but I don't know. I don't know how I could do that."

"My husband is the Dean for Academic Affairs at Northern Virginia. I can ask him what they could work out for you."

When Blake made the suggestion, it had seemed so impossible she hadn't thought about it since. Now, talking with someone who might know what to tell her to do, she found the idea very appealing.

"I always liked to study," she said wistfully. "I got some French books last summer and have been reading them. That's what I wanted to do, study French literature. But then . . ." she left the sentence unfinished.

"Well, let me talk with Stan, my husband, see what he says. Tell me again, and I'll write it down — what was the name of your school, and how close were you to finishing? Maybe I should get the name of the convent school in Paris as well."

Trang Sen gave her the information. "But the school isn't there anymore, the one in Saigon," she reminded her. "And I don't really know anything about the one in Paris."

"That's okay. We'll just see how this goes. I'll see what Stan says and give you a call." She looked at her watch. "My goodness, the children will be coming back from music class. I've got to get going." She stood up and offered her hand to Trang Sen. "I'll be in touch. Meantime, you can be sure Kenneth is doing beautifully."

Trang Sen thanked her again, said goodby, and walked back home, a dozen images running through her head. She could see herself sitting at the kitchen table, surrounded by books, or in a classroom, listening to a lecture with all her attention, single-minded for the first time in years. She remembered how clear she had felt, how purified, in those weeks after Tet, before Billings reappeared. Now, perhaps, she could feel that way again, swept clean of complicated emotion. Like a nun, she thought.

And Second Son, she was very proud of him. She had worried about his losing the companionship of his cousins, but he was doing really well. Though he had no playmates at the moment, he didn't seem to mind. A loner. Like me, she recognized.

Second Son WAS stretched out on the sofa reading. She had gone into the kitchen to fix supper when Billings let himself in.

Surprised, she came back into the living room. He hadn't been there in over a month. Sometimes she almost forgot about him, and Second Son seldom asked for him anymore.

"Arthur." She was so out of the habit of expecting to see him, she couldn't think of anything to say.

Second Son didn't have that problem. He jumped up and ran to his father. "Pa-pa! You're back!"

As if he's been away on a trip, she thought. She was disconnected, watching from a distance.

Billings picked up his son and gave him a bear hug. "You're getting so big, pretty soon you'll be picking *me* up!"

Second Son giggled at the idea.

Billings put him down and let himself be pulled over to the sofa. "So how've you been, young fellow? What are you reading?"

Second Son picked up the Spiderman comic book and began an involved re-telling of the story.

Trang Sen remained standing at the kitchen door, very aware that so far Billings had hardly acknowledged her. Months ago, she would have asked if he wanted to stay for supper, but tonight she couldn't bring those words out. Though he was apparently unaware of it, in her mind he had become a stranger in this place.

He left Second Son to a new Spiderman adventure and came over to her, kissed her on the cheek and gave her a quick hug. "So what's for dinner?"

"Not much, very simple, for Second Son and me. Just soup noodles with beef."

"Enough for me to join you?" He went past her and lifted the pot lid, sniffed the rich broth.

"Yes," she said, "if you like."

So the three of them sat down together at the table. Most of the conversation was between Billings and Second Son. She still felt very far away.

After dinner Billings plopped down on the sofa and looked around for the day's paper, apparently intending to stay awhile. Trang Sen cleared the table and settled Second Son there to do the bit of homework Mrs. Gilmartin always assigned.

She put the leftover noodles in the fridge and washed the dishes, checking on Second Son's progress from time to time. That over, "Bedtime," she announced.

"Can't I stay up and talk with Pa-pa some more?"

Billings looked up from the paper. "Let the little guy stay up a while. It's been a long time since I've seen him."

Trang Sen relented, thinking at the same time, *And whose fault is that?* Aloud she said, "Go get your school book and show Pa-pa how well you're doing. You can read him one story, and then you do have to go to bed."

As Second Son ran into the bedroom to find the book, she said to Billings, "His teacher asked me to come talk with her last week. She says he's very smart."

"Hmm, takes after his mother. I'm glad to hear it."

Second Son returned, curled up beside Billings and read the story.

"Off to bed with you now," commanded Trang Sen. "Pa-pa will come say goodnight when you've brushed your teeth and put on your night clothes."

Obedient, Second Son disappeared into the bedroom. In a few minutes he called for his father.

Trang Sen was sitting in the easy chair. Billings closed the bedroom door, came over and perched on the chair arm, reached out his hand and smoothed her hair back. "You're looking especially beautiful tonight," he whispered.

Still in that distant place, she neither responded nor resisted.

He knelt in front of her and put his arms around her, drawing her to him and beginning to kiss her gently.

She had forgotten those kisses, how they aroused her. This time, after so long, they evoked longing as well as awakening an intensifying desire. She couldn't resist them, closed her eyes and with her own lips found his mouth, the soft part of his neck below his ear, the little indentation at the bottom of his throat.

He lifted her and carried her to the sofa, lay beside her. "Ah, honey, ah, honey, you don't know how I've missed you."

Something deep inside, untouched by her heightening passion, noted, *The first time he's seemed to know he's been away so long.* She didn't think any more after that.

She watched him silently as he sat up and began buttoning his shirt. He finished dressing, leaned down and kissed her. "I can't stay now, but I'll be back, if not tomorrow, soon. I love you so much. Hang on a little longer, that's all I ask."

He let himself quietly out the door. She stayed there a long time, emotionless.

HE DIDN'T COME back the next day, or for more than a week after that. She was angry with him, as that one visit had revived Second Son's awareness of his father's absence. "Do you think he'll come back?" was his constant question.

Blake dropped by on the weekend, and Second Son mentioned the visit to him.

Blake raised his eyebrows at Trang Sen.

She shrugged and blushed a little. "He had supper with us one night." She wouldn't have told Blake about the visit.

"And I read to him," added Second Son. "He liked that. He promised he'd come back when he kissed me goodnight."

"So what did you read?"

"I'll show you. D'you want me to read it to you, too?"

"Sure, I'd like to hear it."

Second Son went to get the book.

"Is this starting things all over again?" Blake asked.

"I don't know. He was here last week, and we haven't seen him since. It's reminded Second Son to miss him."

"Too bad," Blake commented as Second Son came back into the room.

Before he left Blake promised to take Second Son to see *Star Wars*. The boy had begged Trang Sen to take him, and she had refused, shuddering. "I don't want to see anything like that."

But Blake was enthusiastic. "You bet we can go. We'll just leave your mom home with her old book. She doesn't know what she'll be missing. Tell you what, I'll come by Friday about six, and we'll hit a McDonald's before the movie starts. How will that be?"

"Yes, and I'll have a Big Mac, and a chocolate shake, and fries." Second Son was ecstatic.

Blake turned to Trang Sen. "That okay with you, Mom?"

Trang Sen nodded, smiling. "Mom? What is this 'mom'?"

"The all-American word for Ma-ma. Don't you like it?"

She didn't think that needed an answer, reflected that Blake was in a funny mood.

Mrs. Gilmartin CALLED and said,"I talked with my husband. He's not sure what you may need to make up before you can start taking credit courses, but he's almost certain something can be worked out, based on what I told him."

"Oh, thank you. Do you really think . . . ?" But she was too keyed up to finish the sentence.

"Now don't worry. I'm sure this is going to happen. What we'd like to do is have you and Kenneth come over for a meal. We thought a cook-out, while the weather is still nice. Our kids are older, but I think we can make sure Ken has a good time. That will give you and Stan a chance to talk a bit informally. And we both can get to know you."

"Thank you, you're very kind."

"We'll enjoy doing it. How about the Saturday after this one? And is there anyone else you'd like to come with you?"

She thought of Blake, but "No, just" — she hesitated over the name — "ah, Kenneth and me."

"Okay, I have your address from Kenneth's record. Stan or I will pick you up about four. Is that okay?"

"Yes, fine, thank you."

"Let me give you our phone number. Do you have a pencil and paper?"

"Wait a minute . . . please," she remembered to add.

She hung up the phone. So much happening at once, she could hardly take it in. Do all teachers do things like this?

But Blake, when she asked him, said no. "Most of them just do their job and that's it. She must be a very special person. Actually, I've heard a good bit about Northern Virginia and what Gilmartin has helped do with that school. Absolutely outstanding. You're lucky to have this connection."

"Do you think I'll really be able to go to college there?"

"Sounds like it to me. I don't think he'd be willing to talk with you if he didn't think there was a way to work something out."

Blake and Second Son left for McDonald's and the movie. She reheated some left-overs and had settled down with a book when she heard the key turn in the lock. Her first thought was, *He'll be angry when he finds out Second Son is with Blake.*

"Hello, honey." He came over, bent down and kissed her, then looked around. "Where's Ken?"

"Gone to a movie with Blake. I didn't know you were coming tonight," she added, somewhat anxiously.

"Actually, that's fine. I want to talk with you, and it'll be easier if he's not here." He sat down beside her, put his arm around her. "Things are going to get better for us. It's been a tough road, but I'm almost at the end of it."

She waited, silent.

"I know I've neglected you and Ken, but a lot has been happening. To put it simply, my marriage has fallen apart. She — my wife — kept getting more and more unreasonable. Then last spring my middle boy was in a bad accident . . ."

"Oh, Arthur," she broke in, "I'm sorry."

"Yes, well, it looks as if he's going to be okay, but it's been a long haul. The kid he was with was charged with drunk driving. Actually, of the two of them Randy's the lucky one. He at least isn't going to have that kind of thing hanging over his head."

Trang Mai's difficulties must have happened about the same time as the accident. A glimmer of understanding, if not sympathy, emerged at this possible explanation for Billings's indifference.

He was going on. "I guess that accident was the final blow, at least for Laura. I don't need to go into the details, but we're getting a divorce."

Once, she thought, *I would have cared. But now* . . . The announcement washed over her like a cold wave, its implications left her untouched.

"So, finally, sweetheart, we can be together again. It's going to take a few more months for this to be final, and I have to be careful in the meantime — can't stay here, for instance. But after that, as soon as I'm legally free, you and I can get married."

She should be glad. She made an effort to imagine them actually living together, the three of them, no waiting for him, no frustratingly brief visits. She tried to recapture the feeling associated with their good times in Saigon. But instead she remembered that terrible time when Billings would have destroyed Eldest Brother. Another memory emerged to rankle — Billings's scornful put-down of the little house where they had lived while he was away. And, here, the way he treated her, like she was his property. She remembered what Blake had said. She could make a choice.

He was looking at her, puzzled. "I thought you'd be excited."

"Arthur, I . . ."

"What is it, is this too sudden?"

She shook her head, less in response than like a swimmer coming out of deep water. "I don't want that anymore."

"Don't want what?"

"To marry you," she whispered, looking down at her hand he was holding. She pulled it away.

"Of course you want to marry me. And Ken, I can be a better father to him now."

She shook her head again. "Too much has happened, too many things, not right."

"I'm sorry about all that, but it will be different now, I promise."

"Too late."

"I shouldn't have sprung it on you like this. It's too much of a surprise. You'll feel differently after you get used to the idea."

He never even considered I would say anything but yes, she realized angrily. "No, never."

"Look, take a few days to get used to this," he repeated. "I never thought how unexpected my news might be." He leaned over and kissed her. "Why don't I go now, and give you time to get accustomed to thinking of yourself as my wife." He smiled, sure of himself and her.

That possessive smile intensified her resentment. "I'll never be your wife. I don't want that now."

"But —"

"No."

"I told you I'm sorry about the way things have been. I'll make it up to you."

"Too late," she said again.

She stood up, and he rose too, tried to put his arms around her. She pulled away.

"Trang Sen," he began, "you're being unreasonable."

Her anger burst out. "*I'm* being unreasonable? After the way you've treated us? I've learned to live here, no help from you. To speak English, find a job, no help from you. To put Second Son in school, no help from you. I don't want to marry you. I want you to leave and not come back. I want the key."

He stood looking at her a moment, his face blank. Then, "Surely —" he began.

"No, give it to me." She held out her hand.

There was something about her stone-hard insistence that he couldn't oppose. Silently, he took the key out of his pocket and handed it to her.

She closed her hand around it, opened the door. "Leave," she said again.

He remembered that other time, in Saigon after her miscarriage, when she went to stay at the tailor shop, then came back to him. "Take your time, honey," he said to her, as he had said then, certain that the same thing would happen this time. After a final attempt to put his arm around her stiff shoulders, he went out.

She felt the key, its metallic coldness growing warm against her palm. A kind of blankness took the place of feeling, a comforting emptiness. She sat down and stared at the wall where she had tacked up Second Son's efforts from art class. In one crayoned sketch, he had drawn three figures standing in front of a building that was oddly reminiscent of the little tailor shop. He had labeled them "mother, father, boy."

So many things to think about, to put together now, on the other side, as it seemed to her. What to say to Blake, and, more importantly, to Second Son. *I don't have to say anything tonight.* Blake, going away soon. *I'll miss him.* But he would come back. For this time she wanted to make her own way, for herself and Second Son.

So many possibilities. She could go to California, join Kim Hoa and the others. But, much as she missed Kim Hoa, like a lost part of herself, this was where she wanted to be.

And next week she would meet Dr. Gilmartin, and that could lead to something new, something that at the same time promised finally to fulfill a desire so old she couldn't remember not having it.

She thought of those years in the village, smiled at the memory of her encounter with the American beside the river, her first American. How fascinated she had been. Looking back now, it seemed that was the beginning of everything. *And here I am,* she thought, *living in America myself, becoming an American.* Regardless of all the pain and sorrow, all the loss it had taken to get to this place, this moment, she was where she wanted to be. She was sure of it.

Waves of memory washed over her, relentless — her struggle to keep studying, the endless obstacles; her mother's disapproval, her family's need for her to take the place of her brothers; the war itself. And later, Billings, and their love that had thwarted her, turned her away from the deepest part of herself. She was angry at all of them, at Billings most of all.

Then she remembered Kim Hoa's words, in the desolate aftermath of Eldest Brother's narrow escape — "Billings gave you the opportunity." And, as she reflected, she saw that all the barriers had also been opportunities. Even the war, the biggest barrier of all. *It brought me here, where somehow I belong.*

It seemed important then to treasure one thing about Billings, one good thing. That rainy night he found her after Tet, the gentle way he pushed the damp hair from her face, the clinging sogginess in the air — that dampness that would forever be part of her memory of Saigon — the dim reddish light from the burned-down candle on the table. One good thing, that time.

Eldest Brother. She was filled with an almost unbearable longing for him, a pang of hope that he was safe and well. Someday, perhaps, she could find him again. She pulled the Sartre book out of her stack of French authors, recalling that fearful time after Tet when Eldest Brother had given it to her. She could almost feel his hand on her arm, the old remembered gesture of comfort for whatever grief had overcome her.

She opened the book to *The Flies*. A creased paper fell out, and she picked it up. "*Ma chère soeur.*" Her brother's note. She scanned it quickly, tears prickling her eyes. "Our long and righteous struggle is nearly over. I am sure that you rejoice with me . . . There will be great danger for those who pinned their hopes on the Americans . . . no place for them in the new Vietnam. . . ."

No, she thought, *no place for me there. Only here.* But she also knew, as she had sensed so long ago, that she would never completely belong to either place. She slipped the paper back into the book and, through her tears, focused on the text. Buoyant and clarified, she reread her favorite passage, changing the wording slightly to claim it: "I can no longer live under his law. I am condemned to have no other law than my own. . . . I can follow only my own road. For I am my own self, Jupiter, and each of us must create her own road."

Yes, I must follow my own road, obey my own law. There is no other way. Even if I'm a woman.

Especially if, she thought, smiling slightly.

About the author

Sarah-Ann Smith earned a degree in international relations at American University in Washington and pursued a career with the U.S. diplomatic corps. Her tours of duty took her to Taiwan to study Mandarin Chinese and to the American Consulate in Hong Kong. She also worked at "Foggy Bottom," the legendary headquarters of the U.S. State Department.

Friendships with a number of Asian students piqued Smith's interest in Southeast Asia; her fascination intensified as they voiced their critiques of U.S. policy at the height of the Vietnam War. Years of professional and personal focus on Asian political and cultural life impelled her to write about it in this, her first novel.

Smith's life after the Foreign Service has focused on writing and teaching. In addition to *Trang Sen*, she has published numerous essays and op-eds and has taught courses on China and Southeast Asia at universities in Maryland and North and South Carolina.

Also available from Pisgah Press

Mombie: The Zombie Mom	Barry A. Burgess
$16.95	illustrations by Jake LaGory
Letting Go: Collected Poems 1983-2003	Donna Lisle Burton
$14.95	
Unbelievable: Faith, Reason, & the Search for Truth	Joseph R. Haun
$16.00	w. A. D. Reed
MacTiernan's Bottle	Michael Hopping
$14.95	
rhythms on a flaming drum	Michael Hopping
$16.95	
I Like It Here! Adventures in the Wild & Wonderful World of Theatre	
$30.00	C. Robert Jones
Lanky Tales, Vol. I: The Bird Man & other stories	C. Robert Jones
$9.00	illustrations by Jennie Jones Branham
Fragments	Martin A. Keeley
$16.00	
Oscar & the Royal Avenue Cats	Martin A. Keeley
$15.00	
Red-state, White-guy Blues	Jeff Douglas Messer
$15.95	
A Green One for Woody	Patrick O'Sullivan
$15.95	
Reed's Homophones: a comprehensive book of sound-alike words	A.D. Reed
$10.00	
Killer Weed	RF Wilson
$14.95	

To order:

Pisgah Press, LLC
PO Box 1427, Candler, NC 28715
www.pisgahpress.com